Women's Empowerment in India:

Philosophical Perspectives

(An Anthology of Research Papers Presented in the National Seminar on 'Problems and Prospects of Women's Empowerment and Gender Inequality: Some Issues in Applied Ethics' Sponsored by the Indian Council of Philosophical Research, New Delhi and Conducted in March, 2002 by the Department of Philosophy, B.R. Ambedkar Bihar University, Muzaffarpur-842001 (Bihar).

Chief Editor

Professor Sachindra Kumar Singh

Pro VC, Kameshwar Singh Darbhanga

Sanskrit University, Darbhanga, Bihar.

Editor

(English Section)

Professor Hari Narain Pandey

(Hindi Section)

Dr. Saroj Kumar Verma

ORIGINALS

Delhi-110052

Published by

ORIGINALS

(an imprint of Low Price Publications)

A-6, Nimri Commercial Centre,

Ashok Vihar Phase-IV, Delhi-110052

Phone: +91-11-27302453 Fax: +91-11-47061936

e-mail: info@Lppindia.com

website: www.Lppindia.com

Marketed by

Low Price Publications

Delhi

Published in India 2010

ISBN 10: 81-8454-095-7

ISBN 13: 978-81-8454-095-6

Printed at

D K Fine Art Press P Ltd.

Delhi-110052

PRINTED IN INDIA

Contents

Foreword

It has come as an expansive deference of the Baba Saheb Bhim Rao Ambedkar Bihar University, Department of Philosophy to me in approximately 12 years old retirement as a teacher from its sister department of political science to have been asked to write the foreword to the anthology on Women's Empowerment in India: Philosophical Perspectives which it is scheduled to publish. The deference is expansive because I, a Political Science man having been mainly concerned with international politics, do not find myself deserving it. Yet I am humbly responding, taking this deference as a spiritual culmination of the affections continually showered on me for nearly half a century by about a score of brotherly and sisterly Philosophy Department colleagues-some having commanded my deference, some my friendship and some my elderly love. It has stirred me a little when one of them, decades ago, had invited me to contribute to their maiden Departmental venture, the *Chintan*. It stirred me again a couple of years back or so to be invited to write a piece for a souvenir edited for the Department by a class friend of mine and retired Head of it. It is stirring me for the third time now rather in a quaking way.

It does not embarrass me in any way to commence this Foreword at a note of personal high appreciation for Dr. Sachindra kumar Singh's academic stewardship of which this anthology is only one example, though, no doubt, both academically and socio-politically glittering. The anthology, treasuring the explorations of a somewhat massive national seminar on a very live and pertinent social issue of the day has as may be seen, very meaningfully fructified in a series of perspectives---philosophical, socio-philosophical, social-thought-traditional, ethical, existentialist, feminist and medico-technical. Some 46 academics explorers have joined the exercise and the produce of their collective toil is not only being academically disseminated but is also being transmitted to society to serve it in tackling one of its standing problems which has continued to be elusive and has been negatively making it evasively stayput.

The readership that the anthology may enlist on its publication will benefit quite a lot from its philosophic generalities regarding women's social positioning in this country, socio-philosophic insight on the past of the same as also in its current social and political realities, reminders regarding the relevant national social-thought traditions with their messages of pertinence and help today, the ethical imperatives underlined with reference to the gender discrimination problems, the existentialist sensitivity as found warranted, the feminist arousals perceived and the socio-medical remedies suggested against the heinous consequences of our social maladies ensuing from gender discrimination.

The anthology ought to be of great interest and help to the country's sensibly live and striving socio-political circles pushing forward the fight for, and mitigation of, gender sadism and discrimination rampantly continuing to incapacitate us as a national community.

It may and ought to be an anthology dear to the hearts of our educated and educating mothers, sisters, daughters and afflicted partners in our social strife for achieving gender equality.

I have no doubt at all that by publishing this highly valuable anthology, the Department of Philosophy of this University will earn a good deal of academic and social esteem for itself and for the university of which it is an apexual structure.

It comes as a happy chance coincidence to me to have scripted this Foreword on the Teacher's Day of the year 2005, for the day symbolically enshrines the high esteem in which our nation holds a great teacher like Sarvapalli Radhakrishnan who once towered Philosophy as an academic discipline in this country.

D N Mallik
Professor and Head (Retired)
Department of Political Science,
B R Ambedkar Bihar University,
Muzaffarpur-842001

Introduction

Sachindra Kumar Singh

This anthology is a wrap-up of the 46 papers, which the 3-day National Seminar on Women's Empowerment in India, sponsored by the Indian Council of Philosophical Research (New Delhi) and conducted by the B.R. Ambedkar Bihar University (Muzaffarpur) Department of Philosophy, in March 2002, could solicit.

The *Introduction* is aimed at underlining the sense that the seminar could develop on the matter with what may be viewed as a bunch of 'Philosophical Perspectives.' Those perspectives have been identified and have further been categorized as parts of the anthology. One of the parts needs to be doubly sub-categorized. Some liberty has been taken in adopting the yardstick for identifying and categorizing these perspectives and the same is based on the understanding that women's empowerment is meant to improve their social lot against prevailing deprivations and discriminations so as to capacitate them to acquire social equality and social freedom of choice and action with, of course, commensurate responsibility also on their part as the co-efficient of that equality and freedom.

Of the 46 papers, 32 were in English and 14 in Hindi. The anthology has avoided attaching significance to the bilinguality of communication since it is concerned only with the various philosophical perspectives they convey.

In all, 7 main categories of 'perspectives' have been identified as reflected in the papers (taken as articles for this anthology). Accordingly, the anthology has been organized in terms of 7 parts: I. General Philosophical Perspectives, II. Socio-Philosophical Perspectives, III. Social Thought Perspectives, IV. Ethical

Perspectives, V. Existentialist Perspectives, VI. Feminist Perspectives and, finally, VII. Medico-Technical Perspectives. The category of 'Socio-Philosophical Perspectives' (Part II) needed being sub-categorized at two layers: at the first layer, with reference to India's 'Social Past' (Section-2) and its social 'Contemporaneity' (Section-ii) and, at the second layer, 'Contemporaneity' had to be sub-categorized further with reference to 'Social Problems' (II-ii-a) and 'Political Issues' (II-ii-b).

The category of 'General Philosophical Perspectives' (Part I) embeds generalities of approaches and opinions borne in 13 of the articles. In her article, Abha Singh holds the view that women's empowerment in India can be real and substantive only if they set their own agenda for development. Tandra Patnaik, in hers, looks at women's empowerment as intrinsic and, essentially, a matter of their self-growth. On the other hand, S.N. Chaudhary takes that empowerment as just a real extension of social values like liberty and justice to them. Banking on the Marxist perspective, R.K. Singh posits that women's empowerment is likely to materialize really only if women are liberated as an exploited social class. Believing that this country's ancient past presented a much happier state of affairs for its women, C.D. Jha has no hesitation in striking a note of pessimism on the ongoing efforts for empowering them. To R.K. Sinha, redemption appears lying in men and women, the two sides of social life, supplementing each other. Decline in women's status n this country, according to V.S. Singh, owed considerably to foreign invasions and what the Indian women need today is education, lessons in practical morality and socio- political awakening. Holding that the Indian women's social position in the ancient past was dignified, Navin Kumar's remedial line is similar to Singh's. Shail Kumari asserts in her article that notwithstanding the ongoing global efforts to empower women, in India, they have first to wage a struggle to bring about changes in their own attitudes. Alok Tandon focuses on a series of desired efforts—political, socio-structural, cultural and religious, if women in India are to get empowered. Drawing inspiration from what he sees as man-woman partnership model of women's social status in ancient India, Rajeshwar Singh takes an interesting philosophical position that, there being a man within every woman and the vice-versa, it would be women's highest fulfillment if every woman discovered the man within herself. Holding a somewhat different view, H.S. Singh, is inclined to believe that there has always been a gender discrimination in society irrespective of lofty claims to the contrary and, according to him, it is only through their own awakening that Indian women can change men's mentality for the sake of their own empowerment. In the thirteenth article, that being the last one of part I, in almost a similar vein, Rajeeva Kumar spots the male-female sex difference lying at the root of gender discrimination prevailing in society and accounting for women being used as a commodity.

In part II, 20 articles bear on 'Socio-Philosophical Perspectives' with reference to Indian women's empowerment—4 of them going back to their 'Past' and 16 concerned with their 'Contemporaneity' respectively in Section-i and Section-ii of this part. 12 of these 16 bear on 'Social Problems' in sub-section (a). and the remaining 4 on 'Political Issues' in sub-section (b). Among those who look to the past of socio-philosophical perspectives, Indu Kumari, surveying the status of women in ancient India critically, posits that they enjoyed their social due fully and have been deprived of it with the passage of time. Sunil Kumar Singh is of the opinion that the age-old Indian social tradition has suffered a lot of vitiation on account of a blind imitation of the materialistic West. Men and women, for him, form the two pillars of society and they have their conjunctive rights together and, as such, he advocates a right kind of implementation of the relevant Hindu precepts. Shyam Kishore Singh goes into the Jainist precepts and emphasizes equality of status between men and women for resecuring the stability of the latter's position in society. Damodar Singh goes into how the Mughals in India socially treated the gender issue and finds that they made discriminations. Among the 12 articles relating the 'contemporaneous' social problems in India to 'socio-philosophical perspectives' (sub-section-ii-a), Kanupriya, in her article, goes into the plight and prospects of divorcees among women in the Hindu society and wishes them to become self-revolutionary enough to break the conservative social framework. With reference to the rights of women in Islam, M.R. Kazimi holds that, under certain Quranic precepts, social equality is permitted to women and feels that what is desirably needed is a progressive education in that context. Rekha Singh underlines the factors of female foeticide in India these days and believes that a stringent legislation is needed to nullify the trend. H.N. Pandey examines the causes of that problem, sees remedies in the corrective roles of the government, society, doctors, religious preachers and voluntary social organizations as also in appropriate deterrent laws. Viewing gender discrimination as a stigma on the Indian society, Nirmala Kumari Jha uncovers the forms of such discrimination and they, according to her, may be done away with social awareness and conducive milieu for women's development. B.V.S. Bhanusree, linking the status of women in India with the role of education, draws inspiration from the status of women in this country obtaining in the Sutra and Epic periods, regrets the way the deterioration in their status reached a nadir in the sati practice and sees the remedy lying in better and better education for women. Rashmi Rekha underlines the self less contribution of Sister Nivedita in empowering the women of modern India by spreading education amongst them. Kamala Kumari focuses on the role of education and economic self-dependence in women's empowerment in India. Indra Kumari looks at attitudinal change as the chief factor of gender equality and advocates that Indian women should shed their fear and inhibitions through education. S.K. Verma, concentrating on the Indian contextuality, surmises that women in this country, without allowing themselves to be used as a commodity, ought to acquire the right to decide for themselves, choosing their own model, and men ought to be flexible for cooperating with women who may not necessarily look for total independence. Drawing from the fact that, with the passage of time, Indian women have become more and more enlightened, getting more and more elitist. Yogini Nighoshkar suggests that their elitism be harnessed to women's empowerment. Poonam Singh has found of interest and value the Indian women's struggle against exploitation as depicted in Amar Kant's stories. Sub-section (b) of section-ii of part II bears 4 articles relating to some 'Political Issues' as a shade of 'Socio-Philosophical Perspectives' in India. Among them Prabhakar Prasad Singh's concentrates on the consciousness, which the Indian women gained during the freedom struggle as lying at the root and underlines the desirability of a fresh historical evaluation of the interaction between the social reforms of the nineteenth century and the women's movement in this country. In his article Y.V. Satyanarayana scrutinizes gender difference, which has continued to matter adversely in Indian women's participation in the country's political bodies and processes and sees remedies in their proper education, etc. In his response to India's politics for women as one of the two demographic segments of it, D.N. Mallik goes into the hurdles it has been pitiably facing for the last few years, calls for liberal-realistic flexibility on the part of Indian women themselves in acting unitedly for their reserved representation in all legislative bodies and institutions based on social quotas and ephasizes that political measures be viewed as vital steps in social engineering. In the next, rather an informed and research oriented article, Anil Kumar Ojha goes tabularly into the political representational status of women under the republican constitution of this country, traces the political issues of their representation back to the thirties of the freedom struggle, takes a comparative peep into women's political representation reflecting their empowerment as obtaining somewhat diversely in several European countries and underlines the recent political crosscurrents in this country of about half a dozen hues at work as are generating a stalemate of hopelessness. Incidentally, though inadvertently, Mallik's call for our better half stands vindicated by Ojha's findings.

Part III of the anthology is given to the 'Social Thought Perspectives' in India bearing on women's empowerment. They are somewhat different from the 'Socio-Philosophical Perspectives' covered in part II, which are social practice—referring and problem-specific. In fact the former has been picked up from more massive and broader contexts of the Indian philosophical-spiritual thought for being related to women's empowerment. So projected, Part III contains 3 articles. In one of them, S.B.P. Sinha focuses on the Vedantic perspective of the Indian social thought, urges practical Vedanta to be adopted as a highly desirable input in the present-day Indian social dynamics and hopes that the Vedantic thought unity of all existence can well be inclusive of gender forms. In the second article of this part, Swami Brahmeshwarananda looks to Swami Vivekananda in relation to women's empowerment in India. The country's national growth, according to him, needs a harmonious development of both men and women as that could be vital for the growth of children as well. He surmises that women have to be worshipped as mothers. In the third article of this part, Anima Kumari explains the Gandhian approach to Indian women's empowerment as rejecting the view that the female side of society is weaker. On the contrary, it has to be seen as the nobler side and women ought to resort to Satyagraha against all forms of injustice they encounter.

Part IV, carrying 3 articles reflecting 'Ethical Perspectives' on women's empowerment in India, has one from Sadanand Prasad Singh. He views it as a critique on the issue of gender equality in the vein of an exercise in applied ethics. The contention is that woman, as a mother, can bc of considerable help in reducing the crime graph of society by assisting the police and generating self-confidence in daughters and may as well turn to be instrumental in promoting communal harmony. In the second article of this part, Sachindra Kumar Singh analyses women's right to maternity in biological, social and ethical perspectives. He refers to Plato's works, the Shaiva philosophy and recent scientific researches in these contexts and appreciates the New Education Policy of the country for its emphasis on the role of education for women's equality. Viewing female as an ethical issues, in the third article of this part, M.P. Chaurasia traces the origin of this evil social practice back to the days of Mughal invasion, holds amniocentesis accountable for sex determination as a catalytic agent in encouraging it and advocates special rights for women as a stopper.

The single article forming Part V of the anthology on 'Existentialist Perspectives' is from Shiv Bhanu Singh wherein the author presents an existentialist view of gender inequality. In his opinion, the psychology of sex differences is natural and the pertinent approach advocated by Dorothy Parker is considerably balanced.

Given to 'Feminist Perspectives' Part VI carries 3 articles. Asha Mukherjee relates women's empowerment in India to feminist ethics, which rejects a priori premises of male superiority and attaches importance to the role of females in various walks of life. Asha emphasizes the role of NGO's and governmental organizations. S. Shyam K. Singh relates women's empowerment in India to gender justice, which calls for the women's right to maternity to be protected. Rashmi Rekha has shown through a journey to the life of Sri Sri Sarda Devi as to how spirituality is more powerful a tool of empowerment of women than any known material tools.

Part VII, bearing 'Medico-Technical Perspectives' carries 3 articles, each authored by a medico. In her article, Rangila Sinha makes out that violence is carried against the female from the womb to the tomb and explains that measures needed to stop this depend on the role of the government, the NGO's, the private sector and the religious leaders. R.U. Sinha, viewing gender discrimination as socio-medical problem, underlines a series of measures to be taken up at political, bureaucratic, judicial and social levels. In the third article of this part, K.K. Singh goes into the gender bias, female feticide and infanticide, which undermine women's empowerment. He points out that an Act of 1971 in India provided for termination of pregnancy and amniocentesis has added fuel to the fire. He asserts that enough of provisions exist under the Indian Penal Code to deal with menaces like feticide and infanticide and believes that such menaces call for a radical change in the country's social vision.

Whereas it is gratifying for this anthology to have a clear one third of contributors from among female academicians, it is regretted that indexes could not be organizationally managed. That would have added to its worth. Any other organizational clumsiness, found creeping up in it, may further be condoned large-heartedly.

Sachindra Kumar Singh
Professor and Head
Department of Philosophy,
B R Ambedkar Bihar University,
Muzaffarpur-842001

Part I

General Philosophical Perspectives

Chapter 1

Towards Women's Empowerment

Abha Singh

Human beings are born male and female according to the biological sex given to them. However, they are divided into masculine and feminine genders by being taught how to behave as males and females, and moreover, inculcate the particular ways of life prescribed for each gender by the society which nurtures them from birth.

Gender inequality i.e., the disparity between women and men and the disadvantages of women are not, of course, unique to India. There is much evidence of extensive gender based inequality even in the elementary matters of health care and nutrition in many regions across the world. But fairly detailed comparisons of mortality rates, morbidity rates, hospital care, nutritional attention etc. have been made in India. It proves that despite variations between regions within India, they clearly confirm fairly decisive picture of women being systematically deprived vis-a-vis men throughout the country.

In India, discrimination against women starts in the foetus, proceeds through systematic under nourishment in childhood and deprivation of education in adolescence, and ends in domestic violence and bride burning. In a scenario where the number of women to men is decreasing alarmingly—unlike any other nation in the world—they are all victims of original discrimination that a girl child faces at the fetal, natal and post natal stages which decides whether she is 'empowered' to live at all.

Possession of power by a person has the authority to discriminate. Genderdisation of human beings is the primary structure through which this authority is exercised. It has assigned roles and functions to human being on the basis of sex and these have been accepted as inherent to the person. The roles assigned to the male sex give access to and control of resources required for a subsistence and growth and those assigned to female sex are only derived from and secondary to the roles of the male. This ensures that the women can seldom possess power and whatever authority she exercises is delegated to her by the man in her life.

Discrimination against women and their oppression is a heinous crime not merely against women but it is a sin against humanity. "It is a serious crime against human civilization. If the family or home is the cradle of civilization, culture and development, and if influence of mother in a family surpasses all other forms of influence, the pain and the groanings of that mother will remain unresounded in the hearts of her children. It will definitely affect the happiness of the whole family ".[1]

Gender roles oppress man as well as woman because they do not respect the nature of the person. Gender assigns roles, responsibilities and functions to the person based on sex irrespective of whether that is what the person wants or is capable of. Capacity is considered to be inherent in the masculinity or the feminity of the person. Through a system of rewards, to mark approval and punishments to mark disapproval, this power structure has been perpetuated.

Not being vested with any power directly, women do not possess the means of changing this situation by emancipating themselves physically, mentally and emotionally, since they do not possess the resources to support their efforts. They have been denied education, mobility and means of production. They have been denied getting identified or recognized as individuals voicing themselves. The followers of every religion have ensured that women be personalityless and voiceless. The situation is in no way better today.

Women have been nurtured in the belief that man by nature is better informed, can counter violence can provide a shield, safety and security. These beliefs are well ingrained in women. They have accepted that, because of the difference in sex, nature has ordained for them only the secondary subservient roles which are prescribed according to the expectations of men. As secondary roles do not have a direct economic value those who perform these roles are not counted as productive. Hence a woman's value in her own eyes is less than that of the man. We can therefore understand why the life of the woman was never valued highly. Its worth depended on the convenience or contribution she could make to man in the form of helping him to realize his roles and satisfy his desires.

In the backdrop of the social scene cited above a paramount question crops up in any normal brain. Should sex/gender bias be assumed to be unavoidable? In order to find out a satisfactory answer to this question it appears better to think over one's own position in life. Above all, one finds oneself as a human being whose thoughts and beliefs are influenced by one's settings in the family and society. Quite likely, given another setting and influence one could have lived, acted and thought quite differently. Thereupon, the issue of genderdisation of humanity gains paramount ethical importance as ethics belongs to the self-understanding of every human being.

The ideal is a 'happy life'. Happy life does not intend the narrow egoistic satisfaction of individual needs but the enrichment or protection of life by mutual give and take policy. Thus ethics is a vision which shapes on as person who is responsible for co-existence with other persons. Now the question is how to define the person. This is a philosophical question about one's own being and about the being of other persons as well. Peter Kemp explaining the concept of person writes, "... I am a person from the moment. I discover myself and understand myself as a will-to-life and at the same time discover others as a condition for expanding the capacities of my own life. A person is then a self-conscious physical being who lives by receiving something from and giving something to other self-conscious physical being".[2] Thus the concept of person implies an autonomous will. Hence autonomy supposes, on the one hand, a separation from others by which an individual has specific personality and, on the other hand, an association with others by which others recognize one's self as autonomous. However, self-autonomy can be interpreted in terms of capacities such as responsibility, accountability, independence etc. Ethical interpretation of human well-being presupposes the individual's capacity to develop and pursue one's own conceptions of the good. Maeve Cooke perhaps had this idea in mind when he wrote: "The autonomous self is held to be in some sense self-directing, It must be able in some sense to see itself as author of its own life history and of its constructions of personal identity".[3] Self must be responsible and accountable for its actions. Meaning thereby, the self must take issue with external forces that influence its life and make query in a responsible and accountable way, regarding their inevitability.

Self-authorship implies independence. By independence is meant objectivity which forbids over-reliance on the opinions and judgments of others in one's views of the world, relationships to others, self-definitions and narrative constructions of identity; it also calls for the attempt to free oneself from the pernicious influence of one's own earlier life.[4] Self-authorship also comprises of purposive rationality and capability to evaluate or select from among a range of options, those which the self judges to be desirable from the point of view of its self-identity. Hence strong evaluation demands certain creative powers, dispositions such as flexibility and open mindedness and faculties such as memory and imagination. It also has a social material dimension. If the self is autonomous to select goals on the basis of its strong evaluation, it must have at its disposal certain material goods such as food, clothing and accommodation and descent upbringing and education that enable the requisite powers, dispositions and faculties to flourish. Strong evaluation is possible only when sufficiently diverse options are available. If the self can choose only from among trivial options or if all the choices are potentially horrendous or evil, then strong evaluation is not possible.

Finally, self-authorship is central not just to the concept of personal autonomy but to that of public or political autonomy. Citizens are held to be politically autonomous to the extent they see themselves as authors of their own laws. Political theorists such as John Rawls and Habermas have emphasized the internal connection between personal autonomy and political autonomy. The thesis here is that the development of personal autonomy is impeded by lack of public autonomy and that political autonomy is justified through reference to the value of personal autonomy. But the personal autonomy of women in Indian society is considerably impaired by economic and social disadvantages as well as by forces of manipulation and control resulting into their seclusion from public life and their lack of political power.

Above discussion compels us to hold that gender inequality is rooted in denial of autonomy to women in India and the voices of women's liberation often sound wired and cacophonous. Nevertheless India cannot remain unaffected by the influence of women's liberation movement in view of urbanisation, industrialisation and modernisation. Since there is no basic difference in the mental capability of men and women, women do not differ from men in their capability of choosing rational goals in their self-interest and in their choice of reasonable means for the achievement by those goals. Although the biological factor connects women with child bearing which makes her weak, at least for the time being, and thereupon paves the way for her exploitation. Thus the base of gender discrimination is inherent in human biology, but it can be conditioned. Women should have the same opportunities as men to manifest most of the abilities they have. Social options for men must be extended to women so that they can compete on equal terms. As Ferguson writes:

> If men and women make different choices as to how to develop what economists call "human capital" that is their skill and abilities, including their formal education and job training, this is due not to innate gender prejudices and skill e.g. that men are more competitive and aggressive and women more nurturant and submissive. Rather it is realistic option that society and individual circumstance provide.[5]

Therefore, people must be assessed as individuals and should not be lumped into 'female' and 'male'. The roles occupied by males and females must be kept flexible to enable people to do what they are best suited for. Inequality based on an obvious difference between males and females produces a divided society with a sense of superiority on the one side and a sense of inferiority on the other. Therefore, sexual inequality has more divisive effect than any other form of inequality. It also creates a feeling of hopelessness among women since their sex is not the product of their own action and there is nothing they can do to change.

Hence, the issue of women's empowerment is not concerned with a group of people we like to be benefited, but with a type of injustice we want to see eliminated. However, it is sad to note that thinkers like John Rawls whose *Theory of Justice* has, in fact, done much to draw attention to the political and ethical importance of individual freedom, avoids the issue of justice between men and women. Perhaps the most distinguishing feature of John Rawls' *Theory of Justice* is that all human beings are seen as rational maximisers. He advocated an optional share of available utilities/ welfare/entitlements to all. His principle of justice safeguards the priority of individual liberty, subject to similar liberty for all. His accounting of inequality concentrates not on distribution of utility, but on that of 'primary goods'. These are the means such as income, wealth, liberty etc. that help people to pursue their respective objectives freely.

But equal distribution of primary goods is practically not possible due to the freedom enjoyed by two people according to their different status in the society. Conforming with this idea Amartya Sen writes:

> ....making comparisons of the primary goods different people have, is not quite the same as comparing the freedoms actually enjoyed by different persons, even though the two can be closely related. Primary goods are means to freedom, but they cannot represent the extent of freedom, given the diversity of human beings in converting primary goods into the freedom to pursue their respective objectives. Given the variation in sex, age, inherited characteristics, environmental differences etc. that may prevail among and within groups of people, an equal distribution of primary goods may go with very unequal levels of freedom.[6]

Equal holdings of primary goods may make people of weaker sex less free to pursue their own well-being, unless they get special facilities in participating in the choice of common social institutions and in influencing general political decisions.

Special facilities or affirmative action should not be limited to seat reservation in educational or political institutions. Reservations were originally conceived as a means of creating social equality. Certainly reservations are politically expedient to the extreme but women's empowerment through reservation is merely a hallucination. Reservations should be accompanied by a multiprolonged effort for all round development of women. The task should not be left to the government but shared by the society at large.

Empowerment of women through reservation in parliament is a mockery of women's problem. Will the increase of women parliamentarians reduce the incidence of female foetus abortion? Can it reduce the number of female infanticide? Will it stop discrimination between boys and girls? Will it lessen demands for dowry, maltreatment to daughter-in-laws, wife bashing, deaths in contrived accidents and neglect of widows? The answer to every question is simply no. And the reason is neither poverty nor lack of education. Recent demographic survey shows that the female birth rate is decreasing fast in so called educated and will to do states such as Punjab and Haryana. "Amniocentesis based female foeticides are the highest in Haryana and Punjab amongst the educated middle class families who believe in the small family norm and exercise their son-preference, by routinely getting rid of higher birth order girl foetuses".[7] Subsequent discrimination too prevails as brutal sense of son-preference in a rational world- view where the daughter's utility and value addition is meant for some other family, not one's own.

Anyway, the goal is the liberated woman, the complete woman, self-reliant, confident of her relations with and position vis-a-vis men, freed from the guilt complex of being natural. A complete woman—not just a complete woman for a complete man but one who could demand and get the complete man, a woman who would set her own agenda and know how to fight for it. Therefore, the need is total change in our outlook. Hence a workable solution could be to put economic, political and educational power within the reach of women with good guidance and support so that they could take up the cause on their own.

References

1. Gregory D. Souza, "Gender Discrimination: Reason and Remedies", *Journal of Dharma,* vol. XX, No. 1, p. 64.
2. Peter Kemp, "From Ethics to Bioethics", *Questioning Ethics,* ed. Richard Kearney and Mark Dooley, (Rautledge, London & New York), pp. 284-85.
3. Maeve Cooke, "Questioning Autonomy", *Ibid.,* p. 266.
4. *Ibid*., p. 267.
5. Ann Ferguson 'A Feminist Aspect Theory of Self, *Women, Knowledge and Reality,* ed. Ann Garry, and Marilyn Pearsall (Unwin, Hyman, Boston, 1989), p. 95.
6. Amartya, Sen, "Individual, Freedom", *The Times of India,* Patna, 16th Oct,, 98.
7. Amrit Srinivasan, "India's Missing Women", *The Times of India,* Patna, 28th April, 2001.

Chapter 2

Empowerment of Women: What it Should Mean?

Tandra Patnaik

A woman is a human being—no sane person will contest this fact. Yet gender-bias is an integral ingredient of our social fabric—this again is an undeniable fact. These two contradictory realities can co-exist if we willy-nilly accept the inferiority of women's status in the social hierarchy. Biologically she belongs to the same species as man i.e., homo-sapiens, yet socially, politically and culturally she is denied certain rights and privileges enjoyed by her male counterparts. This predicament is will reflected in the Beijing. Declaration on the occasion the 4th world conference on women held in 1995. It states, "Women's rights are human rights."[1] The charter promises to ensure "full implementation of human rights of women and girl child as an inalienable and indivisible fart of all human rights.[2] The charter also foresees that women can be brought to the level of human beings by the process of 'advancement' and 'empowerment'[3] That is why in recent times we hear a lot about women's empowerment. But very few are clear about what empowerment should mean? Is it intrinsic or extrinsic? In other words, is empowerment a process of power being thrust on women by an outside agency, or is it supposed to grow from within? Unless we clarify this basic question, the word 'empowerment' sounds like a cliche. My paper aims to explore this question keeping the Indian context in the background.

At first hand, it appears that we can better understand this issue if we address ourselves to the Feminists' approach to the problem of gender bias. It is well known that Feminism is not the name of single set of ideas and beliefs. Till 1970s Feminists demanded equal rights for women by emphasizing on aggressive imitation of masculinity. This form of feminism is now replaced by a form of liberalism, which presupposes a form gender-neutral theory of equality and justice. But the neo-Feminists take a different stance. For them, the identity of woman as a 'distinct class' should not be sacrificed at the alter of gender-neutrality. So they insist on the preservation of women's identity on the basis of 'distinct female' characteristics and 'distinct female instinct'. The various versions of such Feminist theories, however, do not take us very far in our analysis of what empowerment should mean? In case of India, Feminist movements are largely confined within the bounds of the elite class. At the same time, a section of modern women seem to be strongly influenced by such theories. The gender-neutral approach implicitly suggests the acceptance of the male personality as role-model. Those who follow this version of Feminism believe that in order to be empowered women must be more assertive and aggressive. Even, in the matters of dress codes, they follow the male. The yuppie and dink culture emulated by a certain section of professional women are the manifestation of this gender-neutral model of Feminism. On the other hand, the neo-Feministic model builds its theory of 'distinctness of woman as class'. But more the self-consciousness about feminity and feminine-power, the more there is the projection of woman as an object of attraction. The elite Indian women revel in the 'celebration women's sensuality.' The Indian advertising world, especially, the visual media, has banked upon this concept in their projection of women as independent, yet unabashedly self-conscious about their sensuality. The life style and the ideals projected by the Feminist theories in India cannot be called empowerment. Hence, we have to look elsewhere for a more viable model.

I propose to examine here Amartya Sen's Developmental model[4] and explore it's feasibility in the context of empowerment of women in India. What makes this theory more relevant in the Indian context is the recognition of the fact that the problem of gender-inequality is more rooted in social attitudes than in psychological and genetic factors. Besides, unlike Rawls,[5] Sen does not dismiss the problem of gender-bias. Rawls theory, though initially attractive, is based on the presupposition that women's right is not very distinct from the general issues of human rights as a whole. Moreover, for Sen, women's empowerment is not basically a form of women's 'well farism'. It is not just enough that state society guarantees the welfare of women. The very notion of women's welfare is rooted in the notion of the woman as an 'agent'. Though both women's welfare and woman as an agency are interrelated, yet, true welfare cannot be realized unless and until the woman is recognized as an independent agent having some definite role in the society. As Sen clarifies, "the most immediate argument for focusing on women's agency may be precisely the role such an agency can play in removing the inequities that depress the well- being of women".[6] His agency- centered approach allows women not to see themselves just as the recipients of welfare-enhancing help, but as active agents of change. Moreover, understanding the agency-role of woman helps her to recognize herself as a responsible person who can act or refuse to act and can choose to act in one way or the other.

Empirical research shows that relative respect for women's well-being is strongly influenced by the following variables: (1) women's ability to earn an independent income (2) her ability to find employment outside home (3) her ability to have ownership rights, and (4) to have literacy and be educated participants in decisions within and without the family. These variables may seem divergent and disparate, but according to Sen, they have in common one positive contribution, viz., "adding force to women's voice and agency-through independence and empowerment".[7] In Indian society, women's subjugation, in most cases, is due to women's economic dependence on the male members of the family. Till date the male child is coveted as he is seen as a potential bread-earner and the future caretaker of the family. By this I do not try to overlook other social and cultural factors that determine the inferior position of women in the family. Women's role in managing the family chores, bearing and rearing of off springs are seen as non-productive. But working outside home and earning an independent income makes her contributions to the family more 'visible'. Similarly, working outside the family gives her a lot of exposure that makes her confident. Education makes women more skilled and informed; and property-rights allow her to be a powerful participant in family decisions. Thus, in-spite of being divergent, these four variables can have a 'unified empowering role'. This, in-turn, can have, as Sen hopes, "far reaching impacts on forces and organizing principles that govern divisions within the family and society as a whole".[8] However, Sen admits that the problem is largely rooted in the social psyche which strongly influences our pattern of family living. The principles that govern the division of role in the family decided by the congruent and conflicting roles that men and women play in family life. The family affairs smoothly run on the basis of certain *implicitly* agreed pattern of behaviour. This 'cooperative conflict' influences the 'deal' that women get in family regarding division of roles. An empowered woman can bargain for a better 'deal' by which both the parties can gain. Sen believes that "the impact of greater empowerment and independent agency of women....includes the correction of the iniquities that blight the lives of women vis-a-vis men".[9]

Now let us look at the social realities in India in the backdrop of Sen's theory. First and foremost, in India, most of those who are associated with women's movement believe that empowerment means delegation of power to women. For them, it is a form of extrinsic empowerment, where women are supposed to be the recipients of certain facilities and rights granted to them either by the society or by the government. In this regard the state has taken enough steps to empower women by its reservation policy in different job sectors, educational institutions and local political bodies. The 73rd and 74th constitutional amendment acts, 1992, proclaimed that not less than 33% of seats will be reserved for the women in local political bodies. But in reality, as is obvious from our experience and media reports, most of these candidates contesting elections do not come out even to canvass for their candidature. This job is often left to their men-folk. As a result, when they are elected these women do not act as the real decision-makers. This type of empowerment thrust upon women neither leads to advancement, nor to the sense of respect and dignity that are the corner stones of women's empowerment. Similarly, reservations of all kinds, be it in job sector or in educational institutes, promote a sense of diffidence amongst women. In recent times we notice that girls are coming out with flying colours in all sorts of examination. They are doing equally well at different levels of urban job sectors. So the potential trapped within women can flower provided they get equal opportunity. Hence, reservation policy may seem to be counterproductive at a psychological level. I strongly feel that women should not be empowered through the process of granting of reservation and quotas. Without intrinsic empowerment, this sort of extrinsic empowerment do not lead us anywhere.

How intrinsic empowerment is to be achieved remains a puzzling question. Let us take, for examples, the plight of women who satisfy all the four conditions enumerated by Sen i.e., (1) women's ability to earn, (2) to find employment outside home, (3) to have property-rights and (4) to be literate. In urban areas, we notice that there is growing trend amongst men to prefer working women as their wives. These women are educated, with an independent income of their own. But are they really empowered? Till today parents of highly qualified women with a handsome pay packet are expected to give dowry (most often cash) to the equally qualified, and sometimes even less qualified grooms. Similarly, the dowry deaths that are regularly reported in newspapers, include educated and sometimes, employed girl. These women have a voice that is muffled by the family members and more prominently, by the other women members of the family. The emerging economic structure in recent times has provided new opportunities to women in the job market. But women, in this case have to face a lot of pressure from both the sides i.e., the peace of job and the family. The job market is a male-dominated field. Here, the woman has to work four times harder to get a foothold in the place of her work. Besides, as a person she is put to real test by her efficiency in performing multiple and conflicting roles. These could be those of a worker, a mother, a wife, a hostess and the individual simultaneously, or at different times, thus, generating a lot of tension due to conflicting forces. Of course, every individual is expected to play multiple, and sometimes, conflicting roles in life. But such role conflicts are more taxing in case of women. She has to be assertive and sometimes aggressive in her work place, while back home she is expected to be a docile, caring and loving woman, conforming to the image of the traditional Indian women. Besides, her household responsibility continues to be the same, despite her being an independent wage earner. The net outcome is stress—a highly expensive experience.[10] The role-stress that she faces has various dimensions which can be put under the following categories, viz., self-role distance, self-isolation, self-ambiguity, role-expectation conflict, role-erosion, role-stagnation, resource-person feedback inadequacy, and finally, the multiplicity of roles.[11] Such role stress can cause immensely painful situations for working women. In India, the social psyche remains largely rigid. As a result, very few concession are made to her in matters of, what Sen calls, 'the principles that govern the division of roles'.[12] He, of course, is aware of such possibilities. While talking of 'cooperative conflicts' and implicit agreements in case of man-woman relationship in the family, Sen observes, "the very nature of family living—sharing a home and leading joint lives—requires that the elements of conflict must not be explicitly emphasized (dwelling on conflict will be seen as a part of failed union), and sometimes, the deprived woman cannot even know the extent of her relative deprivation. Similarly, the perception "productivity are to be assessed may rarely be discussed explicitly".[13] But in my opinion, this problem has to be discussed explicitly. As long as our social psyche revolves round the theory that women really belong to the home, we cannot achieve real empowerment for women. Intrinsic empowerment requires women to pay a heavy price in the current social and cultural atmosphere.

In this paper I have focused on different dimensions of empowerment which is based on the perception of women as the recipient of benefits does not actually lead to real empowerment. What should be targeted is intrinsic empowerment. Conditions like education, economic independence, property rights, etc., will help women gain necessary confidence that, in long run, would concretize the dream of empowerment. But what is urgently needed is a shift in the attitude of family members and a rationally based division in the family.

References

1. *Beijing Declaration* 1995, column 14.
2. *Ibid.*, column 9.
3. The Beijing Declaration makes it explicit (Column 12) that "the empowerment and advancement of women, including right to freedom of thought, conscience, religion, and belief, thus contributing to the moral, ethical, spiritual and intellectual needs of women and men, individually or in community with others and thereby guaranteeing them the possibility of realizing their full potential in society and shaping their lives in accordance with their own aspirations".
4. Amartya Sen, *Development as Freedom,* OUP, New Delhi, 1999.
5. John Rawls, *A Theory of Justice.*
6. Sen, *op.cit.*, p. 191.
7. Sen, *ibid*, p. 191.
8. Sen, *ibid*, p. 192.
9. Sen, *ibid*, p. 193.
10. Jitendra Mohan, "Globalization and Role of Stress among Women", *Globalization culture and Women's Development,* Ed. Rajmohini Sethi, Rawat Publications, New Delhi, 1999, pp. 302-
11. *Ibid.*
12. Sen, *ibid*, p. 193.
13. *Ibid.*, p. 193.

Chapter 3

Women's Empowerment: Retrospect and Prospect

Shyam Narayan Chaudhary

The Concept of "Women's Empowerment" is the outcome of the concept of 'Liberty' or 'Freedom'; which the human race is still striving to achieve in its fullness. Credit might be given to the concept of 'Modernism' and 'Industrial-revolution' for stirring up the conscience of the male-dominated society in this direction. "Women's-Empowerment" means to treat women at equal footing and empower them with such opportunities which may bring them at par with men. It has to be admitted that efforts are being made in this direction around the world, which has certainly brought some difference in the status of women. But, at the same time, it cannot be denied that the plight of women has not been removed so far, and the idea of "Women's Empowerment" still seems to be 'utopian' and a 'pious-wish'. It is painful to note that when science is striving to conquer space and time, the media are still full of the shameful and savage acts of gender-discrimination and atrocities on women in the form of sexual-harassment, leading to rape, murder, dowry-problem coupled with dowry-death, termination of female foetus, mal-nutrition and mal-treatment to female-child, discrimination in wages, deprivation of women in taking the decision of marriage and child-birth and other forms of exploitations; both in and outside the family almost around the world. It appears that man has not freed himself from the animal-instinct of "Might is Right", prevailing in his primitive abode (Jungle), where male being stronger in physical might, considers himself superior to female. The condition is worse in under-developed countries where chains of tradition are more tight than those of the developed nations.

The great psychologist Sigmund Freud[1] considers this 'Superiority-Complex' in men and' inferiority-complex' in females a psychological phenomenon. According to him the deprivation of female of the male-like sex-organ gives birth to the everlasting 'inferiority-complex' in female, while the possession of greater sex-organ in male is responsible for the superiority-complex in them. Freud adds one thing more. According to him female develops passive and sadistic complex, under which she gains pleasure in suffering pain, while male develops active, violent masochistic complex under which he derives pleasure by inflicting pain.[2] Thus, according to Freud women are destined to have inferiority complex, while the matter is just reverse in male. The communist thinker like C. Millet[3] rejects Freudian theory as a bourgeois concept of the patriarchal society.

This attitude of male's superiority had its reflection in literature also. Women was depicted as passive, shy, timid, introvert, mysterious, unpredictable, treacherous and an object of enjoyment: While man was described as active, open, extrovert, responsible, brave, and aggressive. Different religions also were not favourable and sympathetic towards women. With the exception of a few celestial mothers, the women in general have been treated as the "gate-way of hell" and also the "property of men". Strict commandments have been issued for maintaining the "sexual-purity" of women. Even the open-minded Lord Buddha, who did not favour caste-difference, was not favourable for the admission of women in his 'Sangha'. Freud is of the opinion that different social customs for restricting free-mixing of women with men even inside the family are due the fear of incest.[4]

This apathetical attitude of the different socio-religious institutions have been responsible for the worsening condition of women, as a result of which they were denied proper place in social-order. Different religions framed various codes of conduct for maintaining the sexual-purity of women and also for keeping strict loyality to their men. By the tightening of the institution of marriage, these dogmas became all the more, hardened. This gave birth to the backwardness of women in the form of illiteracy, superstition, traditional dogmatism and acceptance of the slavery of men.

In the Indian context the status of women was by and large better in the Vedic period. No Yajna could be performed without the participation of women and they enjoyed almost equal status along with men in the social-order. Vedas are full of the examples of so many learned and and elevated women like Ghosha, Apala, Vishwadhara, Lopamudra, Shachimaulomi, Varabhrini, Surya, Romasha, Shachi, Saraswati etc., who even discovered[5] so many mantras (hymns) like male Rishies. As for example Surya[6] discovered 47 Richas of the 10th Mandal of Rigveda, Romasha[7] discovered 7 Richas of 1st Mandal. Shachi[8] and Ghosha[9] discovered some Richas of 10th Mandal, Apala[10] discovered 7 Richas of the 8th Mandal and Saraswati[11] discovered a Richa of 1st Mandal and so on. The women even went to the battle-field to fight along with men in this period.

In the upanishadic period the position of women began to be eroded. But, in the puranic and epic periods the status of women began to be tightened. The institution of marriage came up with harsh rules for women. While women were asked to be monogamous but no such restriction was imposed on men. During this period Krishna was glorified for having sixteen thousand 'Pat-Ranies' (queens). In Shrimad Bhagavat[12] too women have been called weak (Abla), fraud and selfish. Lord Brahman is the first example of causing sexual harassment to Saraswati,[13] after which he had to lay down his body from which Manu and Satarupa (male-female) arose. The framers of ethical-codes like Manu, Vidura, Chanakya etc. have also not been kind towards women.

The Mahabharata[14] and Ramayana[15] speak a lot about the detoriation of the condition of women in this age, to the extent of giving away Draupadi in gambling, turning of Ahilya into stone, fire-test and final banishment of the legendary Sita. It is this age that the self-immolation by Sati, the consort of Shiva, in the Yajna of his father Yaksha was glorified to the extent that it gave birth to the dreaded system of 'Sati' which could be stopped with the great efforts of Raja Ram Mohan Roy and others after thousands of years.

But we must remember that India had to pay, the price of this apathy towards women. The society became so much indifferent and insensitive that it paved the way of slavery of this land for thousands of years.

It is amazing that Mahammad Gajni who came with some hundreds of soldiers, succeeded in plundering all that he wished; and millions of men and women remained silent spectators.

After a long lapse of many centuries 'Jhansi Ki Rani' came to arouse India from its dogmatic slumber by challenging the foreign intruders. During freedom struggle, the concept of 'Bharat Mata' (Mother-India) tied up in chains, representing the true picture of the Indian women, aroused the spirit of the great freedom fighters. Mahatma Gandhi could foresee that unless the women are brought out from their doors, the concept of freedom would be a myth. Hence, he took a bold step towards the empowerment of women in which after fighting out lot of hindrances he succeeded to a considerable extent and finally freedom could be achieved. The 'Khadi' and 'Charkha' (Spining wheel) movement was directed mostly to this direction. The veiled Indian women, living in traditional environment could come out with their Charkha-spun threads to deposit them and get the price at the collection centers which they called 'congress'. This 'Charkha' became the great source of livelihood of the millions of Indian women, specially the poor and the widows, which popularized the congress. The concept of Marx that "slavery is an economic category" also proved to be correct.[16]

After India gained freedom, equal voting-right had to be granted to women and later on 'Sharda-act' and 'Hindu code bill' were enacted, which went a long way in initiating the process of the empowerment of women. Reservation for women in recently concluded Panchayat election and bill pending in the parliament for the reservation of 33% seats for women in the decision-making bodies like parliament and assemblies are indeed welcome-steps.

It is encouraging to note that women are proving their worth in all the fields wherever opportunity in being provided to them. But still the gender-difference and exploitation of women is going on at an alarming rate. They are lagging far behind in education, employment, male-female ratio, birth-rate, survival of girl child, health, nutrition, political power and status in the family and society. The craving for male-child has not stopped yet, which often leads, to the termination of female-foetus. The concept that "for the continuation of Bansha' (clan) and for achieving heaven a male-child is essential", is at the root of all these evils in which female themselves are equally responsible.

In the international arena too the situation is not all together different. in some form or the other, gender inequality is there and the empowerment of women is still a far-cry. The average male-female ratio in the world is 100:95, while in Korea and Singapore; it is 100:92. In China it is 100:86 and in India it 100:92:5. In Spite of boasting to be the leader of the modern developed world, U.S.A. has not been able to empower any woman as its President in its long history. Same is the case more or less with other countries, including communist block. The condition of women in the Islamic countries is the worst, where no serous effort is being made to improve their condition. Thus, gender-differentiation is a global phenomena and there is only a difference in degree in the different parts of the world.

Prospect

It is heartening to note that inspite of the gender-differentiation being faced by women, the voices are being raised against it around the world for a long time. In ancient Greece Lisistrata gave a call for sexual-strike against men for ending war. Again, during the French-revolution, women marched in procession raising slogans in favour of liberty and faternity. The Socialist International held in 1910 in Copenhegen announced "women's-day" for starting the movement for women's right in which 100 women from 17 countries participated. In the year 1911 "International women's day" was observed in Austria, Denmark, Germany and Switzerland on March 19, in which one million men and women participated and demands for voting-right, right to work, vocational-training and stopping gender-discrimination to women were raised. In Russia the first International Women's day was observed on 28th February in 1913. On the same day, in U.S.A. also, first national women's movement was celebrated. The women's movement gained such a momentum later on, that in 1945 the United Nations proclaimed in its charter 'gender-equality' as a fundamental human-right. In 1975 "first international women's conference" was held. The conference held in Narobe demanded that women should get suitable representation in political decision-making institutions. In India also recently 2001 was declared as the year of women's empowerment.

It cannot be denied that all these efforts on national and international levels have brought some change in the status of women. But it has to be admitted that these efforts have not given desired results so far, and a lot more has to be done. The authoritative-tendency of male and the traditional-minded women, having blind faith in social and religious dogmas, are the main impediments in the way of women's-Empowerment. Hence, following few steps have to be taken, if we are really serious about women's empowerment:—

1. The programme for universalisation of education up to +2 level with special stress on girls-education, should be taken up on national level as a time-bound programme; in which stress should be given on job-oriented vocational training. Besides, moral education based on human values should be made compulsory at all stages.
2. A planned programme for modernisation and industrialisation should be taken up for raising the standard of living.
3. A planned programme for opening of female-centered cottage-industries should be taken up on large scale to make women financially self-dependent.
4. Laws for giving proper share to women in paternal and husband's property should not only be enacted, but there should be a powerful agency for the strict implementation of these laws.
5. A mass awareness-programme against gender-discrimination and socio-religious dogmas should be under taken at all levels.
6. Separate agencies headed by women for the redressal of the grievances against the atrocities on women in and out side the family should be established and time-bond summary-trials by courts headed by women, should be done.
7. A powerful body headed by woman should be established at different levels to implement the different laws already enacted, like anti-dowry act etc. and also to monitor the actions taken at different levels for the implementation of different laws in favour of women's empowerment.
8. Right to work should be included in the constitution and 'house-wifery' should also be treated as a 'work' for which suitable allowance should be given to the women.

9. The rape-victims should be thoroughly rehabilitated and harsh-punishment in the form of very heavy fines together with at least life imprisonment should be given to the guilty.
10. Persons responsible for the termination of female foetus should be given severe punishment by treating the offerce as murder.
11. Proper awareness-programme for treating girl-child at par with male-child should be under taken.
12. Female-nutrition and health-care programmes should be under taken on a large scale.
13. Marriage and Motherhood should not be treated as the only goal of girl's-life and she should be encouraged to be self-dependent first and to take decision in the matter of her marriage and child-birth thereafter on her own.
14. At least 33% reservation for women should be given in different educational institutions, government and private jobs and also in all the decision-making bodies from the panchayat to the parliament.
15. Irrespective of religious faiths, polygamy should be banned altogether.
16. Mother's name should be mentioned on all documents along with father's name.
17. Care should be taken for stopping the spread of the western perverted culture, which is projecting woman merely as a thing of enjoyment and all sorts of medium of entertainment and advertisement should be thoroughly screened against these filthy and provocative tendencies.
18. An agency consisting of women's organization and government bodies should be established to suggest ways and means for the upliftment of women and also for the stock-taking of the actions-taken on all programmes of women's empowerment at all levels.

Thus, though we have miles to go in the direction of women's empowerment, yet we must be very optimistic about its prospect. It has to be realised that the feeble voices raised for women's empowerment are slowly but steadily taking the shape of a global movement. Even in the societies where the concept of the freedom of women is being treated as ante-religious, voices are being raised in its favour, however feeble it might be. No movement started with strong determination and courage has ever failed and this movement is bound to succeed as it is not a movement for giving anything 'new', but giving the 'due' to women which has been denied to them so far. What is needed is the sustained, determined and planned effort, without caring for the social, religious, political and traditional obstacles; which have to be faced with courage and determination. It is also needed that the educated and empowered women should come out of the boundaries of the traditional socio-religious "Lakshman Rekha" and keep on burning the flames of this movement with determination and courage and also with the confidence of achieving the goal in days to come. Men should also understand that women's-empowerment is not antagonistic to their interest; rather it is a boon in disguise and they should remember and realise the old saying that where women are worshipped, Gods (Virtues) reside there (Narystu Yatra Pujyante Ramante Tatra Devatah); which entails that for the all-round development of human society women's-empowerment is the essential condition. And for women's-empowerment; "Women's-emancipation" "Women's-upliftment" is needed which can be achieved through making determined- honest-efforts

References

1. Sigmund Freud, *A general Introduction to psychoanalysis (Introductry Lectures on Psychoanalysis)*, Penguin Edition, Ch.-III, Lecture 20, pp. 359-60.
2. *Ibid.*, p. 347.
3. K. Millet, *Sexual Politics*, 1970 Also See, Margret Mead, Sex and Temperament in three primitive societies, 1935, E. Borguego, A world of women, 1986.
4. Sigmund Freud, *Totem and Taboo*, Pub., Routledge & Kegan Paul, London, Ch. 1, pp. 1-17.
5. *Vedas* are called 'Apaurusheya' as the Vedic Mantras are said to nave been discovered in the state of 'Samadhi' (trance) by the different Rishies at different times. Besides, the Vedic Rishies were called "Kavayah satya Shrutah" (poets, who were the listners of the truth). Hence, instead of taking shese hymns as written; it would be proper to call them as 'discoveries'.

6. *Rigveda*, 10.85.
7. *Ibid.*, 1.126.7.
8. *Ibid.*, 10.125.
9. *Ibid.*, 10.39, 40.
10. *Ibid.*, 8.91.
11. *Ibid.*, 1.34.
12. *Shrimad Bhagwat,* 6.18.33-35 and 6.18.41-43,7.11.9, 10.
13. *Ibid.*, 3.12.27-33 see also, 9.1.13-32. There is a story of the Vaivashvata Manu whose wife gave birth to a daughter, for which he was so much agrived that he got her changed into a son.
14. i. Mahabharata, Adi Parva, Ch. 122 (The Sexual harassment of the mother of swehaketu before him)

    ii. *Ibid.*, Ch., 82 (Here women have been regarded as the movable property of men, who are destined to be under the shelter of father in childhood, under husband in young age and under son in old age).

    iii. *Ibid.*, Ch., 104 (King Bali sent his wife Sudeshna to the blind Rishi 'Dirghatama' for having sexual contact to produce son. This practice was called 'Niyoga'.

    iv. Ch., 105 (Niyoga by Kunti).

    Ch., 121 (Niyoga by Amba, Ambika etc.).
15. i. *Valmiki,* Ramayana, Aranya Kanda 45, 29, 30, 33.

    ii. Tulasi Das, *Rama Charita Manansa*, Cotemptuous remarks for women:—

    Vala Kanda, 125.2, 3, 133, 12, 143. 23, 243

    Aranya Kanda, 76. 1, 2. 3, 4, 77

    Kishkindha Kanda, 16.4

    Sundara Kanda, 62.3

    Uttar Kanda, 161.1

    (The list is just illustrative, not exhaustive).
16. Karl Marx, *The Poverty of Philosophy*, p. 124.

Chapter 4

Gender Discrimination, Globalisation and the Problem of Women's Empowerment: A Marxist Perspective

R.K. Singh

Over the recent years, few topics have drawn the attention of researchers in social philosophy as well as social sciences, planning groups of government and NGOs' social workers, political activists and reformers as the problem of Gender Discrimination in the wake of Globalisation acclaiming laurel for ameliorating the ostracised state of deprivation along with abominable sex prejudices against women endemic to the male dominated society.

The harassment of women and violence against them is not a new phenomenon. One may trace back its history to the origin of family and private property with the beginning of agricultural period. Though in Vedic period women in India enjoyed high social status which is evident from the excerpts so oft -quoted by the Indologists as well as sociologists.

In his study of "Status of Women", Professor Ram Ahuja has extensively referred to the passages of the ancient Indian scriptures as crucial instances of high status enjoyed by Indian women in ancient times Apastamba, for example, had prescribed:

"All must make a way for a woman when she is treading path".[1]

Manu had also high esteem for the women folk:

"Where the female relations live in grief, the family soon wholly perishes, but where they are not unhappy, the family ever prospers".[2]

He had again said:

"Where women are honoured, the Gods are pleased but where they are not honoured, no sacred rite yields any reward".[3]

Yagnavalkya is said to have had great reverence for the women "the embodiment of all divine virtues on earth".[4]

References are also made to several passages of the *Ramayana* and the *Mahabharata* which underline the lofty ideals about women. While the Vedic and the post-Vedic periods are proud of allowing equal status some time higher to women, the Puranic period presents a gloomy picture of the deplorable status of women deprived discriminated and undrprivileged. With the imposition of the Brahmanical austerities and restrictions , women were subjected to exploitation. Pre-puberty marriage, prohibition of widow remarriage, the Purdah system, the system allowing the status of a God to husbands (Pati Parmeshwar), total denial of education to women, the custom of sati, the practice of polygamy, economically ostacised with the total deprivation of ownership and share of property are the worst marks of male domination over the subjugated and enslaved women folk. Women empowerment was metaphor for misfortune.

However, the Buddhist period and the Medieval period allowed some kind of freedom to women specially in the field of religion, but nothing substantial could be done to promote women's liberation as the economic structure did not undergo any viable change. An impartial probe into changes of women's status brought about by reforms in the British period as also by social movements initiated by enlightened leaders like Raja Ram Mohar Roy and others show that inspite of important role played by them to free the women folk from the shackles of Brahmanical restrictions and repressive taboos which subsequently aroused the awareness, social and political, in women in the pre-independence period, which subsequently ensured their participation in Freedom Movement, could hardly make any breakthrough as the patriarchal economic structure remained intact.

In the post independence period, the scenario of the condition and status of women in India hardly changed. The father of the nation, Gandhijee had also unrealistic and unscientific vision of the status of woman. His male attitude towards women becomes clear when he believes in the natural division of shever of work of men and women. Illiteracy, economic dependence, religious strictures and prohibitions, restriction imposed by caste system, patriarchal hegemony, callous and inhuman attitude of men towards women resulting into foeticide, dowry deaths, rapes and sexual harassment, violence against women in various forms, perpetuation of sex prejudices, denial of equal status and deprivation of equal opportunities have belied the tall claims of the governmental agencies regarding women's upliftment. In her preface, to J. P. Memrial Lecture by Justice Chinappa Reddy "From a man's world to a Human world" eminent sociologist Neera Desai has rightly observed: "It is a man's world is not a rhetoric nor a cliche but a reality faced by half the humanity for millennia".[5]

According to report commissioned by the united Nation published in "Women Development and Empowerment", the Apartheid of Gender "becomes glaring": Women in India. How free? How equal? It is startling how few women in Bihar really have the basic freedom of choice. Over 80 percent in Bihar, Madhya Pradesh, Haryana and Andhra Pradesh and nearly ninety percent in Uttar Pradesh need permissions from male members of the family to visit a friend or relative or to go to the market. Millions of them simply lack the freedom to go out of their house to seek health services they need. According to the report, family members punish women for trivial relations".[6]

The present age beginning with the collapse of the Soviet Union and the end of the cold war leading to a unipolar world has come to be widely known as the age of globalisation. The concept as such is not new for the Marxists as is being claimed since more than a century ago the communist manifesto boldly declared:

"The working men have no country........... They have a world to win. Working men of all countries unite".[7]

What is gruesome and enigmatic about the concept is that in the name of freedom it stands for the hegemonisation of capitalism in a unipolar world. By using the international financial and trade institutions and pursuing policies like economic blockade and sanctions, the USA is out to meddle in the internal affairs of a host of countries. The logic behind all this is nothing else other than

Globalisation. However, one is not to wonder if in the name of freedom Globalisation has come to stand for the supreme hegemony of the capitalist countries all over the world threatening national freedom and sovereignty. It will not be unworthy to retrospect, the lines from the Manifesto itself which clearly elucidate the meaning of 'Freedom'.

"By freedom is meant, under the present bourgeois conditions of production, free trade, free selling and buying".[8] This kind of freedom preys upon the freedom of the immense majority of the masses. It only tantamounts to the slavery of the great Masses.

However, for the present purpose let us venture to the high sounding claims made by the advocates of globalisation in fighting out gender-discrimination thereby ensuring a congenial environment for the women to enjoy freedom. Globalisation as is claimed, has taken long strides to redeem women from male-dominated world by opening up new vistas of greater employment opportunities for them. Claims are being made that in the new world of globalisation women are successfully attaining higher status and are enjoying greater economic freedom. How can it be denied that the number of women labour has increased in recent years? The Ford Foundation Report advocates the impact of globalisation on the empowerment of women. The economic reforms and changes in economic policies have ushered in tremendous progress in improving the condition and status of women. New opportunities have come up to ameliorate the situation in which the apartheid of gender has given way to a new world of freedom for women.

The fabulous mystification of the redemptive impact of globalisation on improving the lot of women falls flat with 'Gender Quake' beginning with the charges of sex-exploitation made by professor Anita Hill against senator Bob Packwood in 1991-92. Neeomi Wolf in her new book "Fire with Fire: The New Female Power and How It Will change The 21st Century" has referred to the exposition of events, the "Gender Quake" that has begun to shake the patriarchal system. It also exposes the myth of women empowerment in the era of globalisation.

As a matter of fact globalisation itself is a new form of patriarchal hegemony which perpetuates discrimination and violence against women. In the name of freedom women are being used as a commodity to be sold in the Market. Through cosmetic and entertainment industries, beauty contests, modeling new markets of nudity and 'cat girls' have propped up. A large number of women from third world countries are being exported to developed countries to be employed as nurses or in most cases as maids and sex workers. The sex industry of Japan earns billions of yens a year. By importing women from their countries Bangladesh, Sri Lanka and many other under developed countries earn billions of dollars to pay off their loans caused by the economic reforms dictated by the interests of the developed countries. Sex-tourism preys upon women and children. Philippines and a few other countries unable to bear the burden of loans have already earned notoriety in the sector of sex tourism. The above brief account of the myths and reality of the impacts of globalisation with regard to women's liberation clearly exposes the surreptitious return of patriarchal hegemony and a glamorous exploitation of women by men.

To make it worse, the return of religious revivalism and fundamentalism in the form of sporadic Sati incidents victimises women, the soft targets of society.

As a matter of fact, globalisation and all forms of religious fundamentalism are the weapons to protect the interest of a particular class, the ruling class. The existing economic and social structure is denying freedom to women.

Hence the claims made by the advocates of globalisation with regard to women's liberation turn out to be new challenges, and threats with all brutality to women's empowerment. Creating a few jobs for women, making constitutional provisions for their political rights, even their access to political power here and there through electoral system hardly make any difference with regard to power and authority of women in general. We have examples of greater atrocities towards women in a state where a woman wields highest political power and authority. Even such power and authority hardly succeed to attain public recognition, often such women in power are used to serve the interest of Socio-economic system where patriarchal hegemony matters.

The question of women's empowerment can be addressed only when we take up the issue of production relations. Justice Chinnappa Reddy rightly observes:

"It is now accepted by all serious social scientists that the vast majority of women have always been economically productive and that the differing degrees and differing forms of power and authority held by different classes cultures and nation depended on the historical changes in production relation".[9]

Hence it is absolutely necessary to consider the point of productive relation as the genesis of power and authority of women in a society. To quote him further:

"So long as production was for consumption women held public authority but with the production of commodities for exchange the public authority women could wield was lost as the new economic relation based on exchange were in the hands of men".[10]

The very base of status low or high of a class is the pattern of economic condition the productive relation attached to that class. It is the change in production relation that necessitates changes in the role of a class. Eleanor Leacock has aptly observed: "Changes in productive relations" brought about "changes not only in degrees of female authority and power but also in the forms taken by authority and power and their relations to one another".[11]

The relationship between production relation and the status of women was explored and scientifically explained by Engels in his celebrated book "The Origin of the Family Private Property and the state". By employing Dialectical Materialism and Historical Materialism Engels elaborately explained that the economic pattern of a particular form of society, the kind of the means of production and production relations ultimately determine the status of different classes of the society including men and women. It was the production relations existing in a particular form of society that determined degradation of the status of women from the dignity of a Matriarch to the servility of the first domestic servant in history. By referring to a number of prehistoric periods as well as Medieval and Modern periods with capitalistic mode of production and examining them Engels concluded that the 'mother right' The Matriarchal form of society was due to the primitive form of economy where the storing of food and the administration of the household were entrusted to women. Engels observed:

"The savage, warrior and hunter had been content to occupy second place in the house".[12]

But later on with the development of property and division of labour the supremacy of women was denied and the patriarchal form of society came into existence. According to Engels, "The administration of the household lost its public character. It was no longer the concern of society. It became a private service. The wife became the first domestic servant, pushed out of participation in social production. The modern individual family is based on the open or distinguished enslavement of the women. In the family, he is the bourgeois: the wife"[13] represents the proletariat.

Under a class divided society women are subjected to double exploitation: firstly, general exploitation of women by men.

The low status of women with all sorts of sex discrimination rests solely on the exploitative form of economy which persists in the present day world.

Hence, the true empowerment of women, their emancipation urgently calls for a radical change in the form of production and productive relation. No amount of legal and constitution reforms, no worship or idols of goddesses, no moral preaching can guarantee women's empowerment.

It is through the overthrow of the exploitative economic system that real emancipation of women can be achieved. Employment of women is a step forward towards emancipation of them. Empowerment and emancipation of women should not be confused with the western concept of women's liberation where it stands for alienating women from men. Emancipation of women on the other hand, is the achievement of equal status with men and not freeing from the since they constitute the inseparable part of a nation. It is through participating in the common struggle of the masses to change the socio-economic system based on all sorts of discrimination and exploitation that women can achieve emancipation. Vinod Mishra, a communist leader of contemporary India observed: "Women's struggle for equality is in fact a struggle in a society. Such a society can only be a socialist society which eradicates private property and class division. Therefore, only under the guidance of communist thought can woman liberation struggle accomplish its ultimate stage".[14]

A revolutionary transformation of the socio-economic system based on exploitation, discrimination and division of classes to Usher in a new order of society proud of a "Kingdom of freedoms" can alone achieve emancipation for women.

References

1. Ahuja, Ram: *Indian Social System*, Rawat Publication, New Delhi, 1997, p. 91.
2. *Ibid.*, p. 91.
3. *Ibid.*, p. 92.
4. *Ibid.*, p. 93.
5. Desai, Neera: Preface to "From a Man's World to a Human World", Lecture by Justice Ghinnappa Reddy published in........centre for Women's Development Studies, 1990, p. 16.
6. A report by the office of the UN Resident Co-ordination in India, published by Times Response Supplement, 8 march 2002, p. 11.
7. McLekhan, Barid, Karl Max: Selected Writings, Oxford University Press, 1977, pp. 235-246.
8. *Ibid.*, p. 233.
9. Reddy, Chinnappa: From a Man's World to a Human World", Centre for Women's Development Studies, 1990, p. 15.
10. *Ibid.*, p. 15.
11. Eleanor, Leacock: *Women power and Authority in Visibility*, Oxford University Press, 1986, pp. 15-16.
12. Marx, Karl and Engel's, Frederick: *Selected Works*, Vol. 3, Progress Publishers, Mascow, pp. 332-33.
13. *Ibid.*, pp. 332-33.
14. Mishra, Vinod: *Selected Works*, Sankalan Prakashan, 1999, p. 164.

Chapter 5

Problems and Prospects of Women's Empowerment

C. D. Jha

The society is advancing very fast with alround socio-economic development but the position of women is not improving alongwith the pace of development. With the growing development and cry to march in the 21st century there is common consensus that women should be given adequate facilities for the development of a sound nation. But all the sayings and calls are useless till the teasing and body-assaults are not stopped. Since the dawn of civilization male dominated society, treated women as sex symbols. All must be aware about the treatment as "Devdasi Pratha" of our country. We all talk about giving equal status to women in all the spheres of life but still this is far from the truth. In recent days even political parties have neglected the reservation of women in election. "Dahez Pratha", torturing of women are normal phenomena. It would be better to examine the fate of women in every walk of life. Gender reason is most vital, which inhances the problems of women. Even women are also enemy of women, what to say of males. None thinks that women are the vital organ of the society. They are regarded as goddesses but face human atrocities in various ways. This is why during the struggle for independence, Mahatma Gandhi realising this, took special efforts to include women in political as well as in economic and social struggles.

After independence, the progress of women and of the society seems to have been retarded. Even after fifty years, examples are galore, where on the one hand the sensitivity over women's issues are lacking and on the other hand atrocities against women are rising.

Women related issues have many dimensions but they can be summarised as violence, denial and deprivation. Violence can be in parental or matrimonial house or at work-place, or elsewhere in the society. Denial comes as denial of the right to be born, or denial of nutrition, education, health, home, property etc. Deprivation results from debarring them from several opportunities of empowerment—political, economic or career-wise.

These are the problems? But what about the systems designed to solve these problems? How effective are they? For example, a review of legal system shows that right from the judicial system to police investigation, to medico-legal recordings to the system of evidence have been twisted in the hands of advocates. Everywhere we find systematic insensitivity. Similarly in social, economic and political systems, we find insensitivity to the women's aspirations for realising their potential.

All this provides the working ideology for National Commission for Women which was formed by Indian Government .The most important and operative part i.e., section '10' of the Act makes provision of investigation in all matters relating to safeguard of women from torturing. The Commission has some programmes for granting funds to voluntary organisations, academicians and other bodies. The programme of legal literacy camps has been designed to organise a 3 days legal awareness for a group of nearly 50 women by any organisation. The 'Parivarik Mahila Lok Adalat' (P.M.L.A.) is designed to give fund to voluntary agencies which can work along with District Family Court or the District legal Aid Service Authority to provide counseling to the disputing parties. The other programme includes public hearing under which hearing is given to a group of 30 or more women who are affected by a typical situation at one or more places. Funding is also given for holding seminars, workshops, on topics relevant and important for women's problems and also for the academicians to carry out surveys and other studies.

So the terms "Gender Justice", "Women-Empowerment" and "Women-Welfare" are in limelight in the social and economic developmental programmes of both developed and developing nations. The debate on gender-justice to women-empowerment was at the central stage in the international arena in 1994 in Cairo and during fourth International Conference on women at Beijing in 1995.

The Government of India has taken numerous measures and is making honest endeavours to raise the status of women and establish gender equality. The constitutional obligations as well as different plans programmes and policies have laid emphasis on women-empowerment. Article 15 of the constitution prohibits any discrimination on the ground of sex. While Article 15(3) classifies that this provision will not prevent the state from making any special provision for women. Article 42 of the constitution envisages for securing just and human conditions of work and for maternity relief. The directive principles of state policy also urges that the state shall direct its policy towards securing an adequate means of livelihood for women and for insuring equal pay for equal work for both men and women. The idea of setting up of a National Council for empowerment of women is an encouraging step in this direction and similarly setting up a National Resource Centre for Women is other step for development of women.

But the numerous welfare measures regarding status of women have not been adequatly implemented and the position of women-empowerment varies from region to region, state to state and even between rural and urban areas. It also varies from one community to the other. The fruits of women welfare measures are being largely enjoyed by the highly educated women and women belonging to socially, economically and politically advanced upper strata of urban society. Even then the women are not adequately represented in the legislative, executive and judicial wings of the government.

In India, women's representation in Parliament and state Assemblies has never gone beyond eight to ten percent. Not only in legislative sphere but also in the executive and judicial spheres women are thinly represented. In the social sphere there is 'Gender Isolation' and Gender Oppression'. Being isolated in social sphere women are less represented in I.A.S., I.P.S. sports and business, because of 'Gender stereotypes'.

A society that has effectively implemented women's welfare measures and has ensured gender justice and empowerment of women, has achieved greater social development. In India Kerala is an outstanding example of socially advanced state. Over looking of empowerment of women means dispossession of half of human capital. It means an incomplete attempt for social development and a complete violation of Human Rights for all.

Chapter 6

Gender Discriminations: A Feminist Critique

Ravi Kumar Sinha

The phenomena of gender discrimination in the social, cultural, economic and political fields are evident all over the world, only forms and ways vary. The biological difference between 'male' and 'female' which is naturally ordained and which places women at a disadvantageous position, has been exploited by men since the formation of social structure to their benefit. However, and this seems paradoxical also, the issue of gender discrimination cannot be adequately grasped nor can be satisfactorily addressed to in purely biological terms. In the second sex Simone de Beauvoir argues that the division of sexes is as irreducible, not an historical category. This implies that women's problems could be understood by women only. Contrary to this , the issue of gender discriminations and women's problems require a broader perspective for their proper understanding. A feminist perspective is closely related to "concern with issues affecting women, a concern to advance women's interests, so that, therefore, anyone who shares this concern is a feminist".[1]

Gayatri Spivak, who makes her 'sex' the ground for a question, says that "as a female reader I am haunted by another question".[2] And Virginia woolf observes that women's inheritance is the 'difference of view, the difference of standard. However, it would be erroneous to assume that this 'difference' is something given; it must be produced. Jacques Lacan is closer to the truth when he says that "psyche" of the "unconscious" is "structured" in the symbolic system of a linguistic culture.[3] This is attested by the fact that today even women share 'men's anti-female feelings'[4]—Women's complicity in Dahej and related atrocities supports the view. Shoshana Felman and Elaine showalter mean the same thing when they refer to the strategic or theoretical position of a female reader which "changes our apprehension of a given text, awakening us to the significance of its sexual codes".[5]

It is true that western Feminist theories do provide some insights into the subtle process of Gender discrimination—how biological compulsions made women vulnerable and also dependent upon men, how power and prestige got associates with men's works and how men gained access and exclusive rights to those activities including politics, which invested them with authority. This constitutes an interesting area of socio-psychological study of Indian male psyche that constructed myths and legends specifically the notorious Smritis which are rightly considered responsible for the social and culture degradation of women, denying them rights to education, mobility, freedom of choice in matters of careers and proper health-care facilities. However, it is here that inadequacy and incompetency of the Shobha De—type Indian version of the Western Feminism is evidenced. It does not voice the concerns and problems of the 70% to 80% of the total Indian women living in the rural areas. While in urban areas women constitute 12% to 20% of the total labourer class working on building sites, in the rural areas the figure goes upto 40% in the agricultural sector where they work with men at every stage of cultivation. This certainly goes against the view of such anthropologists as Lionel Tiger and Robin Fox regarding the women who are incapicitated to undertake heavy and demanding works.[6] More importantly, rural communal life provides greater security to the working women; they enjoy a congenial atmosphere which is suggested by the 'song' they sing with men-workers during sowing-harvesting time.

Even in urban areas, in cultured families, the housewife enjoys honour and respectability which cannot be fully measured by those uninitiated in Indian culture. In Indian culture, the "expressive housewife-mother role"[7] has not been invented for the domestic oppression and exploitation of women. In fact, here femininity finds its supreme fulfilment in motherhood. And if women prefer or are assigned, house-bare and less strenuous works, it is because of practical advantage of this division of labour by sex.

In fact, Indian women unlike their western counterparts do not suffer from any sense of identity crisis. In Christianity, there is 'God, the father' and 'Son of God' while women are represented as being responsible for the original sin in the Garden of Eden. One can understand the lament of a noted feminist, Helen Cixous, "that the world of being can function to the exclusion of the mother".[8]

Indian women, on the other hand, are securedly placed in myths and legends. Here, masculine elements are as much contained in woman—in Kali and Durga—as feminine qualities are contained in 'Man'—in the feminine beauty of god and in the very feminine, "Usha", conception of the universe. In the Rig Veda, the figures of Gargi and Maitreyi contesting with Yagyavalkya on the nature of the universe, and the presence of Saraswati, the Goddess of learning, in the pantheon of Gods, are suggestive of the fact, that there is no under privileging of women in Indian culture. It is important that Panini, the great grammarian, formulated the rule of constructing lexical pairs (Samas) in which 'feminine' term should precede the 'masculine', such as Gauri-Shankar, Radha-Krishna and Sita-Ram. This is not to cover up the bewildering rupture in our cultural history first during the Brahmanical and Smriti period, and secondly during the Muslim and Christian invasion when we failed to "clutch"[9] to our glorious roots. This is only to emphasize the fact that all forms of gender discrimination cannot be traced back to religio-cultural heritage. The present backward condition of Indian women is more due to defective planning, massive illiteracy, utter poverty, lack of basic facilities, caste-ridden society and the phenomenon of eradication by the Feminist programmes of the west—the hybrid model or the modes of a unisex society as suggested by Alice Ross,[10] the birth control technique for reversal of role-models, disruption of the institutions of 'marriage' and 'family', and finally insistence on tolerance of homo sexual and lesbian relationships so that, as Kate Millelt[11] would say, "the sex act ceases to be arbitrarily polarized into male and female". These would rather sound preposterous even to the most oppressed of the Indian women, who despite their illiteracy, are well versed in the positive and progressive dimensions of their culture. That is why cultural revisionism becomes irrelevant in case of Indian feminism which seeks to secure respectable social status for women, based on economic and intellectual independence- and all these within the institution of "family".

Marginalization of women and the neglect of feminine qualities gave impoverished human culture. For Virginia Woolf the loss of feminine elements was responsible for "barbarism" in every aspect of modern life. She wants to bring the feminine principle back into an entirely masculinized world in order to humanize it, only then can men and women supplement each other in their pursuit of exploring the mystery of completion and establishing a better world".[12] This understanding comes sensitively closer to Indian ethos, according to which God or divine bliss reigns supreme at those places where women or feminine qualities are worshipped.

References

1. Rosalind Delmar, *'What is Feminism' What is Feminism*, Edited by Juliet Mitchell & Ann Oakley, Blackwell, U.S.A., 1994, p. 12.
2. Gayatri Spivak, *'Finding Feminist Readings: Dante-Yeats'*, Social Text, 3, 1980, pp. 73-87.
3. Jaeques Lacan, *'The Insistence of the letter in the Unconscious'*, In Modern Criticism and Theory*: A Reader*, ed. David Lodge, Longman, London, 1991, p. 82.
4. Dorothy Dinnerstein, *The Mermaid and the Minotaur: Sexual Arrangements and Human Malaise*, New York, Harpur, 1976, p. 90.
5. Shoshana Felman, *Women and Madness: The Critical Phallacy: Diacritics*, 5:4 (1975), 2-10. A Feminist Reading of Balzac, Elaine Showalter: Towards a Feminist Poetics In Women Writing and Writing about Women, ed. M. Jacobus, London, 1979, pp. 22-40.
6. Lionel Tiger and Robin Fox, *The Imperial Animal Seeker & Worburg*, London, 1972, as discussed in Sociology: *Themes of perspectives* by M. Haralambos with R.M. Heald, Oxford University press, Delhi 1980, p. 370.
7. Ann Oakley, *Housewife*, Allen Lane, London, 1974, as Discussed in *Sociology*, pp. 373-74.
8. Helen Cixous, *Sorties In Modern Criticism and Theory: A Reader*, p. 288.
9. T. S. Eliot's *Expression in the Wasteland: "What are the Roots that Clutch"*.
10. As discussed in M. Haralambus's *Sociology*.
11. Kate Millett, *Sexual Politics*, Doubleday, New York, 1970.
12. Bernard Blackstone, *Virginia Woolf*, London 1952, pp. 26-31.

अध्याय 7

लिंग असमानता : एक सर्वेक्षण

विद्या सागर सिंह

अभी हम सभ्यता के विकास की जिस मंजिल पर पहुँचे हैं वह प्रकृति एवं प्राकृतिक नियमों पर शोध एवं चिन्तन का समय है। जहाँ एक ओर विश्व के अधिकाशं विकासशील एवं विकसित राष्ट्राध्यक्षों तथा सजग एवं प्रबुद्ध नागारिकों का ध्यान इस पर केन्द्रित नजर आता है वहीं दूसरी ओर मनुष्य के यानी नर एवं नारी के आत्मिक अलगाव, विषमता, विच्छिन्नता, एकाकीपन और टूटन का भी समय है। यों कहा जायं कि आज का समय मनुष्य एवं मनुष्यता पर विचार करने का है। चूँकि पिछली पूरी सदी हिंसा की सदी थी। और महिलाओं पर अत्याचार एवं हत्या का मामला (दहेज एवं बाह्य सौन्दर्य की कमी के सन्दर्भ में और अधिक) कहर ढाता हुआ महसूस हो रहा है। आज की देहज-प्रथा प्राचीन काल की दहेज-प्रथा का ही विकृत रूप है। आज दहेज माता-पिता के स्नेह एवं वात्सल्य का स्वरूप न होकर वर-पक्ष द्वारा शोषण एवं अपमान का साधन बन गया है। आजकल कन्या के विवाह के पूर्व वर-पक्ष वाले विवाह की शर्त के रूप में बड़ी-बड़ी राशि वसूल करते हैं। साथ ही साथ वे टी0 वी0, स्कूटर, मोटरकार, फ्रिज, वीडियो आदि की भी मांग करने से नहीं चूकते हैं। और चुकती नहीं होने पर उन्हें अपमानित करना, तरह-तरह की यातनाएँ देना और यहाँ तक कि इसके लिए उनकी हत्या भी कर देते है। कुछ ऐसे भी उदाहरण अखबारों, पत्र-पत्रिकाओं एवं अन्य साधनों के द्वारा उपलब्ध हो रहे हैं कि आज महिलाओं की प्रतिष्ठा, उनका मान-सम्मान, उनके माता-पिता के द्वारा दहेज में दी गई राशि के आधार पर ही होता है। उनका यौवन उनकी आकांक्षाएँ सभी दहेज की अग्नि में जलकर भस्म हो जाती हैं। बेमेल विवाह और विलम्ब से विवाह दहेज-प्रथा के स्पष्ट दुष्परिणाम दृष्टिगोचर हो रहे हैं। हमें स्मरण रखना चाहिए कि आनेवाली पीढ़ियाँ उन्हें ऐसे ही याद करेंगी।

युद्ध, आतंकवाद, सम्प्रदायवाद, जातीय तथा नस्लों और सफलतापूर्वक महिलाओं पर अत्याचार एवं संहार पिछली सदी की पहचान रही है। यह मानवीय हिंसा का उदाहरण ही कहा जायेगा। मुझे ऐसा प्रतीत होता है कि अहंकार की तुष्टि एवं आर्थिक विषमता इसका मूल कारण है। इन्हीं दोनों कारकों ने हिंसा को एक नवीन संस्था नवीन तकनीक, मनोवैज्ञानिक योग्यता और अद्‌भूत रचनात्मकता का रूप दे दिया है। वस्तुतः उपर्युक्त समस्याओं के मूल में राजसिक एवं तामसिक अहंकार की तुष्टि के लिये ही आर्थिक मोर्चाबन्दी की गई है और आर्थिक विषमता की बढ़ोतरी से भयावह स्थिति उत्पन्न होती रही है। इस होड़ ने हमारे पूरे अस्तिव को मार डालने की बेहतर क्षमता के साथ जोड़ दिया है। इसकी पुष्टि इस बात से और अधिक युक्तिसंगत ढंग से की जा सकती है कि दुनिया के सभी देशों के रक्षा बजट में बढ़ोत्तरी एवं लोक कल्याण के बजट में कटौती कर दी गई है। इससे भी और अधिक चिन्ता का विषय यह है कि विश्व के लगभग साठ प्रतिशत वैज्ञानिक प्रत्यक्ष या परोक्ष रूप से रक्षा अनुसंधान में लग गये अथवा लगाये गये है। संसार में महिला और पुरुष के बीच असमानता ने इसमें महत्वपूर्ण भूमिका अदा की है। आज महिलाओ के प्रति आसोमा बिन लादेन का प्रतिबंध दुनिया को चौकानेवाला रहा है। यों अफगानिस्तान में तालिबान के पतन के बाद गठित सरकार ने महिलाओं को बराबरी के अवसर देने की प्रतिबद्धता जतायी है। इससे पहले तालिबान शासन काल में महिलाओं को शिक्षा एवं रोजगार से वंचित रखा जाता था और घर से बाहर निकलते समय बुर्का पहनना उनके लिये अनिवार्य था। किन्तु उन्हें यह भी स्मरण रखना चाहिए कि उनका राष्ट्र ही मर्द नहीं है और भी है। स्वयं के बराबर अन्य को भी मानना चाहिए।

अफगानिस्तान की ही नही बल्कि अन्य मुल्कों में भी विषमता दृष्टिगत होती है। पुरुष प्रधान समाज में महिला को उसका वास्तविक अधिकार देने के चाहे जितने भी बयान दिये जायें, पखवारे और महिला सशक्तिकरण वर्ष मनाया जाय, लेकिन यह ध्रुव सत्य है कि हमारे समाज में समस्त सुधारों के बाजजूद बेटे के जन्म पर जैसी खुशियाँ और जश्न मनाये जाते हैं, बेटी के जन्म पर वैसा कुछ देखने में प्रायः नहीं आता। संतानहीन दंपत्ति भी वैद्य, हकीम और डाक्टर से इलाज के दौरान पुत्र-रत्न प्राप्ति की ही मंशा जाहिर करते हैं।

जहाँ तक प्राचीन भारत का प्रश्न है यहाँ की महिलाओं का इतिहास गौरवमय था। वैदिक युग में भारतीय समाज व्यवस्था की धुरी महिला ही थी। जीवन के प्रत्येक क्षेत्र में उनकी सक्रिय भूमिका थी। शास्त्रों के सृजन से लेकर महत्वपूर्ण फैसला लेने संबंधी प्रक्रिया में वे हर मोड़ पर मौजूद थीं। इसलिए समाज में सौहार्दपूर्ण वातावरण था। हरेक क्षेत्र में देश की श्रेष्ठता दृष्टिगत होती थी। सम्पूर्ण संसार विशेष से एशिया,

भारत की प्रगति और चिंतन शैली से गंभीर रूप से प्रभावित था। लेकिन इस विकास प्रक्रिया में विदेशी हमलावरों ने बाधा पहुँचायी। इन विदेशियों ने आपसी भेद-भव लाकर इनकी सभ्यता एवं संस्कृति को नष्ट करने का हर सम्भव प्रयास किया और आपसी वैमनस्यता का लाभ उठाकर भारत को एक बार नहीं अनेक बार रौंदा। देश राजनैतिक रूप से पराधीन हो गया। सामाजिक दृष्टि से पतन के गर्त में गिरा। मिथ्या धारणाओं और अप्रासंगिक रूढ़ियों के बल पर उसे मात्र गृहिणी बना दिया गया। गृहिणी के रूप में भी उसके केवल कर्तव्य ही निर्धारित किये गये। अधिकार के नाम पर तो उनके पास सिर्फ 'जननी' बनना ही शेष रहा।

इस भयावह स्थिति के कारणों का एहसास होते ही आधुनिक समाज सुधारकों ने इन कुरीतियों से महिला समाज को मुक्त करने का प्रत्यन प्रारंभ कर दिया। स्वामी दयानन्द सरस्वती, राजा राममोहन राय, महर्षि कर्वे एवं महात्मा फूले जैसे समाज सुधारक समूची स्थिति के आकलन के आधार पर इस निष्कर्ष पर आये कि महिलाओं को समाज की मुख्य धारा से बाहर रखने के कारण देश में जड़ता और उदासीनता का प्रसार हुआ। पर्दाप्रथा और अशिक्षा प्रमुख जकड़न थी। राजा राम मोहन राय ने सती प्रथा का डटकर विरोध ही नहीं किया बल्कि पर्दाप्रथा जैसी कुरीतियों को बन्द कर शिक्षा पाने के लिए कन्याओं को प्रेरित भी किया। शिक्षा के माध्यम से वे अपने अधिकारों एवं कर्त्तव्यों को समझ पायेंगी और देश का विकास संभव होगा। हिन्दू शास्त्रों में वैसे पहले से ही महिला और पुरुष दोनों को समान महत्व दिया गया है। डा0 जयशंकर मिश्र ने भी लिखा है कि "हिन्दू विचारकों की दृष्टि में स्त्री-पुरुष का भेद नहीं था।"[1]और यदि था तो वह प्राकृतिक मामलों में हीं। सामाजिक, धार्मिक, राजनैतिक एवं नैतिक दृष्टिकोण से दोनों को समान सत्ता के रूप में स्वीकार किया जाता था। इन विचारकों ने तो यहाँ तक कहा है कि जिस कुल में स्त्रियों की पूजा होती है, उस कुल पर देवता प्रसन्न होते हैं और जिस कुल में इनकी पूजा नही होती उस कुल में सर्वकर्म निष्फल हो जाते हैं। हिन्दुओं के सर्वश्रेष्ठ स्मृतिग्रन्थ मनुस्मृति में तो स्पष्ट कहा गया है कि "यत्र नार्यस्तु, पूज्यन्ते रमन्ते तत्र देवताः। यत्रैतास्तु ने पूज्यन्ते सर्वास्तत्राफलाः क्रिया।। शोचयन्ति जायमो यत्र विनश्चत्याश तत्कुलम। न शोचयचन्ति तु यत्रैतावर्धते तद्धि सर्वदा।।[2] यहाँ तो घोषणा के तौर पर स्वीकार किया गया है कि जिस कुल में घर की स्त्रियाँ (जामि) शोक करती हैं, वह कुल शीघ्र ही नष्ट हो जाता है और जिस कुल में या वंश में वे शोक नही करती वह वंश सर्वदा उन्नति करता है। आगे एक स्थल पर यह भी कहा गया है कि उन्नति चाहने वाले मनुष्यों को स्त्रियों के प्रति आदर-सत्कार की भावना एवं क्रिया से सम्पन्न होना चाहिए। इसलिए भारतीय परंपरा में विवाह को अत्यधिक महत्व दिया गया है।

विवाह के प्रसंग में मनुस्मृति की तुलना में नारद एवं याज्ञवल्क्य स्मृति अधिक उदार और व्यावहारिक दृष्टिगत होते हैं। जहाँ तक विधवा विवाह का प्रश्न है नारद स्मृति की तरह याज्ञवल्क्य स्मृति में जो शर्त या व्यवस्था दी गई है वह मनुस्मृति की तुलना में अधिक व्यावहारिक है। इसमें यह उल्लिखित है कि उस समय जिस तरह पुरुष पत्नी की मृत्यु अथवा बाँझ होने अथवा किसी खास बीमारी से ग्रसित होने पर दूसरी शादी कर लेते थे वैसे पत्नी भी खास पारिस्थिति में दूसरे से सम्पर्क स्थापित कर पुत्र उत्पन्न कर सकती थी या विवाह कर सकती थी। इससे उस समय की महिलाओं के महत्व और उनकी स्वतंत्रता का पता चलता है।

लेकिन भारत की परतन्त्रता के साथ-साथ महिलाओं की परतन्त्रता का भी श्रीगणेश हुआ। एक दूसरे के लिए प्रेम, करुणा और बलिदान की भावना ने कालान्तर में विष अथवा घृणा एवं द्वेष का रूप धारण कर लिया। उनका पुरातन सेवा-भाव उन्हीं के लिये घातक बन गया। खासकर इब्राहिम लोदी एवं मुगलों के शासन काल में निर्दयी पुरुषों ने उन्हें बन्धनों में जकड़ दिया। और तभी इन्हें व्यक्तिगत या सामूहिक रूप में चिता भी सजानी पड़ी। राखी की सहायता लेनी पड़ी। और ऐसी दयनीय स्थिति में ही गोस्वामी तुलसीदास को कहना पड़ा होगा कि "पुरुष के बिना नारी की वह स्थिति बन जाती है जो स्थिति पानी के बिना नदी की बन जाती है। या फिर समुद्र के माध्यम से यह कहना कि" ढोल गँवार शूद्र पशु नारी। सकल ताड़ना के अधिकारी"[3] या अनसूयाजी का यह कहना कि स्त्री जन्म से ही अपवित्र है।[4] दरअसल उसी समय में तीन तरह की स्त्रियों की चर्चा करके उन्होंने उनकी स्वतंत्रता का भी प्रमाण दे दिया है। विशेष सावधानी एवं प्रतिबंध की बात जो कुछ दृष्टिगत होती है वह इस्लाम के कारण ही। इस्लाम में नारी को न पहले स्वतंत्रता थी न आज है। पहले नारी को खेत और अंगूर का बगीचा कहा गया है।[5] फिर उन्हें और भूमि की उर्वरा शक्ति को पुरुष के अधीन बतलाया है। इतिहास के अध्ययन से पता चलता है कि नारी की स्थिति बराबर एक-सी नहीं रही। अनेक बार महिलाओं की स्थिति अन्य श्रेष्ठ व्यक्ति व संस्था द्वारा कमजोर बना दी जाती रही है।[6] बाबर और उससे पूर्व इब्राहिम लोदी आदि मुसलमानों का शासन हीं इसके लिए उत्तरदायी है। कुछ शासकों ने इसे महसूस भी किया इसलिए अकबर ने अपने सिद्धान्तों में नरमी का रूख अपनाया। किन्तु फिर औरंगजेब के समय और फिर इनके बाद के शासकों के समय उनकी स्थिति फिर वही हो गई। उनके शासन काल में जिन राज्यों में सैनिक अधिनायक रहे या एक ही नायक के हाथों में सारी उनमें महिलाओं को कभी भी विशेष सुविधाएँ नहीं मिलीं। ऐसी ही स्थिति ईसाई धर्म और पश्चिमी दुनिया में रही। इसलिए सीमोन द बोउवार को बेबल की उक्तियों को उद्धृत

करना पड़ा कि "औरत और सर्वहारा दोनों ही दलित है और दोनों के सामाजिक जागरण की संभावना यांत्रिक सभ्यता में अधिक पायी जाती है।"[7] व्यक्तिगत संपत्ति के लोभ से पुरुष में स्वामित्य की भावना विकसित हुई। वह जमीन का मालिक था, वह गुलामों का मालिक था और तब बना स्त्री का भी मालिक। यहीं से महिला की गुलामी की कहानी शुरु होती है।[8]

महिलाओं में हीन भावनाओं का आगमन निजी सम्पत्ति की अवधारणा से भी हुआ है। यह अवधारणा हिन्दुस्तान की अपनी नहीं बल्कि दूसरे जगहों से प्राप्त हुई है। आज जो हिन्दुस्तान में भी कुछ उदाहरण देखने को मिल जाते हैं वह पाश्चात्य सभ्यता एवं अन्य पूंजीपतियों एवं सामंती व्यवस्था के कारण ही निजी सम्पत्ति की अवधारणा ने ऐतिहासिक विकास क्रम में सामाजिक स्तर पर स्त्री को निंरतर हीनतर स्थिति में पहुँचाया है।[9] पितृ सत्तात्मक समाज तथा संस्थाओं की मौलिक संरचना में निजी सम्पत्ति का मालिक अपनी भी वैयक्तिकता को हस्तान्तरित और विलग करके मात्र अपनी सम्पत्ति को प्यार करता है। उसकी सम्पत्ति हस्तान्तरित होकर पुत्र के हाथ होती है, पुत्री के हाथ नहीं। उनका अस्तित्व तब पुरुष की कृपा यानी पिता की कृपा पर निर्भर था। पिता को पूरा अधिकार था कि वह चाहे जहाँ और जिससे भी बेटी का विवाह करे।[10] किन्तु अब तो भारत में उन्हें कानूनी तौर पर समान अधिकार प्राप्त हो गया है। इसके अतिरिक्त न्यायालय ने यह भी फैसला दिया है कि यदि कोई व्यक्ति ऐसा पाया गया जो भ्रूण का पता लगाने की कोशिश कर रहा हो तो भी वह दोषी सिद्ध होगा और दण्ड का भागी बनेगा। अतः बच्ची समझकर भ्रूण हत्या की बात तो दूर रही उसे पता लगाने वाले भी दोषी माने जायेंगे। हाँ! यदि महिलाओं का जीवन समाप्त होने का खतरा हो या उनसे जर्बदस्ती यौन व्यवहार के कारण गर्भपात करना पड़े तो वह न्यायसंगत प्रतीत होता है। इस संबंध में अपलाइंग ह्यूमनिटेयन एथिक्स द मोरल प्रोवमेल ऑफ एबोरसन शीर्षक के अन्तर्गत द ह्यूमनिटेरियन एथिक्स टू द प्रोवलेम में ठीक ही कहा गया है कि "In general, Humanitarian Ethics has an inherent bias in favour of protecting huuman life, even unborn human life, since the value of life principle is of primary importance in the ethical system. This would mean then, that abortion should be a last resort to be uesd only when there is strong justification"[11] बॉक ने भी इस बात की पुष्टि की है। बॉक की क्राइटेरिया का उल्लेख करते हुए बतलाया गया है कि "I believe that if abortions cannot be avoided and women should try to avoid then to the best of their ability they should be allowed on request up to the twelth week. In other words, I agree with Box's criteria for when taking a human life is most serious and also for when later abortions can be allowed"[12]

दरअसल, जैसा कि समकालीन भारतीय चिन्तकों का कहना भी है कि मनुष्य के व्यक्तित्व का विकास विभिन्न चरणों में आयु पर्यन्त होता रहता है। अतः इस कारण गर्भ से मृत्यु पर्यन्त के शरीर और आत्मा पर उत्तम संस्कार डालना और शुभ संकल्प लेना व्यक्ति और समाज, पुरुष और महिला के हित में आवश्यक हो जाता है। यदि महिलाओं में असमानता का भाव जागृत होगा तो उसका प्रभाव उनके बच्चे एवं बच्चियों पर पड़ेगा ही। इसलिए उनमें हीन भावना का उदय होना या उनमें हीन भावना पैदा करना नैतिकता के विरूद्ध है। उनका उचित सम्मान करने में ही राष्ट्रा और विश्व का कल्याण संभव हो सकता है। इसलिए 1975 में ही अन्तर्राष्ट्रीय महिला वर्ष का भारत में उद्घाटन करते हुए तत्कालीन प्रधानमंत्री श्रीमती इन्दिरा गाँधी ने 16 फरवरी 1975 को नई दिल्ली में 'राष्ट्रीय महिला दिवस' पर कहा था कि 'ऐसा कोई काम नहीं है जिसे महिलायें पुरुषों के साथ कन्धे से कन्धा मिलाकर नहीं कर सकती'।

आज भी भारत, इंगलैण्ड और रूस को छोड़कर विश्व में जितना अधिक शोषण महिलाओं का हो रहा है उतना किसी अन्य का नहीं होता। वैसे तो यह शोषण राजनैतिक एवं सामाजिक स्तर पर भी है किन्तु सर्वाधिक शोषण सामाजिक स्तर पर है। दुर्भाग्य की बात यह है कि महिला हीं महिला का सबसे बड़ी शत्रु बनती जा रही है। दहेज का मामला हो या राजनैतिक मामला हो या सामाजिक सभी में महिला का हस्तक्षेप रहता ही है। और कम से कम उन देशों में जो विकसित और विकासशील है। परम्पराओं के साथ महिला को जितना अधिक जोड़ दिया गया है या महिला उनसे जितनी अधिक जुड़ी हुई है, उसके कारण न केवल उसके अधिकारों का हनन होता है बल्कि वह शोषण का एक जरिया भी बन जाता है। यदि इस समस्या का समाधान खोजना है तो विश्व को इस बात पर विचार करना ही होगा कि महिलाओं को राजनैतिक, सामाजिक, सांस्कृतिक एवं आर्थिक स्तर पर स्वतन्त्रता कैसे प्राप्त हो? इसके लिए उन्हें शिक्षित करना अनिवार्य है। उन्हें व्यावहारिक नैतिकता की सीख लेनी चाहिए।

भारत की सरकार ने कानूनी तौर पर इस दिशा में संतोषजनक कोशिशे की हैं। स्थानीय निकायों में महिलाओं के लिये भागीदारी सुनिश्चित कर एक ठोस और रचनात्मक कदम उठाया है। सम्पूर्ण देश में अब स्थानीय निकायों के चुनावों में महिलाओं ने भाग लिया और महत्वपूर्ण स्थान ग्रहण कर सक्रिया भूमिका अदा कर रही है। यह विश्व के लिए अनुकरणीय है। राष्ट्र की आर्थिक समृद्धि एवं आम लोगों के जीवन स्तर को उन्नत बनाने के लिए महिलाओं को आत्मनिर्भर बनाना होगा।

इसके लिये बिना किसी भेदभाव के रोजगार का अवसर उपलब्ध कराने के साथ-साथ उन्हें सामाजिक एवं राजनैतिक रूप से और जागरूक बनाने की आवश्यकता है। चूँकि इसके अभाव में महिलाओं की ऊर्जा एवं प्रतिभा का अवमूल्यन होता रहेगा, व्यावहारिक नैतिकता की बात पागलों का प्रलाप बनकर रह जायेगा। व्यावहारिक नैतिकता को जमीनी एवं कारगर सिद्ध करने के लिए स्त्री-पुरुष के बीच परस्पर विश्वास एवं विवेक का समुचित उपयोग करना आवश्यक है। ईमानदारी से साथ देना और ईमानदारी से साथ लेना दोनो के लिए अनिवार्य है और ईमानदारी से परिश्रम करना इसका सबसे बेहतर उपाय है।

संदर्भ

1. डा0 जयशंकर मिश्र, प्राचीन भारत का सामाजिक इतिहास, बिहार हिन्दी ग्रन्थ अकादमी पटना, 1983 ई0, पृ019.
2. मनुसमृति - 3.56-57.
3. गोस्वामी तुलसीदास, (टीकाकार हनूमान प्रसाद पोद्दार) श्री रामचरित मानस (सचित्र, सटीक मोटा टाइप,), गीता प्रेस गोरखपुर सं0 2054 सुन्दरकाण्ड, पृ0 751.
4. वही, अरण्यकाण्ड, पृ0 610.
5. सीमने द बोउवार (अनु0 डा0 प्रभाखेतान), स्त्रीः उपेक्षिता हिन्द पॉकेट बुक्स, दिल्ली 1991, पृ0 72.
6. वही पृ0 74
7. वही पृ0 44
8. वही पृ0 44
9. वही पृ0 56.
10. वही पृ0 57.
11. जेक्स पी0 थिरोक्स (कॉपीराइट), एथिक्सः थ्योरी एण्ड प्रैक्टीस, कोलियर मैकमिलन पब्लिशर्स, लंदन 1977, पृ0 344.
12. वही (द मोर मोड्रेट पोजिसन ऑन एबोरसन), पृ0 336.

अध्याय 8

नारी सशक्तिकरण : वर्तमान व्यावहारिक सन्दर्भ में एक विश्लेषण

नवीन कुमार

प्रस्तुत आलेख में मैंने नारियों के गौरवपूर्ण इतिहास एवं समाज में उसकी महत्वपूर्ण भूमिका पर संक्षेप में प्रकाश डालते हुए उसके प्रति किए जा रहे शोषण को स्पष्ट करने का प्रयास किया है। पुनः राजनीति, शिक्षा एवं आर्थिक स्वावलम्बन के क्षेत्र में उसकी भागीदारी एवं इससे संबंधित समस्याओं को दर्शाते हुए उन सुझावों को प्रस्तुत करने का प्रयास किया है जो आज के व्यावहारिक सन्दर्भ में महिलाओं के सशक्तिकरण के प्रयास में कारगर कदम साबित हो सकते हैं।

सर्वप्रथम यहाँ नारी के गौरवपूर्ण इतिहास का उल्लेख करते हुए यह बतलाया जा सकता है कि नारी ब्रह्म-विद्या है, श्रद्धा है, शक्ति है, पवित्रता है, वह सब कुछ है जो इस संसार में सर्वश्रेष्ठ के रूप में दृष्टिगोचर होता है। नारी कामधेनु है, अन्नपूर्णा है, सिद्धि है, ऋद्धि है, और वह सब कुछ है जो मानव प्राणी के समस्त अभावों, संकटों का निवारण करती है। नारी एक सनातन शक्ति है। वह आदिकाल से उन सामाजिक दायित्वों को अपने कन्धों पर उठाए आ रही है जिन्हें केवल पुरुषों के कन्धे पर डाल दिया जाता तो वे कब का लड़खड़ा गया होता। यहाँ यह बतलाया जा सकता है कि वेद से लेकर आज तक नारी का इतिहास गौरवमय रहा है। 'अर्धनारीश्वर' भगवान शिव की कल्पना नारी के गौरव का ही प्रतीक है।

वेदों की तरह ब्राह्मण ग्रन्थों में भी नारी की महिमा का बखान करते हुए उसे सावित्री कहा गया है। महाभारत के अनुशासन पर्व में भीष्म पितामह ने कहा है—"स्त्री को सदैव पूज्य मानकर उससे स्नेह का व्यवहार किया जाना आवश्यक है। जहाँ स्त्रियों का आदर होता है, वहाँ देवताओं का निवास होता है तथा इनकी अनुपस्थिति में सभी कार्य पुण्यरहित हो जाते हैं।"[1] वस्तुतः नारी समाज का वह स्तम्भ है जिसके बिना समाज का निर्माण नहीं हो सकता। नारी के अभाव में कोई

भी पारिवारिक, धार्मिक अनुष्ठान अथवा सामाजिक दायित्व को पूरा नहीं किया जा यसकता। नारी ने अलग-अलग सीमा में रहकर इस समाज को उन्नति के शिखर पर पहुँचाने की जिम्मेदारी से भी अपने आप को अलंकृत किया है। वस्तुतः नारी करुणा, उदारता, कोमलता, मातृत्व-वत्सल आदि भावनाओं से इस समाज को सुशोभित कर, उसे सुविधाएँ प्रदान करके, नवजीवन का संचार करती हैं इसीलिए उसे 'प्रकृति की बेटी' कहा गया है। इस तरह यदि हम नारियों के चरित्र पर गहन दृष्टि डालते हैं तो पता चलता है कि ईश्वर ने नारी को अनेक रूपों में जगद्कल्याण की भावना से समाज को अर्पित किया है, जैसे—माँ के रूप में यशोदा, त्याग के लिए पन्नाधाय, भक्ति की पराकाष्ठा मीराबाई, पत्नी के रूप में सीता, सावित्री जैसी अनेक नारियाँ समाज में प्रकट हुई और समाज को रास्ता दिखाकर, एक दिशा देकर अपनी अमिट छाप छोड़ गई है।

इस प्रकार स्पष्ट है कि समाज के विकास में नारियों की भूमिका, उनका महत्वपूर्ण सहयोग प्रारम्भ से ही रहा है। नारी की महत्ता को लेकर यहाँ हम निम्नलिखित पंक्तियों को उद्धृत कर सकते हैं—"भारत में अत्यंत प्राचीन काल में ही स्त्रियों को आदरपूर्ण स्थान प्राप्त था तथा उन्हें शक्ति, ज्ञान और सम्पत्ति का प्रतीक माना जाता था। उन्हें दुर्गा, सरस्वती एवं लक्ष्मी के रूप में आराध्य माना जाता था।"[2] डॉ0 राधाकृष्णन ने भी सामाजिक जीवन के क्षेत्र में नारी के महत्व को स्पष्ट करते हुए बताया है—"जब आकाश बादलों से काला पड़ जाता है, जब हम अन्धकार में बिल्कुल अकेले होते हैं, प्रकाश की एक भी किरण नहीं दीख पड़ती और जब सब ओर कठिनाइयाँ ही कठिनाइयाँ होती है, तब हम अपने आपको किसी प्रेममयी नारी के हाथ में छोड़ देते हैं।"[3] इसी तरह मनुस्मृति में 'यत्र नार्यस्तु पूज्यन्ते, रमन्ते तत्र देवता'[4] जैसे वाक्यों के द्वारा नारी की महत्ता का बखान किया गया है।

इस तरह नारी की गौरवपूर्ण गाथा का उल्लेख करने के पश्चात हम यहाँ यह कह सकते हैं कि शुरू से लेकर आज तक व्यावहारिक दृष्टिकोण से समाज के विकास में नारी की सहभागिता साफ तौर पर देखी जाती है। इस तथ्य से भी इन्कार नहीं किया जा सकता है कि जब-जब समाज ने नारी को उचित अवसर तथा अधिकार प्रदान किये हैं तब-तब नारी ने विश्व के समक्ष श्रेष्ठ उदाहरण प्रस्तुत किया है। मैत्रेयी, गार्गी, आंडाल, विश्वपारा, केशा आदि विदुषी स्त्रियाँ शिक्षा के क्षेत्र में अपने बहुमुल्य योगदान के लिए आज भी पूजनीय हैं। आधुनिक काल में महादेवी वर्मा, सुभद्रा कुमारी चौहान, महाश्वेता देवी, अमृता प्रीतम, अरून्धती राय आदि स्त्रियों ने साहित्य तथा राष्ट्र की प्रगाति में अपनी महत्वपूर्ण भूमिका अदा की है। रजिया सुल्तान, लक्ष्मीबाई, शिरिमाओं भंडारनायके, इन्दिरा गाँधी आदि स्त्रियाँ प्रगति के मार्ग

पर संघर्ष और सुनेतृत्व की स्पष्ट मूर्तियों के रूप में स्थापित हुई। कला के क्षेत्र में एम0 एस0 सुब्बुलक्ष्मी, लता मंगेशकर, देविका रानी, वैजयन्तीमाला, सुधा चन्द्रन, सोनल मानसिंह, मीरा नायर आदि स्त्रियों को योगदान वास्तव में प्रशंसनीय है। इनके अतिरिक्त अन्य क्षेत्रों जैसे-चिकित्सा, अभियान्त्रिकी, बैंकिग, प्रशासन आदि में भी स्त्रियाँ अपनी सक्रिय तथा विकासोन्मुखी भूमिका निभा रहीं है। इसी तरह आज प्रायः सभी क्षेत्रों में महिलाओं की सहभागिता उजागर होती है। महिलाओं के लिए कठिन माने जाने वाली रक्षा सम्बन्धी सेवाओं में भी श्रीमती किरण बेदी, अन्ना मल्होत्रा, आदि जैसी कई महिलाओं ने अपनी कार्यकुशलता से लोगों को काफी प्रभावित किया है। इसी तरह भावना गर्ग और विजयलक्ष्मी विदारी जैसी नारियों ने भी शिक्षा के क्षेत्र में इतिहास रचकर पुरुष के इस दंभ को तोड़ा है कि महिलाएँ पुरुषों की अपेक्षा कम बुद्धिमान होती है। इस प्रकार हम देखते हैं कि नारी को जहाँ भी अवसर मिला है उसने अपनी भरपूर कोशिशों से कुछ-न-कुछ नया कर गुजरने का प्रयास किया है और यही हमारी संस्कृति की पहचान रही है।

इस तरह नारियों की सहभागिता का उल्लेख करने के उपरांत हम यहाँ यह कह सकते हैं कि ऊपर में हमने जिन महिलाओं की सहभागिता का उल्लेख किया है वह सहभागिता वर्तमान में चंद नारियों के किस्से है जिससे संपूर्ण समाज का विकास संभव नहीं है। अतः प्रस्तुत लेख के माध्यम से हम यह देखने का प्रयास करेंगे कि आखिर क्यों चंद महिलाएँ ही आगे बढ़ने में सफल हो सकीं तथा किस तरह हम सभी महिलाओं को विकास के इस मार्ग से जोड़ें ताकि महिला सशक्तिकरण का हमारा जो प्रयास है वह अधिक से अधिक सफल हो सके? इस प्रश्न पर विचार करने के उपरांत हम यह पाते हैं कि वस्तुतः नारियों के समाज के प्रति महत्वपूर्ण योगदान के बावजूद प्रायः सभी समाजों में नारियों का शोषण किसी-न-किसी रूप में होता आया है। 'ढोल, गँवार, शूद्र, पशु, नारी। सकल ताड़ना के अधिकारी।।[5]' रामचरितमानस की यह चौपाई नारियों के प्रति हमारे समाज की संकुचित मानसिकता को अभिव्यक्त करती है। इसी तरह नारियों की वेदना को इंगित करते हुए लगभग 400 वर्ष पूर्व तुलसीदासजी ने लिखा था–

'कत विधि सृजीं नारी जग माहीं। पराधीन सपनेहुँ सुखु नाहीं।।'[6]

इस तरह शुरू से लेकर आज तक नारी का शोषण होता रहा है, चाहे इसका कारण सदियों से चली आ रही परम्परा हो या बाजार को मजूबती प्रदान करने के लिए अपनाए गए आधुनिक तकनीक हो या फिर लोगों द्वारा अपनाए गए धर्म के विभिन्न आयाम हों। डॉ0 अल्तेकर ने भी स्त्रियों की सामान्य स्थिति में आयी गिरावट के संबंध में बतलाया है–"आर्य-गृह में अनार्य स्त्री का प्रवेश स्त्रियों की सामान्य स्थिति

की अवनति का मुख्य कारण है। यह अवनति ईसा के करीब 1000 वर्ष पूर्व से धीरे-धीरे अति सूक्ष्म रूप में प्रारम्भ हुई और करीब 500 वर्ष पश्चात् काफी स्पष्ट मालूम पड़ने लगी।"[8]

इसके अलावे आज के भी कुछ तथाकथित बुद्धिजीवियों, लेखकों, प्रिंट मीडिया, इलेक्ट्रॉनिक मीडिया आदि ने नारी को दोयम दर्जे का नागरिक समझा है। डॉ0 धर्मवीर भारती ने अपनी पुस्तक 'हिन्दी की आत्मा बनाम संस्कृति का खात्मा' में इस बात का जिक्र किया है कि किस तरह संस्कृति के प्रकाण्ड विद्धानों ने अपने लेखन द्वारा नारी जाति को अपमान, उपेक्षा एवं शोषण का शिकार बनाकर उसे शताब्दियों पीछे कर दिया है। इसी तरह आज पूँजीवादी भी अपने उत्पादों को बेचने के लिए उनका इस्तेमाल कर रहा हैं। मनुष्य के अन्दर दमित कामवासना को उत्तेजित कर उनका भावनात्मक शोषण कर रहा हैं। नारी के अर्द्धनग्न शरीर को उत्तेजक रूप में अपने उत्पाद के साथ समस्त प्रिंट मीडिया और इलेक्ट्रॅनिक मीडिया के द्वारा हर घर में प्रस्तुत किया जा रहा है और मजे की बात यह है कि अभिभावक भी अपने बच्चों, जिसमें किशोर और युवा भी शामिल हैं, के साथ उन भौंडा विज्ञापनों का रसास्वादन करते हैं।

यह ठीक है कि धीरे-धीरे परिस्थितियाँ बदल रही है किन्तु इसके बावजूद इस सच से इन्कार नहीं किया जा सकता कि शुरू से ही पुरुष अपने अहं के कारण नारी को बहन, बेटी, माँ, पत्नी आदि से भिन्न भूमिका में स्वीकार करने से हिचकता रहा है। अभी तक जितनी भी परम्पराएँ बनी हैं सब में पुरुष का हाथ रहा है और इसी के पीछे पुरुष की वह मानसिकता भी रही है जो नारी को सदैव काबू में रखने का प्रयास करती रही है। सहनशीलता, कोमलता, लज्जा, पर-निर्भरता आदि जैसे गुणों से जकड़कर पुरुष समाज ने कमोवेश यही प्रयास किया है कि उसका बौद्धिक विकास नहीं हो पाए, वह आर्थिक, सामाजिक और राजनीतिक दृष्टि से अधिक सजग एवं स्वावलम्बी न बन पाए। इसके अलावे भी भारतीय नारियों के शोषण के कई ऐसे रूप हैं जो कानून के शिकंजे से बाहर है और जिनके लिए विधवा विवाह, बाल-विवाह, बेमेल विवाह, लड़कियों को बेचना, भ्रूण-हत्या, बहुओं को जला देना आदि अनेक अमानवीय कृत्य परम्परानुमोदित बन चुके हैं। सबसे बड़ी विडम्बना तो यह है कि नारियों के प्रति परिवारिक अत्याचारों में सास, ननद आदि के रूप में नारियाँ प्रमुख रूप से भाग लेती है। इससे ऐसा लगता है कि अगर नारी-नारी का दुश्मन न हो तो सुधार की सम्भावना अधिक हो सकती है। आज मध्यम वर्ग की महिलाएँ सबसे अधिक संघर्षरत दीख पड़ती हैं। जो दफ्तर में काम करने वाली महिलाएँ हैं उन्हें साथ-साथ घर का भी कार्य देखना पड़ता है। उसी तरह कहीं-कहीं घरेलू कार्य करने वाली महिलाओं को 'सोसायटी वूमेन' भी बनने के लिए बाध्य किया

जाता है। इस तरह दोहरे चरित्र को निभाने के कारण वह अपने व्यक्तित्व का सम्पूर्ण विकास नहीं कर पाती है। इसी तरह के शोषण से समाज को मुक्त करने के लिए आज महिला सशक्तिकरण जैसे आन्दोलन की आवश्यकता प्रतीत होती है।

यहाँ यह उल्लेख करना उचित ही प्रतीत होता है कि स्वतंत्रता-प्राप्ति के बाद प्रायः सभी क्षेत्रों में महिलाओं की भागीदारी बढ़ी है। महिला शिक्षा के विस्तार हेतु चलाए गए भिन्न-भिन्न कार्यक्रमों, योजनाओं आदि से महिला शिक्षा की तस्वीर उज्जवल बनी है। 1951 में जो महिला साक्षरता दर 8.86 प्रतिशत थी वह आज लगभग 34.16 प्रतिशत पर पहुँच गयी है। महिलाएँ आज बस कडंक्टर से लेकर पायलट तक तथा एक सामान्य शिक्षिका से लेकर अन्तरिक्ष विज्ञान एवं मेरीन इंजीनियरिंग तक के क्षेत्र में अपनी उपस्थिति बखूबी दर्शा रहीं है। इस तरह आज अधिकांश क्षेत्रों में उसकी सशक्त उपस्थिति हुई है। कई कानूनी अधिकार जैसे-हिन्दू लॉ, उत्तराधिकार अधिनियम, हिन्दू कोड बिल, दहेज निषेध अधिनियम और भारतीय दंड संहिता के कई संशोधनों आदि से नारियों को मिले अधिकार उन्हें सशक्त करने में अहम भूमिका निभा रहीं हैं। इस ओर संकेत करते हुए जैसा कि डॉ0 शिवभानु सिंह ने भी लिखा है–"आज समकालीन युग में विश्व में लिंगीय समानता की स्थापना को सर्वाधिक प्राथमिकता दी जा रही है तथा मानवधिकार-संरक्षण के समर्थकों ने स्त्रियों के प्रति होने वाले किसी भी प्रकार के अन्याय, शोषण, अत्याचार या भेदभाव का जबर्दस्त विरोध करना प्रारम्भ किया है। पश्चिम से शुरू हुए नारी-स्वातन्त्रय आन्दोलन ने आज सम्पूर्ण विश्व की महिलाओं को आंदोलित किया है तथा उनमें व्यापक रूप से सामाजिक एवं रातनीतिक जागरूकता उत्पन्न की है। यही कारण है कि इक्कीसवीं सदी के मुहाने पर खड़े हम जीवन के प्रत्येक क्षेत्र में पुरुषों के साथ कन्धे से कन्धे मिलाये स्त्री को खड़े देख सकते हैं।"[9] इस तरह स्पष्ट है कि बदलते परिवेश ने एक शिक्षित, स्वतंत्र, अधिकार संपन्न, स्वावलंबी नारी की छवि का निर्माण किया है जो पुरुष के कंधे से कंधा मिलाकर आगे बढ़ने को तैयार हैं। आज हमारे पास महिलाओं की प्रगति के कई आँकड़े और चेहरे हैं, जैसे-पहली महिला प्रधानमंत्री इन्दिरा गाँधी, पहली महिला आई0 पी0 एस0 किरण बेदी, आई0 ए0 एस0 अन्ना मल्होत्रा, अंतरिक्ष में जाने वाली पहली भारतीय महिला कल्पना चावला, पहली भारतीय मिस यूनिवर्स सुष्मिता सेन, गोल्डन लायन पुरस्कार पानेवाली पहली भारतीय महिला मीरा नायर (फिल्म मानसून वेडिंग) आदि कई नाम है जिनपर भारतीय महिलाएँ गर्व कर सकती है।

वस्तुतः नारी सशक्तिकरणः उसकी चेतना एवं अपने अधिकारों के प्रति जागरूकता से पूरी तरह जुड़ा हुआ है। नारियों पर आज दोहरी जिम्मेदारी है–

1. अपने विचार परिवर्तन की, और
2. परिवार और समाज के विचार परिवर्तन की।

इस दिशा में निःसन्देह आज महिलाओं में एक नई जागृति, अधिकारों के प्रति जागरूकता, शोषण के विरुद्ध आवाज उठाने की शक्ति एवं अत्याचार के विरोध में डटे रहने का साहस आया है। परन्तु इसके बावजूद इस बात से इन्कार नहीं किया जा सकता है कि तमाम आर्थिक, सामाजिक और वैज्ञानिक प्रगति के साथ-साथ हर कदम पर स्त्री की भागीदारी के बावजूद उसकी मूल लड़ाई 'समाज में अपने वर्चस्व की लड़ाई' आज भी कमोवेश वहीं की वहीं है। चंद महिलाओं का नाम गिनाकर हम हर साल 8 मार्च को 'महिला दिवस' मनाए जाने की सार्थकता को स्थापित नहीं कर सकते है और ना ही यह कहा जा सकता है कि हमने इस क्षेत्र में अपना लक्ष्य पा लिया है। यही कारण है कि सन् 2001 को महिला सशक्तिकरण के लिए के लिए चुना गया था ताकि इस क्षेत्र में बेहतर-से-बेहतर सफलता प्राप्त किया जा सके और इन्हीं सबों को लेकर आज देश में सभी जगह महिलाओं के समुचित विकास एवं सशक्तिकरण के लिए अनुकूल वातावरण बनाने का प्रयास किया जा रहा है। इसी आधार पर लोग 21वीं सदी को 'महिलाओं की सदी' की संज्ञा से विभूषित करने लगे हैं। महिलाओं की आर्थिक, सामाजिक और राजनीतिक स्थिति को सुदृढ़ बनाने के लिए आज कुछ-न-कुछ प्रयास हर जगह और हर स्तर से किए जा रहे हैं। इस क्रम में देश में त्रिस्तरीय पंचायतों में महिलाओं की भागीदारी के लिए की गयी व्यवस्था एक क्रांतिकारी कदम है। 73वें और 74वें संविधान संशोधन के परिणामस्वरूप देश की ग्रामीण एवं नगरीय दोनों प्रकार की पंचायतों में महिलाओं के लिए एक तिहाई आरक्षण की व्यवस्था हो जाने से लगभग 14 लाख महिलाओं को जनप्रतिनिधियों के रूप में विभिन्न प्रकार के उत्तरदायित्व एवं अधिकार प्राप्त हुए हैं। किन्तु इस स्थिति को किसी भी तरह से संतोषजनक नहीं माना जा सकता है।

अतः महिला सशक्तिकरण के अभियान को पूर्णतया सफल बनाने के लिए आज आवश्यकता इस बात की है कि नारी को पुरुष की तरह ही सभी क्षेत्रों में समर्थ, सक्षम और सशक्त बनने का अवसर दिया जाए क्योंकि इस तथ्य से प्रायः सभी सहमत है कि किसी भी स्वस्थ एवं विकसित समाज के निर्माण में स्त्री एवं पुरुष दोनों की बराबर की सहभागिता तो होना परमावश्यक है ही, साथ ही साथ नैसर्गिक सिद्धान्त तथा पर्यावरण संतुलन की दृष्टि से भी ऐसा अनिवार्य माना जाता है। इसके लिए यह आवश्यक है कि हम महिला दिवस के औचित्य को समझते हुए उन पर सार्थक पहल करें। सर्वप्रथम महिलाओं की शिक्षा पर विशेष ध्यान देने की आवश्यकता है क्योंकि शिक्षा व्यक्ति में स्वाभिमान की भावना जगाती है और उनके कार्यक्षेत्र की

सीमा का विस्तार करती है। एक पुरानी कहावत है कि यदि एक पुरुष शिक्षित होता है तो एक व्यक्ति शिक्षित होता है, लेकिन यदि एक महिला शिक्षित होती है तो पूरा परिवार शिक्षित होता है। इसी तरह विश्व विकास रिपोर्ट 1998-99 स्पष्ट करती है कि महिला शिक्षा आर्थिक विकास में मददगार होने के साथ ही, प्रजननता को कम करने, बच्चों के उचित पालन-पोषण तथा माता एवं बच्चों के बेहतर स्वास्थ में सहायक होती है। अतः महिला शिक्षा पर अत्यधिक जोर देने की आवश्यकता है।

पुनः इस बात की भी आवश्यकता है कि अतिशीघ्र राजनीति के सभी स्तरों पर आधा उत्तरदायित्व उन्हें सौंपा जाए और साथ-ही-साथ आर्थिक, प्रशासनिक, न्यायिक तथा विकास के सभी क्षेत्रों में उनकी 50 प्रतिशत भागीदारी सुनिश्चित करने हेतु सभी स्तरों से व्यापक प्रयास किए जाएं। अगर वास्तव में महिलाओं की स्थिति सुधारनी है, उन्हें शोषण-उत्पीड़न से मुक्ति दिलानी है तो कोरे आश्वासनों के बजाए हमें कुछ सार्थक काम करना होगा। जब तक कथनी और करनी का अन्तर नहीं मिटेगा तब तक इस दिशा में ठोस काम नहीं हो पाएगा। भारत पेट्रोलियम निगम लि0 ने पूरी तरह से महिलाओं द्वारा संचालित देश के पहले ऐसे पेट्रोल पम्प की शुरूआत कर एक अच्छी पहल की है। इससे महिलाओं को रोजगार के अवसर मिलेंगे और वे आत्मनिर्भर बनेंगी। महिलाओं के विकास के लिए उनका आत्मनिर्भर होना जरूरी है। अगर साल भर थोड़ा-थोड़ा ठोस काम भी होता रहे तो महिलाओं की स्थिति में और सुधार लाया जा सकता है।

अतः आज इस बात की विशेष आवश्यकता प्रतीत होती है कि देश में सरकार एवं विभिन्न संस्थाओं के द्वारा चलाए जाने वाले महिला आन्दोलनों को खुले दिल से अपना समर्थन दिया जाए और लोगों में इसके प्रति जागरूकता पैदा करने का भरपूर प्रयास हो। प्रत्येक स्तर पर ऐसी व्यवस्था करें जिससे महिला समानता और सशक्तिकरण की योजनाएँ सिर्फ सरकारी स्तर पर और कागजों तक ही सीमित न रह जाए। उनकी गरीबी, निरक्षरता, आर्थिक असमानता, राजनीतिक व्यवस्था, निर्णय लेने की प्रक्रिया में उपेक्षा, संसाधनों के सीमित उपयोग, पारिवारिक और सामाजिक स्तर पर होनेवाली हिंसा से बचाव आदि के समाधान के लिए न हमें केवल लक्ष्य निर्धारित करना होगा बल्कि उन लक्ष्यों की प्राप्ति के लिए हमें आवश्यक संसाधन भी जुटाने होंगे। साथ ही हमें महिलाओं के प्रति अपनी संकुचित मानसिकता को बदलते हुए कथनी और करनी के बीच व्याप्त अन्तर को समाप्त करना होगा। पुरुष का अहं कभी-कभी नारियों के विकास में बाधा पहुँचाता है और उसे अधिकार सम्पन्न बनने से रोकता है। अतः इसके लिए नारियों को भी स्वयं सजग एवं जागरूक होना होगा। अपने अधिकारों की रक्षा के लिए लड़ना होगा और अपना अधिकार खुद प्राप्त करना होगा तभी नारी सशक्तिकरण की सार्थकता सिद्ध हो पाएगी।

संदर्भ

1. महाभारत, अनुशासन पर्व, 46/5.
2. डॉ0 शिवभानु सिंह, 'भारतीय समाज में लिंगीय समानता', संदर्शन, भाग-24, 2000, पृ0 44-45.
3. डॉ0 राधाकृष्णन, 'भारतीय समाज में स्त्रियों की स्थिति', भारतीय समाज तथा सस्कृति-गुप्ता एवं शर्मा, साहित्य भवन, आगरा, 1993, पृष्ठ 315.
4. मनुस्मृति, अध्याय-3, श्लोक-55.
5. रामचरितमानस, सुन्दर काण्ड (दोहा सं0 58 के बाद चौपाई सं0 3 में उद्धत), गीता प्रेस, गोरखपुर, पृ0 855.
6. रामचरितमानस, बाल काण्ड (दोहा सं0 101 के बाद चौपाई सं0 3 में उद्धत), गीता प्रेस, गोरखपुर, पृ0 115.
7. मनुस्मृति, अध्याय-9, श्लोक-3-4.
8. डॉ0 ए0 एस0 अत्तेकर, 'द पोजीशन ऑफ वूमेन इन हिन्दू सीवीलाईजेशन', पृ0 345.
9. डॉ0 शिवभानु सिंह 'समाज दर्शन का सर्वेक्षण', शारदा पुस्तक भवन, इलाहाबाद, प्रथम संस्करण, 2001, पृ0 395.

अध्याय 9

लैंगिक असमानता : एक अध्ययन

शैल कुमारी

चूँकि राष्ट्रीय अध्ययन संगोष्ठी में प्रयुक्त लिंगभेद/असमानता संपूर्ण विषय का दूसरा हिस्सा है। संगोष्ठी का प्रथम संयुक्त नारी सशक्तिकरण की समस्याएँ और समाधान है, लिंगभेद दूसरा संयुक्त है, दोनों संयोजक अनुप्रयुक्त नीतिशास्त्र के निर्गमन हैं जिन पर हम अपनी ओर से कुछ कहना चाहते हैं। लिंग-भेद अथवा लिंग आधारित असमानता से हमारा तात्पर्य—"समान परिस्थितियों में स्त्री-पुरुष के समान कार्यों, कार्यक्षमताओं का, दोनों की आकांक्षाओं का, जीवन के विभिन्न क्षेत्रों में दोनों का दर्जा तथा दोनों की भूमिकाओं का अलग-अलग मापदंड से मूल्यांकन करना तदनुसार असमान व्यवहार करना ही लिंग-भेद है।"

हालाँकि, बौद्धिक स्तर पर स्पष्ट हो जाता है कि स्त्री-पुरूष में जो प्राकृतिक भेद है वह स्वाभाविक है और सृष्टि प्रक्रिया की मूल बात है। अन्य जितने भी भेद हम कर लें सभी कृत्रिम हैं फिर भी, व्यावहारिक स्तर पर हम इस कृत्रिमता को स्वीकार नहीं करना चाहते हैं : हमारी यही मनोवृत्ति लिंग-भेद/असमानता की जन्मदात्री है।

सामाजिक विज्ञान ने मानवीय समाज का सूक्ष्म अध्ययन कर बहुत सारे महत्वपूर्ण तथ्यों की खोज की है, आधुनिक समाज को पुनर्गठित कर नयी दिशाएँ निर्धारित की हैं। इसके शोध से लिंग-भेद एवं इससे उत्पन्न समस्याओं का अध्ययन एक बहुचर्चित विषय बन गया है। फिर भी, लैंगिक असमानता संबंधी समस्या का उन्मूलन इतना आसान काम नहीं है। विश्व जनमानस इस संदर्भ में चिंतित एवं क्रियाशील प्रतीत होता है, परन्तु यह मात्र बौद्धिक विषय तक ही सीमित रह जाता है, क्योंकि इस दिशा में उठाए गए कदम वांछित परिणाम उत्पन्न करने में प्रभावी सिद्ध नहीं होते। फरव्र का विषय है कि यथेच्छ बौद्धिक प्रयास अभी भी जारी हैं। उदाहरण के तौर पर विश्व के सर्वोच्च संगठन संयुक्त राष्ट ‸ संघ का प्रयास सराहनीय है। साथ ही इससे यह भी संकेत मिलता है कि यह असमानता मानवीय

समाज के लिए बहुत बड़ा कलंक है जिसका निदान समाज के स्वास्थ्य हेतु नितांत आवश्यक है। लिंग-भेद जन्य असमानता के प्रति चिंतित संयुक्त राष्ट्र संघ ने महिलाओं की स्थिति में सुधार की आवश्यकता महसूस करते हुए अंतरराष्ट्रीय महिला दिवस, वर्ष एवं दशक निर्धारित कर हमें इस दिशा में कुछ करने को प्रेरित किया है।

वस्तुतः विश्व की गंभीरतम समस्याओं में लिंग-भेद की समस्या चिन्तनीय है। दुर्भाग्य की बात है कि आबादी की पचास प्रतिशत स्त्री वर्त्तमान सहस्त्राब्दी में भी विभिन्न असमानताओं की शिकार है। क्या ऐसी परिस्थिति में एक स्वस्थ मानव समाज की कल्पना की जा सकती है? मंद बुद्धि भी इस बात से सहमत नहीं हो सकती कि स्त्री की उपेक्षा कर मानव-समाज में प्रगति लायी जा सकती है। स्त्रियों की दशा में सुधार के अभाव में मानव-मूल्य की स्थापना का कोई अर्थ ही नहीं हो सकता क्योंकि किसी भी तरह की प्रगति, मानवता एवं मानव-मूल्य के अभाव में निरर्थक है। यह विडम्बना नहीं तो और क्या है कि एक ओर विज्ञान सूक्ष्म से सूक्ष्मतम वस्तु के अध्ययन में तल्लीन है और व्यापक अंतरिक्ष की टोह में क्रियाशील है, तो दूसरी ओर स्त्री जो मानव-समाज के अस्तित्व का उत्स है, वह उपेक्षिता है तथा स्वस्थ दृष्टिकोण की अपेक्षा उसे पुरूष-प्रधान समाज से है।

इसमें कोई शक नहीं कि दुनिया भर के बुद्धिजीवियों ने इस संदर्भ को प्राथामिक दी है और समय-समय पर संगोष्ठी एवं सम्मेलन का आयोजन किया है। वे बौद्धिक स्तर पर भरसक प्रयास करते हैं और बहुमूल्य सुझाव भी देते हैं ताकि लिंग-भेद की विरूपता समाप्त हो। फिर भी जमीनी सच्चाई बिलकुल भिन्न है। स्त्री होने के नाते मैंने इस भेद की अनुभूति स्वयं की है। भेद की शिकार होने पर अधिकांश पुरुषों के घड़ियाली आँसू भी मैंने देखे हैं। सूक्ष्म अवलोकन एवं अध्ययन के आधार पर कहा जा सकता है कि विकसित समाज (उच्चवर्ग) भी इस बिन्दु पर न्यायसंगत नहीं है और स्त्रियाँ समानता तथा न्याय जैसे सामाजिक एवं राजनैतिक आदर्शों का लाभ प्राप्त करने से वंचित है। जहाँ तक भारतीय समाज में स्त्रियों की समस्या की बात उठती है—तो इसकी स्थिति अन्य देशों के अपेक्षाकृत दयनीय है। भारतीय संविधान के निर्माताओं ने भी संविधान की प्रस्तावना[1] में स्पष्ट उल्लेख किया है कि संविधान का प्राथमिक लक्ष्य है—समानता स्थापित करना और इसमें भारतीय नारी निर्विवाद रूप से सम्मिलित है। नस्ल, जाति, लिंग, धर्म तथा जन्मस्थान के आधार पर मौलिक अधिकारों[2] से किसी को भी वंचित नहीं किया जा सेता है। परन्तु दुर्भाग्य की बात है कि आधी शताब्दी से अधिक समय बीत जाने पर भी हमारे संविधान निर्माताओं के सपने खंडित ही हैं। समाज की पारंपरिक एवं पुरातनपंथी पुरूष इस दिशा में प्रमुख

बाधक की भूमिका निभाते हैं। हम इन्हें स्त्रियों का, स्त्री-समाज का और अंततोगत्वा संपूर्ण मानव-समाज का सबसे बड़ा शत्रु कहते हैं। जहाँ तक भारतीय संविधान द्वारा प्रदत्त वोट डालने और चुनाव लड़ने की बात है तो दोनों के अधिकार एक जैसे हैं, परन्तु स्त्रियों ने इसे विभिन्न देशों में 1917, 1920 तथा 1928 के लगातार संघर्ष द्वारा प्राप्त किया है।[3] तथापि तथ्य यह है कि महिला आंदोलन के अधिक मजबूत होने तथा राजनैतिक सहभागिता की माँग जोरदार होने के बावजूद न तो लोकसभा में महिला-प्रतिनिधित्व का प्रतिशत बढ़ा है, और न महिला उम्मीदवारों तथा मंत्रियों की संख्या बढ़ी है। विभिन्न राजनैतिक दल इस स्तर तक नीतिविहीन हो गये हैं कि 33% महिला आरक्षण का बिल पास होने का मंत्रोच्चार, करते रहने के बावजूद महिला आरक्षण बिल पास नहीं करवा सके।

उपर्युक्त लिंग-भेद की सच्चाई देखने के लिए भारतीय समाज का सूक्ष्म अवलोकन अनिवार्य है जहाँ इसकी सामान्य प्रवृति में लिंग-भेद के उदाहरण सर्वत्र मौजूद हैं। अधिकांश परिवार पुत्री के जन्म से उस तरह खुश नहीं होते जैसी खुशी पुत्र-जन्म से पाते हैं। वैसे समाज के कुछ प्रगतिशील[4] लोग इस खाई को पाटने के लिए स्वतंत्रतापूर्व से ही प्रयासरत हैं परन्तु उत्तर आधुनिक युग में भी जन-सामान्य को मान्य नहीं हुआ एक मात्र पुत्री का जन्म लेना। मात्र पुत्री को जन्म देकर जनसंख्या नियंत्रण को लगाम लगाने वाली माताओं का, न केवल अपने परिवार में बल्कि अपने व्यक्तिगत अनुभव के आधार पर मैं कह सकती हूँ कि अन्य लोगों द्वारा भी, उपहास किया जाता है। पुरूष वर्चस्व उस मोड़ तक पहुँचाता है जब पति की दूसरी शादी पुत्र-पैदा हेतु कर दी जाती है। जबकि यह वैज्ञानिक तथ्य है कि पुत्री जन्म का कारण पति की जैविक भूमिका है। इस तरह इससे पारिवारिक कलह उत्पन्न होता है, परिवार टूटता है, साथ ही ऐसा मानसिकता का दुष्प्रभाव सामाजिक एवं राजनीतिक क्षेत्रों में भी देखा जा सकता है। समाज वैज्ञानिकों5 ने इस संदर्भ में कई शोध किए हैं और महत्त्वपूर्ण बिन्दुओं का संकेत कर अपने उपाय सुझाए हैं, परन्तु भेद की जड़ें इतनी मजबूत हैं कि आनन-फानन में मिटाना आसान कार्य नहीं है। जैसे—19वीं शती में मनोवैज्ञानिक फ्रॉयड, समाजशास्त्री एंगेल्स, राजनैतिक और आर्थिक चिंतक मार्क्स ने तत्कालीन समाज-व्यवस्था तथा पूर्व स्थापित सामाजिक मूल्यों पर करारा प्रहार किया है जिसने इस विषय पर नये सिरे से सोचने के लिए हमें बाध्य किया है। प्रसिद्ध दार्शनिक जे0 एस0 मिल0 अपनी रचना 'The Subjection of Women' में महिला-विकास के राह में बाधक सभी समस्याओं के निराकरण की बात करते हैं।6 20वीं शती के पूर्वार्द्ध में नारी अधीनीकरण नारीवाद

को पनपाने में सहायक सिद्ध होता है जो उत्तरार्द्ध आते-आते नारी स्वतंत्रता आन्दोलन को बढ़ावा देता है। 1980-85 में दो और विश्वस्तरीय महिला महासभाएँ हुई। इन सभाओं का वैश्विक प्रभाव हमने प्रत्यक्ष देखा है। इसके पीछे कारण यही था कि महिला संबंधी विभिन्न समस्यों का सटीक ढंग से कोटिबद्ध किया गया तथा विभिन्न समस्याओं का विस्तृत विश्लेषण किया गया।

भले ही हम पर विदेशी विचारों से प्रभावित हो जाने का इल्ज़ाम ठोक दिया जाए, हम 1995 ई0 के संयुक्त राष्ट्र संघ द्वारा बिजिंग में आयोजित चतुर्थ विश्व महिला महासभा के आभारी हैं। बिजिंग सम्मेलन में महिलाओं ने एक नई उपलब्धि हासिल की है कि " स्त्री के अधिकार मानवाधिकार हैं।" विगत सौ वर्षों में राष्ट्रीय तथा अंतरराष्ट्रीय स्तर पर अनेक महत्वपूर्ण परिवर्तन हुए हैं और इनका प्रभाव भारत की सभ्यता तथा सांस्कृतिक दृष्टिकोण पर पड़ा है। अपनी प्राचीन सभ्यता और संस्कृति पर गौरवान्वित होने वाला भारत, अपने ज्ञान के घमंड से मदोन्मत्त होने वाला भारत, लैंगिक असमानता के उदाहरणों से भरा पड़ा है। उदाहरण स्वरूप हम पितृसत्तात्मक समाज-व्यवस्था में विवाह की प्रथा को ले सकते हैं क्योंकि विवाह पश्चात् स्त्री को परिवार की सम्पत्ति जैसा ही समझा जाता है, लेकिन स्त्री अपने परिवार की पुश्तैनी सम्पत्ति पाने के हक से कई जगह, कई कारणों से, अक्सर वंचित रह जाती है।

इस संदर्भ में विश्व-विश्रुत भारतीय मूल के नोबेल पुरस्कार विजेता अमर्त्यसेन का उल्लेख करना समीचीन होगा, जिन्होंने 'Many Faces of Gender Inequality' शीर्षक लेख में तीसरी दुनिया/विकासशील देशों में व्याप्त लिंग-भेद का प्रतिपादन किया है। उपर्युक्त निबंध में लिंग-भेद पर आधारित सात प्रकार की असमानताओं का वर्गीकरण करते हुए लैंगिक असमानता को वे[7] समस्याओं का संग्रह मानते हैं। यहाँ हम उनका केवल नामोल्लेख कर रहे हैं–

(i) मृत्यु दर में असमानता
(ii) जन्म दर में असमानता
(iii) बुनियादी सुविधाओं में असमानता
(iv) विशेष अवसरों की उपलब्धता में असमानता
(v) पेशागत असमानता
(vi) स्वामित्व की असमानता
(vii) घरेलू असमानता

हालाँकि श्री सेन द्वारा किये गये वर्गीकरणों ने लिंग-भेद के कई आयामों को घेरने में सफलता पायी है, फिर भी कई बिन्दु जैसे राजनीति, महिलाओं की प्रतिष्ठा, गरीबी इत्यादि पहलू छूट गये से लगते हैं।

तीसरी दुनिया खासकर उत्तरी अफ्रिका तथा ज्यादातर एशियाई देशों में स्वाथ्य, सुविधा और पोषक आहार में पुरुषों की अपेक्षा महिलाओं के साथ भेदभाव किये जाने से महिलाओं का मृत्यु-दर अधिक हैं। जहाँ तक स्त्री एवं पुरुषों के जन्मदर संबंधी अनुपातों की बात हम करते हैं तो वर्तमान सांख्यिकी के आँकड़े स्पष्ट करते हैं कि महिलाओं का जन्मदर पुरुषों की अपेक्षा कम है। भारत और दक्षिण एशिया में उदाहरण मौजूद हैं। महिलाओं के जन्मदर में कमी लाने में भ्रणू परीक्षण की उपब्धता ने मदद की है। तथ्य यह है कि अधिकांश लोग भ्रूण परीक्षण से जान चुके होते हैं कि भावी संतान पुत्री है तो भ्रूण हत्या करवा दी जाती है, क्योंकि माता-पिता सहित परिवार के सदस्यों का जो खुशी पुत्र के जन्म लेने से मिलती है वैसी पुत्री के जन्म लेने से नहीं होती।

यदि इस घिनौनी और जघन्य हत्या के कारकों की खोज हम करें तो—पुत्री के विवाह में होने वाला दहेज का खर्च और माता-पिता के मृत्योपरान्त मुखाग्नि रीति के पीछे हमारी वही पुरातन परम्परा है, जिसे आज भी सम्पूर्ण मानवता के शत्रु परम्परावादी महिला और रूढ़िवादी पुरुष ढोते चले आ रहे हैं। यह उत्तर आधुनिक युग के पितृसत्तात्मक पुरुष प्रधान समाज का कटु सत्य है। इस तरह भ्रूण हत्या की संख्या में वृद्धि लिंग-भेद का अमानवीय उदाहरण है। इसके प्रचलन ने जैव-आचारशास्त्रियों का ध्यान आकृष्ट किया है और वे इसके औचित्य पर गहन अध्ययन करने लगे हैं। उन्होंने इसमें मानव-मूल्यों के ह्रासोन्मुख प्रवृत्ति के लक्षण देखे और नवजात शिशु एवं भ्रूण में वास्तविक व्यक्ति लक्षित किया है।[8] उन्होंने व्यक्ति के दो वर्ग किए—

(क) वास्तविक व्यक्ति और

(ख) संभाव्य व्यक्ति

नवजात शिशु एवं भ्रूण को संभाव्य व्यक्ति की श्रेणी में रखा और मानववादी दर्शन को इस तकनीकी युग में प्रष्ठिापित करने के लिए अपने विचार दिये कि संभाव्य व्यक्ति को भी वास्तविक व्यक्ति की तरह व्यवहार दिया जाना चाहिए। उपर्युक्त अध्ययन से स्पष्ट हो जाता है कि जैव-आचारशास्त्रियों ने लिंग-भेद के कारण भावी मानव समाज की दिशाहीनता पर रोक लगाने का प्रयास किया है।

19वीं तथा 20वीं शती में यह तथ्य भी हमारे समक्ष आया है कि विकसित देश अमेरिका भी लिंग-भेद/असमानता से ग्रस्त है। यहाँ मेरे मन में एक प्रश्न बार-बार कौंध रहा जिसका उत्तर उपस्थित शिक्षाविदों से जानना चाहती हूँ—जब महिलाएँ दिमागी शक्ति में, क्षमता में, कार्य कुशलता में पुरुषों के बराबर स्वयं को साबित कर रही हैं, तो फिर क्यों अवसर आने पर इन्हें हाशिये पर ढ़केला जाता है? एशिया

महादेश में प्राचीन सभ्यता संस्कृति का संरक्षक कह स्वयं को महिमामंडित करके अपने ज्ञान पर गौरवान्वित होने वाला, ज्ञान के घमंड में खुद को सर्वश्रेष्ठ कहने वाले भारत में तीसरी सहस्त्राब्दी का धुर सच हम चारोओर समाज में देखते हैं कि अधिकांश क्षेत्रों में माता-पिता द्वारा पुत्रियों को अधिकाधिक शिक्षा देने के पीछे उनकी की शादी की बेहतर संभावना मात्र ही तलाश रहे हैं न कि उन्हें अपना मालिक स्वयं बनने देने के लिए।

दार्शनिकों द्वारा दिये गए उपर्युक्त विचार इस बात के संकेत हैं कि वर्तमान विकसित विश्व में अब भी लिंग-भेद का अभिशाप विद्यमान है। इसकी जड़े इतनी मजबूत हैं कि आधुनिक तथाकथित प्रगतिशील समाज के लिए इसका उन्मूलन एक दुरुह कार्य है। साथ ही एक स्वाभविक जिज्ञासा जगती है कि यह लिंग-भेद कब और किस प्रकार मानव सभ्यता एवं संस्कृति के इतिहास में अपना पैर जमाने लगा? वर्तमान ऐतिहासिक शोध के आधार पर यह बताना तो कठिन है कि किस प्रकार स्त्री और पुरुष की सृष्टि हुई? वैसे पौराणिक साहित्य के आधार पर अध्येताओं ने इस संबंध में कुछ पता लगाने का प्रयास किया है, परन्तु वे निर्विवाद तथ्य नहीं हैं। फिर भी इतिहासकारों ने मानव-सभ्यता एवं संस्कृति के विकास क्रम में इस बात का संकेत किया है कि मानव-समाज के प्रारम्भिक काल में समाज मातृसत्तात्मक था। यह स्वाभाविक भी प्रतीत होता है। मानव-संसाधन की स्थिति एवं प्रारंभिक विकास में स्त्रियों की भूमिका का अवमूल्यन नहीं किया जा सकता है। यह संभव है कि मानव सभ्यता के विकास से सामाजिक कार्यों की जटिलता बढ़ी और मध्यकाल आते-आते कार्यों के बँटवारे के क्रम में स्त्रियों को घरेलू कार्य का भार प्राप्त हुआ। इसमें स्त्रायों का कार्यक्षेत्र सीमित हो गया और अन्य महत्त्वपूर्ण कार्यों में उनकी उपेक्षा हो गयी। इस तथ्य को फ्रेडरिक एंगेल्स ने अपने निबंध में स्वीकार किया है9 कि महिलाएँ अपनी अवनति में जन्मदात्री और पूज्या होते-होते घरेलू नौकर का दर्जा पा गयी हैं। इसके बाद उनके लिये अन्य क्षेत्रों में अपनी प्रतिभा प्रदर्शन का अवसर कम होता गया। इस तरह स्त्रियाँ निम्न कार्य करनेवाली सामाजिक सदस्या बन गयीं तथा लिंग-भेद का शिकार होने लगीं। आधुनिक काल में मानववादी दर्शन का प्रादुर्भाव हुआ बुद्धिजीवियों में मानवमूल्यों के विकास की आवश्यकता का नवबोध उत्पन्न हुआ। स्त्रियों के कार्यों का मूल्यांकन किया जाने लगा तथा समाज के समग्रविकास के लिए इनकी भूमिका आवश्यक महसूस की गई, क्योंकि समाज की आधी आबादी स्त्रायों की थी। राजनीति में प्रजातंत्र एवं समानता के आदर्श स्थापित किए गए और स्त्री शिक्षा की आवश्यकता पर बल दिया जाने लगा।

विदा हुई 20वीं शती हर दृष्टिकोण से विश्व इतिहास में एक विशिष्ट शताब्दी के रूप में प्रादुर्भत हुई। नारी मुक्ति एवं विकास के लिए बहुत प्रयत्न किये गये परन्तु वांछिज फल प्राप्त नहीं हुए। भारत में तो स्थिति अपेक्षाकृत निराशाजनक ही है। सह शिक्षा के प्रचलन के बावजूद सभी क्षेत्रों में नारियों का प्रतिशत जनसंख्या की दृष्टि से पुरुषों की अपेक्षा बहुत कम है। अध्ययन का क्षेत्र हो या नौकरियों का, स्त्रियों में इसकी पृष्ठभूमि में कार्य करने वाले कारणों का पता लगाना आवश्यक ही नहीं अनिवार्य है क्योंकि यह भारतीय समाज के विकास के समक्ष बहुत बड़ा प्रश्न-चिन्ह खड़ा करता है एवं भारतीय मानसिकता के पिछड़ेपन का द्योतक है। इस संदर्भ में यह स्पष्ट रूप से कहा जा सकता है कि पुरूष-प्रधान समाज के द्वारा नारियों की उपेक्षा एवं सशंकित परम्परा प्रेमियों द्वारा वर्तमान विकास के आदर्शों की खंडित स्वीकृति इसके दो प्रमुख कारण हैं। अगर इन दोनों कारणों के औचित्य पर दृष्टि डाली जाय तो इन्हें अनुचित एवं अवैज्ञानिक कहा जाएगा। आधुनिक मनोवैज्ञानिक तथ्यों ने प्रतिस्थापित किया है कि लड़कियों का मानसिक विकास लड़कों की अपेक्षा जीव्रगति से होता है। सृजनशीलता भी लड़कों की अपेक्षा लड़कियों में अधिक है। इसी प्रकार शिक्षा के विभिन्न क्षेत्रों में महिलाओं ने अपनी कार्य कुशलता, कौशल द्वारा सिद्ध कर दिया है कि दिमागी काम में भी ये पुरुषों से इक्कीस हैं, मनोवैज्ञानिक रूप से ज्यादा मजबूत हैं। विश्वजन मानस को जेहन में रखना होगा कि अनुसंधाकर्त्ता, टेक्नोलॉजिस्ट, व्यवसायी और विभिन्न सरकारें जिस 'पाई चार्ट' का अब तक व्यवहार करते रहे हैं उसे प्रसिद्ध नर्स फ्लोरेंस नाईटिंगेल ने खोजा था। 17वीं शताब्दी में मुमताज महल की मौसी नूर महल ने प्रथम बार फूलों से इत्र निकालने का यंत्र बनाया था। इसी शती की कल्पना चावला को हम कैसे भूल सकते हैं। इतिहास भारतीय महिलाओं की राष्ट्राध्यक्षा जैसे—बेग़म रानी, चाँद बीबी, रजिया सुल्तान, झाँसी की रानी लक्ष्मी बाई की गवाही आज भी देता है। इस पर और अधिक विवेचन की जगह हम कहना चाहते हैं कि आधुनिक अन्वेषणों एवं औचित्य के आधार पर UNESCO जैसे विश्व संगठन के हम पक्षधर हैं जो लिंग-भेद के उन्मूलन हेतु सतत प्रयत्नशील हैं। इस संदर्भ में 1968 में प्रकाशित UNESCO के उस प्रतिवेदन का हम समवेत स्वर से सराहना करते हैं जिसमें किसी प्रकार के भेद को मानवाधिकार की स्थापना के लिए अस्वीकृत किया गया है।[10]

विगत शताब्दी के प्रयासों की कमी को दूर करने के लिए तीसरी सहस्त्राब्दी के प्रांरभ ने अधिक संवेदनशील दिखायी है एवं महिलाओं की असमान स्थिति को समाप्त करने के लिए 'महिला सशक्तिकरण' का सिद्धान्त देकर लिंग-भेद की समस्या के निदान का स्तुत्य प्रयास किया है। सामाजिक दार्शनिकों ने खोजा है कि

महिलाओं की अवनति बहुत-सी सामाजिक जटिलता एवं दुर्बलता का कारक है। अस्तु नारी सशक्तिकरण के अभाव में किसी भी समाज की नींव मजबूत नहीं हो सकती। यह सहज अनुमान्य है कि समाज की आधी आबादी अर्थात् स्त्री को अविकिसत रखकर विकसित समाज की कल्पना नहीं की जा सकती है। शारीरिक शौर्य का मदान्ध पुरुष यह न भूले कि मात्र नारी को ही बच्चा उत्पन्न करने का प्राकृतिक उपहार अथवा विशेषधिकार प्राप्त है। क्या अस्वस्थ और उपेक्षिता नारी स स्वस्थ संतान जन्म ले सकती है? जैव-वैज्ञानिकों के नवीनतम शोध स्पष्ट करते हैं कि गर्भस्थ शिशु के उचित विकास के लिए माँ के स्वास्थ्य की देखभाल अनिवार्य है। चिकित्साविज्ञान इसके लिए गर्भाधान के समय से ही भावी संतान के प्रति कार्य करने की सलाह देता है। यह ठोस आधार है कि जैव-नीतिशास्त्री भ्रूणहत्या को अमानवीय अपराध के रूप में देखते हैं और इसे मानवता के आदर्श एवं वर्तमान सामान्य चिकित्सीय चेतना के विरुद्ध मानते हैं।[11]

कभी-कभी कार्यस्थल अथवा शिक्षण-प्रशिक्षण संस्थाओं में महिलाएँ यौन-उत्पीड़न की शिकार होती हैं। लेकिन कार्यस्थल पर यौन उत्पीड़न के विरद्ध महिला संगठन की क्रांतिकारी लड़ाई अब अनुप्रयुक्त नीतिशास्त्र का विषय बन गया है। अनुप्रयुक्त नीतिशास्त्र के अन्तर्गत गभपात के संदर्भ में महिलाओं के अधिकारों के साथ ही यौन उत्पीड़न की समस्या स्वयं में एक चर्चित समस्या है। हाँ, हम, फरव्र कर सकते हैं कि स्वतंत्रता की पचासवीं वर्षगाँठ के पूर्व भारत के उच्चतम न्यायालय ने अपने महत्त्वपूर्ण निर्णय में कार्य-स्थल पर यौन-उत्पीड़न रोकने के लिए कई निर्देश दिये हैं। इससे कामकाजी महिलाओं को राहत मिली है।

निष्कर्ष

उपयुक्र्त विवेचन से सहज अनुमान्य है कि लिंग-भेद एक सामाजिक अभिशाप है। इसके समापन से अन्य सामाजिक अभिशापों से स्वयमेव छुटकारा पाया जा सकता है। इस समस्या की जड़ समाज में इतनी गहरी और पुरानी है कि वैधानिक प्रयास एवं सहानुभूति काफी नहीं है। समाज की रूढ़िबद्ध धारणाओं को बदलने के लिए महिला के साथ पुरुष भी अपनी वर्चस्ववादी मानसिकता छोड़े। समाज की मानसिकता में परिवर्तन लाने के लिए वास्तविक एवं कारगर उपाय करने पड़ेंगे। इसके लिए समाज की निष्ठा एवं ईमानदारी के अतिरिक्त महिलाओं की चेतना को जाग्रत करने की आवश्यकता है। इसके लिए इन्हें कदम-दर-कदम अपने अधिकारों के लिए धैर्य के साथ लड़ाई लड़ना होगी। महिलाओं को स्मरण रखना चाहिए कि दार्शनिक एवं वैज्ञानिक आधार पर हम पुरुषों के समक्ष कुछेक प्राकृतिक अंतर के अतिरिक्त किसी भी तरह न्यून नहीं हैं। दर्शन और धर्म-दर्शन के दृष्टिकोण से अगर

आत्मा को आधार अनाया जाय अथवा जीवविज्ञान के Cell को आधार बनाया जाय तो नारी-पुरुष दोनों में कोई भेद नहीं है। इस प्रकार वांछित स्थिति प्राप्त करने के मार्ग में किसी प्रकार का वैचारिक या वैधानिक बाधा नहीं है। अतः इस नरात्मक स्थिति को दूर करने के लिए मेरी ओर दार्शनिक सुझाव है कि महिलाओं को सर्वप्रथम स्वयं आगे बढ़कर अपने अधिकार की लड़ाई लड़नी होगी तथा पुत्री-पत्रु के बीच समानता का वातावरण निर्मित कर अपने बच्चों का पालन-पोषण करना होगा। माता-पिता ही अपनी समुचित शिक्षा और व्यवहार के द्वारा संतान में लिंग-भेद के बीच जमने से रोक सकते हैं। इसके अलावा वैधानिक प्रयास को और अधिक मजबूत बनाने की आवश्यकता है। समाजशास्त्रियों एवं विधि-निर्माताओं को अनछुए पहलों पर विचार करना होगा। मसलन सम्पत्ति के विक्रय में पत्नी के दस्तखत को भी अनिवार्य बनाया जाये ताकि सम्पत्ति के उत्तराधिकार के क्षेत्र में महिलाओं की सक्रिया भागीदारी की प्रवृति बढ़े जिससे महिलाओं में न्याय और समानता के बोध की क्षमता में वृद्धि हो।

संदर्भ

1. Basu, Durga Das. Commentary on the Constitution ofI n d i a . (S.C. Sarkar & Sons Ltd. Calcutta 12,) Third edition 1955, preamble, p. 42.
2. Encyclopaedia of India Women, Vol.3 p. 753

   और

   The Constitution of India, Part-III & Article-15 (i).
3. The New Encyclopaedia Britannica, Vol. 19, p. 912.
4. Sharma, Radhakrishana, Nationalism, Social Reform and Indian Women (A Study of the Interaction between our National Movement and the Movement of Social Reform among Indian Women, 1921-1937.
5. Reddy, O. Chinnappa, From a man's World to a Human World, Centre For Women's Development Studies, 1990, p. 9-32.
6. Mill, J. S. On Liberty, Representative Governments, TheSubjection of Women : Three Essays, London : Oxford University Press, 1971
7. Sen, Amartya, "Many Faces of Gender Inequality." (Frontline, New Delhi, Nov. 9, 2001).
8. The Encyclopedia of Bioethics, p. 826.

9. Marx, karl and Engels, Fredrich, 'The origin of the family, private property and the state', Selected works, vol-3, progress publishers, Moscow.

10. UNESOC Chronicle, June 1968, Vol-XIV, No.-6, p. 217.

11. The Encyclopedia of Bioethics, p.1-4.

अध्याय 10

नारी सशक्तिकरण : एक पुनर्विचार

आलोक टंडन

नारी सशक्तिकरण अब महज़ अकादमिक बहस का मुद्दा नहीं रह गया है। अपनी आधी आबादी को निर्जीव और पंगु रखकर कोई भी देश-समाज विकसित होने का दावा नहीं कर सकता। संस्कृतिवादी, पुरातनपन्थी लोग समय-रथ को पीछे खींचने का चाहें जितना प्रयास करें, आज की नारी पारम्परिक सोंच के दकियानूस दायरे को तोड़कर चहुंमुखी विकास की ओर अग्रसर है। नारी अस्तित्व और नियति के पुराने आख्यान अप्रासंगिक हो गये हैं। उसे एक प्रजननकारी कोख समझने की सामन्तवादी मानसिकता का खुलेआम समर्थन करने का साहस अब उसका शोषण करने वालों में भी नहीं है। गई सदी में नारी प्रश्न पर जो व्यापक बहस चर्चा हुयी है उसके परिणाम स्वरूप एक मुक्ति कामी चेतना का निमार्ण हुआ है। नयी सदी में यही चेतना, नारी-सशक्तिकरण के रूप में अभिव्यक्ति हो रही है। निश्चय ही इसके व्यापक परिणाम हमारे घरेलू-सामाजिक जीवन पर होंगे। इसके मूर्त होने से पहले ही इससे जुड़े विविध वैचारिक पक्षों की जानकारी और समीक्षा इस लेख का उद्देश्य है, जिससे सामाजिक न्याय से जुड़े इस महत्वपूर्ण सामाजिक आन्दोलन के प्रति एक समझदारी पूर्ण दृष्टिकोण बनाया जा सके।

नारी आन्दोलन से जुड़ी सरकारी, अर्द्ध-सरकारी और गैर-सरकारी एजेन्सियों द्वारा नारी सशक्तिकरण का मुद्दा एक नारे के रूप में जिस शोर के साथ उछाला जा रहा है उसमें विचारणीय गम्भीर प्रश्नों के छूट जाने का भय है। यह सही है कि गैर-बराबरी समाप्त करने की अवधारणा अब सशक्तिकरण की अवधारणा में बदल गयी हे किन्तु क्या दोनों में कोई अन्तर नहीं है? क्या नारी सबलीकरण की अवधारणा वैचारिक रूप में अधिक पुष्ट है? भूमण्डलीय पूंजीवाद ने स्त्री-शोषण के नये रूप उपस्थित किये हैं, क्या अवधारणा उनसे निपटने में सक्षम हैं? याकि भूमण्डलीय बाजार स्वयं

सबलीकरण का सफल हथियार है? यहीं यह सवाल भी महत्वपूर्ण है कि सशक्तिकरण के लिये स्त्री की भागीदारी कैसे सुनिश्चित हो? स्वाभाविक है कि यह प्रश्न भी पूछा जाये कि सबलीकरण का मात्र राजनीतिक पक्ष ही क्या महत्वपूर्ण है? सामाजिक और आर्थिक सबलीकरण के क्या रूप हो सकते हैं? व्यावहारिक रूप से किसी नतीजे तक पहुंचने के लिये यह जानना भी जरूरी है कि आखिर नारी-सशक्तिकरण का सशक्त वाहक कौन हो सकता है? इन प्रश्नों की गम्भीर मीमांसा इसलिये भी जरूरी है क्योंकि वैचारिक स्पष्टता के अभाव का आरोप नारीवादी आन्दोलनों पर बराबर लगाया जाता रहा है। स्पष्ट रणनीति के अभाव में न्याय के लिये जूझने वाले अन्य वर्गो का सहयोग जुटा पाना भी दुष्कर है।

(I)

नारी सशक्तिकरण की अवधारणा को समझने के लिये नारी-मुक्ति आन्दोलन के ऐतिहासिक विकास पर दृष्टि डालना आवश्यक है। इसे तीन चरणों में स्पष्ट रूप से देखा जा सकता है। इनके अनुरूप विकसित हुये तीनों माडलों की चर्चा यहां अपेक्षित है। प्रथम चरण को अठारवीं शताब्दी के मध्य से उन्नीसवीं शताब्दी के मध्य तक माना जा सकता है। सैद्धान्तिक रूप से इस दौरान औरत-मर्द के बीच सम्बन्धों की गैर बराबरी को लेकर मूलभूत प्रश्न उठाये गये और यह स्थापना की गयी कि वर्ग और जाति के समान ही लिंग को भी सामाजिक न्याय के विवेचन में एक स्वतंत्र स्थान दिया जाना चाहिये। इस दौरान सारा जोर महिलाओं को, मर्दो के समान में बराबर अधिकार पाने के हक पर दिया गया। यह सब उदारवादी नागरिक अधिकारों के वैचारिक ढांचे के अन्तर्गत था। पुरुषों के समान ही नारियों को भी समान कार्य के लिये समान वेतन, चिकित्सा सुविधाओं, गर्भपात के कानूनी अधिकार आदि के लिये समाज और राज्य की ओर से प्रयत्न किये गये। यह माना गया कि सारी दुनियां की स्त्रियों की समस्यायें और उनके हल एक समान हैं क्योंकि पितृ-सत्तात्मक समाज ही नारी शोषण का आधार है जिसका अन्त नारी-पुरुष के बीच कानूनी असमानता दूर करके ही सम्भव हैं। इसे 'नारी कल्याण माडल' भी कह सकते हैं।

ईस्टर बोसेरप की पुस्तक **'Women's Role in Economic Development' (1970)** को हम 'नारी-विकास माडल' का आरम्भिक स्त्रोत मान सकते हैं। उसने दर्शाया कि कार्य संपादन, संसाधनों की उपलब्धता और लाभों के बटवारे में लैंगिक असमानता है। आगे के शोधकार्यों से यह स्पष्ट हो गया कि यद्यपि दुनिया की पचास फीसदी आबादी महिलाओं की है, वे लगभग दो तिहाई कार्य घंटों का निष्पादन करती हैं, आय का दसवां हिस्सा ही उन्हें प्राप्त होता है और वे सम्पत्ति

के मात्र एक प्रतिशत भाग की स्वामिनी हैं। इस प्रकार की लैंगिक असमानता को दूर करने के लिये नारी विकास की विशिष्ट योजनायें संसार के अनेक देशों (जिनमें भारत भी शमिल था) में बनाई गयीं। किन्तु इन प्रयत्नों की समीक्षा से यह पता चला कि ऐसी योजनाओं से महिलाओं को बराबरी का स्थान नहीं मिल सका। पहले से बनी हुयी सामाजिक असमानतायें और मजबूत हुयीं। कुछ विद्वानों का मत था कि ऐसा विकास के पूंजीवादी-पितृसत्तात्मक माडल के रहते स्वाभाविक ही था। जो भी हो, इस तथ्य ने लिंग-संवेदी विकास की नीतियों और उसे दर्शाने वाले लिंग-संवेदी सूचकांक को जन्म दिया। अब सारा जोर महिलाओं को विकास कार्यक्रमों में भागीदार बनाने पर दिया जाने लगा, न कि सिर्फ उन्हें विकास के फायदों तक ही सीमित रखा गया, जैसा कि पहले होता था। नारी की पहचान आर्थिक विकास की एक सक्रिय एजेन्सी के रूप में गयी। इस प्रकार हम देखते हैं कि नारी-विकास माडल भी दो चरणों में पूरा हुआः नारी और विकास और लिंग और विकास। पहले में जहाँ। विकास नीतियों में नारी कल्याण पर समुचित ध्यान दिया गया वहीं दूसरे में लिंग भेद को ही योजना का आधार बनाया गया।

यद्यपि लिंग-न्याय के प्रति विकास योजनाओं को संवेदनशील बनाने में उपरोक्त माडल का योगदान सराहनीय रहा किन्तु उसकी अपनी सीमायें हैं। औरतों की कुछ व्यावहारिक जरूरतें उनकी जैविक संरचना, जीवन स्थितियों, भूमिकाओं, कार्यों और जिम्मेदारियों से जुड़ी होती हैं। इनमें जच्चा-बच्चा सुविधायें, पानी, ईंधन के साधन, बच्चों के देखभाल की सुविधायें आदि आती हैं। इसके अतिरिक्त उनके कुछ सामरिक हित भी हैं जो लिंग भेद पर आधारित अन्यायपूर्ण सामाजिक ढ़ाचें को विनष्ट करने की नीतियां अपनाने की जरूरत पर बल देते हैं। इसी भेद को ध्यान में रखते हुये सामाजिक-नारीवादियों ने नारी - विकास माडल की आलोचना यह कह कर की है विकास माडल व्यावहारिक जरूरतों की पूर्ति के नाम पर सामरिक हितों की अवहेलना करता है। उपरोक्त माडल की सबसे तीखी आलोचना यह कहकर की गई कि इसमें शक्ति के आयाम की अनदेखी की गई है। ऐसा मुख्य रूप से आर्थिक विकास को प्रधानता देने के कारण हुआ है। कुछ अध्ययनों से यह भी स्पष्ट हुआ कि आर्थिक रूप से महिलाओं का उठता स्तर उन्हें आवश्यक रूप से खुशी और समान सामाजिक स्तर नहीं प्रदान करता। कई स्थितियों में तो उनकी स्थिति और भी खराब हो जाती है क्योंकि उन्हें परम्परागत भूमिकाओं के साथ-साथ ही नयी आर्थिक जिम्मेदारियां भी निभानी होती हैं। इसलिये आवश्यक है कि निर्णय में उनकी भागीदारी सुनिश्चित हो। इसके लिये उनका घरेलू और सामुदायिक शक्ति संरचनाओं में सक्रिया रूप से भाग लेना आवश्यक है। इसकी पहचान ने ही 'नारी सशक्तिकरण' की नयी अवधारणा के लिये मार्ग प्रशस्त किया।

(II)

नारी सशक्तिकरण या सबलीकरण अपने शाब्दिक अर्थ से ही शक्ति के आयाम की अन्य आयामो पर प्रमुखता की ओर इंगिता करता है। इसके अन्तर्गत यह माना जाने लगा है कि नारी सबलीकरण की कुंजी उसके स्वयं तथा शक्ति-संरचना के ऊपर नियन्त्रण में छिपी है। शक्ति-संरचना पर धीरे-धीरे बढ़ते नियंत्रण के साथ ही अन्य स्तरों पर लिंग समानता-भागीदारी, संसाधनों की प्राप्ति, भौतिक कल्याण आदि, स्वाभाविक रूप से स्त्री को प्राप्त हो जायेगी। नारी सशक्तिकरण का अर्थ घरेलू और सामुदायिक दोनों शक्ति-संरचनाओं में नारी की शक्ति को बढ़ाना है। एक तरफ से यह औरत और मर्द के बीच शक्ति संबंधों में मूलभूत बदलाव है जिससे महिलायें अपने जीवन पर अधिकाधिक नियंत्रण पा सकें और पुरुषों का उन पर से नियंत्रण कम हो सके। प्रसिद्ध समाज शास्त्री आन्द्र बीते भी मानते हैं कि नारी सबलीकरण के पीछे मुख्य धारणा शक्ति संबंधों के पुनर्निधारण द्वारा समाज परिवर्तन है। इसे ही एन्थोनी गिडिन्स ने 'Transformative Capacity' कहा है और कुछ अन्य समाज शास्त्रियों ने इसे 'power over' के स्थान पर 'power to' से परिभाषित करना चाहा है। किसी भी दृष्टि से नारी सशक्तिकरण का यह माडल शक्ति केन्द्रित ही है और जो हर स्तर पर लैंगिक असमानता का शनैः शनैः ह्रास करता है। यह नारी-विकास माडल से अधिक व्यापक है क्योंकि यह केवल सामाजिक कल्याण या आर्थिक बराबरी को महत्व नहीं देता अपितु आर्थिक, सामाजिक, राजनैतिक, मनोवैज्ञानिक सभी पहुलओं को एक सूत्र में पिरो कर उन पर विचार करता है।

नारी सशक्तिकरण की यह अवधारणा सबलीकरण के लिये उस आलोचलात्मक विवेक को प्राप्त करने को प्रमुखता देती है जो शोषण, दमन और अन्याय में छिपे संरचनात्मक पहलुओं को ठीक से पहचान सके। इस प्रक्रिया में तीन कड़ियां हैं। पहले में भौतिक सुविधाओं, आहार, मृत्यु दर, जनसंख्या अनुपात, शिक्षा, वेतन, रोजगार, परिवार और समाज के निर्णयों में भागीदारी तथा अपने श्रम, आय और जीवन पर आत्म-नियंत्रण में जो लिंग भेद के कारण असमानतायें हैं उनकी व्यापक चेतना फैलाई जाती है। दूसरी कड़ी यह बोध जगाना है कि ये असमानतायें ईश्वर या प्रकृति प्रदत्त नहीं हैं, अतः उन्हें बदला जा सकता है। तीसरी कड़ी उपरोक्त समझ के आधार पर लिंग समानता के उद्देश्य को प्राप्त करने के लिये महिलाओं को संगठित करना है।

नारी सशक्तिकरण के लक्ष्य-प्राप्ति के लिये दो तरीके सुझाये जाते हैं। पहला है राज्य द्वारा कानूनी और प्रशासानिक उपायों द्वारा नारी की शक्ति का उन्नयन। दूसरा है महिलाओं द्वारा स्वयं संगठित होकर शक्ति प्राप्त करना। एक रास्ता ऊपर से नीचे की ओर जाता है तो दूसरा नीचे से ऊपर की ओर। सैद्धान्तिक दृष्टि में दोनों में

भिन्नता होते हुये भी व्यावहारिक दृष्टि से दोनों की द्वन्द्वात्मक एकता स्वीकारनी पड़ती है क्योंकि अक्सर संगठित होकर मांग करने के पश्चात ही कानून बनाये जाते हैं और कानूनों को अमली जामा पहनाने के लिये संगठन की आवश्यकता होती है।

हमारे उपरोक्त विवेचन से यह स्पष्ट है कि नारी-सशक्तिकरण माडल अपने पूर्ववर्ती नारी-विकास माडल से कई महत्वपूर्ण बातों में काफी भिन्न है। जहां नारी-विकास माडल एक सामाजिक-आर्थिक परियोजना है, वहीं नारी-सशक्तिकरण माडल मुख्य रूप से एक राजनैतिक परियोजना है। पहले में आर्थिक क्षेत्र में नारी के स्थान को ऊँचा उठाने पर बल दिया गया है तो दूसरे का मुख्य जोर नारी को राजनैतिक रूप से सशक्त करने पर है। दोनों की नाप के लिये अलग-अलग सूचकांक भी गढ़े गये हैं (GDI और GEM) हालांकि विश्लेषणात्मक दृष्टि से दोनों भिन्न हैं किन्तु तथ्यात्मक दृष्टि से दोनों जुड़े हुये भी हैं। यदि नारियां राजनैतिक रूप से शक्तिशाली हो जाती हैं तो वे उसका उपयोग अपने विकास के लिये कर सकती हैं। इसी तरह यदि उनका सामाजिक-आर्थिक विकास हो जाता है तो वे शक्ति प्राप्ति के लिये प्रयत्नशील हो सकती हैं। इस तरह से हम कह सकते हैं कि दोनों तरीके एक दूसरे के सम्पूरक हो सकते हैं—अन्तर केवल इतना है कि आप किस आयाम को प्राथमिकता देते हैं—आर्थिक या राजनैतिक?

(III)

आइये देखें कि नारी सशक्तिकरण के जिस माडल की चर्चा हम ऊपर कर आये हैं उसकी संयोजना में कोई खोट तो नहीं? उदारवादी नजरिये से देखने पर साफ जाहिर होता है इसमें पुरुषों की सभी स्तरों पर उपेक्षा की गई है। इसका परिणाम पुरुषों का लिंग न्याय के सवालों से कट जाने में हुआ है। इतना ही नहीं कई बार यह पुरुष को शत्रु के रूप में भी चित्रित करता है। इस प्रकार नारी सशक्तिकरण आन्दोलन एक लिंग-युद्ध में बदल जाता है जिसमें काम-सम्बन्धों की सफलता और पारिवारिक शान्ति की बलि चढ़ जाती है। यहीं यह बात भी नहीं भूलनी चाहिये कि संयुक्त परिवारों के उदाहरणों से स्पष्ट है कि स्त्री भी स्त्री के शत्रु की भूमिका निभाती है।

संरचनात्मक दृष्टि से नारी सशक्तिकरण का उपरोक्त माडल तात्विक रूप से असंरचनात्मक, विशिष्ट वर्ग केन्द्रित और मनो-केन्द्रित दिखाई देता है। यह स्त्रियों का आन्तरिक विवेक जगाने पर अत्यधिक बल देता है। किन्तु क्या पुरुषों के विवेक को जगाये बिना और उनकी मनोवृत्ति में परिवर्तन के बगैर लिंग सम्बधों को न्याय पूर्ण बनाया जा सकता है? शायद नहीं। इसके अलावा, स्त्री पुरुष दोनों के मन का बदलना आवश्यक तो है किन्तु पर्याप्त नहीं, आर्थिक और राजनैतिक संरचनात्मक परिवर्तन भी बराबर से जरूरी है।

मार्क्सवादियों ने नारी सशक्तिकरण की धारण पर यह आरोप लगाया है कि यह नारी की पुरुष पर आर्थिक निर्भरता के सामाजिक सत्य की अनदेखी करता है जो समपत्ति सम्बन्धों की संरचना में अन्तः निर्मित है। जब तक लिंग आधारित सम्पत्ति संबंधों को नष्ट नहीं किया जाता, मात्र चेतना में परिर्वतन से कुछ होने वाला नहीं। यदि बहस के लिये यह मान भी लिया जाये कि नारी सशक्तिकरण का माडल संरचनात्मक तत्वों की अवहेलना नहीं करता तो भी यह राजनैतिक संरचना को आर्थिक संरचना पर वरीयता प्रदान करता है। इस तरह यह दोनों के बीच एक कृत्रिम पूरी करता है जबकि, मार्क्सवादी दृष्टि से, आर्थिक संरचना में परिवर्तन किये बगैर राजनैतिक परिवर्तन मात्र भुलावा है।

एक महत्वपूर्ण आलोचना, संरचनात्मक दृष्टि से, यह की जाती है कि नारी सशक्तिकरण माडल में सभी स्त्रियों को एक ही सामान्य कोटि के अन्तर्गत रखा गया है जबकि यह यथार्थ नहीं है। स्त्रियों के बीच व्यापक आन्तरिक विभेद हैं। उदाहरण के लिये शहरी और ग्रामीण औरतों, कार्यशील और घरेलू औरतों, पढ़ी लिखी और गैर पढ़ी लिखी औरतों के परिवेश, जरूरतों और हितों में काफी भिन्नतायें हैं। प्रश्न उठता है कि नारी सशक्तिकरण की चर्चा करते समय हम किस वर्ग की नारी के बारे में बात कर रहे? यह बात छिपी नहीं है कि नारी सशक्तिकरण का आन्दोलन शहरी, पढ़ी-लिखी, कार्यशील, मध्यम/उच्च वर्गीय महिलाओं द्वारा अपने हितों में प्रयोग किया जा रहा है। इसमें ग्रामीण, अपढ़ निम्नवर्गीय महिलाओं का प्रतिनिधित्व लगभग नहीं है। आश्चर्य की बात नहीं कि पिछड़ी जातियों, अल्पसंख्यक वर्गो की महिलाओं को समुचित लाभ न मिल पाने के आरोप के कारण नारी आरक्षण विधेयक संसद में अभी तक अटका पड़ा है।

सांस्कृतिक दृष्टिकोण से नारी सशक्तिकरण माडल की आलोचना यह कह कर की जाती है कि यह पश्चिम केन्द्रित है और पूर्व के देशौं, जिनमें भारत भी है, की संस्कृति के अनुकूल नहीं है क्योंकि यह लिंग सम्बन्धों को मर्यादित करने में धर्म की भूमिका की अनदेखी करता है। भारतीय सांस्कृति परिदृश्य पश्चिम से कई महत्वपूर्ण रूपों में भिन्न है। सांस्कृतिक रूप से पुत्र को पुत्री पर वरीयता, पुत्री को पराया धन समझना, पिता का पुत्री-विवाह का उत्तरदायित्व, पतिव्रत धर्म का आदर्श और मातृत्व को ही नारीत्व का सर्वेपरि मानदण्ड मानना आदि सांस्कृतिक विशेषतायें भारत में लिंग सम्बन्धों का संचालन करती हैं जिन पर नारी सशक्तिकरण का वर्तमान माडल समुचित विचार नहीं करता। यहीं पर यह भी नहीं भूलना चाहिये कि इन सभी सांस्कृति कुरीतियों का पालन करने में भारतीय महिलायें पुरुषों से आगे रहती हैं भले ही इसे उन पर पितृ सत्ता के शिकंजे की मजबूती के रूप में ही क्यों न देखा जाये।

लगभग सभी परम्परागत धर्मों ने लिंग-असमानता को औचित्य प्रदान किया है। कहीं-कहीं किसी विशेष मुद्दे पर उन्होंने प्रगतिशील भूमिका भी निभाई है। लेकिन नारी सशक्तिकरण का माडल धर्म की सामान्यतः लिंग-न्याय विरोधी भूमिका को न कवेल नजरअंदाज करता है अपितु उससे निपटने का भी कोई रास्ता नहीं सुझाता।

भारतीय सन्दर्भ में जब हम नारी-विकास और नारी सशक्तिकरण माडलों की समीक्षा करते हैं तो उनकी असफलता ही दृष्टिगोचर होती है। दोनों ही राज्य की अभियोजनायें रहीं हैं और वहीं तक सफलता पा सकीं जहाँ तक उन्होंने पितृसत्ता को चुनौती नहीं दी। इसलिये कहा जा सकता है नारी सशक्तिकरण का आन्दोलन एक जन आन्दोलन का रूप इसलिये भी नहीं ले सका क्योंकि इसने भारतीय सांस्कृति यथार्थ को ठीक से नहीं समझा और न पितृसत्ता की संस्कृति को भीतर से कोई वास्तविक चुनौती दी।

(IV)

नारी सशक्तिकरण माडल की ऊपर की गई आलोचना से यह स्पष्ट ही है कि उसमें कई गहरी कमियाँ हैं। वह शक्तिकरण का एक आयामी दृष्टिकोण है, उसकी नीति भी इकहरी है और लक्ष्य प्राप्ति के लिये वह एक पक्ष पर ही निर्भर है। इसलिये शक्तिकरण की वर्तमान अवधारण पर पुनर्विचार की जरूरत है। चूंकि इसका ढ़ांचा टकराव का है इसलिये सोंचना होगा कि क्यों केवल नारी-शक्तिकरण की चर्चा की जाये क्यों नहीं लिंग-शक्तिकरण को लक्ष्य बनाया जाये? लिंग समानता के स्थान पर लिंग-न्याय की बात करना क्या उपयुक्त नहीं होगा? और यदि यह उचित है तो फिर उसे प्राप्त करने के लिये कौन से उपाय करने होंगे?

केवल नारी पर केन्द्रित नारी-सशक्तिकरण के स्थान पर लिंग-सशक्तिकरण की अवधारणा किसी एक पुरुष या स्त्री के शक्तिकरण पर आधारित नहीं है। यह तो लिंग सम्बन्धों के असन्तुलन की ओर ध्यान दिलाकर उनको इस तरह बदलने पर बल देती है कि उन्हें एक सीढ़ीकर व्यवस्था से अधिक समतापूर्ण व्यवस्था बनाया जा सके। यह नारी-शक्तिकरण के विरूद्ध नहीं है किन्तु यह नारी-पुरुष सम्बन्धों को टकराव की दृष्टि से नहीं अपितु संपूरकता की दृष्टि से देखती है और उनमें नया संतुलन कायम करना चाहती है। यह नारी शक्तिकरण की तरह एक पक्षीय नहीं है, पुरुष के विरोध के स्थान पर उसका सहयोग पाने पर बल देती है।

लिंग समानता के स्थान लिंग-न्याय को वरीयता देने के पीछे कारण यह है कि समानता का प्रत्यय कई ढंग से व्याख्याति किया जा सकता है। बराबरी किसकी? अवसरों की, अधिकारों की या स्थितियों की? तीनों ही रूपों में यह अप्राप्य आदर्श है। इसके स्थान पर शक्तिकरण के लिये बराबरी से कुछ ज्यादा ही अपेक्षित

है—नारियों को विशेष उपायों द्वारा आगे लाना जिससे उन्हें न्याय मिल सके। समानता का मानदण्ड प्रायः पुरुषों की स्थिति के अनुरूप ही होता है जबकि न्याय का आदर्श पुरुष मानदण्डों को अतिक्रमित करके लिंग सम्बन्धों को नये ढंग से परिभाषित करने की सम्भावनायें खोल देता है। शक्तिकरण का अर्थ नारी के नारी के लिये पुरुष जैसा होने का प्रत्यन नहीं हैं, पुरुष व्यवहार का सब कुछ ग्राह योग्य नहीं है।

सशक्तिकरण की अवधारणा को दो रूपों में समझा जा सकता है—एक आयामी और बहु आयामी। राजनैतिक शक्ति पर केन्द्रित नारी सशक्तिकरण का माडल एक आयामी है क्योंकि यह नारी के अपने शरीर, यौनिकता और संस्थागत सांसाधनों पर नियंत्रण तक सीमित है जबकि सबलीकरण की बहुआयामी अवधारणा नारी सशक्तिकरण के लिये अधिक सम्भावनापूर्ण है। राजनैतिक आयाम के अलावा शक्तिकरण के सामाजिक, आर्थिक, मनोवैज्ञानिक, सांस्कृतिक आयाम भी महत्वपूर्ण हैं। ये सभी आयाम एक दूसरे सें इस तरह गुंथे हुये हैं कि किसी एक को अन्य के स्थान पर ज्यादा महत्व देने से काम चलने वाला नहीं। अतः सशक्तिकरण की बहुआयामी अवधारणा, जो नारियों की सभी प्रकार की क्षमताओ के बढ़ाने पर बल देती है, को एक आयामी राजनैतिक शक्ति केन्द्रित अवधारणा के स्थान पर अपनाने की आवश्यकता है।

यह मानते हुये कि नारी सशक्तिकरण के लक्ष्य की प्राप्ति के लिये महिलाओं में चेतना जगाने, संगठन बनाने और आन्दोलन करने का अपना महत्व है लेकिल मनोवृत्तियों में परिवर्तन के लिये अन्य उपायों की भी मदद ली जानी चाहिये। शिक्षा सामान्य रूप से और स्त्री-शिक्षा विशेष रूप से ऐसा ही एक तरीका है, विशेषकर तब जब पाठ्यक्रम लिंग-न्याय के प्रति संवेदनशील हो। इसके अलावा एक और तरीका लिंग-न्याय के प्रति संवेदनशील सामाजीकरणक की नीति हो सकती है। परम्परागत रूप से सामाजीकरण पितृ सत्ता के प्रति पक्षपाती रहा है। आज जरूरत है इसे लिंग-न्याय के प्रति संवेदनशील बनाने की। इस कार्य के लिये बच्चों का पालन-पोषण इसी दृष्टि से किये जाने की आवश्यकता है। माँ को केन्द्र में रखकर इस कार्य को करने में लाभ की सम्भावना अधिक है क्योंकि माँ की भूमिका बच्चे के सामाजीकरण में पिता से अधिक महत्वपूर्ण है। यह विधि दूरगामी प्रभाव डालने वाली है, सुरक्षित है और इसमें टकराव की गुन्जाइश भी कम है।

हमारे पूर्व विवेचन से यह तो स्पष्ट ही है कि नारी सशक्तिकरण के लिये ससंरचनात्मक परिवर्तन की उतनी ही जरूरत है जितनी कि मनोवृत्तियों में परिवर्तन की। संरचनात्मक परिवर्तन के लिये राजनैतिक और आर्थिक उपायों का अपना महत्व

है। नये कानून और संविधान में परिवर्तन जहाँ राजनैतिक संरचना में परिवर्तन लाते हैं वहीं आर्थिक विकास की योजनायें आर्थिक रूप से प्रभावशाली हथियार हैं। लेकिन सामाजिक सहयोग के बिना दोनों का यथेष्ठ लाभ नहीं मिल पाता। फिर भी भारत ७३वां और ७४वां संविधान संशोधन विधेयक पंचायती व्यवस्था में महिलाओं को उचित प्रतिनिधित्व देकर अच्छी भूमिका निभा रहा है। किन्तु हमें यह नहीं भूलना चाहिये कि आर्थिक राजनैतिक शक्ति के पुनः व्यवस्थित होने मात्र से नारी सशक्तिकरण का लक्ष्य प्राप्त नहीं हो जायेगा। इसके लिये सांस्कृतिक मूल्यों में भी परिवर्तन लाने के उपाय करने होंगे। पदाक्रमित लिंग व्यवस्था के संस्कार सामान्य जनता के मन में गहरे हैं जिसे बदलने के लिये धार्मिक परम्पराओं की उन उपधाराओं का समर्थन जुटाना अनिवार्य है जो लिंग-न्याय का समर्थन करती हों। अतः कह सकते हैं कि नये रूप में विवेचित उपरोक्त नारी सशक्तिकरण के लक्ष्य की प्राप्ति के लिये बहुआयामी कदम उठाने होंगे।

चूंकि पितृ सत्तात्मक व्यवस्था के अनुपालन में मर्दों की भूमिका बहुत महत्वपूर्ण है, इसलिये उस व्यवस्था को बदलने के लिये नारियों से अधिक पुरुषों को चेतनाशील बनाने की जरूरत है। इसके अलावा पुलिस, न्याय व्यवस्था, कारागार एवं प्रशासन की अन्य व्यवस्थाओं में कार्यरत पुरुषों को भी इस दिशा में शिक्षा देने की आवश्यकता है।

अब समय आ गया है जब हम समझें कि लिंग-न्याय का लक्ष्य पुरुषों को छोड़कर नहीं प्राप्त किया जा सकता। जब तक नारी और पुरुष मिलकर लैंगिक सम्बन्धों को वर्तमान ऊँच-नीच ढ़ांचे को चुनौती नहीं देते, न्यायपूर्ण लैंगिक सम्बन्धों की स्थापना सम्भव नहीं है। हो सकता है व्यक्तिगत स्तर पर कोई स्त्री और पुरुष आपस में न्यायपूर्ण सम्बन्धों को जी रहे हों किन्तु वास्तविक चुनौती तो उसे संस्थागत स्तर पर प्राप्त करने की है। तभी नारी सशक्तिकरण का सपना सच होगा।

अध्याय 11

नारी-तत्त्व : एक दार्शनिक अनुचिन्तन

राजेश्वर सिंह

आर्ष ऋषियों ने विश्वरूपिणी महाशक्ति प्रकृति की संकल्पना अशेष सौन्दर्यमयी नारी एवं परम कल्याणमयी जननी के रूप में की है। नारी की कोमलता और मधुरता में उन्होंने महाशक्ति के प्रकाश का साक्षात्कार किया। वीर्य और ऐश्वर्य का सौन्दर्य और माधुर्यरूप में प्रकाश ही नारीतत्त्व है। इस नारी-तत्त्व के बहिर्भाव में सौन्दर्य और माधुर्य, कोमल और शांत गुण-समूह लीला कर रहे हैं जो स्नेह और ममता, प्रेम और सेवा के द्वारा त्रिविध आधिभौतिक, आध्यात्मिक एवं आधिदैविक दुःखों से संतप्त प्राणियों को ऐकान्तिक एवं आत्यन्तिक मुक्ति प्रदान कर सर्वदा संतृप्त करती है। आभ्यान्तर में यही नारी तत्त्व अनन्त शक्ति सम्पन्न ऐश्वर्य रूपी वीर्य की भावभूमि है जिस पर पुरुष-तत्त्व का प्राकट्य होता है। सुप्रशान्त, सुकमनीय, सर्वरसघन, लीलायितगति नारी शक्ति से ही विश्व की समस्त शक्तियों का जन्म होता है; समस्त खण्डशक्तियों का उद्भव होता है। जब परस्पर प्रतिद्वन्द्विनी शक्तियों का एकाकार होता है तो नारी तत्त्व का विकास प्रारम्भ होता है।

भारतीय तत्त्वदर्शी साधकों ने विश्वविधायिनी अनन्त वैचित्र्यप्रसविनी महाशक्ति का एक ऐसी महानारी के रूप में साक्षात्कार किया जिसमें कर्मशक्ति; संरक्षणशक्ति, उत्पादिनी शक्ति और संघटिनी शक्ति सभी नित्य परिपूर्णता से प्रतिष्ठिता हैं। अतएव वह प्रेम, सौन्दर्य, माधुर्य और आनन्द से मण्डित होकर प्रकट है। कर्मक्षेत्र में उसका हिंसा-भाजन कोई प्रतिद्वन्द्वी नहीं है। उसके ज्ञान में कोई आवरण तथा विक्षेप नहीं है, उसकी संकल्प-सिद्धि में कोई अन्तराय नहीं है, उसमें अपने पराये का भेद नहीं है। देवता और असुर सभी उसकी संतान हैं। सब प्रकार की शक्तियों में उसी की शक्ति लीला कर रही जिसका समायोजन वह स्वयं करती है। प्रस्तुत शोधपत्र में नारी तत्त्व एवं उसकी शक्ति के सम्पूर्ण कलेवर को 'दर्पण संक्रान्तमिव विम्बम्' की भाँति संक्षिप्त रूप में अपने अनुचिंतन का विषय बनाया जा रहा है।

इस अनुचिंतन के लिए वेद, उपनिषद एवं सांख्यीय दृष्टि को निकष के रूप में अंगीकार किया गया है।

I

मानव सभ्यता एवं संस्कृति के आदि ग्रन्थ वेदों में नारी-तत्त्व की समग्रता का दिग्दर्शन प्रशस्त रूप में प्राप्त होता है। धन की देवी लक्ष्मी, शक्ति की दुर्गा और विद्या की सरस्वती हैं; इसी प्रकार अदिति, ऊषा, इन्द्राणी, इला, भारती, होला श्रद्धा आदि वैदिक देवियाँ अनेक तत्त्वों की अधिष्ठात्री हैं। इन्हें कहीं देवमाता और कहीं देवकन्या बताया गया है। इन सब में अदिति देवी का उल्लेख सबकी अपेक्षा अधिक है। वे सर्वशक्तिमती, विश्वहितैषिणी,[1] सर्वग्राहिणी और स्वाधीन मानी गयी हैं। अदिती ही जन्म और उसका कारण है। कहीं-कहीं अदिति के साथ दिति का भी उल्लेख है—'अदिती दिति च'। इसी दिति को पुराणों में दैत्यों की माता कहा गया है। ऋग्वेद में कई स्थानों पर सीता की स्तुति देवी कह कर की गयी है—'सौभाग्यवती सीता' हम तुम्हारी स्तुति करते हैं। तुम हमें धन और सुन्दर फल दो। पूषा सीता को नियमित करे।[2] सरस्वती देवी, पतितपावनी, सत्य की ओर प्रेरित करने वाली, शिक्षिका और ज्ञानदात्री मानी गयी हैं।[3] इस प्रकार ज्ञान शक्ति का संवर्धन नारी-तत्त्व के बिना सम्भव नहीं है।

नारी-तत्त्व की इस संकल्पना ने भारतीय समाज को जो नैतिक एवं सांस्कृतिक संवल प्रदान किया है, वह चिरकालाबाधित है। उसकी प्रगति-प्रेरणा में कहीं भी उच्छृड.खलता को अवसर नहीं है। इस संकल्पना में सदाचार की मर्यादित मानभूति पर प्रधावित होने की संपूर्ण स्वाधीनता अवश्य है। पश्चिम के प्रकाश में प्राप्त प्रगति के नाम पर हमने पतन की ओर पथ-क्रमण किया है, वह हमारी संस्कृति की सम्मुन्नति में नहीं अपितु समाधि में ही सहायक बना है। ऐश्वर्यशालिनी ललनाओं को हतश्री बना देने वाली पाश्चात्य अपसंस्कृति से नारी-तत्त्व का विकास सम्भव नहीं है। सम्प्रति, तथाकथित प्रगतिवादी पांसुल के पंजे से प्रताड़ित नारी को यर्थाथतः प्रगति के पथ पर अग्रसरित करने की प्रेरणा हमारे आर्ष ऋषियों की महान् देन है—जो लक्ष्मी, दुर्गा एवं सरस्वती के रूप में अभियुक्त हुयी है।

दैवी संसृति के अनन्तर मानव-जगत् पर दृष्टिपात करने से विदित होता है कि आर्यलोग नारियों का बड़ा सम्मान करते थे। वे घर को नहीं नारी को ही घर मानते थे और गृहस्थधर्म के पालन में नारी की ही प्रधानता समझते थे। उनके विवाह का प्रयोजन था नारी के साथ रह कर धर्मानुष्ठान और यज्ञ-सम्पादन। नारी के बिना गृह का अस्तित्व ही कहाँ है और गृह के बिना गृहस्थ धर्म का सम्पादन ही कैसे हो सकता है। वैदिक साहित्य में जाया की महिमा, गरिमा तथा शोभा स्थान-स्थान पर गायी गयी

है–'कल्याणी जाया सुरणं गृहे ते'[4] (तुम्हारे घर में कल्याणी सुषमामयी जाया है।) 'जायेदस्तं मधवन् सेदुयोनिः'[5] (हे इन्द्र! जाया ही घर है, वही पुरुष का विश्राम स्थल है।) ये सभी उद्‌गार नारी के सम्मानित स्वरूप के द्योतक हैं। इसके अतिरिक्त संतान पुत्र हो या पुत्री दोनों ही आर्य लोगों को प्रिया थे। वे पूषा देवता से कमनीय कन्या के लिए प्रार्थना करते थे। कन्याओं का उनके यहाँ बड़ा आदर होता था। कन्या का विवाह हो जाने पर उससे जो पुत्र होता था उसको अर्थात् अपने दौहित्र को वे अपने धन का उत्तराधिकारी भी बनाते थे। पुत्र अथवा पौत्र के अभाव में दौहित्र को ही यह अधिकार मिलता था। घर में गोरक्षा का प्रधान कार्य इन्हीं के हाथ में था। दूध, दही, घी आदि की व्यवस्था कन्याएँ ही करती थीं। कन्याएँ कलश में जल भरकर भी लाती थीं। वे माता-पिता को पानी नहीं भरने देती थीं। खेत की रखवाली का कार्य भी वे ही करती थीं। कन्या की रक्षा पिता करते थे पिता न हो तो बड़े भाई पर उसकी रक्षा और विवाह आदि का भार रहता था। आमरण अविवाहित रहने वाली कन्या पिता के धन में हिस्स पाती थी। वृद्धावस्था तक नारी अपने घर में प्रभुता रखती थी।[6] स्त्री को अपने लिए धन का कुछ नियत भाग प्राप्त होता था, जिस कोष से वह ब्राह्मणों को दान दे सकती थी।[7]

ऋग्वेद के अनुशीलन से ज्ञात होता है कि आर्यों में स्त्री शिक्षा का यथेष्ट प्रचार था। स्त्रियाँ वेदाध्ययन करतीं और कविताएँ भी रचती थीं। वे अपनी त्याग-तपस्या से ऋषिभाव को भी प्राप्त होती और मंत्रों का साक्षात्कार करती थीं। ऋग्वेद के अनेक सुक्तों का आविष्कार स्त्रियों द्वारा ही हुआ है।[8] स्त्रियाँ संग्राम भी किया करती थीं। रथ हांका करती थीं। मद्‌गलपत्नी इन्द्रसेना ने बड़ी दक्षता से युद्ध में रथ हांका था और इन्द्र के शत्रुओं का विनाश बड़ी वीरता से किया था। अस्त्र संचालन कला में वह पारड्.गत थी। अपनी वीरता से उसने शत्रुओं के छक्के छुड़ा दिये थे और अपहृत गौओं को उसने छुड़ाया था।[9] दौत्यकार्य भी स्त्रियों के द्वारा सम्पादित किया जाता था। सरमा नामक स्त्री इन्द्र की ओर से पणि असुर के पास दूती बनकर गयी थी। सरमा और पणि संवाद पढ़कर तत्कालीन स्त्रियों की बुद्धि-प्रखरता पर किसे आश्चर्य न होगा।[10] इस प्रकार वैदिक साहित्य का अवगाहन करने पर अनेक ऐसे दृष्टान्त प्राप्त होते हैं जिसमें नारियों को पुरुषों के समकक्ष ही नहीं अपितु उससे कहीं अधिक अधिकार एवं सम्मान प्राप्त थे।

वस्तुतः जिसे देश अथवा समाज का साहित्य स्वस्थ एवं जीवित होता है, उसी देश या समाज में प्रगतिशील सामंजस्य एवं वैभवशाली विकास की पराकाष्ठा प्राप्त होती है। वैदिक समाज में नारी की सहभागिता के विविध आयाम इस बात को पुष्ट करते हैं। हजारों वर्ष बीत जाने पर भी भारत को इस बात का गर्व है कि नारी-तत्त्व

के विकास की सर्वाङ्.गीण संकल्पना के कलाधार वेदों में स्त्री-पुरुष की समान सामाजिक का समुन्नत समन्वय संपादित हुआ है। अवश्य ही पराधीनता की पिछली दो शताब्दियों में हमारी अपनी आत्म विस्मृति ने पर-प्रेरणा से पथ-भ्रान्त बना दिया है; जिस सामाजिक संकल्पना से प्रकाश पाकर विश्व की संस्कृति अपने को उज्जवल देखने को विवश बनती थी, उस संरचना को स्वतः की आत्मा-प्रवंचना ने अवश्य ही विपथगामिता का अनुयायी बना दिया है। जिससे प्रेरित होकर किसी भी समाज ने प्रगति साधना की है, उसका 'मूल' कितना विशाल, कितना समुन्नत होना चाहिए, जो निरन्तर शताब्दियों नहीं, सहस्राब्दियों से समानरूप से अनेक उत्थान-पतनों के आते-जाते रहने पर भी संसार को प्रगति और प्रकाश प्रदान करता आ रहा है। आवश्यकता इस बात की है कि हमें अपने वैभवशाली अतीत से प्रेरणा लेकर नारी-अस्मिता एवं उसके गौरवगाथा को पनुः स्थापित करना होगा।

II

उपनिषदों में नारी-तत्त्व की अभिव्यंजना विशद रूप में हुई है। वह नारी-तत्त्व सर्वशक्तिमान, सर्वधार श्री सर्वेश्वर प्रभु की शक्ति है जो माया, प्रकृति, अजा, इच्छा, ह्रीं, धी, श्री आदि अनेक शब्दों से उपनिषदों में वर्णित हुई है। यद्यपि उपनिषदों के अनेक वाक्यों में परमात्मा को निर्गणु, निष्क्रिय एवं अकर्ता बतलाया गया है तथापि अधिकार वाक्य सर्वाधार, सर्वनियन्ता, सर्वगुणाकार ही बतलाते हैं। द्विविध वाक्यों का मुख्य अभिप्राय यही है कि परमात्मा दिव्यगुणी है, उसे कथमपि गुणहीन नहीं कहा जा सकता। ऐसी स्थिति में जब प्रलयकालीन सद्रूप परमात्मा के गुण, शक्ति आदि भी सद्रूप ही रहते हैं एवं 'इदं' शब्द वाच्य समस्त जगत् भी सद्रूप ही बन जाता है, तब नारी पृथक कहाँ रही? वह भी उस समय सद्रूप ही थी। सब कुछ एक (अ ई क) था अर्थात् जिस प्रकार व्याकरणशास्त्र में अकार, ईकार और ककार तीनों वर्ण मिलकर 'एक' ऐसा अद्वितीय शब्द बनता है, वैसे ही प्रलय काल में भी अ-श्री वासुदेव, ई-श्री महालक्ष्मी और क-जीव समूह ये सब भी एक सत् अथवा आत्म शब्द वाच्य एक ही तत्त्व कहलाते हैं। अस्तु, सद्रूप में शक्ति (प्रकृति) और शक्तिमान परमेश्वर दोनों ही सत् हैं और दोनों का युगल अनादि-अनन्त है। कारण शक्ति के बिना शक्ति का पृथक अस्तित्व नहीं रह सकता। ये दोनों अन्योन्यापेक्षी हैं। उस शक्तिमान की वह महाशक्ति ज्ञान, बल, क्रिया आदि अनेक रूपों से उसकी सहकारिणी एवं सहधर्मिणी बनी रहती है।[11] वही शक्ति परा एवं अपरा प्रकृति भी कहलाती है[12] और वंशी (प्रभु) का अंश भी कहलाती है।[13]

वस्तुतः नर-नारी की परस्परपूरकता दार्शनिक तत्त्व चिन्तन के द्वारा उपनिषदों में कथात्मक रोचकता के साथ अभिव्यक्त हुयी है जो वर्तमान समय में नारी के महत्त्व को अंगीकार करने के लिए बाध्य करती है। वृहदारण्यक उपनिषद् के अनुसार-सृष्टि

के आरम्भ में बस वही शक्ति-शक्तिमान का एक युगल था। उस एक ही विराट विग्रह में सभी शक्तियाँ निहित थीं, तथापि तत्तद्रूपों में विभक्त होकर अभिव्यक्त हुए बिना उस पुरुषावतर नर (ब्रह्म) को असंतोष ही रहा; असन्तोष ही नहीं—वह नर भयभीत भी होने लगा, क्योंकि एकाकी को भय होना स्वाभाविक है।[14] तब वह पति-पत्नी के रूप में विभक्त हो गया।[15] सुख एवं आकाश ब्रह्म के दो रूप थे[16] (कं ब्रह्म खं ब्रह्म) वे भी दोनों में विभक्त हो गये अर्थात सुख-विशेषांश पति (नर) में रहा और आकाश-विशेषांश पत्नी (नारी) में रहा। अतएव नारी बिना नर शरीर अर्ध-युगल कहलाता है इस अपूर्णता की पूर्ति नारी के द्वारा ही हो सकती है (अयमाकाशः स्त्रिया पूर्यत)[17] वास्तव में नर और नारी दोनों एक ही तेज की दो ज्योतियाँ हैं, दोनों का समान रूप से महत्त्व है।

एतदर्थ, तत्त्व विमर्श के माध्यम से उपनिषदों में नारी-तत्त्व को परब्रह्म परमेश्वर की भिन्नाभिन्नात्मिका शक्ति माना गया है। नररूप, सर्वाधार सर्वशक्तिमान् श्रीसर्वेश्वर एवं जगत् की उत्पत्ति-स्थिति लयकारिणी नारीरूपा भगवती श्रीसर्वेश्वर-इन दोनों की मनमोहिनी नित्यविहार-विहारिणी युगल जोड़ी सदा-सर्वदा से ही अटल है। जैसे इन दोनों का 'एक तेज द्वै नाम' माना जाता है, उसी प्रकार इन्हीं दोनों के अंशरूप लौकिक नर-नारियों को भी 'एक तत्त्व द्वै नाम' समझना चाहिये। नारी नर के लिये अनुपम सहकारिणी है; क्योंकि यदि नर जीव रूप से विचरण करता है तो नारी बुद्धि बनकर सहयोग करती है। यदि नर दिन बनकर श्रम द्वारा तपता है तो नारी रात्रि बनकर उसके श्रम को हरती है। यदि नर मन बनकर संकल्प-विकल्प करता है तो नारी वाणी बनकर उसका समाधान करती है। यदि नर सूर्य बनकर जगत् को प्रकाशित करता है तो नारी द्यौ बनकर उसको अवलम्ब देती है। यदि नर इन्द्र बनकर जलवृष्टि करता है तो नारी पृथ्वी बनकर उस जल से प्राणियों का पोषण करती है। परब्रह्म की संसाररूपी यज्ञशाला में नर 'होता' है तो नारी अग्नि है जो आहुतियों के स्थूलांशो को भस्म करके शुद्ध दिव्यांशों को 'होता' के उद्देश्यानुसार तत्तद्देवों की सन्निधि में पहुँचा देती है। जिस प्रकार सांख्यशास्त्र में प्रकृति और पुरुष द्वारा अंध-पंगु[18] के दृष्टान्त से समस्त जगत् का संचालन सिद्ध किया गया है उसी प्रकार नर-नारी द्वारा भी लोक-सचांलन की प्रक्रिया उपनिषदों में बतलायी गयी है।

III

वेदों एवं उपनिषदों के साथ ही साथ गीता में भी नारी-तत्त्व का सुतरां सम्पादन किया गया है। गीता में एक गुरुतर एवं गूढ़तर बात कही गयी है—

अपरेयमितस्त्वन्यां प्रकृतिं विद्धि में पराम्।
जीवभूतां महाबाहो ययेदं धार्यते जगत्।।[19]

यहाँ पुरुष और प्रकृति द्वैत नहीं है। केवल प्रकृति ही है। परा और अपरा। जीवनमात्र परा प्रकृति है और देह, मन, प्राण, इन्द्रिय, पृथ्वी जल, तेज आदि सब अपरा प्रकृति है—जड़ प्रकृति है। चित् प्रकृति ही पुरुष है और वह पुरुष भी प्रकृति ही है। पुरुष रूपा प्रकृति और नारी रूपा प्रकृति-दोनों ही प्रकृति हैं। पुरुष तो एक ही हैं। उस परमात्मा पुरुष में ही समस्त जगत् 'सूत्रे मणिगणाइव' अनुस्यूत है। 'द्रष्टा दृशिमात्रः शुद्धोऽपि प्रत्ययानुपश्य'[20] इस पातंजल सूत्र में प्रकृति-पुरुष का निगूढ़ रहस्य भरा है-महत्तत्त्व नामक बुद्धि जो प्रकृति का सर्वोत्तम विकास है, उसमें पुरुष प्रतिबिम्बित होता है। बुद्धि पुरुष के द्वारा प्रतिसंविदित होती है। इसीलिए बुद्धि परुषाकारा बनती है एवं पुरुष का अभिमान ग्रहण करती है, तदन्तर पुरुषभाव को प्राप्त होती है। बुद्धि, पुरुष से पूर्णतः पृथक होने पर भी पुरुष-आभासित होने पर पुरुष बन जाती है। दर्शन की भाषा में इसे 'ग्रहीता पुरुष' कहते हैं। इस पुरुषभाव के अविवेक को मिटाना ही समस्त साधनाओं का मूल उद्देश्य है। पार्थिव पुरुषगण प्रतिनिधि-पुरुष हैं, अविवेकजन्य पुरुष हैं। वस्तुतः वहाँ प्रकृति ही है, पुरुष नहीं। वह सत्य तत्त्व नारी है। पुरुष अभिनयकर्ता है-नटवद् व्यवतिष्ठाते लिंगम्।[21] 'पुरिशेते इति पुरुषः' अर्थात् जो पुरि = क्षेत्र (प्रकृति) में रहता है उसे पुरुष कहते हैं। जब तक वह प्रकृति में रहता है तभी तक संसार है—यावत् संसरति तावत् संसारः[22] और अन्ततः 'लयं गच्छति'। इसलिए 'पुं' चिह्न का नाम लिंग है। अर्थात् जो रहता नहीं हैं, विलीन हो जाता है। यहाँ गीता के शांकरभाष्य में एक प्रश्न उपस्थापित किया गया है कि यह संसार क्या है और पुरुष उसमें किस कारण से है? उत्तर में आचार्य शंकर कहते हैं कि 'सुखदुःखसंभोगः संसारः पुरुषस्य च सुखदुःखाना संभोक्तत्वं संसारित्वम्' (गीता, शां. भा. 13/20) पुरुष-जीवात्मा प्रकृति में स्थिति है, प्रकृति को अपना स्वरूप मानता है, इसलिये वह प्रकृति से उत्पन्न हुए सुख-दुःख और मोह रूप से प्रकट गुणों को मैं सुखी हूँ, दुःखी हूँ मूढ़ हूँ, पण्डित हूँ? मानता हुआ भोग करता है, संसरण करता है। (गीता-13/21) स्त्री-चिह्न का नाम 'योनि' है अर्थात् कारण या तत्त्व है। नारी में ही जीव का जीवन-तत्त्व प्रतिष्ठित है। नारी ही जीवन का कारण है।

उपर्युक्त दार्शनिक तत्त्व गवेषणाओं के निहितार्थो का अनुचिन्तन आवश्यक है। विशुद्ध प्रकृति एवं विशुद्ध पुरुष की दार्शनिक गवेषणा अधिमानसिक होने से अशक्य है। तब इन दोनों के मिथुनीकृत रूप की गवेषणा ही हमारे अनुचिन्तन का लक्ष्य है। इस संदर्भ में चण्डी के ऋषि की यह उद्भावना श्लाघनीय है कि—

'ब्रह्मशगुहविष्णुनां तथेन्द्रस्य च शक्तयः, शरीरेभ्यो विनिष्क्रम्य तद्रूपैश्चण्डिकांययुः।
यस्य देवस्य यद्रूपं यथाभूषणवाहनम्, तद्वेव हि तच्छक्तिरसुरान् योद्धुमाययौ।।[23]

गीता भी कहती है कि इस संसार में जो कुछ स्थावर जंगम यानी चर और अचर वस्तु उत्पन्न होती है वह सब क्षेत्र और क्षेत्रज्ञ से संयोग से ही उत्पन्न होती है–

यावत्संजायते किंचित्सत्त्वं स्थावरजंगमम्।
क्षेत्र क्षेत्रज्ञसंयोगात्तद्विद्धि भरतर्षभ।।[24]

उक्त उद्भावना से यह बात सिद्ध हो जाती है कि इस मिथुनीकृत जगत् में नर-नारी की आत्यन्तिक पार्थक्त तात्त्विक विगलन मात्र है। प्रत्येक पुरुष ही नारी है और प्रत्येक नारी ही पुरुष है, जीव-जीवनमात्र ही युगलित है। व्यक्तिमात्र ही मिथुनीकृत है। हमारी शक्तिरूपिणी रमणी हमारे ही भीतर छिपी है। हमारे देह-मन में निमग्न है-निविष्ट है। हम उसे पाते नहीं, देखते नहीं; परंतु चाहते हैं। हमारे अंतर में उसकी संगलालसा है। इसी लालसा के वश में होकर हम बाह्य जगत् में नारी की खोज करते हैं। यही बात नारी के लिए भी है। उसके साथ भी एक मनोरम पुरुष युगलित है। प्रत्येक अपने ही भीतर अन्तरनिहित दिव्य अर्धांश के रूप-रस-सौरभ से व्याकुल होकर कस्तूरी मृग की भाँति मिथ्या भ्रमण (संसरण) कर रहे हैं। हमारी वांछित रमणी तो हमारी ही प्राणमयी, मनोमयी होकर हमारी ही अंतरतमा होकर हमारे ही भीतर नित्य विराजित है। हम निर्बोध हैं जो उसे बाहर खोज-खोज कर अभिश्रान्त-कलान्त हो रहे हैं। हम जिस क्षण उसे पहचान पायेंगे, उसी क्षण हमारे प्राण-मन सदा के लिए आनन्द-चिन्मय-रस में अभिसिक्त हो जायेंगें और इसी के साथ सच्चिदानन्द-रसमय अमृत पुरुष के साथ नित्य प्रेम-साम्मिलन सम्पन्न हो जायेगा। रासपूर्णिमा की अमिय-ज्योत्स्ना के विकसित होते ही मिथ्या पुरुषाभिमान दूर हो जायेगा और रागमयी दिव्यरसवैभवा रमणी प्रकट हो जाएगी। यही पार्थिव पुरुष-जीवन का परम सत्य है। नारी जीवन में तो यह और भी गम्भीरतर सत्य रूप में प्रतिभासित होता है। नारी अपने चिराकांक्षित पुरुष की उपासना करके, अपने गहन-गम्भीर पुष्पसौरभपूर्ण हृदयकुंज में चिन्मय पुरुष का अनुसंधान करके, अमृतमयी होकर नित्यानन्दसौन्दर्य के राज्य में अपने नित्य सुख-सुधा के साथ मिल जाती है। यही नारी जीवन की परम सिद्धि है।

संदर्भ

1. सायण के मत से नारि का भाव नरों का उपकारक अथवा शत्रु न होता है। 'नृणां महावीरार्थिनामु पकारित्वात् नारिः। न अरिः नारिः' (सायण तै. आ. 4/2/1)।
2. ऋग्वेद-4/57/6-7.
3. वही-1/3/10-12.
4. ऋग्वेद-3/53/6.

5. वही-3/53/4.

6. वही-10/85/44.

7. वही-10/85/29.

8. वही-1/126/7.

9. वही-10/102/2-11.

10. वही-10/108/42.

11. 'परास्य शक्तिर्विविधैव श्रूयते स्वाभाविकी ज्ञान वलक्रिया च', श्वेता.-6/8.

12. अपरेयमितस्यत्वन्यं प्रकृतिं विद्धि मे पराम्।
जीवभूतां महाबाहो...............।। गीता-7/5.
(अनुवादक-श्री हरिकृष्ण दास गोयन्दका गोविन्द भवन-कार्यालय, गीताप्रेस, गोरखपुर, सं. 2053 बीसवाँ संस्करण)

13. मयैवांशो जीवलोके जीवभूतः सनातनः। गीता-15/7. (अनुवादक-श्री हरिकृष्ण दास गोयन्दका गोविन्द भवन-कार्यालय, गीताप्रेस, गोरखपुर, सं. 2053 बीसवाँ संस्करण)

14. साऽबिभेत्तस्मादेकाकी विभेति स हायमीक्षांचक्रे। वृहदा.-1/4/2.

15. स इममेवात्मानं द्वेधापातयत, वृहदा.-1/4/3.

16. छान्दोग्य उप.-4/10/5.

17. वृहदा.-1/4/3.

18. पड्.ग्वन्धवदुभयोरपि संयोगस्तत्कृतः सर्गः। ईश्वर कृष्ण कृत सांख्यकारिका- 21, चौखम्वा संस्कृत प्रतिष्ठान, वाराणसी,, 1990.

19. गीता-7/5. (अनुवादक-श्री हरिकृष्ण दास गोयन्दका भवन-कार्यालय, गीताप्रेस, गोरखपुर, सं. 2053 बीसवाँ संस्करण)

20. योग सूत्र-2/20, व्याख्याकार डॉ. रमाशंकर त्रिपाठी, कृष्णदास संस्कृत सीरीज-70, 1999.

21. सां. का.-42.

22. माठरवृत्ति सां. का.-42, ईश्वर कृष्ण कृत सांख्यकारिका की माठरवृत्ति-21, चौखम्वा संस्कृत प्रतिष्ठान, वाराणसी,, 1990.

23. दुर्गा सप्तशती-8/13-14.

24. गीता-13/26. (अनुवादक-श्री हरिकृष्ण दास गोयन्दका गोविन्द भवन-कार्यालय गीताप्रेस, गोरखपुर, सं. 2053 बीसवाँ संस्करण)

अध्याय 12

लिंग असमानता : एक विश्लेषण

हिमांशु शेखर सिंह

स्त्री और पुरुष दोनों सृष्टि, समाज एवं राष्ट्र के स्तम्भ हैं। दोनों के सहयोग से ही सृष्टि संपन्न होती है। परिवार और राष्ट्र का ढाँचा तैयार होता है और उसकी मजबूती के लिए परस्पर सहयोग की अनिवार्यता है। आज विश्व इक्कीसवीं सदी में अपना कदम रख चुका है। आज जहाँ चारों ओर विज्ञान एवं तकनीक के विकास का बयार अपने चरमोत्कर्ष पर पहुँच रहा है वहीं मानव अपने तर्कबुद्धि तथा अपने ही बनाये हुए आयुधों एवं विलासिता संबंधी उपकरणों के जाल में फँसता चला जा रहा है। फलस्वरूप स्वार्थवाद को बढ़ावा मिल रहा है एवं परार्थ की भावना घटती जा रही है। आधुनिकता के इस दौड़ में सबसे बड़ा धक्का स्त्रियों को लगा है। जीवन के हर क्षेत्र में स्त्रियाँ हाशिए पर पहुँचती जा रहीं हैं और उन्हें अनेक प्रकार की समस्यों का सामना करना पड़ रहा है।

इस संक्षिप्त शोध-पत्र के माध्यम से मैं लिंग असमानता से सम्बद्ध कुछ यथार्थवादी एवं नैतिक प्रश्नों के समाधान ढूँढ़ने की चेष्टा करूँगा। यहाँ मेरा लक्ष्य प्रमुख रूप से लिंग असमानता की समस्या के उस पक्ष को उजागर करना है जिसका संबंध भारतीय नारियों के जीवन से है। इस निंबध को सुविधा के दृष्टिकोण से दो भागों में विभाजित किया गया है। पहले भाग में लिंग भेद तथा लिंग असमानता का अर्थ और दूसरे भाग में लिंग असमानता से संबंद्ध कुछ व्यावहारिक एवं नैतिक प्रश्नों के समाधान हेतु सुझाव देने का प्रयास किया जाएगा।

लिंग भेद तथा लिंग असमानता का अर्थः प्राचीन काल से लेकर आज तक ससंसार के सभी वर्गों को सुविधापूर्वक समझने के लिए संसार के सभी प्रमुख भाषाओं में शब्दों का 'लिंग-भेद' होता रहा है। 'लिंग-भेद' को परिभाषित करने पर देखते हैं कि ये दो शब्दों के योग से बना है–लिंग+ भेद। 'लिंग' संस्कृत भाषा का एक शब्द है जिसका अर्थ होता है 'चिह्न' या 'निशान' एवं 'भेद' का अर्थ होता है 'प्रकार' या

'श्रेणी'। इस प्रकार लिंग भेद का शाब्दिक अर्थ श्रेणियों का चिह्न हुआ। लिंग को हिन्दी व्याकरण में परिभाषित करते हुए कहा गया है कि "संज्ञा के जिस रूप से व्यक्ति या वस्तु की जाति का बोध हो सके 'लिंग' कहते हैं।"[1] उपर्युक्त परिभाषा से स्पष्ट होता है कि 'लिंग' किसी संज्ञा का ही होता है। 'संज्ञा' किसी वस्तु, व्यक्ति या स्थान के नाम को कहते हैं। वह वस्तु, व्यक्ति या स्थान या तो स्त्री जाति का होगा या पुरुष जाति या जड़ जाति का। तात्पर्य यह कि प्रत्येक 'संज्ञा' या तो पुल्लिंग होगी या स्त्रीलिंग। चाहे वह प्राणीवाचक होगी या अप्राणीवाचक।

उपर्युक्त विवेचन से स्पष्ट है कि लिंग-भेद का प्रयोग भाषा को सरल एवं स्पष्ट बनाने तथा विश्व के सभी वस्तुओं को अच्छी प्रकार से समझने में सुविधा के दृष्टिकोण से किया गया है। फिर लिंग-भेद और लिंग असमानता इन दोनों के अर्थों में भी अंतर देखा जाता है। लिंग-भेद का प्रयोग, जैसा कि ऊपर लिखा गया है कि भाषा को स्पष्ट एवं सरल बनाने तथा संसार की सभी वस्तुओं को सुविधापूर्वक समझने के दृष्टिकोण से किया गया है। परन्तु किसी जाति या वर्ग के बीच चिह्नों के आधार पर सामाजिक, आर्थिक एवं व्यावहारिक स्तरों पर अनुचित अंतर को लिंग असमानता कहा गया है।[2] इस प्रकार लिंग-भेद और लिंग असमानता में भी स्पष्ट अंतर देखा जाता है। फिर आध्यामिक दृष्टिकोण से भी देखा जाए तो पुरुष और स्त्री के मध्य कोई विभेदक रेखा नहीं देखने को मिलती है। 'पुरुष' दो शब्दों के योग से बना है—पुर+ष। 'पुर' का अर्थ है 'निवास स्थान' या 'क्षेत्र' और 'ष' का अर्थ 'रहने वाला' या 'क्षेत्रज्ञ'-'पुरि शेते इति पुरुषः'। यह सृष्टि एक निवास स्थान या क्षेत्र है और इसमें रहने वाले सभी प्राणी पुरुष या क्षेत्रज्ञ हैं। शरीर के लक्षणों के आधार पर उनमें कोई भी भेद-भाव करना अनुचित है। जैसा कि श्वेताश्वतर उपनिषद में कहा गया है कि 'यह जीव न तो स्त्री है, न पुरुष है और न नपुंसक ही है। यह जिस-जिस शरीर को ग्रहण करता है उस-उस से जुड़ जाता है'।[3] मध्यकाल के महाकवि दार्शनिक संत कबीर भी स्त्री और पुरुष के मध्य किसी भी प्रकार के अंतर को अस्वीकार करते हुए कहते हैं कि 'हम अपने शरीर में रमने वाले जीव को, उस अविनाशी चेतन को स्त्री, पुरुष या नपुसक नहीं कह सकते, क्योंकि स्त्रियत्त्व, पुरुषत्त्व या नपुंसकत्त्व शरीर के लक्षण हैं, जीव के नहीं।'[4] संत कबीर 'को पुरुषा को नारी'[5] का प्रश्न कर शारीरिक लक्षण के आधार पर भेद-भाव करने वालों की कटु आलोचना भी करते हैं। गोस्वामी तुलसीदास भी सभी जीवों को ईश्वर का अंश मानते हुए सभी के कल्याण की बात करते हैं। उपर्युक्त विवेचन से स्पष्ट है कि चाहे वह व्याकरणीय आधार हो या आध यात्मिक आधार हो, किसी भी आधार पर लिंग असमानता को प्रश्रय देना समाज के लिए घातक ही सिद्ध होगा।

लिंग असमानता से संबद्ध व्यावहारिक एवं नैतिक प्रश्नों के समाधान हेतु सुझाव : किसी भी समाज में नारी की स्थिति ही उसके उन्नत और संस्कृत होने का प्रमाण है। आज अगर हम अपने सामाजिक स्थिति के ऊपर ध्यान केन्द्रित करें तो स्पष्ट रूप से स्त्री और पुरुष के बीच लिंग असमानता की बातें हर स्तर पर देखने को मिलती है। ऐसी बात नहीं है कि प्राचीन युग में लिंग असमानता नहीं थी। लिंग असमानता के आधार पर स्त्रियों का शोषण हर युग में होता रहा है। परन्तु आज जितना विभत्स रूप धारण किये हुए है प्राचीन काल में ऐसी स्थिति नहीं थी। प्राचीन काल में स्त्रियों को काफी सम्मानजनक स्थिति प्राप्त थी। समाज में नारी को आदर की दृष्टि से देखा जाता था। ऋग्वेद में नारी अर्थ-वाचक 'मेना' शब्द का प्रयोग हुआ है--'मानयन्ति एनाः पुरुषाः'[6] 'मेना' शब्द संस्कृत के 'मान्य' शब्द से व्युत्पन्न हुआ है। मान्य को ही 'मान' या 'मर्यादा' कहा गया है। मनु भी नारी को मान्य या मर्यादा स्वीकार करते हुए कहते हैं कि 'जिस कुल में स्त्रियों की पूजा होती है उस कुल पर देवता प्रसन्न होते हैं और जिस कुल में स्त्रियों को अपमन किया जाता है उस कुल के सभी कर्म निष्फल हो जाते हैं। अतएव स्त्रियों का अपमान नहीं करना चाहिए।'[7] हमारे धर्मग्रंथों में 'अर्द्धनारीश्वर' की कल्पना इस बात का प्रमाण है कि स्त्री और पुरुष के बीच कोई विभेदक रेखा नहीं खींची जा सकती। दोनों का अहअस्तित्व है। प्राकृतिक नियम के अनुसार विभिन्न जीवों में अपने वंश को चलाने के लिए नर और मादा का सृजन होता रहा है। हम जिस जगत् में निवास करते हैं उसे 'ब्रह्माण्ड' कहा गया है। जिसका शाब्दिक अर्थ होता है 'ब्रह्म का अंडा'। अगर जगत् ब्रह्म का अंडा है तो इसका विकास होना स्वाभाविक है। 'वृहत्वात् ब्रह्म' अर्थात जिसका विकास हो, वही ब्रह्म है। इस विकास क्रम को आगे बढ़ाने के लिए 'नर' और 'मादा' दोनों का सहयोग समान रूप से अपेक्षित है।

प्राचीन काल में नारी को उचित सम्मान देने हेतु विवाह प्रथा का आरम्भ हुआ। विवाह पारिवारिक जीवन का आधार होता है। प्रत्येक स्त्री और पुरुष का यह परम कर्त्तव्य होता है कि वह संस्कार को सम्पन्न करें। याज्ञवल्क्य ने ठीक ही कहा है कि 'नारी माता बनने के लिए और पुरुष पिता बनने के लिए ही उत्पन्न किए गये हैं।' वेदों में भी कहा गया है कि धर्म का आचरण पुरुष अपनी पत्नी के साथ करे।'[8] वही व्यक्ति पूर्ण पुरुष है जो पत्नी और संतान से युक्त है।[9] हमारे शास्त्रों में स्त्री को अर्धांगिनी तथा धर्म-पत्नी की संज्ञा दी गई है जिसका अर्थ है कि पुरुष का आधा भाग उसकी पत्नी है, अर्थात् बिना विवाह हुए पुरुष का व्यक्तित्व अधुरा है। विवाहोपरांत ही उसका व्यक्तित्व पूर्ण माना जाता है। रामायण में भी पत्नी पति की आत्मा मानी गयी है। विवाह के बाद पति और पत्नी के बीच अविछिन्न संबंध

उत्पन्न हो जाता है जो किसी प्रकार से समाप्त नहीं किया जा सकता। हमारी हिन्दू विधि में भी विवाह को पवित्र संस्कार मानते हुए कहा गया है कि हिन्दू विवाह संविदा नहीं बल्कि एक पवित्र संस्कार है जो धार्मिक अनुष्ठानों को सम्पन्न करके पूर्ण किया जाता है और जन्मजन्मांतर कायम रहता है।[10] परन्तु आज के विद्वानों ने पुराने आदर्शों एवं समानताओं को असमानतओं में बदलकर तलाक प्रथा को जन्म दे दिया।

ऐसी बात नहीं है कि वैदिक युग या महाकाव्यों के युग में नारी पूर्णरूप से स्वतंत्र थी या उन्हें पुरुष के समान हर क्षेत्र में समान अधिकार प्राप्त था। स्त्री और पुरुष के बीच भेद-भाव का संकेत प्राचीन काल में भी देखने को मिलता है। प्राचीन युग में भी स्त्री को पुरुष के अधीन माना जाता था। मनुस्मृति में कहा गया है कि 'स्त्री को बचपन में पिता के अधीन, युवावस्था में पति के अधीन और वृद्धावस्था में पुत्र के अधीन रहना चाहिए।[11]' मनु स्त्रियों के चरित्र के ऊपर भी संदेह करते दीख पड़ते हैं। स्त्रियों के चरित्र का विवेचन करते हुए उनका कहना है कि स्त्रियाँ पुरुष के सुन्दर रूप की परीक्षा नहीं करती, युवावस्था आदि के आधार की भी विशेष चाह नहीं करती, किन्तु केवल यह पुरुष है इसी विचार से उसके साथ संभोग करती हैं।[12]

पितृसत्तात्मक और पुरुषप्रधान सामाजिक व्यवस्था में स्त्री की सुलभ आकांक्षाएँ किस प्रकार पुरुषप्रधान व्यवस्था से टकराती थी और उसके सामने घुटती थी इसका महाकवि दार्शनिक गोस्वमी तुलसीदास ने 'रामचरितमानस' में बड़ा ही मार्मिक चित्रण प्रस्तुत किया है–

जननी उमा बोलि तब लीन्ही। लै उछंग सुंदर सिख दिन्ही।।
करेहु सदा संकर पद पूजा। नारिधरमु पति देउ न दूजा।।
बचन कहत भरे लोचन बारी। बहुरि लाई उर लीन्ह कुमारी।।
कत बिधि सृजीं नारि जग माहीं। पराधीन सपनेहुँ सुख नाहीं।।[13]

यहाँ एक ओर मैना नारिधरम की शिक्षा दे रही है तो दूसरी ओर पुरुष पराधीनता के प्रति उनका दर्द स्पष्ट उभर कर सामने आता है। सीता की भी मानसिक व्यथा पुरुषप्रधान व्यवस्था के भीतर नारी की पराधीनता और विवशता से है। स्वयंवर की बात कर उन्हें पति चुनने का अधिकार तो दिया गया, परन्तु स्वयंवर कहने मात्र का स्वयंवर है, क्योंकि स्वयंवर की शर्त पुत्री नहीं; बल्कि पिता तय करते हैं। इस व्यवस्था के प्रति सीता की आत्मकुंठित होती भावनाएँ एवं सामाजिक कुव्यवस्था के पंक में फँसी छटपटाती नारी हृदय की आकांक्षाओं की दम तोड़ती पीड़ा मानस के निम्न पंक्तियों में देखी जा सकती है–

अहह तात दारूनि हठ ठानी। समुझत नहिं कछु लाभु न हानी।
सचिव समय सिख देइ न कोई। बुध समाज बड़ अनुचित होई।।[14]

लंका में युद्ध के दौरान लक्ष्मण को शक्तिकरण लगने पर स्वयं श्रीराम जो कहते हैं उससे उस समय के पुरुषप्रधान सामाजिक व्यवस्था के भीतर स्त्री-पुरुष के आनुपातिक संबंध और स्थान का पता चलता है। नारी गँवाने की तुलना में भाई गँवाने के अपयश का डर उन्हें ज्यादा है–

जैहऊँ अवध कवन मुहु लाई। नारि हेतु प्रिय भाई गँवाई।।
वरू अपजसु सहतेऊँ जग माहीं। नारि हानि विशेष छति नाहीं।।[15]

इस प्रकार की भेद-भाव भरी बातें और भी कई शास्त्रीय ग्रंथों में देखा जा सकता है।

स्पष्ट है कि नारियों के प्रति सम्मान और अपमान, उदारता और अनुदारता, श्रद्धा और तिरष्कार की धारा सदियों से बहती चली आ रही है। इस पुरुष प्रधान व्यवस्था के काल रूपी पंजों में जकड़ी उनकी सुलभ भावनाएँ एवं आकांक्षाएँ सदियों से अवगुंठित एवं शोषित होती रही है। यह असमानता धीरे-धीरे आगे बढ़ती हुई आज विकराल रूप धारण कर चुकी है। पारिवारिक, सामाजिक, आर्थिक हर क्षेत्रों में स्त्रियाँ आज शोषण का शिकार हो रही हैं। स्त्रियों के जन्म लेने के पहले ही गर्भ में पता लगाकर भ्रूण-हत्या कर दी जाती है। अगर जन्म हो जाए तो जन्म के समय ही इनका परिवार दुःखी हो जाता है। पारिवारिक पालन-पोषण में भी उन्हें द्वितीय दर्जे का माना जाता है। पढ़ाई-लिखाई में उन्हें कम अवसर प्राप्त होते हैं। पढ़-लिखकर भी इस पुरुष प्रधान समाज में उन्हें रोजगार चुनने की स्वतंत्रता प्राप्त नहीं है। शादी में भी अपनी पसन्द या नापसन्द का अवसर नहीं के बराबर ही दिया जाता है। शादी के बाद ससुराल में उन्हें अपने पति और उनके परिवार वालों से जो आदर और सत्कार मिलता है यह आये दिन समाचार पत्रों में पढ़ने और टी0 वी0, रेडियो आदि में सुनने को मिल जाता है। अपने पिता के घर से अधिक दहेज न मिलने पर सुहाग गीतों के बदले व्यंगवाणों से उनका स्वागत् किया जाना, पति के परिवार में कोई दुर्घटना अगर घटती है तो स्त्री को ही इसके लिए दोषी मान कर उसे कुलक्षणी की संज्ञा दिया जाना, इसके बाद अगर लड़की को जन्म दे दे तो फिर उसका जीना दुभर कर दिया जाना; देखने और सुनने को मिलता है। कभी-कभी तो उन पर चरित्रहीन का भी कलंक लगा दिया जाता है और इन सब परिस्थितियों में उन्हें इतनी यातनाएँ दी जाती है कि वे आत्महत्या तक करने को मजबूर हो जाती हैं। अगर वे आत्महत्या नहीं करतीं तो कहीं-कहीं उनकी हत्या भी कर दी जाती है।

आज इन कारणों से स्त्रियों का पारिवारिक जीवन नरक बनकर रह गया है। परिवार में प्रेम की जगह घृणा का वास होने लगा है। इसका दंष्प्रभाव परिवार के बच्चे और बच्चियों पर भी स्पष्ट रूप से पड़ता है। कलह, द्वेष और वैमनष्यता के माहौल

में सन्ततियों का उचित विकास नहीं हो पाता और आने वाली पीढ़ियों को भी इसके दुष्परिणाम भुगतने पड़ते हैं।

आज राष्ट्रीय एवं अंतर्राष्ट्रीय स्तरों पर महिला सशक्तिकरण की बात काफी जोर-शोर से उठायी जा रही है। इनके पक्ष में अनेक कानून भी बन रहे हैं और कानून का उल्लंघन करने वालों के लिए कठोर दण्ड की भी व्यवस्था की गई है। परन्तु फिर भी महिलाओं के स्तर में कोई भी उल्लेखनीय सुधार होता दिखाई नहीं पड़ता है। इसका मुख्य कारण है कि कानून तो बना दिया जाता है परन्तु कोई भी कानून व्यावहारिक रूप नहीं ले पाता है। यह कानून मात्र कागजी दिखावा बनकर रह जाता है। इसे व्यवहार में लागू करवाने वाले स्वयं इसका उल्लंघन करते देखे जा सकते हैं। आज जरूरत है कि पुरुष अपनी मनः स्थिति को बदले और ईमानदारी पूर्वक स्त्रियों के अधिकारों को समझे एवं उसे बराबरी का दर्जा दे। वे स्त्रियों को दासी या भोग्या नहीं समझकर जीवनसंगिंनी के रूप में लें। अगर पुरुष ऐसा नहीं करते तो समस्या ज्यों की त्यों बनी रहेगी। लिंग असमानताओं के आधार पर कानून बनते रहेंगे और स्त्रियाँ अत्याचार का शिकार होती रहेंगी। जिन्हें हमारे धर्मग्रन्थों ने 'शक्तिस्वारूपा' कहा है वे यों ही लुटती रहेंगी, रोती रहेंगी और सिसकती रहेंगी तथा मैथिली शरणगुप्त की इन पंक्तियों की याद दिलाती रहेंगी कि—'अबला जीवन हाय तुम्हारी यही कहानी, आँचल में है दूध, आँखों में पानी।'

आज अपने अधिकारों के लिए नारियों को भी स्वयं जागृत होना चाहिए। उन्हें अपने परिवार में पहले अन्य स्त्रियों के साथ भेद-भाव को मिटाना चाहिए। मेरा अनुभव है कि स्त्री को परिवार में कष्ट देने में सबसे बड़ा हाथ स्त्रियों का ही होता है। परिवार में सास-बहु, ननद-भौजाई, भाइयों की पत्नियों के बीच वैमनस्यता एवं कटुता जगजाहिर है। उनके छिद्रान्वेषी एवं एकाकी प्रवृत्ति के कारण परिवार में अशांति और कलह का वातावरण व्याप्त रहता है। सबसे पहले उन्हें मिटाया जाना चाए। इसके लिए उन्हें भी पहले अपनी मानसिकता को बदलना चाहिए। उन्हें परिवार एवं समाज के प्रति अपने कर्त्तव्यों के साथ-साथ अपने अधिकारों के प्रति भी सजग होना पड़ेगा। उन्हें पुरुषों को यह एहसास दिलाना होगा कि इस जीवनरूपी रथ का एक सबल पहिया वे भी हैं उन्हें किनारा करके आदर्श परिवार, समाज य ा राष्ट्र का निमार्ण नहीं हो सकता। इसके लिए उन्हें अपने मूल स्वरूपों का जागृत करना चाहिए। नारी को चन्द्रमा का प्रतीक माना गया है। जिस प्रकार चन्द्रमा में शीतल, अमृत और प्रकाश तत्त्व विद्यमान होते हैं, उसी प्रकार नारी के मूल स्वरूप में ये तीनों तत्त्व विद्यमान हैं। इसीलिए प्रकृति ने उन्हें माँ बनने का गौरव प्रदान किया है तथा शास्त्रों में जगत्‌जननी जगदम्बा के रूप में प्रतिष्ठत किया गया है।

उन्हें अपने क्षुद्र स्वार्थों का त्याग कर इस प्रकृति या ईश्वर प्रदत्त गुणों में निखार लाना चाहिए। हमारे शास्त्रों में पुरुष को भी सूर्य का प्रतीक माना गया है। जिस प्रकार सूर्य में ऊर्जा, चेतना और जीवनशक्ति मूलतत्त्व के रूप में भरे होते हैं उसी प्रकार पुरुष के मूलस्वरूप में ये तीनों तत्त्व विद्यमान हैं। नारी अगर मनः प्रधान होती है तो पुरुष बुद्धि प्रधान होता है, पुरुष अगर विचार प्रधान होता है तो नारी भावना -प्रधान होती है, पुरुष पुष्प है तो नारी सुगंध है, पुरुष विश्वास है तो नारी श्रद्धा है। सृष्टि का विकस सिर्फ ऊर्जा, चेतना और जीवन शक्ति से नहीं हो सकता इसके लिए शीतल, अमृत और प्रकाश की भी आवश्यकता है। दोनों के पारस्परिक सामंजस्य एवं सहयोग से ही एक आदर्श परिवास, समाज या राष्ट्र का निर्माण हो सकता है। अक्सर हम कहते हैं कि अमुक परिवार बड़ा ही आदर्श परिवार है। अगर हम उस परिवार के मूल में झांक कर देखें तो स्पष्ट रूप से वहाँ उतना ही बड़ा समझौता दिखाई देता है। इतिहास में भी वे ही पुरुष और नारी श्रद्धा एवं आदर्श का पात्र बने हैं जिन्होंने अपने जीवन में विभिन्न परिस्थितियों से समझौता एवं सामंजस्य करते हुए, संयम और त्याग का परिचय देते हुए, परिवार और समाज में प्रेम तथा सौहार्द बढ़ाने का प्रयत्न किया है।

अपनी स्वतंत्रता और समानता के अधिकार को प्राप्त करने के लिए स्त्रियों को और कठिन परिश्रम करने की जरूरत है। यदि उन्हें कोई अधिकार देता है तो कुछ और बात है यदि इसे वह स्वयं प्राप्त करती है तो कुछ और बात होगी। स्वयं सक्षम बनकर इन असमानताओं का दूर करना स्त्रियों एवं समाज दोनों के लिए हितकर सिद्ध हो सकता है और तभी व्यावहारिक नैतिकता का औचित्य भी सिद्ध हो सकता है। नहीं तो नारी सशक्तिकरण पत्र-पत्रिकाओं, पुस्तकों, गोष्ठियों एवं सभाओं की चर्चा मात्र बनकर रह जाएगा।

संदर्भ

- आधुनिक हिन्दी व्याकरण और रचना, वासुदेव नंदन प्रसाद, भारती भवन पब्लिकेशन, पृ0-119.
- Oxford Dictionary, Edition-2001, page-663.
- नैव स्त्री न पुमानेष न चैवायं नपुंसकः। यद् यच्छीमादते तेन तेन स भुज्यते।। श्वेताश्वतर उ.-5/10.
- त्रिया पुरुष कछु कथ्यो न जाई। सर्वरूप जग रहा समाई।। बीजक रमैनी-77/2.
- बीजक रमैनी-75/2.
- ऋग्वेद निरूक्त-3/21/2.

7. मनुस्मृति-3/56.
8. याज्ञवल्क्य स्मृति-1/77.
9. मनुस्मृति-9/61.
10. हिन्दू विधि, यू. पी. डी. केसरी, सेन्ट्रल लॉ पब्लिकेशन, इलाहाबाद, पृ.-31.
11. पिता रक्षति कौमारे भर्ता रक्षति यौवने। रक्षन्ति स्थविरें पुत्रा न स्त्री स्वातन्त्रमर्हति।। मनुस्मृति-9/3.
12. मनुस्मृति-9/14.
13. रामचरित मानस बालकाण्ड—101/2-5.
14. रामचरित मानस बालकाण्ड—258/1-3.
15. रामचरित मानस लंकाकाण्ड—61/11-12.

अध्याय 13

लिंग-भेद की विडम्बना

(एक व्यवहारिक नीतिशास्त्रीय विश्लेषण)

राजीव कुमार

"आधुनिक समाज लोगों का नहीं, मात्र पुरूषों का समाज है।"

हेनरिक इब्सन

"किसी समाज की सांस्कृति उपलब्धि का प्रमाण उस समाज के नारियों की स्थिति में ढूँढ़ा जाना चाहिए।"

महात्मा गॉधी (यंग इण्डिया-1918)

यह एक सर्वविदित तथ्य है कि लिंग-भेद की धारणा ने सभ्यता के आरम्भ से ही नारियों की गुलामी की भूमिका तैयार कर दी थी। तब से लेकर आजतक, यानी उत्तर आधुनिक काल तक विभिन्न रूपों में नारी-उत्पीड़न की समस्या विद्यमान है। इस लेख में हमार लक्ष्य इस गंम्भीर समस्या की तह में जाना है और यह दिखाने का प्रयास करना है कि आखिर वह कौनसी विचारधारा है जिसके तहत पुरूषों नें नारियों पर अपनी श्रेष्ठता की घोषणा की दी, साथ ही, वह कौन-सी मजबूरी थी जिसके तले स्त्रियों ने बिना विरोध के उनकी अधीतना स्वीकार कर ली। यह कितनी मजबूत धारणा है कि समय-समय पर आयी विचार क्रान्तियों में भी यह समूल नष्ट नहीं हुई थी और अपना चोला बदलकर नए-नए रूपों में फिर-फिर प्रकट होती रही। नैतिक और धर्मिक आदेश इसका कुछ भी नहीं बिगाड़ सके बल्कि इसी ने धर्म और नैतिकता का नकाब की तरह इस्तेमाल किया। आधुनिक प्रजातांत्रिक समाज के समानता, स्वतंत्रता, न्याय आदि के फिकरे सामनें व्यर्थ सिद्ध होते से नजर आते हैं। आज जब हम 21वीं सदी में प्रवेश कर चुके हैं और अपनी आँखों में समातावादी मूल्यों आधारित एक सुन्दर, स्वस्थ समाज का सपना लेकर आगे बढ़ने हेतु अतीत से पाथेय की तलाश कर रहें हैं तो हमारा सामना सदियों पुरानी लिंग-भेद की इस गंभीर समस्या

से होता है। यह समस्या अमरबेल की तरह सम्पूर्ण सामाजिक व्यवस्था पर छायी हैं। अतः हमारा लक्ष्य उक्त धारणाओं के विश्लेषण द्वारा यह दिखाना है कि ये धारणाएँ एक तरह से अर्थहीन हैं, श्रान्तिजन्य हैं और शाश्वत प्राकृतिक नियमों एवं नैतिक मूल्यों की गलत पक्षपातपूर्ण ब्याख्याा के परिणाम हैं।

हमारी खोज समाज में प्रचलित इस धारणा से शुरू होती है कि पुरूष श्रेष्ठ है और नारी उसकी अधीनस्थ। आखिर किसने इस धारण को जन्म दिया? किसने यह मान्यता स्थापित की कि पुरूष को हुक्म देने का हक है और स्त्री उसे मानने का बाध्य है? या पुरूष शासन कर सकते हैं और महिलाएँ नहीं? हमने सृष्टि की कल्पना परमात्मा के नृत्य के रूप में की और परमात्मा को अर्धनारीश्वर कहा, तो फिर यह स्वामी और अधीनस्थ का भेद कहॉ से आया?

प्रकृति ने सृष्टि की प्रक्रिया को निंरतर गतिमान बनाए रखने के लिए दो तरह के प्राणियों की रचना की-स्त्री और पुरूष, एवं दोनों को विलक्षण मनोदैहिक विशेषताओं से युक्त बनाया। दोनो को एक दूसरे का पूरक बनाया। उसमें न कोई हेय है और न कोई श्रेय। बल्कि दोनों के मिलने से सृष्टि की पूर्णता है। फिर मनुष्यों ने अपना समाज बनाया, अपनी सभ्यता-संस्कृति विकसित की। समाज को सुचारू रूप से चलाने के लिए मर्यादाएँ निर्धारित की। स्त्री-पुरूष की मनोदैहिक विशेषताओं के आधार पर कर्म-विभाजन किया गया। पर ज्यों-ज्यों सामाजिक संरचना जटिल होती गई, इसमें एक विचित्र प्रवृत्ति पनपती गई-समाज पुरूष प्रधान होता गया। स्त्रियों को दोयम दर्जे का प्राणी माना जाने लगा। धीरे-धीरे पुरूष सभी-चीजों का स्वामी बन बैठा। वह सामाजिक व्यवस्था का केन्द्र बन गया एवं स्त्रियॉ उपेक्षित होकर परिधि पर आ गई। इस व्यवस्था को आज का नारी मुक्ति आंदोलन "Phelio-Centricism" कहता है ऐसी भीषण दुर्घटना इस कारण से घटी कि नर-नारी के बीच पाए जाने वाले प्राकृतिक एवं स्वाभविक अंतरों को सामाजिक स्तरीकरण का आधार माना गया। सेक्स-डिफरेंस को जेंडर-डिसक्रिमनेशन का आधार बना दिया गया। चूँकि पुरूष शारीरिक दृष्टि से सबल था, और गर्भ धारण आदि प्राकृतिक व्यस्तताओं से मुक्त था, नारियों की सुरक्षा उसके पास थी, अतः पुरूषों ने अपने हक में प्राकृतिक अंतर को सामाजिक अंतर का आधार बनाने का योजनाबद्ध अभियान चलाया और कुछ ही शताब्दियों में नारी की सारी मनोदैहिक विशेषताएँ उसके दासकरण, शोषण और उत्पीड़न के उपादान बन गई। प्राकृतिक अंतरों का समाजीकरण कर सभ्यता के इतिहास में सबसे निन्दनीय युग का आरम्भ किया गया। ये समाजीकृत अंतर शास्त्रों के अभिन्न अंग बन गए और बाद में चलकर नारी को हीन और पुरूषों को श्रेष्ठ बताने में इन्हीं शास्त्रों की जुदाई दी जाने लगी।[1]

नर-नारी की पारस्परिक प्राकृतिक भिन्नताओं के सामाजीकरण की आधारभूत मान्यता मंशा यह रही है कि पुरूष प्राथमिक श्रेणी का होने के कारण एसी भिन्नताआ का मानक हैं। जो भी पुरूष से भिन्न है वह निम्न है और निम्न होने का कारण शासनीय और शोषणीय हैं। युगों से चला आ रहा नारी का शोषण आज इतना आश्चर्यजनक नहीं लगता जितना ये तथ्य कि स्वयं को एक तरफ रक्षक, पालक और शासक, घोषित व स्थापित करने वाले ने कभी अपना आधारभूत मान्यताओं पर पुनर्विचार नहीं किया। कभी अपने आपसे प्रश्न नहीं पूछा कि स्वयं को श्रेष्ठ मानने का उसके पास औचित्य क्या था? हक्सले लिखते है “यह मानना या कहना कि स्त्री पुरूष से निम्न है एक असत्य उक्ति ही नहीं, निष्ठुर कृति भी है”[2] प्रत्येक शासक यह मानकर चलता है कि शासित को उसके शासन की आवश्यकता है और उसका शासन करने का अधिकार स्वाभविक एवं प्रकृति प्रदत है। भले ही वह शासन शासित के लिए जानलेवा क्यों न साबित होता हो। जो शासक को भाता है, सुविधा पहुँचाता है, सुख देता है वही नैतिक है, न्यायपूर्ण है, धर्मिक है और शास्त्र-सम्मत भी है। नारी को अर्धांगिनी मनाने वालों ने कभी नहीं माना कि पुरूष भी स्त्री का अर्धांग है।

जहाँ तक कानून और राज व्यवस्था के नियमों का सवाल है तो ये नियम व्यक्तियों के बीच मौजूदा संबंधों को मान्यता देने पर आधारित होते हैं। ये नियम एक भौतिक तथ्य को कानूनी अधिकार में तब्दील कर देते हैं। इसलिए जिन्हें शासित होने के लिए विवश किया गया था, कानून एवं राज व्यवस्था ने उन्हें कानूनी तौर पर शासित का दर्जा दे दिया। जैसे प्राचीन ग्रीक एवं यूरोप में दास प्रथा को कानूनी तौर पर बैध दिया गया। प्राचीन समय में बहुत से पुरूष और सभी स्त्रियाँ दास थीं। हमारे देश में भी अधिसंख्य पुरूषों एवं स्त्रियों की स्थिति दासो-गुलामों से अच्छी नहीं थी उसमें भी महिलाओं की अनकही दासता का कोई अन्त ही नहीं था।

भारतीय समाज की स्थिति एक अर्थ में और भी दयनीय रही। बुद्ध, जिसने तात्कालीन समाज में प्रचलित सभी प्रकार के अंधविश्वास, वर्ण भेद, जाति विशेष के आधिपत्य, निरंकुश राजतांत्रिक शासन व्यवस्था आदि सबको झकझोर कर रख दिया था, वे भी नारी अधीनता के मामलेंमे पुरूष सत्तात्मक समाज के साथ हो लिए। यहाँ तक कि नारियों को अपने संघ में प्रवेश पर प्रतिबंध लगा दिया। बाद में प्रति-बंध हटा भी तो उसमें बुद्ध की अनिच्छा ही थी। सांस्कृतिक पुर्नजागरण के दूसरे अग्रदूत महावीर ने तो स्त्री-जाति मात्र को यह कहकर ठुकरा दिया कि स्त्रियाँ मुक्ति की अधिकारिणी नहीं हैं। मुक्ति के लिए उन्हें अगले जन्म में पुरूष होना पड़ेगा।

निश्चय ही महापुरूषों की नारी संबंधी उक्त धारण ने स्त्रियों की गुलामी को और पक्का कर दिया। जिस समाज में स्त्रियों के बारे में यह कहा जाता हो कि "वह समस्त रूपों में बंधन कारी है"। (समस्त भावैःखलु बंधनं स्त्रियः[3]), और "वह नरक का द्वार" (द्वारं किमेकं नरकस्य नारी[4]) उस समाज में स्त्रियों के स्थिति की कल्पना सहज ही की जा सकती है। अगर स्त्रियों को मौका मिलता तो वे कहती कि पुरूष तो साक्षात नरक ही हैं, क्योंकि उसने उनकी जिन्दगी को नारकीय बनाने में कोई कसर नहीं छोड़ रखा है। पर शायद किसी ने कभी भी पुरूष को नारी की दृष्टि से देखने की कोशिश नहीं की। इतना ही नहीं नारी को नारी की दृष्टि से समझने की भी चेष्टा नहीं की गई। अतः हमें नारी के चरित्र, स्वभाव और उद्देश्यों के संबंध में लिखित जो कुछ भी मिलता है वह प्रायः नारी को पुरूष की दृष्टि से देखने और नारियों के दमन का एक लज्जाजनक अभिलेख मात्र है।

नारियों की अधीनता के पक्ष में एक धारणा 'शक्ति के नियम' की है। अठारहवीं सदी में तर्क को जितनी मान्यता दी गई थी, उन्नसवीं सदी नें उतनी ही महत्ता मूल मानवीय प्रवृत्ति को दी गई। यानी, मनुष्य के भीतर की खूबियों एवं खामियों को प्रकृति की इच्छा या ईश्वर का आदेश मानकर स्वीकार कर लिया गया। यही कारण था कि महिलाओं की समाज में जो स्थिति थी उसे सहज ही उचित मान लिया गया। ध्यान रखना होगा कि समाज के नियम-कायदों को हम अनुभव के आधार पर ही अपनाते है। यदि स्त्रियों पर पुरूषों की सत्ता एवं वर्चस्व स्त्री और पुरूष दोनों की सत्ता के तुलनात्मक अध्ययन के आधार पर पुरूष को श्रेष्ठ जानकर स्थापित किया गया होता तब तो स्त्रियों की अधीनता समझ में आती है। लेकिन स्थिति ठीक इसके विपरीत है, पहली बात तो यह है कि स्त्रियों को अधीनस्थ का दर्जा देने वाली व्यवस्था एकतरफा सिद्धांत पर आधारित है। इसके विपरीत व्यवस्था कभी स्थापित ही नहीं हुई। अतः यह कहना पक्षपातपूर्ण है कि स्त्रियाँ बराबरी की हकदार नहीं हैं।

ओकली जैसे ब्रिटिश समाजशास्त्री का स्पष्ट मानना है कि "जैविक कारणों से कठिन शारीरिक श्रम वाले कार्यो को करने में महिलाओं की अक्षमता एक मिथ हैं। लिंग भूमिकाएँ संस्कृति द्वारा निर्धारत होती है। यह सार्वभौतिक नहीं हैं। मानव संस्कृति में बहुत विविद्यता है, और यह विविद्यता मानवनिर्मित है न कि जैविक शक्तियों पर आधारित।"[5]

एक बात और, स्त्रियों पर पुरूषों का प्रभुत्व कुछ भिन्न किस्म का है। यह पूर्णतः बल पर आधारित नहीं हैं। इसे मानने के लिए महिलाओं को विवश नहीं किया जाता बल्कि बिना किसी शिकायत के वे स्वयं ही उस प्रभुत्व को स्वीकार कर लेती हैं।

ऐसा मूलतः इस कारण संभव हो पाता है कि पुरूष वर्चस्ववादी समाज स्त्रियों के दिमाग को गुलाम बनाने की प्रक्रिया उनके बचपन से ही शुरू कर देता है। उन्हें पुरूषों की भाँति आत्मनिर्भरता एवं आत्मसंयम की शिक्षा न देकर समर्पण, परनिर्भरता, वफादारी, पवित्रता का पाठ पढ़ाया जाता है। उन्हें सिखाया जाता है कि पति के लिए, बच्चों के लिए, जो जितना त्याग करे, कष्ट सहन करे वह उतनी ही महान नारी होती है। फलतः इस खोखली आदर्शवादी शिक्षा के सम्मोहन में स्त्रियों को गुलामी, गुलामी की तरह नजर ही नही आती्। सचमुच पुरूषो का यह स्वार्थ ही् है् कि उन्होने विनम्रतापूर्ण समपण, व्यक्तिगत इच्छा के हनन को यौन-आकर्षण के अभिन्न अंग के रूप में रखा ताकि मनोवैज्ञानिक रूप से स्त्रियाँ इतनी समर्पित हो जाए कि वे यौन-स्वेच्छा एवं स्वतंत्रता के बारे में सोच भी न सके, उन्हें अपने त्याग और पराधीनता में ही सुख का अनुभव हों।

जे0 एस0 मिल कहते हैं–"यदि कभी स्त्रियों के बगैर पुरूष होता या ऐसा समाज जिसमें स्त्रियों पुरूषों के अधीन में न होतीं तो शायद दोनों के बीच मानसिक एवं नैतिक भेदों के बारे में कुछ मालूम हो पाता। आजकल जिसे स्त्री-स्वभाव कहा जाता है वह नितांत गढ़ी हुई धारना है, जो कुछ अर्थो में बलात् दमन और कुछ अस्वाभाविक प्रोत्साहन का परिणाम है।"[6] तथ्य यह है कि स्त्रियों की रूचि और उनकी सामर्थ्य के बारे में बराबरी के स्तर पर कभी सोचा भी नहीं गया।

पुरूष प्रधान समाज द्वारा बनाई गई सभी संस्थाओं में विवाह एक ऐसी संस्था है जो नारी-उत्पीड़न के लिए सबसे अधिक उत्तरादायी है। प्राचीन भारतीय इतिहास में अभिजात्य वर्ग की लड़कियों द्वारा स्वयंवर के कुछ उदहारण मिलते है जिसमें उन्हें अपने अनुरूप पति ढूँढ़ने की स्वतंत्रता होती थी। पर सामान्यतः लड़कियॉ आम वस्तुओं की तरह या तो बेची जाती थी या उसका पारस्परिक आदान-प्रदान होता था या पिता द्वारा कन्यादान में दी जाती थी। पहले तो अक्षत कौमार्य और पवित्रता की भ्रमपूर्ण धारणा के आधार पर बाल-विवाह के द्वारा शरीर व समझ विकसित होने के पहले ही उसे बच्चों एवं घर की जिम्मेवारियों से जकड़ दिया गया, पुनः धर्म और नैतिकता की अफीम की गोली खिलाकर, पविव्रता का पाठ पढ़ाकर, उसे घर की दीवारों में कैद कर असूर्यपश्या बना दिया गया। दूसरी तरफ पुरूष एक से ज्यादा विवाह कर सकते थे, वेश्या और रखैल रखना समाज द्वारा स्वीकृत था।

वस्तुतः पितृसत्तात्मक परिवार में स्त्रियॉ वस्तु की भॉति समझी गई। उसके स्वतंत्र अस्तित्व को संबंधों की आड़ में नकारा जाता रहा। बचपन में उसका मालिक पिता होता था। जवानी में पति एवं पति के अभाव में पुत्र[7]। सम्पत्ति के वितरण

में नारी को कहीं जगह नहीं मिली। पिता की सम्पति का उत्तराधिकारी पुत्र होता था। पति के मरने पर सत्पत्ति पुत्र की होती थी, पत्नी की नहीं। गौर करने पर पता चलता है कि समानता, स्वतंत्रता, न्याय एवं नैतिकता-किसी भी कसौटी पर विवाह का उक्त स्वरूप खड़ा नहीं उतरता। बर्टेंड रसेल का भी मानना है कि विवाह और नैतिकता के बीच पूर्ण सामंजस बना पाना करीब-करीब असंभव ही है।[8]

प्रजातांत्रिक व्यवस्था स्वतंत्रता, समानता, न्याय एवं हर कार्यो में जनता की समान भागीदारी-जैसे सिद्धातों पर आधारित है। पर ऐसी व्यवस्था में भी लिंग-भेद की समस्या का कोई सम्यक, समाधान निकलता नजर नहीं आता। महिलाएँ उक्त प्रजातांत्रिक मूल्यों के आधार पर आज भी अपने अधिकारों के लिए लड़ रही हैं। समाजशास्त्री विलियम जे गूड के अनुसार "सारी दुनियाँ में महिलाएँ समानता के अधिकार का दावा कर रही है, काम के क्षेत्र में भी, परिवार के अंदर भी। उनका यह विद्रोह समानता की विश्वव्यापी माँग का हिस्सा है।"[9]

पर क्या इस संघर्ष का कुछ सार्थक परिणाम निकला? यह सच है कि इस व्यवस्था में सरकारी, गैर सरकारी, स्तर पर महिलाओं के जागरण, समान भागीदारी, शिक्षा-स्वास्थ्य एवं आर्थिक स्वतंत्रता की बड़ी-बड़ी बातें की जाने लगी, योजनाएँ बनने लगीं, पर व्यवहारतः परिणाम अपेक्षा से काफी कम निकला। आजादी के 54 वर्ष बाद आज हम महिलाओं की स्थिति को सहज देख सकते हैं। ऑकड़े बताते है कि घर से लेकर संसद तक, स्कूल से लेकर दफ्तर तक देश की आधी आबादी किस हाल में रह रही हैं? महिला सशक्तिकरण के नारे के बीच समाज, राजनीति एवं प्रशासन में औरत कहाँ तक आगे बढ़ पाई है। आकड़ों के जाल में बिना उलझे इतना तो कहा ही जा सकता है कि महिलाओं के फैसले लेनेवाली भूमिका का सवाल आज भी कमोबेश उतना ही अनुत्तरित है। राजनीति, न्यायपालिका, सिविल सेवा में उनकी उपस्थिति आज भी निराशाजनक है। बड़े-बड़े उपक्रमों में भागीदारी की बात छोड़िए, साधारण पारिवारिक स्तर पर 80-90% महिलाओं को रिश्तेदारों एवं दोस्तों से मिलने के लिए घरवालों की इजाजत लेनी पड़ती है।

भारतीय समाज के परिपेक्ष्य मे देखा जाय तो हम पाते हैं कि हमारे संविधान के उपबंध भी कुछ विरोधाभासी है, एक तरफ वह सभी नागारिकों को कानून की दृष्टि में समान मानता है और धर्म, जाति, लिंग आदि के नाम पर भेदभाव को गलत बताता है तो दूसरी ओर, सभी सम्प्रदायों को अपने धर्म के प्रचार-प्रसार एवं नियमन के स्वतंत्रता की गारंटी देता है। धार्मिक स्वतंत्रता की यह व्यवस्था महिलाओं से वैसे बहुत से अधिकार छीन लेती है जो उसे समानता के मौलिक अधिकार के तहत मिलनी चाहिए थी।

करीब दो-तीन दशक पहले विश्व व्यवस्था में एक क्रान्तिकारी मोड़ आया जब राष्ट्र की सीमाओं को लॉघते हुए पूँजी का प्रसार पूरे विश्व में होने लगा। कम्प्यूटरी करण और सूचना तकनीक ने इस क्रान्ति को हवा दिया और सम्पूर्ण विश्व एक ग्लोवल-विलेज के रूप में सिमट गया। बाजारवाद तेजी से हावी होने लगा। पुनः एकबार लगने लगा कि नारी-मुक्ति का प्रयास अब सफल होकर रहेगा। इसके पीछे तर्क यह था कि पहले नारी-जागरण को नारी-मुक्ति का प्रमुख उपाय माना जाता था। पर बाद में ऐसा लगने लगा कि शिक्षा तबतक आवश्यक परिणाम नहीं ला सकती जबतक स्त्री आर्थिक रूप से आत्मर्निभर न हो जाय। भूमंडलीकरण के युग में बढ़ते बाजार के प्रभाव ने रोजगार के अनगिनत अवसर पैदा किए। महिलाओं को पुरूषों के समान नौकरी के अवसर मिलने लगे। श्रम-प्रधान प्रौद्योगिकी से उत्पादन के निचल स्तर पर महिलाओ को काम मिलने लगा। अर्थात्, बाजार ने महिलाओं का इस्तेमाल सस्ते एवे लचीले श्रम के रूप में किया। उत्तर-औद्योगिक-भूमंडलीकृत-समाज में लगातार निचले पायदानों पर सुलभ हो रहे इस रोजगार को अर्थशास्त्र "फेमिनाइजेशन ऑफ सर्टेन जॉव सेगमेंट्स"[10] की संज्ञा देता है।

लेकिन बाजार का अपना एक व्यावसायिक नीतिशास्त्र (कमर्शियल एथिक्स) है, जो लाभ-हानि की शब्दावली में सोचने को विवश है। इस भूमंडलीकृत बाजारवाद को चाहिए था—सस्ता श्रम और उपभोक्ताओं का विशाल बाजार, जहाँ तैयार माल खप सके। इसके लिए औरत के सौन्दर्य को उपभोक्ता संस्कृति का केन्द्र बनाया यगा। पश्चिम में पिट चुकी सौन्दर्य प्रतियागिताओं में नई जान डाली गई और तीसरी दुनियॉ की औरतों को विशेष रूप से सुन्दर घोषित किया गया, जिसका शीघ्र लाभ उन्हें यह मिला कि मध्यवर्गीय लड़कियों एवं गृहणियों के रूप में असंख्य नए उपभोक्ता मिल गए। भूमंडलीकरण ने औरतों के ऐसे इस्तेमाल के वक्त नर-नारी विषमता के सामाजिक पहलू पर कोई ध्यान नहीं दिया और अपने फायदे को ध्यान में रखते हुए इसने औरत की पारम्परिक छवि को कायम रखा, उसकी सुन्दरता के संस्थागत इस्तेमाल को वैश्विक आयाम प्रदान किया।

पर इस चकाचौंध करने वाले शो-केश के पीछे का दृश्य बहुत ही वीभत्स और घिनौना है। पूँजी की अबाध गति के कारण विकासशील देशों की अर्थव्यवस्था विदेशी र्ज के बोझ तले दबती जा रही है। उनके कृषि एवं उद्योग उन्हें कर्ज उतारने के लिए पर्याप्त विदेशी मुद्रा नहीं दे पा रहे हैं। फलतः ऐसे देशों ने पर्यटन एवं मनोरंजन के नाम पर स्त्रियों का निर्यात शुरू किया। वे अमीर देशों में घरेलू नौकरों एवं वेश्याओं के रूप में कार्य करने लगीं। अजनबी धरती पर अपना श्रम और देह बेचकर इन महिलाओं ने अपने देश के लिए बड़े पैमाने पर विदेशी मुद्रा कमाया। आज कौन नहीं

जानता कि सेक्स टूरिज्म कई एशियाई देशों के लिए आमदनी का मुख्य श्रोत है। सॅयुक्त राष्ट्र का अनुमान है कि 1998 में चालीस लाख औरतों का निर्यात हुआ और इससे अपराधी गिरोहों ने सात अरब डॉलर कमाया।

औरतों का ऐसा अपमान और भीषण शोषण किसी भी युग में नहीं हुआ जैसा कि महिला सशक्तिकरण के इस ग्लोबलाइज्ड अभिमान में हुआ है। इसके पहले औरत अपने घर-परिवार में अपने पुरूषों के शोषण का शिकार हुई, उसके साथ व्यभिचार हुआ, उसे उसके श्रम का मूल्य नहीं मिला, कार्य स्थल पर उसका यौन-शोषण हुआ, लेकिन ऐसा कभी नहीं हुआ कि अन्तराष्ट्रीय स्तर पर बड़े-छोटे देशों ने अपने-अपने स्वार्थ में करोड़ो औरतों को आयात-निर्यात की मडी में बेचा हो। दास प्रथा में औरत के साथ मर्द भी दास की तरह बिकता था लेकिन भूमडलीकरण के इस दौर में औरत को मर्द के बिकाउपन से अलग करके विशेष रूप से बेचा जा रहा है। आज वह अपने परिवार के लिए ही नहीं वरन् पूरे अर्थतंत्र के लिए गुलामी कर रही है। यह दुनियॉ की गरीब औरतों पर क्रूरतम हिंसा का कहर है। सास्किया सीसैन इसे "भूमंडलीकरण का प्रतिभूगोल"[11] कहती हैं।

जहॉंतक पावर-वूमेन का सवाल है, तो सबसे पहले यह कहा जा सकता है कि दूनियॉ की सम्पूर्ण श्रम शक्ति में 45% हिस्सा औरतों का है। भूमंडलीकरण से निकली यह पावर वूमेन इन करोड़ो औरतों के एक प्रतिशत भाग का भी प्रतिनिधित्व नहीं करती हैं। पुनः आज का पुरूष प्रधान परिवार इस नई स्त्री "पावर वूमेन" को इस तरह दबाव में लाता है कि अपना कैरियर छोड़ कर विवाह करके घर गृहस्थी के काम में वापस चली आती है और यह सोचने लगती है कि सुखद दाम्पत्य व बच्चों का भविष्य भी औरत का एक कैरियर है। इन महिलाओं के लिए दूसरा विकल्प अर्थात् कैरियर के साथ घर गृहस्थी, और भी उबाने वाला है। वह घर और दफतर की दोहरी जिम्मेवारियों मे पिस जाती हैं। सारांशतः, भूमंडलीकरण ने पितृसत्ता के कुछ नए रूप रचे हैं। इसमें परम्परा और धर्म के अलावा आर्थिक उदारीकरण और वैचारिक आग्रहों को भी नई पितृसत्ता का जनक बना दिया है जबकि इन दोनों को औरत की आजादी का संभावित जरिया माना जाता था।

उपर्युक्त विवरण यह बोध कराने के लिए पर्याप्त है कि नारी का शोषण कितना व्यवस्थित और पारम्परिक है, साथ ही आधुनिक परिप्रेक्ष्य में कितना वीभत्स भी। युग बदल गए, परिस्थितियॉ बदल गई, सामाजिक परिवेश बदल गए लेकिन आजतक हमारा नारी-बोध नहीं बदला। नारी से हमारी अपेक्षाएॅ नहीं बदली। हमनें अपनी परम्परा की गाथा गाई है, अपने शास्त्रों की गरिमा दर्शायी है। अपनी तथाकथित उच्च

संस्कृति का ढ़ोल पीटा है, किन्तु आजतक अपने नारी-बोध को जॉचने-परखने की व्यवस्थित और व्यापक चेष्टा नहीं की क्योंकि पुरूष उसके कुप्रभाव से कभी त्रस्त नहीं हुए। गाँधी जी ने ठीक ही कहा है कि "समान बौद्धिक क्षमता से युक्त और समान स्वतंत्रता की अधिकारिणी नारी पुरूष के हर कार्य में बराबर का हिस्सेदार होने की योग्यता रखती है।"[12]

अतः ऐसा नहीं है कि नारी का समुचित मूल्यॉकन करने वाले विचारक पैदा ही नहीं हुए। दुर्भाग्य की बात यह है कि सही चिंतन मुख्य धारा का चिंतन कभी नहीं बन पाया। राष्ट्रकवि दिनकर का यह कहना काफी प्रासंगिक है कि मानव अपने महापुरूषों को सिर्फ वाचिक सम्मान ही देता है जबकि वह मूलतः लकीर का अंधा फकीर बना रहता है–

"बुध हों कि अशोक, गाँधी हों कि ईसु महान्
सिर झुका सबको सभी को श्रेष्ठ निज से जानें
मात्र वाचिक ही उन्हें देता हुआ सम्मान
दग्ध कर पर को स्वयं भी भोगता दुःख दाह
जा रहा मानव चला अब भी पुरानी राह।"[13]

संदर्भ

1. आर्य परंपरा में नारी-(पेज 5) आर0 पी0 शर्मा, मित्तल प्रकाशन, दिल्ली
2. वही (पेज 6)
3. श्रृंगार शतक (श्लोक न0 2)- भतृहरि शतकम्, सुबोध प्रकाशन, 1987
4. वही (पेज 152)
5. P. No.-390,391 Sociology: Themes and Perspectives *By M. Haralambos with R.M. Heald, Oxford University press, Delhi 1984*
6. Subjection of Women *By J.S.Mill*
7. मनुस्मृति-(5 : 148) चौखम्भा, वाराणसी 1982
8. "Marriage and Morals" *By B.Russell* के सार पर आधारित।
9. Page No. 139,140, The Family *By William J Good, Printice Hall, New Delhi. 1987*
10. कैन मार्केट ऑल्टर जेंन्डर रिलेंसन्स, टेक्नॉलाजी एण्ड डेवलपमेंट, सेज, दिल्ली (खण्ड 3 अंक 1) 1999

11. वूमेंस बर्डन : काउन्टर ज्योग्राफीज ऑफ ग्लोबलाईजेसन एण्ड फेमिनाइजेसन ऑफ सरवाइवल, जर्नल ऑफ इन्टरनेशनल ऑफेयर्स, वसंत अंक 2000 (संख्या 2)

12. यंग इण्डिया 1918

13. कुरूक्षेत्र षष्ठ सर्ग; पेज 81, डा0 रामधारी सिंह दिनकर; राजपाल एन्ड सन्स, दिल्ली-1981

Part II

Socio-Philosophical Perspectives

Section I

Chapter 14

A Critical Survey of Status of Women in Ancient India

Indu Kumari

Like other civilizations of the world, history of Hindu civilization can be traced back to pre-historic times. The early history of men has followed more or less the same lines all over the world; with of course slight local variations. It is said that the civilization began with the Neolithic folk who were the ancestors of the bulk of the pre-Aryan inhabitants of India. The most important development of this period was the growth of a highly developed urban civilization in the valley of the river Indus. The ruins of Mohenjo—Daro and Harappan reveal that the people were not forest-dwellers like the Aryans. What is very interesting about them are them are the figures of dancing girls which reveal that the art was not unknown to them.

The religious literature of ancient India, the four Vedas, the two great epics and the Puranas throw considerable light on the social status of women after the Aryan invasions have taken place. The Vedas contain hymns which reveal that the Aryan who came and settled in India, 15 centuries before the Christian era, allowed their women to enjoy great freedom in the field of education and self development. They were not regarded as subordinates but as a co-partners of men in the manifold activities of life, social, religious and domestic. The nature and mode of their education were moulded by the religious beliefs of the Aryans. The sacrifices, the most important religious rite of the Rigvedic Hindus could not be performed by man without the co-operation of his wife. The gods did not accept the sacrifices offered by a bachelor. At the time of performance of the sacrifice, the priest poured, the priest poured 'soma' on the sacrificial fire and uttered the mantras (hymns) and his wife, surrounded by her female followers decorated the alter. The chanting of 'soma lyrics' was usually carried out by the wife and in the absence of the husband, the wife performed the sacrifice. Moreover, women were allowed to perform the *ashwamedha* (horse sacrifice), the most solemn religious function of the time.

The Vedas reveal that the Aryans worshipped certain aspects of nature which were represented as women by them. According to Hindu view of life, women were not considered as incapable of having such revelations which are the results of one's pursuit of the highest truth and its realization on the basis of ascetic austerities and meditation. Through penance and self-culture, the mind was raised to the highest level from the lowest and 'truth' and 'knowledge' was directly revealed to the 'seers' or 'Rishis' and 'Rishikas' The femal-sages (Rishikas) attained this 'Brahmavidya' or 'Knowledge of Brahman' The Rigveda knows of the following Rishikas viz., 1. Romasa, 2. Lopamudra , 3. Apla , 4. Visavara and several others mentioned in the tenth Mandala.

Visavara was the daughter of a king named Kakshivan who was also a 'Rishi' and composer of hymns. A hymn composed by Visavara, incorporated in the fifth chapter of the Rigveda, is said to contain the nucleus of later Vedanta philosophy. Rigvedic learned women were called Brahmavadinis. Rigveda mentions about unmarried, learned and young girls who were married to learned bride-grooms.

In the early Vedic age or Rigvedic age (c.1500-1000 BC), the basic unit of the society was a large patriarchal joint family. Women seem to have enjoyed equal status with men and received Upaniyan an education and observed Brahmacharya like boys; studied the Vedas and some of them even rose to the rank of 'seers' composing Vedic hymns; attended popular assemblies and could offer sacrifices along with their husbands. The institution of marriage was well-established with the monogamy as the general rule, though polygamy and polyandry are also indicated in some cases. No child marriage was allowed and the marriageable age seems to have been 16 to 17 years; Girls enjoyed freedom of choice in their marriage. No 'Sati-system' was prevalent but widow-re-marriage prevailed practice of 'Niyog', in which a childless widow could cohabit with her brother-in-law until the birth of son, was also in vogue and incest was a taboo; dowries and bride prices were taken.

The Aryans were keen on the perpetuating their fight against their enemies. So, the birth of a daughter was naturally not much welcome. They, however, reared the daughters with equal care and treatment. The girls were admitted to Upanayana and Brahmacharya along with their brothers. Apparently, no distinction was made in imparting education to boys and girls.

The Aryans developed a healthy social life. The family was regarded as a unit. Women were held in equal respect. They were honoured in home and respected outside. In intellectual and spiritual life, they occupied the same position as men. There was no 'Parda system' nor was 'Sati' prevalent. During later Vedic period, their position deteriorated. Women could not inherit property. Birth of daughter was regarded as a source of misery. They could not attain sabha Polygamy was prevalent. There were instances of child marriage.

Being entitled to undergo Upanayana and Brahmacharya, girls led a life of discipline in their paternal homes under the supervision of elder members the family. The education of women was therefore, a domestic matter but both its physical and mental aspects received attention. If they wished, some of them could even remain unmarried and devote themselves to the quest of knowledge. Some educated women used to take up to teaching profession and spent their time in imparting education to the girls, who were usually taught by the male members of the family. The wives of some saints were well-versed in Vedic texts and in the absence of their husbands taught the pupils with equal ability and zeal.

The Vedic people did not neglect material or practical aspects of life and, therefore, prescribed such training (other than the religious one) as would enable women to take up such duties as were allotted as mothers, wives and daughters.

In the ancient Hindu period, the real values of a women as a women, a man's companion and helpmate in life, and also as wife and mother were realized. In short, dignity and status of women in society were never questioned and they were offered all kinds of facilities or opportunities for being useful members of the family and the community. The Aryans ideal of women was indeed non-discriminatory. The presence of women was not considered as an impediment to devotion or salvation. All the great sages were married and had spiritual companions as their wives. But this ideal state of womanhood did not last forever and a gradual decline in the social position and education of women took place in the later Hindu period of the Sutras and Purans.

In ancient India, a tendency to curtail religious rites and privileges of women developed in the next period of thousand years which is the age of epics, Sutras and Smritis Ramayana and Mahabharata are the two great epics of India. Next to the Vedas, the two great epics are the most famous books in Sanskrit literature. Whereas the Vedas were meant for the Brahmins only, the epics appeal to women of every class. Heroines like Draupadi and Sita, Savitri and Damyanti are the ideals of Indian womanhood, just as Rama and Lakshman, Bhima and Arjuna are the ideal heroes. The epics reveal that women could still perform the horse-sacrifice and were the spiritual companions of their husbands. When Dasratha decided to perform horse sacrifice for the birth of a son, he had to appeal to his queens to co-operate with him.

The epics further show that men had great regard for women as wives and mothers. Rama once said, *'Lakshman is my right arm, and the princess of Mithila my shadow. In fact, it is impossible to leave Sita, as it is for the wise man to abandon his glory'*. The just and good, Yudhisthira said to his brother, 'Bhimsen', 'O Bhimsena, beware of ill-treating a woman'. Two types of women are depicted by the epics (i) Sita, Savitri, Druapadi and Damayanti, who led a family life and rose to prominence by practicing diligently all the virtues and duties prescribed for them as wives and mothers. Kaushalya is described as a 'woman of all goodness' and Kaikeyi as refined in nature and virtues. To Sita, devotion to Ram was the soul duty in life and to Draupadi a measerable life in the forest in the company of her five husbands. (ii) The austere and ascetic and ascetic women like Anusuya Swyamparbha and Ahilya received great spiritual and moral powers by devoting themselves to Tapas or austerities.

It is evident from the above account of women in the epics that the conception of womanhood had not changed much since the days of the Vedas. The learned and ascetic women like Anusuya etc. are the descendents of the 'Brahmavadinis' whereas Sita, Savitri, Damyanti, the resplendent heroines and representatives of the Sadyavadhus. The religious literature of ancient India, therefore, testifies that women were not treated as inferior beings but they held an equally important place with men in religious and social life and they could not reach heaven without being accompanied by their married consorts.

When men and women entered into matrimony, they were placed on an equal level, in theory, but in practice the wife was considered as a subordinate partner because the patriarchal society was then established. They could not have separate property though they were supposed to be considered joint owners of all that belonged to the new household. In certain matters, however, women were not dependent on men. For example, young women could marry on their own choice, could receive education and move freely in society. They were held in high esteem because their activities as helpers of men were needed by the society. The wife was called 'Sahadharmini', the 'Ardhangini' which indicate their important place in the lives of men.

But there are two references in sacred literature which prove that women were absolutely dependent on men on certain matters and were subject to glaring inequalities. There is a hymn in the Rigveda which points out that confirmed gamblers used their wives as wagers in the game. It means that some Vedic people clung to the pre-historic idea of treating women as mere chattel. It must, however, be admitted that this was an exceptional case and a protest was raised against this practice. The second reference is in the Mahabharata where the just and honest Yudhisthira offered queen Draupadi as a wager in the game of dice but no protest was made against this move either by the king or the priests.

Religious, social and cultural changes do not take place all of a sudden but extend over many years. When the ancient Hindu period terminated with the rise of Buddhism in the sixth century BC, great changes took place in the life of Indians. The majority of the Kshatriyas and Vaishyas adopted the new faith and consequently, the Brahmans became more conservative and watchful about their religious rites. In order to keep their race pure, they advocated stricter rules of chastity for women and tried to marry off theirs daughters as soon as they matured. Thus early marriage stood in the way of women's education and the 'Upanayan' ceremony was gradually stopped. This was the beginning of the decline of Indian womanhood.

Therefore, to an Indian woman, marriage became the only sacrament and came to be solely dependent on man and had to remain under his protection as a daughter, sister, wife and mother.

Manu, the ancient law-giver whose legal treaties were composed some-time between 200 BC to 200 AD refers to women's subordinate place in society. Women must be subordinate to the males of their families. He further says that women who are destitute of strength and destitute of knowledge of the Vedic texts are as impure as falsehood itself.

Apart from 'Manusmrit' or 'Manavadharma Shastra' certain references which prove that changed values in society and religion impaired the status of women. The status lay down definite rules for Upanayans which gave the right to study the Vedas. Even in Vedic times, marriage was almost a universal institution and most of the girls were married at the age of 16 to 18 years. But in the latter Hindu period marriage became compulsory for all girls. They were debased by their exclusive adoration of the husband, a creature similar to themselves and subject to human weakness. In fact, the cult of husband-worship started from the time of the great epics. Sita, Savitri, Damayanti and Draupadi are notable devotees to their lords, Rama, Satyabana, Nala and the Pandavas respectively. A devoted Aryan's wife was ready to sacrifice her life for the love for her husband. But in early times, the husband and the wife were a peerless pair, living complementary to one another, each helping the other in the three stages of life-Garhasthya, Vanparastha and Sannyasa and without the one the existence of the other could not be conceived. The high ideal, however, was bound to be lost because the child needed protection and instead of becoming a companion for her husband, she became a dependant. Polygamy became more common and widow-marriage was tabooed. Thus, women had no share in public responsibilities of any kind, but at home they were important individuals, for which a kind of informal education was strictly enforced upon them by their mothers. According to Manu women must always be cheerful, careful in cleaning utensils and economical in expenditure.

The wife had to manage the collection and spending her husband's wealth. This suggests that she had some elementary knowledge of accounts, which she must have learnt from her father or elder brothers. In fact, a girl picked up elements of whatever she observed. An effective moral institution was given to her and she was taught to be pious, devoted and unselfish like Sita or Savitri. Courtesy, gentleness respect for elders, for family ties were impressed upon her. Inner strength and integrity of character enabled the Hindu women to learn everything and live for others. Girls in rich families were more fortunate because they cultivated some fine arts mentioned by Vatsyayan. The heroines of Sanskrit drama written by Kalidas, Bana and others have been painted as well-versed in literature, music, dancing etc.

In the Ajanta caves which cover a period from second to the seventh century AD, women are seen engaged with books of palm leaves. This shows that in the later Hindu period, there were some enlightened people to challenge the meaningless laws framed by Brahmanas and even the great law-giver had to admit that where women are honoured, the gods are pleased, but where they are not honoured, no sacred rites yield results. In that family where the husband is pleased with his wife and the wife with her husband, happiness will last long.

When so much of restriction was imposed upon the nuns, it can be very easily guessed that laywomen had very little share in public life. It is not known to what extend they were in social practices, but some laywomen like Sujata, Khama mere in practice and performed acts of charity and self-sacrifice.

The negative attitude in the cause of women was new and not at all consonant with ancient philosophy of life.

Traditionally, women since the time of Manu, have been treated like mere chattel. They have no property rights. The cruel treatment of Draupadi was not less shameful. She was being dragged in the open assembly for no fault of her own. She was used as a plaything, rather a deal, by her own husband who played her as a chance or turn. Nothing less was done with Sita. Throughout her life, she honoured and worshipped Rama, believed it to be her virtue, but the very husband exiled her. She respected her husband's words and faced all the odds. Women's existence has been confined all along to mere household chores round the clock, and their general well-being has been taken for granted in this country. Yet a few courageous among them have broken free of these vocations or calling. But such cases are few. In fact, the majority of women folk are pooh- poohed and treated like mere commodities.

In India, women are discriminated from the cradle to the grave. It has become possible to pre-determine the sex of the unborn child, through a technique known as amniocentesis. Discrimination begins even before girls are born.

Female infanticide is another atrocity on women in India. It has been there since the time of Vedas. In some families, people simply kill their new born daughters straightway. Some do it to propitiate gods while others do it for fear of dowry. Still socio-economic and cultural compulsions continue to influence parents to resort to female infanticide. It seems that our society is gripped by mother's guilt for producing a girl child. Ignorantly enough, the mother is blamed for giving birth to a girl instead of a boy. It is due to lack of education economic dependence and ethical unawareness that this discrimination continues. On the other hand it is because of the adamant refusal to understand the truth by man that they alone are responsible for the birth of a girl or boy.

अध्याय 15

हिन्दू-वाङ्.मय में नारी

सुनील कुमार सिंह

किसी भी समाज के दो आधार स्तम्भ होते हैं—नारी और नर। इनमें से यदि कोई बड़ा या छोटा हो, कोई मजबूत हो और कमजोर, तो जीवन-रूपी गाड़ी इन असमान पहियों से नहीं चल सकती। जिस समाज में नर-नारी समान रूप से मर्यादा पाते हैं और आपस से समान ढंग से कर्त्तव्यों का निर्वाह करते हैं, एक-दूसरे का सहयोग करते हैं वह समाज सुखी और सम्पन्न होता है किन्तु नारी की मर्यादा तथा पुरुष से उसकी समानता के अनेक प्रकार के विचार मिलते हैं। कुछ पाश्चात्य विद्वानों ने यह माना है कि नारियों में जन्मजात दोष होते हैं जिसके कारण वे पुरुषों की बराबरी नहीं कर सकती हैं। डॉ0 रुबैक ने यह माना है कि नारियों में जन्म से या स्वभावतः अस्थिरता होती है।[1] फ्रायड की दृष्टि में नारियों में ओर भी दोष हैं। उन्होंने माना है कि नारियों में न्याय की कमी होती है तथा उनके मन में द्वेष-भाव भरा होता है।[2] किन्तु नारी की मर्यादा पर पाश्चात्य विद्वान् रायडन ने भी बल देते हुये कहा है कि नारियों ने ही प्रथम सभ्यता की नींव डाली है और उन्होंने ही जंगलों में मारे-मारे भटकते-फिरते हुये पुरुषों का हाथ पकड़कर उन्हें स्थिर जीवन या घर में बसाया है।[3]

भारतवर्ष वैदिक संस्कृति का पालक देश है। नारी का सदा-सर्वदा आदर करना भारतीय संस्कृति की विशेषता है। भारतीयता की कल्पना नारी सहयोग के अभाव में शशक-श्रृंगवत् है। इसलिये कहा गया है—'गृहिणी गृहमुच्यते'[4] अर्थात् स्त्री ही घर है। भारतीय परम्परा में नारी को शक्ति-स्वरूपा माना गया है। वह पुरुष की प्रकृति मानी जाती है। पुरुष और प्रकृति के संयोग से ही लोक-कल्याण होता है। 'नर' को 'पुरुष' का तथा 'नारी' को 'प्रकृति' का प्रतिकल्पक मानते हुये कहाँ गया है कि दोनों के सहयोग से सृष्टि की रचना हुई है। जैसे पुरुष पर और अपर है वैसे ही प्रकृति भी परा और अपरा। परमपुरुष की पराप्रकृति समस्त जीव-जगत् की जनयित्री है जो निखिल जगत् को धारण करती है।[5] पुरुष के संसर्ग से प्रकृति ही समस्त प्राणी जगत्

को, समस्त विकारों को एवं समस्त गुणों को उत्पन्न करती है।[6] चराचर उच्चावच्च का निर्माण, स्थान और संवरण प्रकृति के द्वारा ही हुआ है, पुरुष तो कूटस्थ, अपरिणामी और क्रियाहीन है। प्रकृति ही शक्ति है, पुरुष शक्तिमान है। शक्ति के बिना शक्तिमान का कोई अस्तित्व नहीं है और शक्तिमान के बिना शक्ति का कोई स्थान नहीं है। शक्ति और शक्तिमान का अविनाभाव संबध है। यही नर-नारी संबंध का मूलतत्त्व है।

नर-नारी की प्रकृति का पर्यालोचन करने पर यह देखा जा सकता है कि इनमें स्वतंत्र भाव से कोई भी संपूर्ण नही है। नर-नारी को चाहता है और नारी-नर को चाहती है। यह नर-नारी का एक-दूसरे के प्रति जो आकांक्षा है, वह उसकी स्वतंत्र रूप से अपनी-अपनी असंपूर्णता को लेकर है। हिन्दू-धर्म में धर्मशास्त्र, साहित्य, शिल्प और भाष्य में अर्धनारीश्वर की कल्पना इस संबंध को बहुत ही सुन्दर रीति से प्रकट करती है। इस से अधिक पवित्र, महान् और उच्च संबंध की कल्पना करना सम्भव नहीं है नर-नारी यदि पारस्परिक संबंध में अपने आधे अंग की भाँति समझे तो यह संसार-जीवन में सुख-शांति का प्रधान कारण बन जाता है क्योंकि ऐसा होने पर उसके दो प्राण, दो हृदय मिलकर एक हो जाते हैं तथा किसी प्रकार की भेद-बुद्धि नहीं रह जाती जिससे शरीर-भिन्न होने पर भी वस्तुतः वे अभिन्न हो जाते हैं। यही समझकर विवाह के समय वर कन्या से कहता है—'यह जो तुम्हारा हृदय है, सो मेरा हो जाय और यह जो मेरा हृदय है सो तुम्हारा हो जाय'[7]। यह भाव यदि हृदय में जाग्रत रहे तो फिर नर-नारी के भेद के आधार पर कोई प्रश्न उठ ही नहीं सकता।

इसे अस्वीकारा नहीं जा सकता कि किसी व्यक्ति या समाज की भलाई-बुराई शुभ-अशुभ और शांति-अशांति प्रधानतया मनुष्य की चित्तवृत्ति अथवा मन के भावों पर निर्भर करती है। प्रचुर धन-सामग्री होने पर भी दम्पती के मन का भाव यदि परस्पर प्रतिकूल होता है तो कभी शांति नहीं होती। दूसरी ओर दुःख के बहुत से कारण विद्यमान रहने पर भी यदि परस्पर अनुकूलता होती है, एक-दूसरे के प्रति गहरा प्रेम होता है तो कोई दुःख नहीं होता, कोई अशांति नहीं होती। इसलिये वैदिक साहित्य में गृह-वातावरण को शांत एवं सुखमय बनाने के लिये नर-नारी के मधुर संबंधों पर अधिक बल दिया गया है। नव वधू गृहप्रवेश के समय अपने पति से कहती है—'तुम एकमात्र मेरे पति होकर अन्य स्त्रियों को नाम मत लो[8] साथ ही नव सधू के लिए यह प्रार्थना की गई है कि वह घर के सभी सदस्यों को नियंत्रित रखे तथा पारिवारिक सुख की कामना करे[9]। हिन्दू-परिवार में 'सहधर्मचरतम्' अर्थात् 'तुम दोनों एक साथ धर्म का आचरण करों', इसी उपदेश को लेकर नर-नारी गृहस्थ जीवन का आरंभ करते हैं। धर्माचरण करने के लिये ही वे अपने इस जीवन को ग्रहण करते हैं। ऐसा करना ही उनका व्रत है। आजकल नर-नारी के समान अधिकार का प्रश्न उठ रहा है। किन्तु, हिन्दू-धर्म में समाज-विज्ञान

का आदर्श दूसरा है। यहाँ नर-नारी का न पृथक् अधिकार (Individual right) है और न समान अधिकार (Equal right) है, अपितु सहाधिकार (Joint right) है। दूसरे शब्दों में, हिन्दू-धर्म कहता है कि मानव के समग्र जीवन को धर्म-साधना में ही लगाकर चतुर्वर्ग (धर्म, अर्थ, काम और मोक्ष) की सिद्धि करनी चाहिये। इसी कारण यहाँ गृहस्थ-जीवन धर्मानुष्ठान के अतिरिक्त और कुछ भी नहीं है। यह धर्मानुष्ठान अकेले पुरुष या अकेली स्त्री से कभी नहीं हो सकता अपितु दोनों कों मिलकर करना पड़ता है तथा जीवन-रूपी मार्ग में मृत्यु-पर्यन्त, कठिन परिस्थितियों में भीं, एक-दूसरे का एक मन, एक विचार होकर साथ देते हैं।

भारतीय संस्कृति के इतिहास का पर्यावलोचन करने पर यह ज्ञात होता हैं कि प्राचीन हिन्दू-समाज में नारी का गृह-कार्य के साथ-साथ लोक-व्यवहार का प्रत्यक्ष अधिकार प्राप्त था। उसे धार्मिक कार्य करने की पूर्ण स्वतंत्रता थी।[10] नारी को साथ लिये बिना यज्ञ पूर्ण नहीं माना जाता था।[11] ऐतरेय ब्राह्मण में नारी को 'जाया' संज्ञा से सम्बोधित किया गया है क्योंकि वह अपने पति को दूसरा जन्म देती है।[12] वैदिक काल में कन्याएँ ब्रह्मचर्याश्रम में रहती हुई विद्या का अध्ययन करती थी।[13] उसे उपनयन संस्कार तथा संध्या करने का अधिकार प्राप्त था।[14] वे यज्ञादि धार्मिक कार्यों में न केवल पति के साथ हिस्सा बटाती थी बल्कि स्वतंत्र रूप से यज्ञ भी करती थी[15] ऋग्वेद के कुछ सूक्त नारी के तत्कालीन दशा को इंगित करता है जिससे यह स्पष्ट होता है कि वैदिक युग में नारियाँ शिक्षित, ज्ञान-सम्पन्न, तेजस्विनी तथा पति-अनुकूल व्यवहार करने को इच्छुक रहती थी।[16] उन्हें समाज में विचरण करने की स्वतंत्रता थी क्योंकि समाज में स्त्रियो के प्रति दुर्व्यवहार को सबसे बड़ा पाप तथा सद्भाव एवं सुरक्षा को सबसे बड़ी शूरवीरता माना जाता था। भारतीय साहित्य के अनुशीलन से ज्ञात होता है कि वैदिक काल में नारी ज्ञान-विज्ञान, कला-कौशल में प्रवीण होने के साथ ही उसे राजनीति एवं युद्ध-कला की भी शिक्षा प्राप्त थी। वह गृहिणी के साथ-साथ पति की सचिव भी थी। परिस्थिति आने पर वह राज-कार्य का संचालन भी करती थी।[17] श्री प्रभु ने स्पष्ट लिखा है कि वैदिक युग में शिक्षा के क्षेत्र में नर और नारी दोनों को समान अधिकार प्राप्त थे और समाज में बराबरी की मर्यादा थी।[18] इस प्रकार वैदिक परम्परा में नारी को सामाजिक, धार्मिक राजनीतिक सभी क्षेत्रों में पर्याप्त अधिकार प्राप्त था। यही कारण है कि प्राचीन काल में भारतीय समाज को विश्व में सर्वाधिक उन्नत स्थिति प्राप्त था। कितनी नारियाँ विदुषी हुआ करती थीं तथा वे वेद मंत्र-द्रष्टा थीं। इन विदुषी नारियों का समाज में काफी सम्मान था। वृहदारण्यक उपनिषद् में एक स्थान पर ऐसे कर्मकाण्ड का उल्लेख है जहाँ गृहस्थ यह कामना करता है कि उनके यहाँ एक विदुषी लड़की उत्पन्न हो।[19] अनेक वेद-मंत्रों के अवतरण में ऋचाओं की दृष्टा के रूप में विश्वतारा, गोधा, सरमा, अपाला, घोषा, शची, लोपामुद्रा आदि ऋषिकाओं को बड़ा

सम्मानपूर्ण स्थान प्राप्त था। इसी प्रकार गार्गी, विदगधा, उद्दालिका, वीचावली, अनुसूया, यामी, सूर्या आदि उस काल की प्रख्यात विदुषियाँ थी। लोला, अववादका, पाटाचारा, सिंहा, वत्सा, जया आदि शताब्दिक स्त्रियों के नार्योचित आदर्श से सभी परिचित हैं। किन्तु धर्मशास्त्र-परम्परा में नारी को पुरूष का अर्धंगिनी बताते हुये उसके अधिकार को थोड़ा संकुचित किया गया।[20] फिर भी नारी को पुरूष के समान ही धार्मिक अधिकार प्राप्त था।[21] नारी को स्मृतिकारों ने 'त्रिवर्ग' देनेवाली माना है।[22] इस प्रकार नारी को धर्म, अर्थ और काम का सामाजिक अधिकार प्राप्त था। उसे सामाजिक स्तर पर काफी सम्मान था।[23] मनुस्मृति में कहा गया है कि नारियों के सम्मान से देवता प्रसन्न होते हैं तथा अपमानित होने पर उसके अभिशाप से परिवार नष्ट हो जाता है। इसलिये समृद्धि की प्राप्ति के लिए नारियों को भोजन, वस्त्र एवं भूषण से सत्कार किया जाना चाहिए।[24] नारियों के मर्यादा के संबंध में याज्ञवल्क्य ने कहा है कि स्त्रियाँ अपने पति, भाई, पिता, जाति के लोग, सास, श्वसुर, देवर तथा बन्धुवर्ग के द्वारा वस्त्राभूषण से सम्मानित होने योग्य है।[25] इस प्रकार धर्मशास्त्र-पराम्परा में भी नारी का समाज में अत्यधिक आदर था एवं कुछ प्रतिबंधों के साथ सामाजिक कार्य करने का पूर्ण अधिकार प्राप्त था। परिवार की अभिवृद्धि का समस्त दायित्व नारियों पर ही था। अस प्रकार हिन्दू सामाजिक व्यवस्था में नारियों को अत्यंत ही गौरवपूर्ण स्थान प्राप्त रहा है।

हिन्दू समाज में नर-नारी को एक-दूसरे का जीवन-साथी माना गया है जहाँ दोनों जन्म-जन्मान्तर साथ रहने की कामना से समाज में अपना योगदान देते हैं। ऐसी स्थिति में नारी से जुड़ी सभी समस्याओं के मूल में नर के साथ नारी भी समान रुप से उत्तरदायी है। औद्योगिक प्रतिस्पर्धा के इस युग में धर्म का स्थान अर्थ ले लिया है। आज नैतिक मूल्यांकन का आधार धर्म न होकर अर्थ हो गया है फलतः अच्छे और बुरे का स्थान लाभ और हानि ले लिया है। जब नैतिक मूल्यांकन का मापदण्ड अर्थनीति से निर्धारित हो तो ऐसी स्थिति में भावनात्मक संबंधों का स्थान गौण हो जाना स्वभाविक ही है। हिन्दू समाज की नींव नर-नारी के भावनात्मक संबंध में ही निहित है। किन्तु आज पाश्चात्यान्धानुकरण से इस भावनात्मक संबंध का स्थान गौण हो गया है। यही कारण है कि आज भारतीय समाज में लिंग-भेद, नारी-भ्रूण हत्या, नारी उत्पीड़न, बलात्कार जैसी समस्यायें उत्पन्न हुई है तथा आज नारी सशक्तिकरण की आवश्यकता महसूस की जा रही है। यदि हिन्दू-धर्म में निहित नर-नारी के धर्मों को सम्यक् रुप से धारण किया जाय तो नारी से जुड़ी समस्याओं।क अंत हो पायेगा तथा ऐसी स्थिति में समाज का सर्वांगीण विकास भी संभव हो सकेगा।

देखा जाय तो प्रकृति की शक्तियाँ दो समानान्तर अथवा पूरक रूपों में कार्य करती रही हैं। नर-नारी का यह परस्पर पूरक संबंध ही प्राणिजगत की निरंतरता को बनाये रखने का माध्यम रहा है। यही जैविक अनिवार्यता दोनों पूरक पक्षों की

शारीरिक, भौतिक एवं मानसिक सीमा-रेखायें निर्धारित करती हैं। जैविक दृष्टि सन्तान की उत्पत्ति एवं उसका पालन-पोषण करना नारी का दायित्व है और इसलिये उसमें वात्सल्य, स्नेह, दया, प्रेम, सौहार्द जैसे अपेक्षित कोमल गुण पाये जाते हैं, जबकि साहस, शौर्य, पराक्रम जैसे कठोर गुण पुरूषों में होते हैं। शायद इसी जैविक भिन्नता के कारण इस संघर्षपूर्ण मानव-जीवन की सामाजिक व्यवस्था पितृसत्तात्मक होती है। और मानव आज युग-युग से चली आ रही संघर्षात्मक वृत्तियों के विध्वंसात्मक भयावह प्रभावों से त्रस्त है और मानव जाति का ही भविष्य संशयग्रस्त है। ऐसे में नारी-सुलभ कोमल गुणों में ही आशा की किरण दिखायी देती है। सामान्यतः नारियों में सहृदयता, सरलता, न्याय, परोपकारिता और दया के भाव होते हैं। सामाजिक प्रगति के लिये इन सदगुणों की स्वीकृति अनिवार्य है। नारी सहभागिता के आधार पर एक ऐसे मानव-समाज की स्थापना संभव है जो रूढ़िवादिता, अंधविश्वास, द्वेष, घृणा, पाखंड, अज्ञान, ईर्ष्या से मुक्त हो और जहाँ समाज के सभी सदस्य परस्पर सौहार्द्र, प्रेम, दया, सहानुभूति के साथ रहकर सहअस्तित्व के स्वप्न को साकार कर सके। इसे अस्वीकार नहीं जा सकता कि पुरूष की भाँति नारी भी परिवार का आधारभूत स्तम्भ है, उसके बिना परिवार की कल्पना भी नहीं की जा सकती। परिवार का स्वस्थ विकास नारी के स्वस्थ व्यक्तित्व पर निर्भर है। सामाजिक समस्याओं के मूल में अधिकांशतः दोषपूर्ण जीवन-दृष्टि रहती है जिसकी आधारशीला बाल्यकाल में परिवार के मध्य रखी जाती है। यदि बाल्यकाल में ही व्यक्ति की जीवन-दृष्टि को स्वस्थ एवं संतुलित किया जाय तो उसके भावी-जीवन में आनेवाली संभावित विकृत्ति को रोका जा सकता है। अतः आवश्यकता है कि समाज में पुरूषों की भाँति नारियों को भी शिक्षित किया जाय जिससे अपनी गोद में वे एक स्वस्थ एवं सम्पन्न भविष्य का निर्माण कर सकें। यदि नारियाँ शत-प्रतिशत शिक्षित हों तो समाज की असंख्य कुरीतियाँ स्वतः समाप्त हो जाएगी।

भारतीय वाङ्मय में मानव जीवन के विभिन्न पहलुओं पर बहुत ही गंभीरतापूर्वक तथा वस्तुनिष्ठता के साथ प्रकाश डाला गया है। यही कारण है कि हजारों-हजार वर्षों से हिन्दू जाति इसका अनुसरण करती हुई अपनी गरिमा को बनाये रही है। परन्तु आज पाश्चात्यान्धानुकरण के कारण हम अपनी संस्कृति से विरत होते चले जा रहे हैं। हमारे यहाँ अर्थ (धन) की महत्ता नहीं है अपितु चरित्र एवं मानवता को उच्चतम स्थान दिया गया है। हिन्दू-धर्म नारियों के आचार पर ही अचल है इसलिए यहाँ नारियों का विशेष महत्त्व है। अतः आवश्यकता है कि नारी अपने सदगुणों को विकसित करते हुये स्वतंत्रता मे निहित इस दायित्व को समझे तथा समाज के प्रति एक संतुलित एवं स्वस्थ दृष्टिकोण को विकसित करें।

संदर्भ

1. डॉ0 ए0 ए0 रुवैक, द साइक्लोजी ऑफ कैरेक्टर, पृ0-609-11.
2. फ्रायड, न्यू इन्ट्रोडक्ट्री लेक्चर्स ऑन साइक्लोजीकल एनालिसिस, पृ0-34.
3. रविन्द्रनाथ मुखर्जी, भारतीय सामजिक संस्थायें, पृ0-474.
4. ऋग्वेद, 3.53.4.
5. श्रीमद्भगवद्गीता, 7.4-5.
6. वही, 13.19.
7. यदेतद्धदय तदस्तु हृदयं मम। यदेतद्धदयं मम तदस्तु हृदयं तव।। (सामविधान ब्राह्मण, 3.9)
8. अथर्ववेद, 7.37.
9. ऋग्वेद, 10.85.26; 10.85.46.
10. ऋग्वेद, 5.3.7, अथर्ववेद, 11.1.13-17, 20.25.3, 20.26.10; यजुर्वेद, 8.1.
11. ऋग्वेद, 18.11.1.5.
12. गोपालकृष्ण अग्रवाल, भारतीय सामाजिक संस्थान, पृ0-274.
13. अथर्ववेद, 11.5.18.
14. यजुर्वेद, 8.1
15. तैतरीय ब्राह्मण, 2.2.2.6.
16. ऋग्वेद, 10.359.2-3.
17. महाभारत (शांतिपर्व), 32-33; रामायण (अयोध्या कांड), 36-38.
18. पी0 एच0 प्रभु, हिन्दु सोशल ऑर्गनाईजेशन, पृ0 258.
19. वृहदारण्यक उपनिषद्, 4.4.27.
20. लिंग पुराण (पूर्वाध), 84.16; मनुस्मृति, 5.155.
21. पराशरस्मृति, 7.17, कात्यायनस्मृति, 19.1-4; वृद्धहारीत0, 8.86; लघुआश्वलायन, 1. 71-72.
22. दक्षस्मृति, 4.1.
23. आपस्तम्बस्मृति 10.11.
24. मनुस्मृति, 3.56-59.
25. याज्ञ0 स्मृति (आचाराध्याय), 82.

अध्याय 16

जैन-आगमों में नारी

श्याम किशोर सिंह

आज के परिवेश में नारी-सशक्तिकरण एक ज्वलंत प्रश्न के रूप में हमारे सामने खड़ा है। इस विषय पर जाने कितनी ही संगोष्ठियाँ हो चुकी है और हो रही हैं। किन्तु प्रश्न उठता है नारी-सशक्तिकरण का आधार क्या हो? क्या नारी-सशक्तिकरण का अभिप्राय यह है कि वह पुरुष के समान शारीरिक रूप से बलिष्ठा हो या पूरुष से प्रत्येक दृष्टिकोण में आगे हो, आदि-आदि। यदि उसे पुरुष से आगे माना भी जाय तो पुनः प्रश्न उठता है कि उसे कितना आगे माना जाए? जहाँ तक नारी-पुरुष-समानता की बात है तो यह हमारी भारतीय संस्कृति में प्राचीन काल से उपलब्ध है। पुरुष और नारी को भारतीय सामाजिक जीवन में दो आधार-स्तंभ के रूप में स्वीकार किया गया है। पुरुष और नारी एक दूसरे के अभाव में अपूर्ण हैं। जिस प्रकार गाड़ी के दो पहिये एक समान होकर मंजिल को प्राप्त करते हैं उसी प्रकार पुरुष और नारी दोनों के सह-अस्तित्व से जीवन रूपी मंजिल को तय किया जा सकता है। विश्व की समस्त विभूतियों में अर्धाश नारी का है। यद्यपि हम व्यवहारिक जीवन में नारी को द्वितीय स्तर पर रखते हैं तथापि यदि शास्त्रों को उठाकर देखें तो भारतीय सामाजिक परिवेश में संभवतः नारी को पुरुष की अपेक्षा उच्च स्थान दिया गया है। चाहे वह वैदिक परंपरा हो या श्रमण, दोनों ही परंपराओं में नारी को सर्वोपरि माना अया है। यदि वैदिक साहित्य यथा-वेद, ब्राह्मण, उपनिषद्, धर्मसूत्र, जिनका समय ईसा पूर्व 2000 वर्ष से लेकर लगभग ईसा पूर्व 300 वर्ष माना जाता है, को देखें तो यह ज्ञात होगा कि नारी को हमारे भारतीय समाज में प्राचीन काल से ही महनीय स्थान प्राप्त है। मनुस्मृति (3/56) में कहा गया है--"यत्र नार्यस्तु पूजन्ते रमन्ते तत्र देवता।" नारी के स्वरूप पर प्रकाश डालते हुए कहा गया है–

कार्येषु मन्त्री, वचनेषु दासी, भोज्येषु माता, शयनेषु रम्भा।
धर्मानुकूला क्षमयाधरित्री षड्भिर्गुणैः स्त्री कुल तारिणी स्यात्।।

कहने का तात्पर्य है कि अपनी विविध भूमिकाओं के कारण नारी एक होकर भी अनेकवत् प्रतीत होती है। जिस प्रकार केन्द्र में रखी हुई कोई वस्तु दिशा भेद से पूर्व-पश्चिम, उत्तर-दक्षिण में दिखाई देती है, उसी प्रकार एक स्त्री किसी की पत्नी होती हुई माता, भगिनी, मंत्री और दासी हो सकती है। वैदिक साहित्यों की तरह जैनागमों में, जिनका समय ईसा पूर्व 5वीं सदी से लेकर ईसा की 5वीं सदी तक माना जाता है, भी नारियों के स्वरूप पर प्रकाश डाला गया है।

इस तथ्य को स्वीकारने में कोई आपत्ति नहीं होनी चाहिए कि विवाह एवं परिवार की संस्था की स्थापना एवं सुदृढ़ीकरण के साथ ही नारियों की सामाजिक स्थिति में उत्तरोत्तर ह्रास होता गया और मातृ सत्तात्मक परिवार एवं समाज पर पितृ सत्तात्मक अवधारण की पकड़ सुदृढ़ होती गई। परिणामस्वरूप भारत में वैदिक काल में जहाँ नारियों को पुरुष के लगभग समकक्ष ही समाज में सहज रूप से स्थान प्राप्त था, वहाँ उत्तर वैदिक काल में कतिपय विदेशी आक्रमणजन्य कुप्रभावों से अपने समाज एवं अपनी संस्कृति के रक्षार्थ अनेकानेक सामाजिक एवं सांस्कृतिक कुण्ठाओं के अवतरण के साथ आर्यों की यज्ञ प्रधान संस्कृति की सहधर्मिनी, अर्द्धगनी, नारी का स्वरूप 'अबला', 'नरक का द्वार' आदि रूप में परिवर्तित होकर समाज की मुख्यधारा से पृथक होकर केवल 'भोग्य' रूप में परिवर्तित होता गया। इस काल में ऐसा माना जाने लगा कि नारी बाल्यावस्था में पिता के अधीन, युवावस्था में पति के अधीन, और वृद्धावस्था में पुत्र के अधीन रहने वाली प्राणी मात्र है। नारी को इस काल में भी 'पूज्या' तो कहा गया किन्तु यह पूज्या स्वरूप उसकी मूर्तिवत गतिहीनता का ही परिचायक प्रतीत होता है जिसका घर की चाहारदीवारी की सीमा में मूर्तिवत स्थापित रहना श्रेयस्कर माने जाने लगा। एक समय तो ऐसा आया जब कतिपय वैदिक ऋचाओं की रचयिता नारी को वैदिक मंत्रों के उच्चारण से भी वर्जित कर दिया गया और पति परायणा मात्र होना उसकी गति एवं नियति मानकर उसे मृत पति के शव के साथ सती होने के लिए भी विवश कर दिया गया।

यह ठीक है कि श्रमण परम्परा पर भी आर्य वैदिक परम्परा की छाप स्पष्ट रूप से दृष्टिगोचर होती है, किन्तु सम्यक रूप से विचार कर देखने पर यह स्पष्ट होता है कि जैन धर्म एवं दर्शन में नारियों की स्थिति पर महत्त्वपूर्ण रूप से चितंन हुआ है और समाज में उन्हें पुरुषों के समकक्ष स्तर प्रदान कर उनकी गरिमा को पुर्नस्थापित करने का गंभीर प्रयास किया गया है, जबकि बौद्ध धर्म की परम्परा में इस दिशा में उतनी रूची नहीं दिखाई गई है।

जैन आगमों में नारी और पुरुष की सामाजिक समता पर बल देते हुए उसके दासी या भोग्या स्वरूप को पूर्ण रूप से नकार कर उसे पुरुष के समकक्ष मानने की बात

की गयी है। इसलिए जैनागमों में नारी चरित्र का उज्जवलत्तम पक्ष ही वर्णित है। 'सूत्रकृतांग निर्युक्ति' में स्पष्ट रूप से कहा गया है कि जो शील-प्रध्वंसक चरित्रगत दोष रियों में पाये जाते हैं वे पुरुषों में भी पाये जाते हैं; इसलिए वैराग्य मार्ग में दीक्षित स्त्रियों को भी पुरुषों से उसी प्रकार बचना चाहिए जिस प्रकार स्त्रियों से पुरुषों को बचने का उपदेश दिया गया है।[1] 'भगवती-आराधना' में भी स्पष्ट रूप से यह कहा गया है कि–स्त्रियों में जो दोष होते हैं वे दोष नीच पुरुषों में भी होते हैं अथवा मनुष्यों में जो बल और शक्ति से युक्त होते हैं, उनमें स्त्रियों से अधिक दोष होते हैं। जैसे अपने शील की रक्षा करनेवाले पुरुषों के लिए स्त्रियाँ निन्दनीया है वैसे ही अपने शील की रक्षा करनेवाले स्त्रियों के लिए पुरुष निन्दनीया है। सब जीव मोह के उदय से कुशील से मलिन होते हैं और उस मोह का उदय स्त्री-पुरुषों मे समान रूप से होता है।[2] स्त्रियों की प्रशंसा करते हुए कहा गया है–जो गुण सहित स्त्रियाँ हैं जिनका यश लोक में फैला हुआ है तथा जो मनुष्य लोक में देवता समान हैं और देवों से पूजनीय हैं, उनकी जितनी प्रशंसा की जाये, कम है। सर्वगुणसम्पन्न साधुओं और पुरुषों से श्रेष्ठ चरम शरीरी पुरुषों को जन्म देनेवाली माताएँ हुई है।[3] तीर्थकर चक्रवर्ती, वासुदेव, बलदेव और श्रेष्ठ गणधरों को जन्म देनेवाली महिलाएँ श्रेष्ठ देवों और उत्तम पुरूषों द्वारा पूजनीया होती हैं। अन्तकृदद्शा और उसकी वृत्ति में कृष्ण द्वारा प्रतिदिन अपनी माताओं के पाद-वन्दन हेतु जाने का उल्लेख है।[4] जैन धर्म में तीर्थकर का पद सर्वोच्च माना जाता है और श्वेताम्बर परम्परा में मल्ली कुमारी को तीर्थकर माना गया है।[5] तीर्थंकरों की अधिष्ठायिका देवियों के रूप में चक्रेश्वरी, अम्बिका पद्मावती, सिद्धायिका आदि देवियों को पूजनीय माना गया है।[6] जैनागमों में उल्लेख है कि न केवल भिक्षुणियाँ ही नहीं बल्कि गृस्थत उपासिकाएँ भी पुरुष को सन्मार्ग पर लाने-हेतु प्रतिबोधित करती थीं। उत्तराध्ययन में रानी कमलावती राजा इषुकार का सन्मार्ग दिखाती है।[7] ये सभी तथ्य इस बात के प्रमाण हैं कि जैनधर्म में नारी की अवमानन नहीं की गई है। चतुर्विध धर्म संघ में भिक्षुणी संघ और श्रामिका संघ को सथान देकर निर्ग्रन्थ परम्परा ने स्त्री और पुरुष समकक्षता को प्रमाणित किया है। अतएव यह स्पष्ट होता है कि जैन संघ का दृष्टिकोण नारी के प्रति अपेक्षाकृत उदार रहा है।

जैन संघ में नारी का कितना महत्त्वपूर्ण स्थान था इसका सबसे बड़ा प्रमाण तो यह है कि प्रागैतिहासिक काल से वर्त्तमान काल तक सदैव ही भिक्षुओं की अपेक्षा भिक्षुणियों की और गृहस्थ उपासकों की अपेक्षा उपासिकाओं की संख्या अधिक रही है। आज भी जैन संघ में लगभग नौ हजार दो सौ भिक्षु-भिक्षुणियों में दो हजार तीन सौ भिक्षु और छः हजार नौ सौ भिक्षुणियाँ हैं।[8] धर्म साधना के क्षेत्र में स्त्री और पुरुष

दोनों को साधना के लिए सक्षम माना गया है। दोनों को ही साधना के सर्वोच्च लक्ष्य मुक्ति-प्राप्ति के लिए सक्षम माना गया है। ज्ञाताधर्मकथा एवं आवश्यकचूर्णि में हम अनेक स्त्रियों के मुक्त होने का उल्लेख पाते हैं।[9] यद्यपि दिगम्बर परम्परा में स्त्री-मुक्ति-निषेध की बात की गई है तथापि षट् खण्डागम और मूलाचार में जो कि दिगम्बरों में भी आगम रूप में मान्यता प्राप्त है, स्त्री-पुरुष दोनों में क्रमशः आध -यामिक विकास की पूर्णता और मुक्ति की सम्भावना को स्वीकार किया गया है।[10] आगमों एवं आगमिक व्याख्याओं, निर्युक्त, भाष्य और चूर्णि साहित्य में कहीं भी ऐसा संकेत नही मिलता जिसमें स्त्री-मुक्ति का निषेध किया गया हो। इससे स्पष्ट है कि न केवल श्वेताम्बरों ने ही नहीं प्रत्युत् दिगम्बर परम्परा के अनेक संघों ने भी स्त्री-मुक्ति एवं स्त्री-दीक्षा को स्वीकार करके नारी के प्रति उदार दृष्टिकोण अपनाय है। स्त्री तीर्थकर की अवधारणा जैन धर्म की अपनी एक विशिष्ट अवधारणा है जो नारी गरिमा को महिमा-मण्डित करती है। यद्यपि हिन्दू धर्म में शक्ति उपासना के रूप में स्त्री को महत्त्व दिया गया है, तथापि जैन धर्म में तीर्यंकर की जो अवधारणा है उसकी अपनी एक विशेषता है। वह सूचित करती है कि विश्व का सर्वोच्च गरिमामय पद पुरुष और स्त्री दोनों ही समान रूप से प्राप्त कर सकते हैं। जैनागमों में नारी-स्वतंत्रता की बात की गई है। ज्ञाताधर्मकथा में राजा द्रुपद द्रौपदी से कहते हैं कि मेरे द्वारा विवाह किये जाने पर तुझे सुख-दुःख हो सकता है, अच्छा हो कि तू अपना वर स्वयं ही चुन ले।[11] ये विचार वैवाहिक जीवन के लिये नारी-स्वातंत्र्य के समर्थक हैं। जैनागमों में वैसे दृष्टांत भी दृष्टिगत होते हैं जहाँ पति द्वारा पत्नी को धार्मिक विश्वास के साथ-साथ खानपान एवं आचार-व्यवहार में स्वतंत्रता प्राप्त थी।[12] धर्म-संघ में भी भिक्षुणी-संघ की व्यवस्था को भिक्षु-संघ से अधिक नियंत्रित नहीं पाते हैं। भिक्षुणी संघ अपने आन्तरिक मामलों में पूर्णयता आत्म-निर्भर था। गण -धर अथवा आचार्य का उस पर बहुत अधिक अंकुश नहीं था।

जहाँ तक पुत्र-पुत्री की समानता का प्रश्न है, जैनागमों में पुत्र-पुत्री के समान महत्त्व की बात की गई है। जैनागमों में हम देखते हैं कि उपासक और उपासिकाएँ पुत्र-पुत्री-हेतु समान रूप से कामना करते हैं[13] पुत्र की प्रधानता की बात हम जैनागमों में नहीं पाते हैं। जैनागमों में पुत्र और पुत्री दोनों की ही उत्पत्ति सुखद बतलाई गई है। धार्मिक आधार पर पुत्र की महत्ता को जैनागमों में स्वीकृति नहीं प्रदान की गयी है। जैन कर्म-सिद्धांत स्पष्ट रूप से उद्घोषित करता है कि व्यक्ति अपने कर्मों के अनुसार ही सुगति-दुर्गति में जाकर सुख-दुःख का भोग करता है। सन्तान के द्वारा सम्पन्न किये गये कर्मकाण्ड पूर्वजों को किसी भी प्रकार प्रभावित नहीं करते।[14]

जहाँ तक विवाह संस्था और नर-नारी समकक्षता का प्रश्न है; जैन धर्म के अनुयायियों में प्राचीन काल से विवाह-व्यवस्था प्रचलित रही, किन्तु निवृत्ति प्रधान

होने के कारण जैन धर्म में विवाह-व्यवस्था को कोई विशेष महत्त्व नहीं दिया गया। जैन-साहित्य के अध्ययन से यह स्पष्ट हो जाता है कि आगामिक काल तक स्त्री विवाह-संबंधी निर्णयों को लेने में स्वतंत्र थी और अधिकांश विवाह उसकी सम्मति से ही किये जाते थे जैसा कि ज्ञाताधर्मकथा में मल्लि और द्रौपदी के कथानकों से ज्ञात होता है।[15] इस प्रकार आगम युग में समान्तया स्त्री को पति का चयन करने की स्वतंत्रता थी। यह उसकी इच्छा पर निर्भर था कि वह विवाह करे या न करे। ऐसी अनेक स्त्रियों के उल्लेख प्राप्त होते हैं जिन्होंने आजीवन ब्रह्मचर्य पालन स्वीकार किया और विवाह अस्वीकार कर दिया। उनमें चन्दनवाला, जयन्ती आदि के नाम उल्लेखनीय हैं। जैनों के लिये विवाह का अर्थ था अपनी वासना को संयमित करना। केवल उन्हीं लोगों के लिये विवाह संस्था में प्रवेश आवश्यक माना गया जो पूर्णरूपेण ब्रह्मचर्य पालन में असमर्थ अथवा विवाह के पूर्व पूर्ण ब्रह्मचर्य-पालन का व्रत नहीं ले चुके हैं। अतएव हम कह सकते हैं कि जैनों ने ब्रह्मचर्य-पालन की आंशिक साधना के अंग के रूप में विवाह संस्था को स्वीकार करके भी नारी की स्वतंत्र निर्णय-शक्ति को मान्य करके उसकी गरिमा को खंडित नहीं होने दिया।

नारी-रक्षा की बात भी हम जैनागमों में पाते हैं। नारी की मर्यादा की रक्षा के लिये जैन-संघ सदैव तत्पर रहता था। निशीथ चूर्णि में कालकाचार्य की कथा इस बात का स्पष्ट प्रमाण है कि आचार्य ने भिक्षुणी की शील-सुरक्षा के लिये गर्द भिल्ल के विरुद्ध शकों की सहायता लेकर पूरा संघर्ष किया था।[16]

जहाँ तक सती-प्रथा का प्रश्न है धार्मिक आधार पर जैन धर्म सती प्रथा का समर्थन नहीं करता है। व्याख्या साहित्य में ऐसी अनेक कथाएँ वर्णित हैं जिनके अनुसार पति के मृत्यु के पश्चात् पत्नी न केवल पारिवारिक दायित्व का निर्वाह करती थी, अपितु पति के व्यवसाय का संचालन भी करती थी। जैनर भिक्षुणी संघ विधवाओं, कुमारियों और परित्यक्ताओं का आश्रय-स्थल था। जब भी नारी पर कोई अत्याचार किये गये, जैन भिक्षुणी-संघ उसके लिये रक्षा कवच बनी, क्योंकि भिक्षुणी-संघ में प्रवेश करने के बाद न केवल वह पारिवारिक उत्पीड़न से बच सकती थी, बल्कि एक सम्मानपूर्वक जीवन भी जी सकती थी। जैन धर्म में सती-प्रथा जैसी कुत्सित प्रथा कभी नहीं रही। यहाँ पति के मृत्यु के उपरांत शरीर त्यागने का उल्लेख तो है, किन्तु उसका स्वरूप सौम और वैराग्य-प्रधान बना दिया गया है। [1] साथ ही जैनागमों में विवाहित स्त्री के अतिरिक्त सभी प्रकार के यौन-संबंध निषिद्ध माने गये।[18] कहने का अभिप्राय है परस्त्रीगमन और वेश्यागमन दोनों निषिद्ध माने गये। ऐसी चर्चाएँ भी जैन साहित्यों में उपलब्ध है।[19] जहाँ तक नारी-शिक्षा का प्रश्न है जैनागमों और आगमिक व्याख्याओं से हमें ज्ञात होता है कि प्राचीन काल में नारी को समुचित शिक्षा प्रदान की जाती थी, किन्तु यह शिक्षा उन्हें घर पर दी जाती थी अथवा वह गुरुकुल

में जाकर अध्ययन करती थी—इसका स्पष्ट उल्लेख नहीं मिलता है। स्त्री गुरुकुल के संदर्भ के अभाव से ऐसा प्रतीत होता है कि उनकी शिक्षा की व्यवस्था घर ही पर की जाती थी, किन्तु बाहर से दासियों एवं गणिकाओं की नियुक्ति शिक्षा व्यवस्था-हेतु की जाती थी ऐसा उल्लेख हमें प्राप्त होता है। सहशिक्षा निर्देश का अभाव आगमों में दृष्टिगत होता हैं। स्त्री-पुरुष दोनों के लिये कर्म-प्रधान शिक्षा का विशेष प्रचलन था। धार्मिक-आध्यात्मिक-शिक्षा उन्हें भिक्षुणियों द्वारा प्रदान की जाती थी। सूत्र कृतांग से ज्ञात होता है कि जैन-परम्परा में भिक्षु को स्त्रियों के शिक्षा देने का अधिकार नहीं था।[20] भिक्षु केवल स्त्रियों और पुरुषों की संयुक्त सभा में उपदेश दे सकता था। स्त्रियों द्वारा धर्मग्रंथों के अध्ययन पर भी कोई प्रतिबंध नहीं था। आगम युग की अपेक्षा आगमिक व्याख्या युग में किसी सीमा तक नारी-शिक्षा के अधिकार को सीमित किया गया था, किन्तु पुनर्जागृति के प्रभाव से आज अधिकांश जैन-सम्प्रायों में साध्वियाँ आगमों के अध्ययन और प्रवचन का कार्य कर रही हैं।

जैन आगमों से ज्ञात होता है कि उस समय नारियों को न केवल गार्हस्थ्य अवस्था में पुरुषों के समान धर्माचरण करने का अधिकार था, अपितु भिक्षुणी बनने में भी उन पर संघ की ओर से किसी प्रकार का प्रतिबंध नहीं था। इनता ही नहीं जैन मान्यता के अनुसार स्त्री तीर्थंकर भी बन सकती थी। मल्ली ने स्त्री होते हुए भी तीर्थंकर पदवी प्राप्त की थी।[21] यहाँ उल्लेखनीय है कि बुद्ध के मतानुसार स्त्री सम्यक सम्बुद्ध नहीं हो सकती थी।[22] अतः यह कहा जा सकता है कि बौद्धों की अपेक्षा जैनों में नारी के प्रति उदार दृष्टिकोण था। मूल जैनागमों में भिक्षुणियों के ऊपर सामाजिक व्यक्तियों के द्वारा अनाचार किये जाने के उल्लेख नहीं मिलते हैं। जैन युग में भिक्षुणियाँ समाज के सदस्यों से सम्मान की अपेक्षा रखती थी तथा अपमानित होने पर उसका प्रतिकार भी किया करती थी। आचार्य भिक्षुओं को भिक्षुणी की शील रक्षा का स्पष्ट आदेश देते थे। भिक्षुणी की शील रक्षा के निमित्त नियुक्त भिक्षु उदण्ड एवं कामुक पुरुषों को मार भी डालते थे।[23] इसके अतिरिक्त आचार्य देश एवं काल की दृष्टि से भिक्षुणी की शील रक्षा हेतु नवीन नियमों का भी सर्जन कर देते थे।

इसे अस्वीकार नहीं किया जा सकता कि जैन-धर्म में अतीत से लेकर वर्त्तमान तक नारी की, और विशेष रुप से भिक्षुणियों की एक महत्त्वपूर्ण भूमिका रही है। जहाँ एक ओर जैन धर्म नारी को सम्मानित और गौरवान्वित करते हुए उसके शील-संरक्षण का प्रयास किया और उसके आध्यात्मिक विकास का मार्ग प्रशस्त किया, वहीं दूसरी ाेर नारी-वर्ग ने अपने चरित्र बल तथा संयम-साधना से जैन धर्म की ध्वजा को फहराया है। तुलनात्मक दृष्टि से भी जैन धर्म एवं अन्य धर्मो में नारी की स्थिति का अध्ययन करने पर ज्ञात होता है कि जैन धर्म का दृष्टिकोण नारी के प्रति अपेक्षाकृत

अधिक व्यावहारिक एवं उदार है। जैन-धर्म में भिक्षुणी संघ ने न केवल नारी को गरिमा प्रदान की, अपितु उसे सामाजिक उत्पीड़न और पुरुष के अत्याचारों से बचाया भी है। यही जैन धर्म की विशेषता है। अतएव निष्कर्षतः कहा जा सकता है कि सैद्धांतिक एवं व्यवाहरिक दोनों ही दृष्टियों से जैन समाज में नारी की स्थिति सुदृढ़ थी एवं नारी को पुरुष के समान जीवन के विभिन्न क्षेत्रों में मान-सम्मान देने का प्रयास किया जाता रहा है।

संदर्भ

1. सूत्रकृतांगनिर्युक्त, गाथा 61
2. भगवतीअराधना; गाथा, 987-88 व 995-96
3. वही गाथा, 989-94
4. अन्तकृद्दशासूत्र-18
5. ज्ञाताधर्मकथा, 8/186
6. पवचनसारोद्धार, भाग-1, देवचन्द लाल भाई, जैनपुस्तकोद्धार संस्था, सन् 1922
7. उत्तराध्ययन सूत्र, 14/38 एवं उत्तराध्ययन चूर्णि, पृ0-230 ऋषभदेव केशरीमल संस्था, रतलाम, 1933
8. चातुर्मास सूची, प्र0अ0भा0 समग्र जैन चातुर्मास प्रकाशन परिषद, बम्बई 1987, पृ0-77
9. आवश्यक चूर्णि, भाग-1, पृ0-181 व 488, भाग-2, पृ0-212
10. (क) षट्खण्डागम, 1.1, 92-93
    (ख) मूलाचार, 4/196
11. ज्ञाताधर्मकथा, 16/85
12. उवासगदसाओं-पृ0-245
13. ज्ञाताधर्मकथा, 1/2/16 विवागसुयं, 1/7/137
14. उत्त्राध्ययन 13/23
15. ज्ञाताधर्मकथा, भाग-1 पृ0-142-143
16. ज्ञाताधर्मकथा, भाग-3, पृ0-234
17. प्रबंधकोश, पृ0 129
18. उपासकदशा, 1, 48
19. जैन, बौद्ध, गीता का आचार दर्शन, भाग-2, डॉ0 सागरमल जैन, पृ0-268
20. सूत्रकृतांग-1, 4, 1, 11.
21. नायाधम्मकहाओ, 1/8/70, 83
22. अंगूत्तर0, 1/19
23. नाया0, 1/8/79

Chapter 17

Gender Issue and the Mughals

Damodar Singh

The present paper is mainly concerned with the problem of examining the gender discrimination in the Mughal India. The importance of the problem lies in the fact that the movement for women's liberation is gaining ground all the world over. The movement, started in the west in the early sixties grew so rapidly that the U.N.O. declared the years from 1975 to 1985 as a decade of women's emanicipation, and 2001 was declared as the 'Year of Women's Empowerment'. The radicalism of the movement has much in common with the other movements of the period such as Black Power, student unrest, and the hippies' rejection of contemporary culture. But the movement for women's liberation has outlasted all the other movements. Its following has increased, its organisations have emerged, and a genuine attempt is being made to develop a theory to guide its politics. The literature of the movement has also progressed in its claim to universal significance and its demands for a revolutionary transformation of society. [1]

For us in India the voices of women's liberation often sound weird and cocophonous. Nevertheless, India cannot remain unaffected from the influence of the movement, in view of the spread of female education, urbanization, industrialization and modernization. It is, therefore, proper to walk down the memory lane and evaluate the position of women in the literary works of the Mughal period. It is with this aim in view that the present paper intends to highlight some of the basic gender discriminations in the Mughal India, and the Mughal Badshahs' endeavour to give women the much needed relief to bring them at par with men.

Discrimination towards the fairer sex is as old as human civilization. Right from the earliest recorded history, after the appearance of civilizations based on class exploitation, it has been realised that women have been relegated to a lower and lower status in the social scale. During the Medieval India women's condition was quite pitiable. This was not because the amount of labour they rendered decreased in comparison to the other half, i.e., men. Just as today, in those days also they performed all the house-hold works—prepared food, nursed children, and helped their men folk in all possible ways. The mid-17th century literature *Zakhiratu'I Khwanin* writes, quite rightly, that in Mughal India the wife of a peasant used to carry bread and yogurt to the husband working in the field.[2] Additionally, she was expected to fetch water "from river, tank and well" and to hand-mill the grain in their houses as well.

In the backdrop of the human biology, which makes women comparatively weak, there has always been gender division of labour. However, this did not exempt the women folks, in Medieval India, from doing hard works. Several hard works were undertaken by them—one of them being spinning. During the Medieval India, handle-spindle was being used; and rotating the hand-spindle was extremely stressful for the fingers. Apparently trying to highlight this hard work of women, in 1301-02 Amir Khusrau aptly remarked the "the needle and the (hand) spindle" was the "spear and arrow" of women.[3] Besides, cotton-seed separation was also considered women's job. Moreover, they actively participated in the taxtile industry by helping the weaver (usually male) to set up loom warp and weft, as well as actively involved in dyeing, labour in Mughal India's important cash crop, i.e., cotton and the textile industry as well.

Women's hard labour was, however, not confined to the domestic industry. Just as today, women in pre-colonical days were assigned the hard labour in building construction.[4] Abul Fazl informs us about it through a couple of paintings, showing women breaking stones or bricks, sieving line and carrying mortor on their heads at construction sites.[5] In this way, there were multiple tasks performed by women in Mughal India.[6]

Inspite of hard input in the word, the women were discriminated when the issue of remuneration arose. Their work remained practically unpaid at home, and they were seemingly immenisly underpaid for their outdoor works. This glaring disparity is found in Allauddin Khilji's (1296-1316) price regulations, wherein the "working men-slaves" were to be given between 10 to 15 *tankas*, and for "working women slaves" the wage was between 5 to12 *tankas*.[7]

In consequence, a major issue of the repression of the women crops up. Taking advantage of the caste system, by cheapening labour of lower castes it was found to be beneficial to the ruling class to lower the cost of remuneration of the fair sex. This helped in sustaining the structure of class exploitation, each supplementing the other.

Traces of inferior status of women are found in both Hinduism and Islam. Manu has given ample proof of gender discrimination prevalent in Hinduism when he says that 'women are impure, wrath dishonest and of bad conduct'; and 'It is the husband who brings good qualities, if any, in the wife'. Further, the inferior status of women is apparently shown by Manu when he says that 'women must always be kept in the dependence of the men'.[8]

Similarly, in the *Qur'an* also there are few glaring and acute instances in which gender discrimination is felt in social relationship. For example, the *Qur'an* accords superiority to men in general by saying that 'men are a degree superior to them (women)' and 'for men the women are like a field to sow'. This superiority of men relates both to the domestic and political fields. In both these fields, *Qur'an* asserts that final decisions should rest with men in general, because men are by nature gifted with wider vision and also because their comparative freedom from certain natural limitations enables them to devote more attention to political affairs.

The following passages of the *Qur'an* exhibit male superiority:

(a) He it is who create you from a single soul, and there from did make his mate that he might take rest in her (VI. 189)

(b) And of His sighs is this; He created for you helpmeets from yourselves that he might find rest in them, and He ordained between you love and mercy. (XXX. 21)

(c) Men are incharge of women, because Allah hath made the one of them to excel the other, and because they spend of their property (for the support of women). (IV. 34)

(d) And they (women) have rights similar to those (of men) over them in Kindness, and men are a degree above them. (II, 228).[9]

The above passages suggest gender discrimination in two ways—firstly, that the female sex must be a source of comfort and peace of mind to its male counterpart, and secondly, in general affairs of life men are partially superior to women.

Consequent upon inferior position of women (cited about), there has been repression of women in the society, Men, how-so-ever high or low he was in the social hierarchy, felt superior to his women; and the women also considered their position as God-given, and, thereupon, accepted their inferior position. Such situation was more prominent in the medieval Indian society. Ostensibly in this backdrop, a prominent early 17th century *sufi* saint, Shaikh Ahmad Sirhindi acclaimed the benevolence shown by God to man, and, thereupon, justified superiority of men over women; and, in case of any adultery, the theologian puts blame conclusively and exclusively on women.[10]

The same spirit of gender discrimination are found in an order of fourth Mughal King Jahangir as well. The king instructed that "Do not grave over the death of daughters. Do not follow the advice of women. Never be complacent and neglectful of their deception and artifice".[11]

The instruction, if true, explicitly shows that the women were considered to be of very inferior character, being undesirable, undependable and unreliable. Here it would be worth noting that nowhere we find any such instruction in Jahangir's memoier, and, more interestingly one should not forget that after Jahangir's marriage with Mehrunissa (alias Nur Jahan) in 1611, the Emperor reposed full faith and trust in her to the extent that thenceforth Nur Jahan became the *de facto* ruler of the Mughal Empire.

It is, therefore, found that due to man's own act of repression, women were found to be weak and ignorant. For example, women were kept illiterate and provided with no facility of education, and, therefore, they were not expected to make adequate contribution to learning and literature. Of course there were some women who did manage to read literature and get education. Some of the prominent figures were Gulbadan Begum (sister of Humayun), Salima Sultan Begum (wife of Bairam Khan and after his death, married to Akbar), and Jahanara (daughter of Shah Jahan). Such educated women were in microscopic minority; and the women in Mughal days were, by and large, far less literate in comparison to their counterpart men. Unluckily, we do not have any data regarding the literary ratio between men and women of Mughal India. However, the 1891 census report, to a certain extent, may serve an indicator to it. According to the census, there was only one literate "female" to every twenty three literate "males".

Gender bias could also be seen in the acceptance of polygamy by the Hindus and Muslims in the Mughal India. It was particularly prevalent in the princely and richer classes of men. The wealthy people kept several wives and concubines, apparently exhibiting the superiority of men over women. The 17th century theologian, Shaikh Ahmad Sirhindi, tried to justify four marriages by men and to keep any number of concubines.

However Akbar, though polygamous himself, raised voice against the tradition of polygamy prevalent in the society, ostensibly considering that it caused high injustice towards women. When 'Ibadat Khana' was established in 1575, for discussing matters with divine and theologians, polygamy was the first issue to be discussed; and, thereupon, in the Ibadat Khana on 3rd October 1578 Akbar personally advocated, the principle of monogramy.[12] Badauni says that in the spring of 1578, Akbar, in fact, issued a decree that 'no one should marry more than one wife, unless she was barren, on the principle of "one God one wife."'[13] However, Abul Fazl tells us of no such order, but he records a saying of Akbar that "To seek more than one wife is to hurt oneself'; One may do so only if the first wife proves to be barren or her offspring does not survive".[14] In this way we find that Akbar did advocate monogamy, and there was no sequel to it in practice. However, protest did come against the polygamy system One may view that Meera Bai's love for Lord Krishna was perhaps a protest, albeit silently, to this orthodox sackles.

Traces of gender discrimination of a different nature could be found regarding marriages of princesses, particularly after Jahangir. Though the kings and princes continued having several wives, the Mughal princesses were being kept unmarried throughout life. The justification was given that marriages could be solemnised between families of equal status, and since such family were very few, the princesses had to remain unmarried. However, more importantly, there was a practical compulsion for such a move. There was high probability that the husbands of the princesses could became a potential contender of the throne, and, therefore, it was found safer to keep the princesses unmarried. The net result was that the lesser important princesses were married off, and the important and powerful ones, like Jahanara and Zebunnissa were, in a way, forced to remain unmarried. Of course these princesses could do nothing, but accept the fait accompli. It is, however, interesting to note that inspite of remaining unmarried, Jahanara got the marriages of hundered of girls solemnised, and, moreover, she was involved in several welfare activities, particularly concerning women. This was perhaps silent protest to the injustice imposed on her.

Regarding marriage itself, another discrimination was the early marriages of girls which was quite prevalent in the Mughal days. Both Hindus and Muslim had fallen prey to it. The 16th Century English traveller, Ralph Fitch (1583-91), while referring to the practice of early marriage of the Brahmin girls in Bengal, says that "their daughters be married at or before the age of ten".[15] Pelsaert, who come to India in the last years of Jahangir (1626), speaking about the early marriages of girls prevalent among Hindus, observes that the 'Hindus (give) Their girls in marriage at the age of only 4 or 5 years'.[16] The mid 17th Century Dutch traveller Manucci, referring to the Hindus, observes that 'often their daughters are married even before they have learnt to talk".[17] Such observation has been substantiated by two more European travellers, namely Withington and Mandelso.

Akbar seems to have disliked early marriage of girls. He was anxious to check this practices as far as possible, seemingly considering it to be injustice towards the small girls. The anxiety was reflected in actual prohibition of girls below the age of puberty, defined as 14or 12 years. Hindu marriages were also covered, in the ban, is shown by the fact that Akbar commented in 1595 on the inequity of marrying off a minor girl especially "under a law where a woman, being so much younger than her husband, cannot marry again".[18] Citing an instruction regarding it, Badauni says that in 1595 the *Kotwal* was directed to permit marriages among ordinary people only after establishing the ages of the two parties; and this greatly filled the pockets of "officials such as the *kotwal's* men, women of distillers and vulgar", Since presumably it was they on whose report would depend whether the marriages could take place or not.[19]

Dowry system, a practice exhibiting the inferior status of women, was rigorously observed in Mughal India. Seventeenth century foreign travellers—Thevenot, Careri, Mandelsco, Manucci and Herbert—have referred to this evil custom, which had become a great hardship to the poor parents of the brides.[20] Marriage presents, to be given by the bride's father to the groom's parents, popularly known as *Jautuka* Bengal and Orissa, and *dahej* in Bihar, Allahabad, and Jaunpur *subas* were common in Mughal India, just as today. On the authority of Abul Fazl, it can be mentioned that the system of dowry seems to have been absent among the Brahmanas of those days.[21] Both Badauni and Nizamuddin refer to the prevalence of this practice among the high class Muslims as will.[22]

The rite sati was yet an another glaring gender bias prevalent in Medieval India. From the accounts of several European travellers, viz. Della Valle, Ibn Batuta, Terry, Pelsaert ans Manucci, it appears that in Medieval India sati was obligatory in some parts of India and in certain cases force accompanied it, though in some parts, e.g. in Rajputana, ladies burnt themselves more willingly than in other parts of India. Muhammad Bin Tuglaq was perhaps the first king who raised his voice against the practice of burning of widow along with the dead body of the husband. Ibn Batuta informs us that the Sultan made it compulsory to obtain a licence or permission to burn the widows.[23] The idea seems to have been to discourage and eliminate the use of force and social pressure. But generally the licence was used as a matter of course.

Possibly Akbar was initially not against sati and in the remarks made by him on the issue on 3 Oct. 1578 in the Ibadat Khana bears testimony to it.[24] During the discussion, Akbar admired the Hindu women's courage in performing sati. It seems, however, that the 0real change came in 1583 when he personally saw to its enforcement after a Rajput officer's death.[25] He, thereafter, ordered to prohibit and prevent any forcible sati. An injunction to the *Kotwal* to the same effect is recorded in *A'in-i-Akbari*.[26]

Akbar's order was, interestingly, found to be quite effective. Throughout the seventeenth century Mughal officials seemed to be honestly attempting to prevent the rite by prohibiting compulsion and advising the victims against it. European travellers, who were generally critical of the Mughal officials, have praised the sincere efforts of officials in this regard. An European traveller, Ovington, who came to India in the last decade of seventeenth century, observed that sati had become a rare event.[27] Though this view clearly seems to be an exaggeration, but it exhibits that there had been substantial achievement towards reducing the number of *satis*.

In this way we see that gender discrimination was prevalent in the Mughal India. However, it was mainly to the credit of Akbar the he tried sincerely to give breather to women. It is quite difficult to analyse as to what extent the various efforts of Akbar to eradicate gender bias were effective. However, one may safely say that all his attempts helped women in sharing the ethical platform.

References

1. See, for example, Juliet Mitchell, *Women's Estate*, New York, 1871; S. Beauvoir, *The Second Sex*, New York, 1972.
2. See S.F. Bhakkari, *Zahiratu'l Khwanin*, pers. text ed. M. Haq, Karachi, 1974, vol. II, pp. 325-26, wherein the author has written an interesting story regarding it.
3. Amir Khusrau, *Hasht Bihist*, pers. text ed. M.S. Ashraf, Aligarh, 1918, p. 28.
4. D. Schlingloff, 'Cotton Manufacturers in India', *Journal of Economic and Social History of the Orient*, vol. XVII, 1971, pp. 89-90; Ishrat Alam, 'Textile Tools as depicted in Ajanta and Mughal Paintings', in A. Ray and S. K. Bagchi, *Technology in Ancient and Medieval India*, Delhi, 1968, p. 130 & plate 29.
5. See the maniacture of MS of *Akbar Nama*, in G. Sen, *Paintings from the Akbar Nama*, Calcutta, 1984, plates 33 & 61.

6. For a detailed information about the works of women in Mughal period, see Shireen, Moorvi, 'Works and Gender in pre-Colonial India', in *Sex-ratios in Historical Perspective 1500-1900*, Milan, 1994, pp. 105-116.
7. Ziya Barani, *Tarikh-i Firozshahi*, pers. text ed. S.A. Khan, W.N. Lees and *Kabir-al Din*, Calcutta, 1862, p. 324.
8. *The Laws of Manu,* Eng. tr. G. Buglera, Oxford, 1866, II. 213-14, V. 147-48, IX. 2, 17, 22, 23.
9. I have used M. Pickthol's translation, *Qur'an*. The chapter and verse numbers are sufficient to trace the references in it.
10. Shaikh Ahmad Sirhindi, *Maktubat-i Imam-i Rabbani*, pers. text ed. Nawal Kishore, Lucknow, vol. I, pp. 190-91; vol. III, p. 70.
11. *Pand-nama-i Jahangiri*, appended to Khwaja Ni'matullah al-Harawi, *Tarikh-i Khan Jahani*, Dacca, 1962, vol. II, p. 703. However, it should be noted that nowhere has Jahangir referred to such sentiments or statements in his memoir.
12. Badauni, *Muntakhab-ut Tawarikh*, Eng. tr. H. Beveridge, Patna, 1979, vol. II, p. 270.
13. *Ibid.*, vol. II, p. 365.
14. Abul Fazl, *A'in-i-Akbari*, Eng. tr. H.S. Jarrett, New Delhi, vol. II, p. 243.
15. Ralph Fitch, in Sir William Foster (ed.) *Early Travels in India*, 1583-1619, Delhi, 1968, pp. 16-18.
16. Francisco Pelsaert (1626), *Jahangir's India*, Eng. tr. W.H. Moreland and P. Geyle, Combridge, 1925, p. 48.
17. Manucci, *Storia do Mogor*, Eng. tr. W. Irvine, London, 1908, vol. III, p. 54.
18. *A'in-i Akbari*, vol. II, p. 242;*Muntakhab-ut Tawarikh*, vol. II, pp. 338, 391.
19. *Muntakhab-ut Tawarikh*, vol. II, p. 391.
20. Sen, *Travels of Thevenot and Careri*, p. 248; Mandelso , p. 62; Manucci, vol. III, p. 61; Herbert's Travels, p. 45.
21. *A'in-i Akbari*, vol. III, p. 339.
22. *Muntakhab-ut Tawarikh*, vol. II, p. 352; vol. III, p. 99; Nizamuddin , *Tabaqat-i-Akbari*, Eng. tr. B. De. Delhi, p. 599.
23. M. Husain, *The Rehla of Ibn Batuta*, Baroda, 1953, p. 21.
24. Abul Fazl, *Akbar Nama*, Eng. tr. Beveridge, New Delhi, 1979, vol. III, p. 256. During the discussion, Akbar admired the Hindu women's courage in performing sati.

25. *Ibid.*, vol. II, pp. 402-403.
26. For the order regarding banning of forced sati, see *A'in-i Akbari*, vol. I, p. 284.
27. J. Ovington, *A Voyage to Surat in the Year 1698*, ed. H.G. Rowlinson, London, 1929, p. 201.

Section-2

Contemporaneity

Sub Section (a)

Social Problem

Chapter 18

Plight and Prospect of Divorcees and Widows in Hindu Society

Kanupriya

Women constitute about half of the country's total population but their status has been inferior to men. For centuries, they have been denied equity and justice—social, economic, political constitutional etc. and have been largely ignored as the weaker sex. Their position has undergone change from the pre-Vedic to modern times. One of the best ways to understand the position and status of divorcees and widows is to study the history of Hindu civlisation from pre-historic times to the present day. During the Vedic Period woman had full freedom for spiritual progress and intellectual development. It deteriorated considerably during the post-Vedic period and further went down during the Mughal period. A woman was sometimes considered a goddess and at other times a slave but never a human being with a personality. During this period, marriage became an irrevocable union. The husband could discard his wife for the simple offence of not being sufficiently submissive. The husband however could discard his wife for the simple offence of not being sufficiently submissive. The wife on the other hand could not take a similar step and marry a second time, even if her husband had completely abandoned her. A greater calamity that overtook the widow in this period was the Sati custom. In the beginning it was confined to the warrior class. It however began to spread wider in society in course of time, as the performance of the Sati came to be regarded as a great religious sacrifice, which deserved to be imitated.

The Aryans, upon their invasion of India 1500 B.C. Introduced the horrific custom of Sati, i.e., the burning of a woman after the death of her husband, when performed singly it is referred to as 'Sati', when performed en masse by all the women and daughters of a town in anticipation of their widowhood, it is known as 'Jauhar'. It is sanctioned by their most sacred texts, and was practiced from the fall of the Semito-Dravidian Indus Valley civilization to the modern age. No doubt the issue attracted the attention of social reforms like Raja Ram Mohan Roy, Dayanand Saraswati, Ishwar Chander Vidyasagar. They believed in reviving the old Vedic society which promised equal status to women.

The recorded cases of divorce, however, are few, as it was not the custom in family for a wedded wife to take a new husband. The ancient Hindu law-giver, Manu, whose philosophy occupies a significant place in the mainstream of Indian ideology and culture, too constantly stresses the inferiority of women to men. According to Manu, a wife must ever remain devoted to her husband and always please him while he is alive. After his death she should never think of any other man. Society, too, held the view that even if the husband was a moral wreak, or was grievously ill-treating his wife, the latter could not claim any relief by way of divorce. We may point out that divorce was permitted to Sudras and other lower castes and it went out of vogue only in the higher sections of Hindu society. Divorce was unknown to high caste Hindus, comprising three Varnas. Marriage bond was indissoluble not only for this life but for lives to come. The older generation usually accepted the life pattern believing it to be preordained by destiny, and tried to make the best of the lot. The Hindu society which was inextricably bound by caste ethics and discipline did not permit its members to go against its caste rules.

For centuries marriage was considered to be the destiny for woman irrespective of the fact whether she was happily married or was miserable due to constant oppression by man in the patriarchal set-up. Marriage is the deepest as well as the most problematic of all human relations. It is a cultural phenomenon which sanctions a more or less permanent union between partners conferring legitimacy on their offspring. Despite this idealized concept, marriage often does not mean companionship or equality for her, rather it turns out to be an institution of oppression for her in various forms.

Strange are the ways of the society. An erring and philandering husband is welcomed back into the family but a woman who has dared to walk the primrose path is beyond redemption. Women down the ages, have been missing out on the joys of life in pursuit of becoming a lady. Natural instincts and desires are suppressed. This artificial conditioning has done more harm than good. However, a possibility of freedom from endless suffering in unhappy marriage appeared with divorce, separation or annulment of marriage under law. Divorce is a process of giving legal recognition to the breaking up of a relationship already shattered by irreconcilable disparity in the character of two persons or by broken faith, and bitter tensions. "Divorce", as Marilyn French says, "like marriage, is morally natural, it is good in so far as it ends a long-term intimacy, it is to be lamented".[1] But certainly divorce gives freedom to woman to get rid of her sufferings due to male-aggression or gender oppression.

In India, traditionally, the matrimonial ties are considered irrevocable. The "Hindu Dharma" expects from a wife complete devotion to her husband. She is known as Ardhangini or Sahadharmini and expected to completely merge her ego with her husband's, and to strictly follow the ideal of Pativrata: "As river merging itself in the ocean loses its identity, so a wife was supposed to merge her individuality with that of her husband............there was no question of raising a word against him even when he was found to be ill-tempered, vicious, diseased or drunkard".[2] Infact, to have a husband is considered the greatest blessing for a woman even if he is evil because society recognises a woman only through her husband. A single woman has no status in society. Hence, Sati still continues to this day, albeit in sporadic cases.

The liberalization of divorce has come as a great help to save women from endless oppression, or torture in marriage. And now apart from the usual ground of adultery, cruelty, greed etc., divorce can be granted on the mutual consent basis, if both the partners agree and are bent upon final separation; this is known as "no-fault" divorce. Though divorce frees women from the agony of an unjust relationship still it does not solve the problems and women have to continue to struggle and suffer on various levels—economic, emotional and psychological. As such the questions arise: Does a sexist society easily accept a woman's freedom? Does a woman find real happiness in her new role as divorce? Does she really become free after divorce? These and some other related issues should be examined.

Divorce which is admittedly a relief from the painful life of a wrong marriage, is hardly enough to re-establish the woman socially and psychologically or financially. Even after divorce, the aggrieved or relieved woman does not find herself in the same situation as before marriage. Despite the wounds inflicted in the unsuccessful marriage which have to be borne for a long time, a woman has to further bear the onslaughts of a harsh society which does not allow her to be free and happy. In the past the role of the divorced woman was to withdraw from the society and hide her shame. The divorcee was avoided by friends, and spoken of in hushed whispers by her relatives. The India society still does not consider divorce to be something good or healthy despite the liberal divorce laws. Divorce in Indian society in general is considered a social stigma and a big scandal for a woman who is treated as if she is accursed with some disease. Probably, this makes most of the oppressed women dare not break their unhappy marriage and silently accept physical and mental torture instead. However, the trends have changed in recent times. Instead of clinging to a sterile and oppressive relationship, few women are asserting themselves and are seeking freedom by way of divorce, even if they have to incur wrath of society or their family. They are coming out of the narrow, dark, slavish, patriarchal bonds, answering the call of their own individuality.

In the traditional society, where a married woman is respected more than a single woman, a divorcee is more or less shunned as if she was a pollution. The husband's social status or official position becomes a touchstone through which the worth of a woman is measured. After divorce, a woman soon realises that it is basically a husband-centred world where a free woman has no place. She often experiences a sense of inability to control or mould her life. While a man feels free from all moral, social and financial responsibilities, a woman feels as if her inner self has gone to pieces.

Gail Putney Fullerton remarks that the final separation is bewildering. "It is like pushing against a door that suddenly gives way". He further says "You think.......that divorce will be the of something that has become intolerable. What you don't know is that you are getting into another way of life that can be just as painful, that divorce is only the beginning".[3] A woman finds herself in troubled waters again. Overburdened with the responsibility of children and home, with no independent income of her own in most cases, a woman has to depend on the little alimony which the court of law grants in her favour as part of divorce settlement. In the case of a working woman, usually alimony is not granted on the grounds that she is earning on her own. But a woman's job is les paying than a man's because in the interest of family she cannot pursue a career and often takes up part-time or less demanding, and hence less-paying, jobs. As a result even though they are working, after divorce women find their financial position not very sound. After divorce, as Marilyn French puts it: "In an overwhelming number of cases...........men become singles and women become single mothers. Women's incomes decline by 73 percent in the first year after divorce; men's incomes increase by 42 percent. The father is better off, the children are often hungry".[4] Germaine Greer, an important feminist of the twentieth century, also observes that the easy divorce laws have increased the financial insecurity of women. She writes: "Women are not signed up for life in the marriage contract because divorce is always possible, but as it stands, divorce works in the male interests, not only because it was designed and instituted by man, but because divorce still depends on money and independent income. Married women seldom have either".[5] A woman, thus, even in purely economic terms suffers greatly in the world of male supremacy. And sometimes the fear of economic hardship alone may hold a woman back in unhappy marriages.

Even on the emotional level, divorce does not bring easy happiness or freedom to women. It turns out to be a traumatic experience, a shock and often disintegrates a poised and amiable woman's balanced personality and disturbs her psyche. Infact, to free oneself from the past, and to soothe the wounds of a broken marriage, one need moral strength and time which ultimately prove to be the healing factors. The social responses also add to the sense of trauma, since a divorced woman is seen as a culprit or as a pitiable creature which increases the sense of deprivation, loneliness and insecurity. Referring to the divorced Indian woman, Tara Ali Baig comments: "Life for the woman who has been deserted or divorced is far more grim.........In many cases they have problems, however, for this is a society that seems to resent the single woman".[6] Thus, after having a happy life full of love, the blow of separation becomes more severe and painful for woman. She feels cracked up. Infact, her whole life was shaped around a man who would not return to her. This feeling totally disintegrates her personality and the emotional vacuum infact deepens. In this context the recent judgment, ruled on Monday 15, 2004, by the Delhi High Court which said that a wife is entitled to half of the matrimonial assets in the event of divorce, as against a fifth at present, is heartening It is a progressive and much needed judgment. So far, divorced women have been almost totally at the financial mercy of their ex-husbands, and can literally find themselves homeless. This judgment will generally empower women. The high court's judgment will come as welcome relief to all the women who are denied their fair share in the eventuality of a divorce. It is a boon not only for the women, who have had to deal with the emotional trauma of a divorce but even for working women, as a job does not necessarily ensure financial independence.

Infact, a free woman exposed to dangers at every level and has to pay a heavy price in terms of her exploitation and harassment. She is often used as convenience, and is sexually harassed, physically exploited and morally demoralized. Fear of loneliness, insecurity, emotional vacuum, financial pressures and unjust division of responsibility make the divorcees realise better than the single persons that married life, at large, is satisfying, and this consciousness makes them plan to return to it by remarriage. They return to marriage in the hope of co-existence, in the hope of a world shared equally by both the sexs. Remarriage, however, can be helpful only if husbands are ready to care and share, otherwise the ordeals of the woman in the patriarchal set-up will continue. Today the higher education has brought significant changes about the practice of remarriage of divorced women. Needless to say that the problem of widow remarriage has been also a serious one particularly among the Hindu society. Historically speaking, they were not supposed to participate in different socio-religious and cultural activities. Association of inauspiciousness with widowhood still continues. The status of widows even today is socially. culturally and economically pitiable. On the whole, widow remarriage historically has been discouraged. Although among lower caste women, it is not a new thing, but in the case of upper caste widows it has always been a rare practice. It is supposed that such widows could not regain their past status when they remarried. Another reason which makes them fear is that by remarrying she can doom the future of her children. Widows who spend their remaining life cherishing the memory of their late husbands and devoting the service of their family, society and country will continue to be revered by society. We should encourage and honour all those, who are genuinely anxious to lead such a life. It cannot be, however, said that the dread of social opprobrium is still preventing a large number of young widows from marrying, in spite of their desire to enter into a fresh wedlock. Since a young widow has a long life ahead, she must remarry if she wants to lead it happily. Hence, the Indian women are to be self-revolutionary for translating their dreams into practical realities by breaking conservative framework for smooth transition.

Divorcees and widows remarrying is taboo among most Hindus. However, with the passage of time, these practices are slowly but surely being accepted by Hindus. With changing attitudes, few Hindu widows are remarrying and this is happily matched by an increasing number of educated Hindu men accepting them as brides again. Changes in our social outlook have brought a great deal of benefit to the usually tradition-ridden Hindu society. But at the same time, one cannot lose sight of the present era which has made inroads into the Hindu society, resulting in the break-up of families. Where one rarely heard of a divorce among Hindu couples in the good old days, it is now a common thing to read in the newspapers accounts of court cases involving Hindu couples. As such some constructive and bold step about divorces to stop this sad deterioration in our social structure is urgently needed. If this is done, the capacity, efficiency and happiness of Hindu women will increase, and as a consequence, our community will be enabled to take its rightful place in the community of nations and make important contributions to the progress and happiness of mankind.

References

1. Marilyn French, *Beyond Power: On Women, Men and Morals,* London, Abacus, 1986 p. 504.
2. Quoted in Promila Kapur, *Marriage and the Working Women In India,* Delhi, Vikas, 1970 p. 9.
3. Gail Putney Fullerton, *Survival in Marriage,* Illinois, Dryden Press Hinsdale, 1977, p. 446.
4. Marilyn French, *Beyond Power: On Women, Men and Morals*, London, Abacus, 1986, p. 505.
5. Germaine Greer, *The Female Eunuch*, St. Albana, Paladin, 1976 p. 320.
6. Tara Ali Baig, *India's Woman Power*, New Delhi, S. Chand, 1976, pp. 130-31.

Chapter 19

The Rights of Women in Islam

M. R. Kazimi

It is commonly alleged that Islam is a religion for man only, that it has not acknowledged woman to be a complete human being and that it has not ordained laws for her which are necessary for a human being. Had Islam granted a woman the status of complete human being, it would not have provided for polygamy, it would not have given the right to divorce to man only. Similarly, it is pointed out that but for denigrating womanhood, this religion would not have made the witnessing of two women equivalent to that of one man; it would not have given the leadership of the family to the husband; it would not have made a woman inheritance to one half of the inheritance of man and, above all, it would not have countenanced that a woman be priced in the name of dowry. Thus list is long. As such, the Islam, the accusation proceeds, provides for discrimination and gives preferential treatment to man, much to the disadvantage of woman.

Are these accusations true? Is there any justification for such provisions? How does slam justify all these? Does really Islam accord woman a status much inferior to man? Does it not contradict the basics of equality, a concept central to Islam? A modest attempt has been made in this paper to seek answer to these questions.

At the very outset, it remains to be pointed out that Islam holds that rights can be equal but it does not emply that they must also be identical. Does nature prescribe the same set of rights and duties for both the sexes? Are both the same biologically and psychologically? In fact, man and woman are equal in being human, but they are of different characteristics and traits. It is sketched out in the very plan of creation. Womanliness of the woman should not be forgotten in any scheme of things. Infact, Islam looks at woman as she is in nature. Islam is not against parity of rights between woman and man but it is against them having the same rights to man and woman in all respects, it has at the same time, not imposed the same duties on both of them on all occasions.

To begin with, Islam has put an end to the practice of looking on woman in a derogatory and debasing manner. The holy *Quran* most explicitly lays down in various verses that 'We created woman from the nature of man and from an essence the same as the essence of man'. Addressing the man the *Quran* mentions at various places that the God created the companion of man from your kind'. It was in order to reject the view that woman was created out of an inferior stock to that of man. It also rejects the view that women are more prone to fall prey to Devil's design than men As regards, Adam and Eve, the *Quran* maintains: 'Satan tempted both of them': 'so he led both of them by delusion'. Islam exonerates the female sex from the accusation that woman is the source of temptation and sin. Again, for every great and pious man, the *Quran* mentions a great and pious woman a long side with him. It makes a special mention of the fact that a woman is blessing for man and is a source of solace and comfort to him.

The holy *Quran* has taken every care to grant financial independence to women. Financial independence is pre-requisite for empowerment. Before going into the details, the following observation of Will Durant may be referred to:

> The first legal step in the emancipation of our grand mothers was the legislation of 1882 by which it was decreed that thereafter the women of great Britain should enjoy the unprecedented privilege of keeping the money thy earned. It was highly moral and Christian enactment, put through by the factory owners in the House of Commons to lure the ladies of England into attendance upon their machines. From that year to this, the irresistable temptation of the profit motives has drawn women out of the drudgery of the home into the serfdom of the shop. (The pleasures of philosophy pp. 131-32)

It was thus the greed to earn more profit by paying less to women that caused the millowners to go for this kind of law which was intended to favour the women. Against this, about fourteen hundred years ago, the *Quran* had ordained: 'To the men a share from what they have earned'. Islam upholds the right of the women to retain and enjoy the fruits of their labour and efforts. At another place the *Quran* lays down: 'To the men a share of what parents and kinsmen leave and to the women a share of what parents and kinsmen leave'. This verse confirms the right of women to inherit. Further, Islam freed women from the bondage of man by making it compulsory for a husband to provide for the comfortable upkeep of any responsibility or obligation in this regard. She is completely free to spend her own earning in any way she likes. In the eyes of Islam, women despite her having a right in agreement wealth of the family, is in no manner, responsible for procuring the necessity of life. If a husband fails to meet the requirements of his wife or ignores her, the wife is entitled to take action against him in a court of Law and to recover maintenance from the man. The reason, why the man has been saddled with all the responsibilities in this regard, not the women are many as explained by profit and his descendants.

Evidently, it appears to be discriminatory to the core that a woman is entitled to only half of the share what a man gets out of inheritance. But it is to be appreciated that woman has been made free of every liability. Islam has exempted women from armed combat (Jehad) and dower and maintenance has been imposed upon men for her benefit. Moreover, if compensation money is to be paid by the relatives of a person, woman has been exempted from contributing.

It is true that due to historical, social and also biological, compulsions, Islam allowed a man to have four wives at a time, it is to be noted that stringent conditions have been imposed for it. It is explicitly laid down that there must never be, for any reasons, discrimination between the wives and the children. The *Quran* explicitly commanded: 'If you fear that you will not be equitable, then only one wife'. According to Islamic injunctions, favouratism in any form or in any manner between the wives is strictly forbidden. The prophet has comedown heavily on those who show inclination towards one at the cost of the other and has clearly stated that such husbands are bound to be consumed by the fire of hell. Those who have polygamy as source of indulgence in sensuality, have really made the Islamic law an excuse for their misdeed. Society has every right to take them to task and to punish them.

Furthermore, though Islam grants the man the right to divorce his wife, 'a right denied to women, but at the same time declared it to be the most detestable action' which is most annoying to God. The prophet declared: get married but do not divorce because the throne of Allah shudders when there is a divorce'. It is also provided that a man should, when he divorces his wife, pay all her dues and something over and above that as an expression of gratitude. Though, the woman has no inherent natural right of divorce, but a stipulatory right, namely in form of a condition contained in the marriage contract, she may have this right. Thus the wives may have this right as an entrusted right. A wife always retains the right to seek separation if she agrees to do away with her right to demand dower.

A fleeting glance over a few of the provisions relating to the rights of woman leaves no one in doubt that Islam treats woman and man as two stars in two different orbits. 'It is not for sun to overtake the moon'. The basic condition for the happiness of both man and woman and, infact, for the whole of the human society is that each of the two sexes should continue to move in their own orbit. Equality and liberty will be of benefit to them as long as neither of them leaves his or her natural orbit and direction. It fact, the *Quran* never neglected the womanliness of woman and manliness of man in the name of restoring the woman to the status of human being and a partner of him in human rights. The *Quran* looked at the woman as she is in nature.

But the plight of the women in Muslim countries present a spectacle, entirely different. They are made to suffer all sorts of deprivations and inequities. The situation in India is no different. Islam in its pure form is not to be blamed for it . A distinction is to be maintained between pure Islam as ordained by the *Quran* and sayings of holy prophet and distored Islam. It is latter, Islam as practiced by king and lords and those clinging to power by any means, fair or foul, in the name of Islam who are to be squarely blamed for this sad state of affairs. There is a wide gap between Islam as preached and Islam as practised which is responsible for all the ills the society suffers from. The position of women in Iran today is to be compared with their position in Afghanistan, other

Muslim countries in close proximity. It has been correctly stated that backwardness of the Indian Muslim women stems not only from the Muslim personal Law or certain "Islamic features", it is very much a product of economic circumstances such as poverty, destitution and, above all, the lack of economic rights.

The National Commission for Women (NCW), in an attempt to bring about improvement in the situation of Muslim women in India, has come out with a number of recommendations some general, some specific, which go beyond the realm of religious reforms. Among the general recommendations are; that information about government programmes be made available to all women, including Muslim women; that facilities must be provided for education among women in general and Muslim women in particular; that Muslim localities must be provided with best teachers, best schools and best infrastructure; that those who dissuade Muslim women from going to school should be imposed with penalties and above all, the society must be made free of all prejudices which inhibit the Muslim women from taking an useful and effective part in the society's welfare and upliftment. Among the specific recommendations, the NCW expressed concern over the biased interpretation of personal law and suggested a forward looking codification of traditional laws governing marriage, divorce or inheritance that took cognisance of the advances made by the Muslim women in other societies (Frontline Sep-Oct. 2000). The various pronouncements of the Supreme Court are pointer in same direction. This task should be taken up in the right earnest at the earliest. Many scholars, with modern outlook like Asghar Ali Engineer, Rafique Zakaria and Tahir Mahmood are veering round this view.

In facts, the single most potent instrument of a dramatic change in the general position of the Muslims and Muslim women in particular is the enthusiastic cultivation of what may be called 'modern' or 'progressive' education. It is quite in keeping with the true teaching of Islam. More and more young men and women from this community are to be encouraged and stimulated into a habit of looking at things from an angle of what their educated mind considers to be rational. The Islam encourages the spirit of drive and initiative. It is well said: "Reform must come from within, not from without. You can not legislate for virtue". (James c. Gibbons)

Chapter 20

Female Foeticide: Factors and Solutions

Rekha Singh

It has been very aptly said that the worth of a civilization can be gauged from the position that it gives to women. Honoured place ascribed to women is one of the several factors that justify the greatness of ancient culture of India. According to ancient Hindu scriptures, religious rites can't be observed with perfection by a man without participation of his spouse. Only married men along with their wives are entitled to perform religious rites on special holy occasions. Woman power has been given due importance in Indian culture. Lakshmi, Kali and Saraswati are the three chief deities whom we worship for wealth and fortune, strength and power and knowledge and wisdom respectively.

The status of women was relegated to background in the middle age which was an era of physical power dominated by men. Women being physically weaker to men slumped into an inferior position. Their status further deteriorated due to Muslim influence. During the Muslim period of history, they were deprived of their rights of equality with men. They were compelled to keep themselves in their houses with long veils on their faces.

With the passage of time, the position of women has deteriorated to such an extent that they are considered as a burden for the family and are killed while in mothers' wombs by those who beget them and should have protected them because of the various factors, some of which are described below:

Male-oriented mind-set

Due to long subjugation of women to men folk, Indian psyche has become male-oriented. Women have been relegated to secondary position in all spheres of life. They have become used to this auxiliary place in the family and society as they are subject to discrimination from their childhood. They have to face discrimination in the matters of food, cloths, education etc. They are also deprived of love and affection of their parents, guardians and elders. They live and grow amidst gender discriminations and illiteracy which made them feel as inferior to men. Their male-oriented mind-set induces them to play an active role in perpetrating gender discrimination against their own class. In the instances of perpetrating harassment and crime against the brides they play a supporting role. They are instrumental in dowry-related evils and crimes. When a young woman after marriage gives birth to a femalc infant, first of all she is cursed by no other person than her mother-in-law. Even in the matter of determination of sex in the pregnancy and subsequent abortion of female foetus women perform their leading role.

Lack of Sex-education

Both men and women in India do not have proper and realistic knowledge of sex. There is no sex-education in the curricula of the educational institutions. A large number of young boys and girls are deprived of schooling. Those who get education in schools and colleges are not imparted scientific knowledge pertaining to sex. Most of the educated boys and girls are either ignorant or have distorted knowledge about sex. Discussions pertaining to sex are considered immoral due to backwardness. Men and women discuss about this aspect of knowledge with their friends in private and get the false or distorted picture of it.

By and large women relate sex with morality because of backwardness and ignorance. This results into their passive role in the matters of sex. They are not fully responsive and active in love making process with their husbands. This unscientific attitude towards sex leaves them dry in sexual pleasures. They are bereft of ecstasy of orgasm in many cases. They should, therefore, shed shyness, inhibition and unscientific knowledge and should play a fully responsive and proactive role with their spouses in order to get optimum enjoyment and satisfaction.

In Indian society, sex is permissible only between wife and husband. Here also women have to face discrimination in two ways.

One, men are generally absolved for pre/extra-marital sexual indulgence by the society whereas the women have to undergo both social punishment and ethical condemnation, but I feel that the punishment and condemnation should be other way round because in such cases it is the men who make proactive or aggressive approaches. Two, the females have to bear the curse of nature when they conceive in the process and are left into lunch by their paramours. Their malaise is exasperated due to their illiteracy, economic insolvency, anti-women mind-set of society and absence of insurance coverage in such cases.

Physical Dependence

Nature has made the women tender, fragile and fair. In the Indian milieu they have to depend on others for their livelihood; giving birth to offspring; and bringing up their children. Physical dependence and gender discrimination make the women feel inferior to the males and by-and-by they also develop male-oriented mind-set. They feel inferior to the males. This feeling of inferiority and physical as well as physiological dependence co-orce them to accept female foeticide with heavy heart.

Economic Dependence

Girls are not allowed to prosecute their studies. They are asked to look after the hearth and home. Uneducated women cannot get jobs. Even some well-educated ones do not have opportunity to go out for various jobs. They are constrained to give up good jobs because of the non-cooperative or negative attitude of their family members. Over all economic dependence is also one of the factors of female foeticide.

Dowry Problems

The rate of dowry demand and dowry deaths is alarmingly high in India. There are laws to prevent demand of dowry and dowry related violence against women but in practice this evil continues unabated. Liberalised economy and consumer boom has resulted a phenomenal growth in dowry related problems. There is unending chain of demands of various costly items and consumer goods. This evil, in fact, is more prevalent among the educated and affluent families. However, unfortunately, the persons belonging to the poor and uneducated class are emulating this social evil at a rapid pace.

It is becoming very difficult to get the girls married to suitable and matching boys because of enormous increase in the demand for dowry. The helpless and hapless parents and guardians shudder at the thought of having a girl child in their family. They are forced to opt for medical termination of female foetuses. In the past at the time of birth of a girl child, she was considered with grace and respect as if goddess of wealth (Lakshmi) has incarnated in her form but today she is treated as a liability, a being to be discarded before birth.

Female foeticide is a legal, social, ethical problem. We can get rid of this cancerous malady if more stringent legislations are enacted and implemented in order to alleviate and eliminate the factors leading to the killing of female infants in mothers' wombs. Persons occupying very high positions in the governmental hierarchy should set examples of arranging simple marriage of their sons withou any dowry. Because, in India, ministers, officers, engineers, judges and lawyers flout the provisions of anti-dowry acts with impunity and set examples for other lesser humans to imitate the dowr system. Highly placed persons should lead by examples so tha good things would percolate to the lower strata of humans' lives.

At the social level, mass awareness programmes against factor of female foeticide have to be launched by the educated and elit groups of persons. The elevated and conscientious women shoul come forward in a big way to educate and convince their specie to follow the spirit and tradition of Kali, Durga, Lakshmi Bai an other illustrious ladies of the yore who played their pivotal role i smothering and extirpating the ills and evils of the society. As mo of the women movements are city-based, there is a need to ope counseling centres for women living in rural areas. They should b provided with the opportunity of learning skills of self-reliance.

Killing of a female foetus is also an ethical problem. Intention abortion of a female foetus amounts to taking life out of her. Wat is indispensable condition for the life of a fish. It we take a fish o of water, it dies after some time. Similarly, a foetus taken out mother's womb before maturity dies instantaneously. This is undisputed case of putting the foetus to death. This is an act murder. So punishment imposed on the perpetrators of fema foeticide should be the same that a murderer is awarded by t court of law. All the persons involved in this heinous crime deserve unequivocal ethical condemnation and they should be punished within the ambit of stringent clauses of law. The government should come forward with comprehensive and rigorous and corresponding follow-up action.

With the adoption of these and some other steps the lost place and prestige of women would be gradually restored and the evil of female foeticide would evaporate naturally. Then men and women would live in co-partnership which is essential for the upliftment and empowerment of women. In the world of business, corporates have started to recognise that closing the gender gap is not only the right thing or politically correct thing to do, but it also makes good business sense. In maintaining male-female balance, the creative energy of women is brought to the fore. They can perform many roles simultaneously and effectively. For any endeavour to succeed it is necessary to harmonise the activity of man and woman both. This is clearly evident from portrayal of the Divine as 'Ardhanareeshwara' (half man-half woman) or 'Shiva-Shakti'. When two forces of opposite sex collaborate on equal terms, massive positive forces would be brought into being.

अध्याय 21

मादा-भ्रूण हत्या : एक समीक्षात्मक अनुशीलन

हरिनारायण पाण्डेय

पुरुष और प्रकृति का द्वैत सृष्टि का सनातन सत्य है। लिंग की दृष्टि से पुरुष पुलिंग एवं स्त्री स्त्रीलिंग है। स्त्री एवं पुरुष दोनों के समागम से सृष्टि-प्रक्रिया प्रारम्भ होती है। पुरुष एवं प्रकृति का एक दूसरे के प्रति आकर्षण सहज, स्वाभाविक एवं सर्जनात्मक है। पुरुष शब्द पौरुष का प्रतीक है तो नारी सौंदर्य की स्वामिनी है। भारतीय नीतिशास्त्रीय दृष्टिकोण के अनुसार धर्म सम्मत् काम ही सेव्य है। काम साधन पुरुषार्थ; क्योंकि वह अभ्युदय एवं निःश्रेयस का साधक है। सन्तानोत्पत्ति समागम का नैसर्गिक प्रतिफल है। शक्ति और सौंदर्य का अहोभाव में तिरोभाव ही सन्तान उत्पत्ति का शाश्वत संकेत है। सन्तान पुरुष को पितृत्व का प्रसाद और नारी को मातृत्व की महिमा प्रदान करती है। वैवाहिक जीवन की सफलता सन्तान उत्पति पर ही निर्भर करती है। सन्तान दाम्पत्य को सार्थक, सरल, समर्थ और सगुण सिद्ध करती है। संतान की अभिलाषा दम्पत्ति का अभीष्ट होता है। संतोनोत्पत्ति दाम्पत्य जीवन में चिर प्रकाश प्रस्फुटित करता है द्वैत का प्रतिफल भी द्वैत होता है अर्थात पुत्र और पुत्री इस द्वैत रूपी वृक्ष के दो पुष्प हैं।

प्राचीनकाल से ही पुत्र के प्रति हमारा आग्रह विश्वविश्रुत रहा है। कन्या संतति की प्राप्ति सामान्यतया विषाद को जन्म देती रही है। पुरुष प्रधान समाज इस व्यथा से मुक्ति का उपाय ढूंढता रहा है। कन्या संतति के प्रति अनाग्रह, उसके लालन पालन, शिक्षा-दीक्षा के प्रति सौततेलेपन का व्यवहार एक कटु सत्य के रूप में हमारे समक्ष समुपस्थित होता है। विभिन्न तकनीकी एवं वैज्ञानिक उपलब्धियों के कारण हमारा जीवन स्तर उत्तरोत्तर विकास एवं प्रगति के पथ पर प्रशस्त है। फलतः हमारा जीवन स्तर ज्यादा समृद्ध एवं विकसित हो गया है। बाजारवाद एवं वैश्विक-क्रांति ने इस जलती आग में घी का काम किया है। आज हम अपनी सुख-सुविधा का कुछ ज्यादा ख्याल रखने लगे हैं। अधिक उपभोक्ता सामग्रियों का भंडारण एवं उससे

अधिकाधिक सुखोपभोग जीवन का लक्ष्य हो गया है। इन सारी अवधारणाओं ने हमें स्वार्थ-केंद्रित एवं अनुदार बना दिया है। नित नूतन सुखों से हमारा आकर्षण इस कदर बढ़ा है कि हम जीवन में मूल्यों एवं संवेदनाओं के प्रति सर्वथा संकीर्ण हो गये हैं।

सामाजिक स्तर पर भी तिलक-दहेज, बच्चों की शिक्षा-दीक्षा पर बढ़ते खर्च, सम्पूर्ण व्यवस्था का पूंजीवाद की ओर उन्मुख होना इत्यादि समस्यओं ने हमारे विवेक को कुंठित कर दिया हैं और हम अपने ही अंग के टुकड़े के दुश्मन हो गये हैं। यहाँ हमारा स्पष्ट संकेत समाज में हो रहे कन्या-भ्रूण हत्या की ओर है, जो आज के इस सभ्य समाज के लिए एक भयंकर विभीषिका बनती जा रही है। देश के विभिन्न भागों में कन्या भ्रूण हत्या की ओर है, जो आज के इस सभ्य समाज के लिए एक भयंकर विभीषिका बनती जा रही है। देश के विभिन्न भागों में कन्या भ्रूण हत्या एक अभिशाप के रूप में साबित हो रहा है। इस कुकृत्य के कारण कुछ प्रदेशों में तो कन्या संतति की संख्या में गिरावट दर्ज की गई है और यह एक महत्वपूर्ण समाजशास्त्रीय समस्या के रूप में हमारे सामने मुँह बाये खड़ी है। कन्यासंतति की संख्या में कमी के कारण समाज में लैंगिक असंतुलन उत्पन्न हो गया है।

स्त्री पुरुष लिंग अनुपात	1901 में	972	-	1000
	1981 में	934	-	1000
	1991 में	929	-	1000
हरियाणा में यह न्यूनतम है	-	875	-	1000
पंजाब में	-	882	-	1000

गुजरात के कुछ भागों में जहाँ सट्टा पद्धति की प्रथा है जो विशेषकर चौधरी रबारीस पटेल एवं प्रजापति समुदाय में प्रचलित है। इस पद्धति के अनुसार जिस भाई को बहन नहीं है उसके विवाह में कठिनाई हो रही है क्योंकि इस प्रथा के अनुसार एक परिवार के भाई बहन की शादी दूसरे परिवार में होती है और दूसरे की पहले परिवार में। इस सामाजिक समस्या के कारण वे लोग दुल्हन खरीदने पर मजबूर हो गये हैं।[1] यह एक ऐसी चुनौती बन गया है जिसके विभिन्न पक्षों पर विचार करना वांछनीय प्रतीत होता है। प्रस्तुत पत्र इस दिशा में एक लघु प्रयास है। अतः यह सर्वथा समीचीन है कि इस समस्या के विभिन्न पक्षों पर संक्षेप में विचार किया जाए। मैं यह मानता हूँ कि इस प्रकार का सैद्धान्तिक विवेचन करना हमारा मूल अभीष्ट है ताकि इस समस्या की भयावहता का प्रतिपादन कर सके तथा इससे संकेतित विभिन्न पहलुओं पर विचार विमर्श हो सके।

इस युग में जब हम जीव नैतिक दर्शन की चर्चा करते हैं और सभी जीव जन्तुओं के संरक्षण संवर्द्धन के लिए विभिनन नैतिक नियमों की बात करते हैं जो हमारे भारतीय नीतिशास्त्र में पूर्ववर्णित एवं चर्चित है। इस आलोक में ऊपरि वर्णित समस्याओं के अध्ययन का औचित्य प्रतिपादित किया जा सकता है क्योंकि जब हम वन्य जीव और अन्य जीव जन्तुओं की रक्षा की व्यवस्था करना चाहते हैं तो मानव के द्वारा उत्पन्न इस कुसमस्या के प्रति हमें ज्यादा संवेदनशील दृष्टिकोण रखना होगा। अतः आज इस चुनौतीपूर्ण समस्या के कतिपय विन्दुओं पर विचार करना हमारा अभीष्ट है।

हमारे धर्मग्रंथों में नारी शक्ति पूज्या, प्रातः स्मरणीया, वंदनीया एवं आदरणीया मानी गई है। मनु[2] ने अपनी मनुस्मृति में यह स्पष्ट उद्घोष किया है कि जहाँ स्त्रियों की पूजा होती है वहाँ सभी देवता निवास करते हैं। और जहाँ ऐसा नहीं होता है उसकी सारी क्रियायें निष्फल होती हैं। मनुजी के अतिरिक्त अन्य प्रातः स्मरणीय श्लोकों में नारी-शक्ति को महिमा-मण्डित एवं गौरवान्वित किया गया है। यह एक सैद्धान्तिक आदर्श है, जो स्मर्तव्य है लेकिन व्यवहारतः जीवन का यथार्थ ज्यादा कटु और नग्न है। व्यवहार में नारी को दोयम दर्जे का नागरिक माना जा रहा है। उसके प्रति सौतेलेपन का व्यवहार किया जा रहा है। कन्या भ्रूण स्थापित होने से लेकर जीवनपर्यंत वह विविध विडम्बनाओं का शिकार होती रही है। यौन अथवा धार्मिक आधार पर उसके साथ अनुचित और असमानता का व्यवहार होता रहा है। यह एक विश्वजनीन समस्या है, जिस पर पाश्चात्य चिन्तकों ने भी पर्याप्त प्रकाश डाला है। एतद्विषयक विचार औचित्यपूर्ण ढंग से उद्धृत किया जा सकता है।[3]

इसके अतिरिक्त भी कन्या जन्म बहुत सारी समस्याओं का कारण माना जाता है—जन्म के बाद से ही उसके लालन-पालन, शिक्षा-दीक्षा, सरुक्षा, उस पर होने वाले व्यय एवं अन्य समस्याओं यथा-विवाह के लिए वर चयन के कारण मानसिक परेशानियाँ, दहेज आदि के लिए अकूत धन (सामर्थ्य) होना—ये सारे कारण दम्पत्ति के लिए शारीरिक, मानसिक, आर्थिक एवं संवेगात्मक शोषण के सोपान बन जाते हैं।

उपरि वर्णित परिस्थियों के आलोक में अध्ययन के औचित्य को पूर्णतः प्रतिपादित किया जा सकता है ताकि इस ज्वलंत समस्या से सम्बद्ध सभी पक्षों पर सांगोपांग विचार किया जा सके। समस्या से जुड़े बहुत सारे पहलुओं पर समीचीन विचार अपेक्षित है। यहा। नारी भ्रूण हत्या के विभिन्न कारणों पर विचार करना आवश्यक प्रतीत होता है—

1. दम्पति की भूमिका
2. चिकित्सक की भूमिका
3. सामाजिक दृष्टिकोण
4. सांस्कृतिक दृष्टिकोण
5. कानूनी दृष्टिकोण
6. शास्त्रीय दृष्टिकोण

दम्पति की भूमिका

पति एवं पत्नी गृहस्थाश्रम के दो सबल स्तम्भ हैं। सन्तानोत्पत्ति वैवाहिक जीवन का प्रथम दायित्व है। सन्तान की कमनीय कामना दम्पति का अभीष्ट होता है। सामान्यतया पुरुष प्रधान समाज होने के कारण पुरुष संतति की अपेक्षा होती है। अपने वारिस के रूप में पुत्र को प्राप्त कर दम्पति आह्लादित हो जाते हैं। पुत्र प्राप्ति के लिए लोग-बाग कई-कई शादियाँ तक कर डालते हैं। हालाँकि अब यह विचार बिल्कुल सीमित उदाहरणों में ही दृष्टिगत होता है। गर्भस्थ भ्रूण की जाँच आधुनिक चिकित्सा विज्ञान ने सुलभ कर दिया है ताकि स्वस्थ शिशु परिवार के लिए वरेण्य वरदान साबित हो सके। दम्पति के मन में पुत्र की इच्छा सर्वदा बनी रहती है। गर्भस्थ भ्रूण की लिंग जाँच के उपरान्त मादा भ्रूण स्थापना से वे विचलित हो जाते हैं। इस भ्रूण की हत्या के लिए वे चिकित्सक के पास पहुँच जाते हैं। यहाँ तक उल्लेख्य है कि यह दृष्टिकोण भी अब कुछ कम हो रहा है।

चिकित्सक की भूमिका

चिकित्सक पेशा सर्वथा उत्कृष्ट होता है जहाँ वह रोगी को मौत के मुँह से छीनने की सामर्थ्य रखता है। रोगी के हृदय में चिकित्सक के लिए अगाध श्रद्धा होती है। और वह उसको सर्वाधिक सम्मान देता है। चिकित्सक को वह अपनी व्यथा निवेदित करता है। चिकित्सक का कार्य जीवन की रक्षा करना है और वह चन्द पैसे के लिए प्रस्तावित भ्रूण की हत्या कर देता है।

सामाजिक दृष्टिकोण

पुरुष प्रधान समाज में स्त्री को अपेक्षाकृत कम महत्वपूर्ण माना जाता है। जिस परिवार में पुरुष संतति नहीं होती है उस परिवार को समाज में सशक्त एवं सबल नहीं माना जाता है। उस परिवार को विभिन्न प्रकार से अनेक अवसरों पर सताया जाता है और वह परिवार शोषित एवं अभिशप्त सामाजिक जीवन जीने को मजबूर हो जाता है। समाज में विभिन्न अवसरों पर पुरुष पात्र की ही तलाश होती है। समाज में पुरुष को श्रेष्ठ एवं सम्मानित स्थान प्राप्त है। वह खुद सुरक्षित माना जाता है और

दूसरे को सुरक्षा प्रदान करता है। विभिन्न सामाजिक एवं सांस्कृतिक अवसरों पर उसकी भूमिका मुख्य एवं महत्वपूर्ण होती है। पुरुष परिवार का कर्ता-धर्ता एवं पालक-पोषक है।

कानूनी दृष्टिकोण

अमिनोसिन्टेसिस जाँच के द्वारा गर्भस्थ भ्रूण के लिंग का पता लगाया जाता है। कानून इसकी इजाजत नहीं देता है। ऐसा करना कानूनी अपराध है और इसके लिए दम्पति सहित चिकित्सक के लिए भी दंड-विधान निर्धारित किया गया है। गर्भस्थ भ्रूण की हत्या 1972 के पहले एक कानूनी अपराध था। बाद में जनसंख्या विस्फोट के कारण इस प्रावधान को हटा दिया गया और स्वेच्छा से गर्भस्थ भ्रूण को विनष्ट किया जाने लगा। इधर जब स्त्री-पुरुष अनुपात में ह्रास हुआ और यह मामला शहर से संसद तक गूँजने लगा तो एक अधिनियम के तहत कन्या भ्रूण जाँच एवं हत्या को दंडनीय अपराध माना जाने लगा।

शास्त्रीय दृष्टिकोण

विहित-अविहित, कर्त्तव्य-अकर्त्तव्य, करणीय-अकरणीय, कार्य-अकार्य, आदेय एवं हेय का प्रमाण शास्त्र है। शास्त्र की शाब्दिक व्युत्पत्ति भी शासन या आदेश का वाचक है। हमारी संस्कृति में पुत्र के प्रति आग्रह का भाव रहा है। कन्या संतति की अपेक्षा पुरुष संतति की कामना जीवन का मूलोद्देश्य रहा है। एतद्विषयक ऐरतरेय ब्राह्म ा के मंत्रद्रष्टा ऋषियों के उद्गार उद्धरणीय हैं। यदि पिता उत्पन्न हुये जीवित पुत्र का मुख देख लेता है तो उस पर अपने सारे ऋण सौंप देता है और अमृतत्व को प्राप्त करता है।[4] प्राणियों के जितने भोग पृथ्वी में हैं, जितने अग्नि में हैं, जितने अग्नि में हैं, जितने जल में हैं, एक पिता के पुत्र में उससे कहीं अधिक है।[5] पिता लोग (अपने-अपने उत्पन्न हुए) पुत्र से बार-बार अत्यन्त (इहलोक और परलोक संबंधी) दुःखों को पार कर जाते हैं। क्योंकि पिता स्वयं ही पुत्र के रूप में उत्पन्न होता है। वह (पुत्र) समुद्र में नाव के समान (पार करानेवाला) है।[6] मल क्या है? अजिन क्या है? श्मश्रु (दाढ़ी मूँछ) क्या है और तप क्या है? हे ब्राह्मणो! पुत्र की इच्छा करो! वही अनिन्दनीय लोक है।[7]

उपर्युक्त उद्धरणों से यह बिल्कुल स्पष्ट है कि हमारे वेदादि ग्रंथों में पुत्र के प्रति असीम एवं अमिट कामना है। साथ ही साथ यह भी द्रष्टव्य है कि कन्या संतति को निंदनीय, कृपण एवं हेय माना गया है—"निश्चय ही अन्न ही प्राण है। वास (कर) शरण (रक्षक) है। हिरण्य (सुवर्णान्द) रूप का संवाहक हैं पशु (गौ आदि, व्यवहार का) निर्वाह करनेवाले हैं। जाया (पत्नी), सखा (मित्र) है। दुहिता (पुत्री) कृपण (दयनीय) हैं। पुत्र ही ज्योति (प्रकाशकारक है) जो पर ब्रह्म में लीन करा देता है।[8] इतना ही

नहीं शास्त्रकारों ने पुत्र प्राप्ति हेतु अगम्या को भी गम्य माना है–"सभी जानते हैं कि पुत्रहीन को लोक (का सुख) नहीं है।"[9] "यह मार्ग बड़े लोगों से प्रशंसित और सुखपूर्वक सेवन करने योग्य है।"[10]

उपर्युक्त उद्धरणों में हमने स्पष्ट रूप से देखा है कि पुत्र प्राप्ति की कामना वैदिक संस्कृति में कितनी प्रबल है। लगता है कि बहुत सारी नैतिक मान्यताओं की तिलांजलि दे दी गई है। अर्थात् साधन-साध्य संबंध पर सम्यक् विचार नहीं किया गया है। ऐसा लगता है कि येन-केन प्रकारेण पुत्र-प्राप्ति ही उनके जीवन का अभीष्ट रहा हैं आत्मा ही पुत्र रूप में उत्पन्न होता है और विवाह का प्रमुख उद्देश्य संतानोत्पति अर्थात् पुत्र प्राप्ति रहा है। ये सारी मान्यतायें समाज में आज भी किसी न किसी रूप में विद्यमान हैं। सामाजिक रूप से पुत्र पिता का उत्तराधिकारी होता है एवं स्वत्वाधिकारी होकर समाज में यश प्रतिष्ठा का अधिकारी होता है। वंशवृद्धि की परम्परा का प्रारम्भ पुत्र ही करता है। पितरों का पिण्ड पानी पुत्र ही प्रदान करता है। पुत्र के द्वारा पिता को यश, नाम एवं ख्याति होती है। पुत्र बुढ़ापे में पिता का सहारा होता है। पुत्र पिता एवं परिवार की रक्षा अपने बाहुबल से आपत्ति में करता है। अर्थात् पुत्र के प्रति अति पिता एवं परिवार की रक्षा अपने बाहुबल से आपत्ति विपत्ति में करता है।

पुत्र के प्रति अति आग्रह के दृष्टिकोण के कारण ही लोग-बाग पुत्र प्राप्ति के लिए कई-कई शादियाँ कर डालते हैं। पुत्र नहीं जनने वाली महिलाओं को समाज में कुछ अप्रतिष्ठा एवं कम सम्मान प्राप्त होता है। कहीं-कहीं तो पुत्रोत्पत्ति नहीं करने वाली स्त्रियाँ प्रताड़ना एवं दंड का भी शिकार होती हैं। उनके साथ अमानवीय, क्रूर एवं बर्बरतापूर्ण बर्ताव दृष्टिगत होता है। लड़की को जन्म देने वाली पत्नी पर जानलेवा हमला तक किया जा रहा है। यह है पुत्र प्राप्ति के प्रति अति आग्रह एवं कन्या संतति के प्रति घृणा, आक्रोश एवं प्राणलेवा हमला एवं तिरस्कार। एतद्विषयक दैनिक हिन्दुस्तान का उल्लिखित विचार औचित्यपूर्ण प्रतीत होता है–".......उड़ीसा में एक युवक ने अपनी पत्नी को मौत के घाट उतारने का प्रयास किया, क्योंकि पत्नी ने लड़की को जन्म दिया था। जैसे ही इस युवक को खबर मिली कि उसके घर दूसरी लड़की का आगमन हुआ है तो वह आग-बबूला हो गया और पत्नी को लहू-लुहान कर दिया। इस युवक ने पत्नी को जान से मारने की कोशिश की। सुधीर ने पत्नी की गर्दन, पेट और दूसरे अंगों पर धारदार हथियार से प्रहार किया"[11] कन्या संतति के प्रति वितृष्णा एवं घोर अत्याचार भाव इस उदाहरण में द्रष्टव्य है। कन्या संतति की अनिच्छा के कई बिन्दुओं को भी अंकित किया जा सकता है। बढ़ती तिलक-दहेज की समस्यायें, कन्या की शिक्षा-दीक्षा में बढ़ता खर्च एवं मनोवैज्ञानिक रूप से जब

तक लड़की के हाथ पीले नहीं होते तब तक परिवार की सुरक्षा में उसे रखना एवं सतत् ध्यान देना। संभवतः उन्हीं समस्याओं से मुक्ति के लिए कन्या भ्रूण हत्या सुलभ एवं सहज साधन बन गया है।

इन्हीं सारे कारणों से हम कन्या भ्रूण हत्या की ओर प्रेरित होते हैं। वैसे तो भ्रूण हत्या ही महापाप और घोर सामाजिक अपराध है। यहाँ हम भ्रूण हत्या से संबंधित शास्त्रीय मान्यताओं पर विचार करना चाहेंगे जहा। इसे निंदनीय एवं त्याज्य माना गया है–

शास्त्र में तो गर्भपात को ब्राह्मम हत्या से भी दुगुना पाप माना गया है।[12]

यत्पापं ब्रह्म हत्याया द्विगुणं गर्भपातने।
प्रायश्चित्तं न तस्यास्ति तस्यास्त्यागो विधीयते।।

गर्भपातिनी स्त्री सन्तान सुख वंचिता होती है। ब्रह्म हत्या से जो पाप लगता है उससे दुगुना पाप गर्भपात कराने से लगता है। इस गर्भपात रूपी महापाप का कोई प्रायश्चित भी नहीं है, इसमें तो उस स्त्री का त्याग कर देने का ही विधान है।

भ्रूणध्नावेक्षितं चैवं संस्पृष्टं चाप्युदक्यया।
पतत्रिणाऽवलीठं च शुना संस्पृष्टमेव च।।

गर्भ हत्या करने वाले का देखा हुआ, रजस्वला स्त्री का स्पर्श किया हुआ, पक्षी का खाया हुआ और कुत्ते का स्पर्श किया हुआ अन्न न खाये।[13]

पूर्वे जनुषि या नारी गर्भपात करि ह्यभूत्।
गर्भपातेन दुःखार्ता साऽत्र जन्मनि जायते।।

जो स्त्री पूर्व जन्म में गर्भपात करती है वह इस जन्म में भी गर्भपात का दुःख भोगने वाली होती है अर्थात् उसकी संतान नहीं होती।[14]

बन्धयेयं या महाभग पृच्छति स्वं प्रयोजनम्।
गर्भपातरतापूर्वे जनुष्यत्र फलं त्विदम्।।

जो कोई स्त्री पूछती है कि इस जन्म में बन्ध्या (संतानहीन) किस कारण हुई तो इसका उत्तर है कि यह पूर्व जन्म में तेरे द्वारा किये गये गर्भपात का ही फल है।[15]

गर्भपातनपापाठ्या बभूव प्राग्भवेऽडज।
साऽत्रैव तेन पापेन गर्भस्थैर्यं न विदन्ति।।

हे अरुण! जो पूर्व जन्म में गर्भपात करती है, इस जन्म में इस पाप के कारण उसका गर्भ नहीं ठहरता अर्थात् वह संतान हीन होती है।[16]

हम यह प्रतिपादित करना चाहते हैं कि हमारी सांस्कृतिक परम्परा में भ्रूण हत्या महापाप माना गया है। पाश्चात्य परम्परा में भी इसकी झलक मिलती है जहाँ सजा के रूप में सम्बद्ध महिला आजीवन गिरिजाघर में प्रवेश से वंचित कर दी जाती है।

विश्वस्तर पर देखा जाए तो भ्रूण हत्या विशेष कर नारी भ्रूण हत्या या कन्या हत्या हमारी चिंता का विषय है जिसका उदाहरण चीन जैसे देशों में भी 19वीं सदी में द्रष्टव्य है।[17] इसके पूर्व भी कन्या शिशु की हत्या मुगलकालीन आक्रमण के समय दृष्टिगत होती है जहाँ उच्च राजघरानों में यह कुप्रथा इसलिए प्रचलन में आई क्योंकि आक्रमणकारियों की बुरी नजर लड़कियों के प्रति थी।

परिवर्तित परिवेश में इस समस्या के समाधान हेतु बहुविध उपायों पर विचार करना होगा ताकि गर्भस्थ नारी भ्रूण की हत्या न हो पाय। भारतीय नीतिशास्त्र में कर्म का सिद्धान्त वर्णित है, जहाँ यह स्वीकार किया गया है, कि हम जैसा करेंगे वैसा भरेंगे। गीता भी स्पष्ट उद्घोष करती है कि हमें अपने शुभाशुभ कर्मों का फल अवश्यमेव भुगतना पड़ेगा। अतः जानबूझकर यह भ्रूण हत्या जो दम्पत्ति की सहमति से की जा रही है, सर्वथा अनैतिक और निन्दनीय है। "सर्वेषु शास्त्रेषु जीवहिंसा विगर्हिता" के आदर्श को चरितार्थ का मूल मंत्र है। जैन नीतिशास्त्र में पंचमहाव्रत का विस्तृत विवरण मिलता है। बौद्ध दार्शनिक इसे पंचशील की संज्ञा देते हैं योग दर्शन में यम की चर्चा करते हुए हिंसा के अभाव को ही अहिंसा कहा गया है।

"लोकाः समस्ता सुखिनो भवन्तु", प्राणियों में सद्भावना हो आदि सूत्रवाक्य सभी जीवों के प्रति सद्विचार, सद्व्यवहार एवं सदाचरण का संदेश देते हैं तो फिर मानव अपनी ही सन्तान की हत्या करे यह कहाँ तक औचित्यपूर्ण हो सकता है? इतना ही नहीं मानवेतर प्राणियों एवं सभी जीव-जंतुओं के प्रति भी दया, करुणा, प्रेम का भाव नीतिशास्त्रीय चिंतन एवं बार-बार आता है। पशु पक्षियों एवं अन्य जीव जंतुओं के पालक एवं पोषक के रूप में हमारी भूमिका सदा सर्वदा स्तुत्य एवं आदरणीय रही है। पर्यावरण संतुलन संरक्षण एवं संवर्द्धन की दृष्टि से वन्य जीवों की रक्षा सुरक्षादि के लिए विभिन्न तरह के दंड विधान बने हैं एवं उनका शिकार निषिद्ध किया गया है। मानव नीतिशास्त्र के अतिरिक्त हमारे यहाँ जीव नीतिशास्त्र की भी चर्चा की जाती है। ऐसी परिस्थिति में यह घिनौनी कुप्रथा का अंत अत्यावश्यक है, अन्यथा एक विकराल सामाजिक एवं राष्ट्रीय समस्या हमारे समक्ष खडी हो जायेगी। कन्या संतति की संख्या इस रफ्तार से घटती गयी तो एक ऐसी स्थिति भी पैदा हो सकती है जहाँ एक पत्नी के लिए कई पतियों का प्रावधान हो सकता है अर्थात् बहुपतीत्व की ओर हम शीघ्रता से अग्रसर हो रहे हैं। कुछ ऐसा ही चिंतन दृष्टिगत हो रहा है निदेशक मणीष झा की चर्चित फिल्म 'मातृभूमि-ए नेशन विदाउट वूमन' में। "फिल्म में एक ऐसी काल्पनिक समाज की कहानी दिखाई गई है जहाँ शिशु हत्याओं एवं भ्रूण हत्याओं की वजह से शादी के लिए लड़कियों की बेहद कमी हो जाती है और एक

परिवार के पाँच बेटों की शादी एक ही लड़की से कर दी जाती है।"[18] यह समस्या की गंभीरता का एक पूर्वाभास है जहाँ इसकी परिणति एक अव्यावहारिक, अनैतिक, अवैज्ञानिक एवं असभ्य निदान के रूप में हो रही है। अतः यह समय की माँग है कि बेटियाँ जन्में और जियें। इस दिशा में एक साहसिक समाधान प्रस्तुत करते हुए प्रसिद्ध समाजसेविका एवं लेखिका मृदुला सिन्हा ने कन्या संतति की रक्षा, पालन-पोषण एवं विभिन्न स्तरों पर उसके सशक्तिकरण की बात की है। इस दिशा में उन्होंने कुछ समाधानों को भी प्रस्तुत किया है जो वांछनीय, विचारणीय एवं अनुकरणीय हैं—"कन्या जन्म देने से भी आवश्यक है जन्मी बेटियों को जीने देना। व्रत त्योहारों से भरे समाज में एक और उत्सव प्रारम्भ करना चाहिए। कन्या-जन्मोत्सव। यही समय की माँग है। तभी कन्या का जन्म बोझ नहीं होगा। बेटा द्वारा मुखाग्नि मिलने पर ही स्वर्ग प्राप्ति होने की धारणा की जगह संतान द्वारा मुखाग्नि का प्रचार-प्रसार होना चाहिए। समाज द्वारा कन्या के जन्मने, स्वस्थ रहने, शिक्षित तथा सुरक्षित रहकर सम्मान पाने का एक नया व्रतोत्सव प्रारंभ करना चाहिए। तभी कन्या-पूजन की सार्थकता होगी।"[19]

माननीय लेखिका द्वारा प्रस्तुत सुझाव निश्चय ही इस जटिल एवं दुरूह समस्या के समाधान में एक सशक्त सोपान होगा। हमारे यहाँ शास्त्रों में भी कन्या पूजन या कुमारी पूजन का प्रावधान हैं नवरात्र के विशिष्ट अवसर पर कुआँरी कन्याओं को विधिवत् आमंत्रित कर उनकी पूजा-अर्चना कर उन्हें मिष्टान्न आदि सुस्वादु एवं पवित्र भोजन ससम्मान परोसकर तृप्त करने का विधान है एवं भोजनोपरांत उन्हें दक्षिणादि भी दी जाती है। लगता है लेखिका का प्रेरणापुंज यह शास्त्रीय प्रथा भी हो सकती है।

नर्स, चिकित्सक, रेडियोलॉजिस्ट आदि अन्य सहायक इस समस्या के समाधान में एक सकारात्मक एवं सार्थक भूमिका निभा सकते हैं, बशर्ते की वे स्वार्थपरता एवं संकीर्णता से ऊपर उठकर व्यापक राष्ट्रहित में सोचें। ऐसा सामान्यतया दृष्टिगत होता है कि येन-केन-प्रकारेण कुछ अर्थोपार्जन के लिए समस्त आदर्शों, सिद्धान्तों एवं मापदण्डों की बलि दी जाती है। यह युग की पुकार है कि सामान्य लाभ से बहुत ऊपर उठकर मानवता की रक्षा के लिए वे आगे आयें। यद्यपि पी0 एन0 डी0 टी0 ए0 एक्ट 1994 में गैरकानूनी ढंग से भ्रूण जाँच को दंडनीय अपराध माना गया है एवं इस कार्य में सम्मिलित होने वाले को प्रथम अपराध के लिए 3 वर्ष का कठोर कारावास, 10,000 रुपये का अर्थ दंड एवं द्वितीय अपराध के लिए उसे और कठोर बनाते हुए क्रमशः 5 वर्षों की सजा एवं 50,000 रुपये अर्थदंड का प्रावधान किया

है। चिकित्सकों के संबंध में भी निर्णय लिया गया है कि जो चिकित्सक इस कुकृत्य में शामिल होंगे उनका निबन्ध समाप्त किया जा सकता है। लेकिन कानून बनाना ओर फिर उसका अक्षरशः पालन होना दोनों दो चीजें हैं। अतः व्यापक मानवहित में राष्ट्रभक्ति की भावना से प्रेरित होकर उन्हें अपने उच्चादर्शों को असली जामा पहनाना चाहिए।

कठोर दंड विधान का प्रावधान

दंड विधान का प्रधान लक्ष्य है कि इससे डरकर अन्य व्यक्ति अपराध न करे और समाज में अपराध पर रोक लगे। अर्थात् इसकी पुनरावृत्ति नहीं हो। मैकेन्जी, अरस्तू, कांट और हीगेल जैसे विचारक निर्विवाद रूप से सहमत है कि अपराधी को दंड अवश्य मिलना चाहिए। ब्रैडले जैसे विचारक इस मत का समर्थन करते हुए स्पष्टतया कहते हैं कि हम दंड इसलिए भोगते हैं कि हम उसके योग्य हैं, किसी दूसरे कारण से नही। भ्रूण हत्या भी एक जघन्य अपराध है और इसे हत्या के दंड विधान के तहत रखकर कठोर दंड का प्रावधान करना चाहिए ताकि इस प्रकार के अपराध की पुनरावृत्ति नहीं हो। कठोर दंड विधान के भय से भी अपराध पर अंकुश लगाया जा सकता है। अतः पाश्चात्य एवं प्राच्य नीतिशास्त्रियों की अनुशंसा के आलेक में उक्त अपराध के लिए कठोरतम सजा का प्रावधान हो। इसाई धर्म में यह उल्लेख आया है कि जो महिला एक बार गर्भपात करा चुकी है उसे गिरिजाघर में प्रवेश से वंचित किया जा सके। सिक्ख धर्मावलबियों ने भी इसे अक्षम्य अपराध मानते हुए इसमें लिप्त व्यक्ति को तनखैया घोषित कर सामाजिक रूप से बहिष्कृत एवं दंडनीय माना है। काँचीपीठ के शंकराचार्य ने भी इसे वीभत्स कृत्य मानते हुए अक्षम्य अपराध की संज्ञा दी है। आशा है इस्लाम धर्मावलम्बी भी इसी समान विचारधारा में शिरकत करते हुए अगर फरमान जारी करें तो समस्या के समाधान की दिशा में एक सार्थक एवं महत्वपूर्ण कदम होगा।

उपर्युक्त पृष्ठों में हमने सविस्तार मीमांसा करते हुए कन्या भ्रूण हत्या की रोकथाम से संबंधित विभिन्न निवारणों पर चर्चा की है। कभी-कभी अवांछित सन्तान गर्भस्थ हो जाती है और फिर उससे मुक्ति का आसान उपाय भ्रूण हत्या ही होती है विशेषकर कन्या की। हमारे ज्योतिषीय ग्रंथों में इस बिन्दु पर विचार कर पुरुष/कन्या संतति प्राप्ति की ओर प्रेरित किया गया है अर्थात् गर्भाधान संस्कार द्वारा गर्भ में पुरुष भ्रूण स्थापित हो और पुनः पुंसवन आदि विभिन्न संस्कारों के द्वारा स्थापित गर्भ से पुत्र प्राप्ति ही काम्य होती है। गर्भाधान मुहूर्त के लिए नक्षत्र वार तिथि लग्नादि का सूक्ष्म विचार किया गया है—"रजोदर्शन के पश्चात् 16 दिनों के भीतर सम दिनों का गर्भाधान पुत्र-प्राप्तिप्रद और विषम दिनों का गर्भाधान कन्या प्राप्ति के लिए कहा गया

है। उसके पश्चात द्वितीय रजो दर्शन तक स्त्री प्रसंग अहेतुक अर्थात् काम तृप्त्यर्थ ही होता है। आधुनिक चिकित्सा पद्धतियों का भी यही मूल सिद्धान्त है"[20] पाश्चात्य प्रसिद्ध चिकित्सक डा0 ट्राल एम0 डी0 के विचार उल्लेखनीय हैं जिन्होंने भारतीय मत का स्पष्टतः समर्थन करते हुए लिखा है–"बहुतायत से साक्षियाँ इस बात की मिलती हैं कि पहले दिनों में गर्भाधान करने से लड़कियाँ और पिछले दिनों में गर्भाधान करने से लड़के होते हैं (पृष्ठ 325)

इस प्रकार हम देखते हैं कि पति-पत्नी में से जो अधिक बलवान होगा उसके अनुसार पुत्र या पुत्री होगी–यह मनुस्मृति का विचार डॉ0 ट्राल के इस विचार से मिलता है कि यदि पुरुष आयु और बल में स्त्री से अधिक है तो सन्तान अधिकतर नर होगी।[21] अन्य संस्कृतियों में भी मनचाही संतान के प्रति आकर्षण भाव रहा ह और इसकी प्राप्ति के विभिन्न विधियों की चर्चा की गई है। "सही समय पर गर्भधारण कर पाईये मनचाही संतान' हाँगकांग। अब मनचाही संतान के लिए न दवा और न दुआ की जरूरत होगी, बल्कि इसे गर्भाधान के सही समय का इस्तेमाल करके हासिल किया जा सकेगा। हाँगकांग के एक व्यापारी ने अपने अनुभव और मामूली परीक्षण करे मनचाही संतान के लिए सही समय बताने का दावा किया है। उसका तकनीक इस तथ्य पर आधारित है कि मानव शरीर साईकिल के हिसाब से काम करता है। चिकित्सा जगत् के विशेषज्ञों ने कुछ संशय के साथ इस तकनीक का स्वागत किया है।"[22] चीन में भी चिकीर्षित सन्तान की प्राप्ति हेतु एक दुर्लभ तालिका की चर्चा की जाती है जिसका परिणाम सर्वाधिक सत्य एवं कसौटी पर खरा उतरा है। "लगभग एक सौ वर्ष पूर्व चीनी वैज्ञानिकों को बीजिंग के पास एक शाही कब्र में एक तालिका मिली थी। इच्छित सन्तान के ज्ञान में यह पर्याप्त उपयोगी हो सकती है। तालिका का एक स्तम्भ-बाँये से दाँये स्त्री की उम्र तथा दूसरा स्तम्भ-ऊपर से नीचे-गर्भाधान का माह प्रदर्शित करता है, इसी प्रकार चिन्ह 'X' पुत्र का तथा चिन्ह 'O' पुत्री का संकेत करता ह। उदाहरणार्थ यदि स्त्री की आयु 26 वर्ष है और गर्भाधान जनवरी माह में हुआ है तो सन्तान कन्या होगी। तालिका की मूल प्रति बीजिंग के पास एक वैज्ञानिक संस्थान में सुरक्षित है। इससे प्राप्त निष्कर्ष 99 प्रतिशत सही सिद्ध हुए हैं"[23]

कन्या भ्रूण हत्या के निवारण हेतु विभिनन पक्षों पर विमर्शोपरांत यह निर्विवाद रूप से प्रतिपादित किया जा सकता है कि यद्यपि मनोभिलषित संतान प्राप्ति के बहुत सारे समाधान भी प्रस्तुत किये गये हैं। तात्पर्य यह है कि अवांच्छित संतति गर्भस्थ नहीं हो सके ऐसी सावधानी अवश्यमेव बरतनी चाहिए। अपेक्षित कन्या

संतति अगर गर्भस्थ हो जाती है तो इसके भ्रूण की हत्या अनैतिक, अधार्मिक, अमानवीय एवं एक गैरकानूनी कदम है। इस अपराध में संलग्न पक्षों को कठोरतम दंड देना चाहिए। इस दिशा में सरकार, स्वयंसेवी संगठन, नेतागण, संचार माध्यम एवं धार्मिक प्रवचनकर्ताओं की महती भूमिका को इन्कार नहीं किया जा सकता है। इसके लिए जनजागरण/जनांदोलन की जरूरत है। हरित क्रांति, श्वेतक्रांति की तरह ही इसके लिए विचारक्रोंति की आवश्यकता है। कानून के प्रति जब तक श्रद्धा-सम्मान का भाव पैदा नहीं होगा इस प्रकार के उच्चादर्शों को साकार करना संभव नहीं होगा। संसद में स्वास्थ्य मंत्री डा0 रामदास ने स्पष्टतः स्वीकार किया कि जब तक समाज में जागरुकता नहीं आयेगी मात्र नियम निर्माण से उक्त समस्या का समाधान संभव नहीं है। ...."उन्होंने स्वीकार किया कि इस समस्या को हल करने के लिए कानून बनाना ही काफी नहीं है, क्योंकि इसकी जड़ें पूर्वाग्रहों से ग्रसित धारणाओं में समाई हुई हैं इसलिए प्रसव पूर्व लिंग निर्धारण और भ्रूण हत्या के विरुद्ध जागरुकता पैदा करने के लिए आकाशवाणी, दूरदर्शन और मीडिया के माध्यम से अनेक प्रयास किए गए हैं।"[24]

अतः यह उल्लेख करना अप्रासंगिक नहीं होगा कि इन सभी प्रावधानों का वास्तविक कार्यान्वयन तभी संभव है, जब लोगों में विशेष रूप से संबंधित पक्षों में इन भावनाओं एवं आदर्शों के प्रति समग्रतावादी दृष्टिकोण का विकास हो और इसके लिए शिक्षा की महत्वपूर्ण भूमिा दृष्टिगत होती है। जनजागरण में वस्तुतः शिक्षा का अमूल्य योगदान है। इसलिए नारी सशक्तिकरण और विशेष रूप से कन्या भ्रूण हत्या के विभिन्न पक्षों के लोगों में इसका प्रचार और प्रसार होना चाहिए। सभी में अपने अधिकार और कर्तव्य के पालन के लिए एक निष्ठा होनी चाहिए। इस आलोक में ऐसी आशा की जा सकती है कि इस सामाजिक व्याधि का बहुत कुछ निराकरण हो सकता है। हमें अपनी प्राचीन भारतीय अध्यात्मवादी पृष्ठभूमि को सतत् स्मरण रखने की आवश्यकता है। इससे भी इस दिशा में हम सब का कार्य सरल हो सकता है।

संदर्भ

1. "There are so many boys in our village who are forced to remain unmarried because they do not have a soster to exchange in teh wedding. They are left with no option but to buy a wife."
—Times of India, Patna, Thursday, July 8, 2004.
2. मनुस्मृति, अध्याय-3, श्लोक-55.
3. "Every human being, regardless of sex, has the right to fulfilment of basic needs, to self determination.......... Quoted from

Vivekananda's feminism in the light of some modern feminist Therories." —Sunil K. Sengupta, The Vedanta Kesari, April 1997, Volume 84, Shri Ramkrishna Math, Mylapore Chennai 6004, India.

4. ऐतरेय ब्राह्मण, अध्याय 33 खण्ड-1, मंत्र-3.
5. वही मंत्र-4.
6. वही मंत्र-5.
7. वही मंत्र-6.
8. वही मंत्र-7.
9. वही मंत्र-11.
10. वही मंत्र-13.
11. हिन्दुस्तान, मुजफ्फरपुर/पटना, गुरुवार 5 मई, 2003. पृष्ठ-10.
12. पराशर स्मृति 4/20.
13. मनुस्मृति 4/208.
14. बृद्धसूर्यारुणकर्मविपाक 477/1.
15. वही, 659/1, 856/1, 921/11, 697/1.
16. वही, 1187/1.
17. "But the principal means of meeting the problem was infanticide specially of girls.....In fact, the killing of baby girls remained a nineteenth century practice".

    —"Encyclopedia of Bioethics, Warren T. Rech, Editor in Chief, George Town University, Complete and Unbridged Edition, 1982, p. 58-61.
18. हिन्दुस्तान, मुजफ्फरपुर/पटना, गुरुवार 5 मई, 2003, पृष्ठ-10.
19. हिन्दुस्तान, मुजफ्फरपुर/पटना, 27 अक्टूबर, 2004, अंगना विशेषांक, पृष्ठ-1.
20. दैवज्ञ श्री रामाचार्य विरचितः मूहूर्त चिन्तामणिः व्याख्याकार केशरपत जोशी, मोतीलाल बनारसीदास, वाराणसी 1992, पृष्ठ-230.
21. व्याख्याकार विद्यामर्तण्ड डा0 सत्यव्रत सिद्धात अलंकार, संस्कार-चन्द्रिकट, नई दिल्ली, संशोधित संस्करण, 2000 ई0, पृष्ठ-113-114.
22. हिन्दुस्तान, पटना, सोमवार 18 अक्टूबर, 2004, पृष्ठ-16.
23. व्याख्याकार विद्यामर्तण्ड डा0 सत्यव्रत सिद्धात अलंकार, संस्कार-चन्द्रिकट, नई दिल्ली, संशोधित संस्करण, 2000 ई0, पृष्ठ-496-497.
24. हिन्दुस्तान, मुजफ्फरपुर/पटना, बुधवार 4 मई, 2005, पृष्ठ-12.

Chapter 22

Gender Discrimination: A Stigma on Indian Society

Nirmala Kumari Jha

Ever since the dawn of independence of our country, women's liberation movement has rapidly been expanded and intensified. It has been mainly focused on the acquisition of a few basic political and social rights, such as the equal right to property, justice, marriage, divorce, liberty and so on. Earlier, the slogan was the upliftment of women, which is presently known as empowerment of women. The terminology has changed, but the ethos has not. If we go some steps backward, we may notice 23rd October as 'Mahila Diwas' in the name of the birthday of Rani Chenamma of South India. 13th February is also marked as National Women's Day in the name of the birthday of Sarojini Naidu well known as Bharat-Kokila, on the recommendation of 'Akhil Bhartiya Mahila Parishad'. History says that 8th March is the symbol of the struggle of women. It was on the 8th March 1857 when the women labourers of a cloth mill of New York took procession for the first time to fix working hours upto the limit of 10 hours while it was 15-16 hours earlier. Though the procession was not so much successful yet it was proved just like a seed in the history of women's liberation. In England, Stuart Mill delivered a lecture in the House of Commons for Women's franchise first time in 1869 and as a result only the tax payer women got the right to vote for Municipal Corporation immediately and in parliament in 1918. As the conference of socialist women took place firstly on 8th March 1910, it was declared as "Women's Day" and the present situation of its culmination is in front of us.

I often come across a very pertinent question; why is there 'Women's Day'? While never heard of 'Men's Day'. And after a series of analysis and deep thinking, I came to the conclusion that the question of upliftment or empowerment has always been raised with regard to the weaker and neglected section of society. When men are already tremendously capable to shape the society as they like, in the patriarchal system, they do not need such type of sympathy from any section of the society. We can say that in our male dominated society, they are already empowered.

In our society, we all live with beliefs and attitudes that women are inferior in status. Some of these are not heard to discover, such as discrimination in male and female child, unequal pay for equal work and the traditional division of labour within the family. "Other attitudes are more subtle: for example, hoping that a couple's first child will be a boy, thinking of a wife's salary as going to buy "extras" rather than as supporting the family".[1]

The traditional middle class families live with a belief to have a male child as more auspicious. Parents are not happy to have a first female child. They are treated just like a burden. The right to life of an unborn female child is a question in many minds. Sex-selective abortions, though legally banned, are in practice even these days. Female foeticide is one of the most dangerous practices in today's civilized society. Preference of a gender foetus can be proved by the census figures of sex ratio. Not are far off the days, gender imbalance will take place and the history will repeat itself in the form of the Mahabharat period (Draupadi was married with five brothers). We may rejoice to celebrate women's day with great pomp and show, still we are no more reasonable from medieval fanatics who seek to hide their excesses against women under the cloak of tradition and superstition. But when a vibrant democracy committed to upholding legal safeguards for all its citizens looks away while these are constantly undermined, there is cause for alarm. Report (United Nations Population Fund) brings out the fact that there is sharp decline in the sex ratio particularly in the northern states of India due to selective sex abortions. The worrying factor is that this is far stronger in urban areas than in rural areas and among literate rather than illiterate women. Obviously economic considerations are no longer the main cause of son's is preference. "A study in Punjab shows that religious and social factors count far more in sex selection. In business families, the son is the natural heir and also the custodian of religious rites".[2]

One may come across the vivid examples of gender discrimination in our society here and there. From the very beginning of childhood, girl child is treated differently. They are given dolls and kitchen-sets to play with. Moreover, they are encouraged to play in-door games. Girls mostly in lower middle class families are discriminated in comparison to boys in providing primary school education. They are forced to drop their education before high school. Though there may be many causes such as economical, social etc. behind this but one of the most markable cause is the forced marriages at a tender age. Situation of girl child is more pitiable particularly in lower class people both in the urban and rural areas. The truth is that they are meant only for household works. We should not hesitate in accepting the fact that these girls are deprived of even primary school education.

Even the picture of the higher middle class families is not very bright. Though they are imparted education and other facilities in accordance with their parent's income, but they are still considered as second grade citizen. They are treated just like creepers seeking support from their male counterparts rather than deep-rooted and strong trees. Unfortunately, most women, even working women, are expected to look towards the male for the simplest of outside jobs. They are provided education not in a true sense. Only going through the formal academic process is not a complete education. We forget the fact that if we educate a man, we educate an individual but if we educate a woman, we educate the whole family. Women, in contrast, are from birth expected to play no role in the decision-making. They are considered as lower developed mind. In our male dominated patriarchal society, women are seldom given the opportunity to show their abilities so that they can evolve into an emotionally mature person. They are not ready to accept the fact that their daughters or sisters or wives are quite capable of taking rational decisions.

Every year there is a substantial increase in the number of dowry deaths. Women become victims of torture because of unceasing dowry demand by their in-laws and husbands. No body has come across the single instance of groom's death, whereas the word evokes memories of the innumerable incidents of bride's death. Dowry has come to be a status symbol, which has acquired the meaning of a business transaction. Girls are subjected to physical torture. Moreover, the greedy dowry seekers poison or burn the brides for bringing more dowry. At times many girls have been compelled to commit suicide. Various laws formulated so far to check the evil of dowry have failed to achieve the desired results. Now, dowry deaths are tried as murder and if proved, punishments are accorded accordingly. But there is need for social awareness among the people.

We often come across the instances of gender discrimination even in the field of employment. Women have been refused to get jobs in many fields duc to physiological and biological reasons; i.e., they are not given equal opportunity. I do mean here to say that from the very beginning, they are deprived of equal opportunity both in the field of education and occupation. They get less remuneration for equal work in comparison to their male counterparts. Theoretical slogan of 'Equal pay for equal work' is often kept in the official records.

In our patriarchal system of society, daughters are not made heirs of their father's property. The discrimination with regard to inheritance is already there. They are not given equal share in paternal property. Even the widows are not liable to such facility. Widows having no child face more miseries. They are treated like waste papers meant for throwing in the dustbin. While widowers in the same society enjoy all facilities of life. Though the courts have been given full power to grant maintenance to women in the case of separation and divorce nut the actual position is known to all of us. In most of cases, women have to face trial for such legal facility.

Though the Indian constitution protects the rights of women giving them parity with their male counterparts without discrimination of sex, but in practice they are deprived of equal opportunity. Right to employment, right to life and personal liberty, educational right, right to marriage and property and so on, are provided in the Indian constitution, but these cannot serve our practical purposes so long as social awareness among the people does not take place.

It is harsh reality that the illiterate mass is unaware of its rights. And if illiterate women are ignorant of their rights, the law itself becomes handicapped. Personal laws, Uniform Civil Codes, Human Rights Commission, *Mahila Ayog* all become farce for want of awareness. So, to educate the illiterate mass through radio, television, street plays, schools, etc. must be the first step, otherwise the ordeal of discrimination will be unending.

References

1. English Jame, *Feminism, Introduction*, p. 2, Published by Rowman and Littlefield, Totown, New Jersey.
2. *The Times of India*, Editorial, No. 158, Vol. XVI, Dated 6th November, 2001.

Chapter 23

The Status of Women in India and the Role of Education

B.V.S. Bhanusree

Swami Vivekananda clearly and rightly pointed out that no society can progress with men alone getting education and opportunities and women being neglected. The prominent modern leaders like Gandhiji and Nehruji believed that if a woman is educated the whole family is educated. Infact, any sensible person never doubts whether women are needed to be educated or not.

The personality and the real status of a woman reflect the amount and the kind of education she received. While rolling back to the Vedic times, one can find the position of women was analogous to what it usually is in early civilized societies. They enjoyed freedom and equality at every aspect of life. Girls were educated like boys and had to pass through a period of Brahmacharya. They also had undergone the sacred thread ceremony (upanayana) along with boys. There were two categories of women in Vedic age, namely the 'Brahmavadins' and 'Sadyovadhus', "the Brahmavadins were entitled to the initiation ceremony (upanayana). They used to tend the holy fires, study the Vedas and beg alms in their homes. The sadyovadhus were given away in marriage after a brisk ceremony of investiture with the holy thread".[1]

The learned men and women could sit together and discuss various matters. As the education of that time aimed at all round development, women were also found truly intellectuals, with good characters and highly cultured Gargi and Maitreyi[2] were said to be the leading philosophers of the time. Many of them used to become distinguished poetesses, and the poems of some of them have been honored by their inclusion in the canonical literature.

There was no seclusion of women; they used to move freely in society, often even in the company of their lovers. Marriages took place according to their choice, usually at a fairly advanced age of 16 or 17. Educated brides of this ate had naturally an effective voice in the selection of their partners in life. In social and religious gatherings they occupied prominent position. Women had an absolute equality with men in the eye of religion; they could perform sacrifices independently and were not regarded as an impediment in religious pursuits. Seeta yajna, Rudrabali and Rudrayaga were exclusively performed by women. The ideal marriage of the Vedic period was a religious sacrament which made the couple joint owners of the household. The widow could if she liked contract another marriage either regularly or under the custom of niyoga.

There was a gradual change in the position of women during the age of the later Samhitas, Brahmanas and Upanishads. In the rich and cultured families there was not much change in their status. But, the system of sending out girls to famous teachers or centers of education came to be discouraged; only near relatives like father, brother or uncle were allowed to teach them at home. As a result, there arose a tendency to curtail the religious rights and privileges of the average women; many functions in the sacrifice which formerly could be performed by the wife alone now came to be assigned to male substitutes. Women used to perform them whenever their husbands were out or they were otherwise preoccupied.

The marriage-age of the bride continued to be about 16 in practice, if not in theory , brides had some voice in the selection of their spouses in life and 'Swayamvara' was fairly common in Kshatriya circles. The marriage ideals and the mutual relations and of the parties continued to be more or less the same as they were in the earlier age. Divorce was permitted to the wife, though the permission was not extensively availed of. Widow had the option of remarriage either with her brother-in-law or with an outsider. But women had ceased to attend public meetings.

Her status as a housewife was raised and maintained well. Without the wife by his side no religious function was performed.

They believed that no oblations offered by the unmarried were accepted by God and maidens and bachelors had no admission to heaven. Another factor is that the Vedic chiefs were anxious to have heroic progeny for the reason that "the non Aryans were probably out-numbering the Aryans and they were anxious to have as strong and numerous an army as far as possible". [3]

During the period between 500 BC and 500 AD, i.e. the age of the sutras, the Epics and the early Smritis, the position of women deteriorated considerably. They suffered as Altekar observes, not merely because they ceased to be productive members of the society. A great calamity awaited them from the presence of sudra woman".[4] When the two races, i.e., Aryans and the indigenous population proceeded to live together peacefully, inter-marriages became inevitable.[5] The non-Aryan wife with her ignorance of Sanskrit language and Hindu religion could obviously not enjoy the same religious privileges as the Aryan consort. Very often the non-Aryan wife may have been the favorite one of her husband, who may have often attempted to associate her with his religious sacrifices in performance to her better educated but less loved Aryan wife. This must have naturally led to grave mistakes and anomalies in the performance of the ritual, which have shocked orthodox priests. They were baffled and thought that she may be a suitable partner in her husband's pleasures but not in religious rituals. But, a mighty king, mad with love for his non-Aryan beloved, who was not to be dictated to by a priesthood dependent upon him for its subsistence. He insisted upon his loving wife to be by his side. In such a condition, eventually it was felt that the object could be gained by declaring the whole class of women to be ineligible for Vedic studies and religious duties. [6]

On the other hand, the growing complexities of the Vedic sacrifices were another factor that tended to make the wife's association in religious rituals a more and more formal affair in course of time. Even the slightest mistake in its performance of in the recreation of its hymns and formula was regarded as fraught with very grave consequences. It required a long training to get the necessary capacity to follow intelligently the minute details of the complicated sacrifice and the average women had not so much time to devote for the purpose. Instead, the Aryans preferred to have early marriages.[7] Owing to different causes at the beginning of this period (c. 500 BC) there arose a tendency to lower the marriageable age of girls, and a consequence to discourage their upanayana and education. Gradually, upanayana has become a formality in the case of girls. At about 200 A.D. it was felt that this meaningless practice should be replaced with the marriage. Towards the end of this period (500 AD) parents could not keep their daughters unmarried after the age of 12.

The discontinuance of upanayana, the neglect of education, and the lowering of the marriage age produced disastrous consequences upon the position and status of women. Early marriage put an effective impediment in the higher education of girls. Brides being too young and inexperienced ceased to have any effective voice in the settlement of their marriages. Love marriages were gradually faded out. Wives with no education and maturity worth the name, naturally could not command respect from their husbands. The matches arranged under such circumstances were often ill-suited and women were often compelled to spend their lives with unsuitable or unworthy partners. Gradually, marriage became an irrevocable union-only so far as the wife was concerned. "This differential treatment" as Altekar observed "was due to the simple fact that women were no longer able to effectively oppose these absurd theories and claims, most of them being uneducated and quite ignorant of their former status and privileges".[8] Purdah system was gradually introduced in the royal families.

The period of 500 years between 200 BC and 300AD was a very dark and dismal one for Northern India. Greeks, Scythians, Parthians, Kushans etc. invaded the futile plains of the Punjab and Gangetic valley one after the other. Political reverses, war atrocities and the decline of population and propriety naturally produced a wave of despondency in society[9] and facilitated the spread of ideal of renunciation. The widow was forced to follow renunciation. She ought to aim at the higher ideal of salvation and not at the lower one of heaven. This is only in the case of the widow, widower was allowed to remarry immediately after the death of his wife.

Practice of sati was revived and more enlogised as an ideal. Consequently, women voluntarily started following sati. They were forced to believe that this is the way to show their boundless spirit of self-sacrifice and love for their husbands.[10]

A school of rationalists opposed the custom vehemently, pointing out its utter futility and stupidity. Consequently, the only direction in which the position of women improved in this period was in the sphere of proprietary rights.[11] By 1200 AD this right was recognized eventually all over the country. Nevertheless, due to the ignorance of girls and lack of education the widow had to undergo the tonsure. By about the 8th c A.D. with the disappearance of Buddhism at this time, the prejudice against the custom gradually disappeared and it was recommended to the widow as a kind of help and protection to her in her ascetic resolve and life. The remodeled pauranic literature was a bit solace as it enunciated the principles of Hinduism in a homely, easy and attractive manner, illustrating them with a number of edifying stories.[12]

After 14th century Bhakti movement brought considerable change in the status of women. Bhakti implies a pure, deep and sincere love for God. No rituals and no mediators are required to unite men with God. Both men and women had the inalienable right to strife for the ultimate goal through deepest love for God. The attitude of the saints of Bhakti movement towards women was not much different. Though they did not object the marital life, they felt that attachment with women may be a great hindrance for the attainment of the highest goal. On the contrary, Mirabai refused to have marital life and gently rejected her husband and walked away royally on her path.[13] No saint was permitted to take sannyasa without the consent of his wife. Besides, if the wife after giving her consent expressed desire to accompany the husband in his new life, she had a right to do so.

All the above saga clearly shows that the changes and fluctuations took place according to the circumstances. Change is natural and essential.[14] One has to understand and to shape the future. As Altekar pointed out, "Hindu society will have to remove a number of cobwebs in its ancient house and change and even revolutionalise some of its customs and institutions in order to accord the proper place which justly belongs to women".[15] It is understood that women began to loose all along the line the moment their education began to be neglected. Having realized that fact the female education should be designed in such a way that it should be a course specially intended for women, calculated to promote a harmonious development of their reason and emotions, enabling them at the same time to become earning members of the family either as part-time or whole time workers in the case of need.

Today with all the doors of her mind opened, the Indian woman is expanding herself into the world of knowledge. She is no longer subservient to man. Gradually, she is tearing the purdah, which imprisoned her body and mind for ages, to pieces and burning the fragments.

Change is native to the land. We should invite the change without loosing the spirit of our culture and respect to our tradition. Now a days, there is no field in which a women cannot enter into. A modern and educated woman proved herself in managing her domestic affairs efficiently, even in times of stress and difficulties. It has been realized all over the world that check on unwanted population growth is a by-product of spread of education. The responsibility of an educated woman is tremendous in this context.

Still a large number of women are not educated in India. They remained only at literacy level. Most of the women are satisfied with only obtaining degrees. They are not able to develop a type of modern mind in a true sense-power of thinking of discrimination, of love, and compassion and dedication to human welfare. She has to realize that the real education is to develop an integrated personality. Education is not simply learning alphabets, repeating and reproducing the matters from the textbooks, and getting degree after degree. The purpose of education is not simply to get good life-partners. It is the study of life, expanding one's own self. It gives us confidence, courage and inner strength. It is the responsibility of the parents, teachers, the society and the government to take care of girls' education. An educated woman should inspire the society with her high thinking, decent behavior and noble and integrated personality.

References

1. K.N. Misra, *Women, Education and the Upanishadic System of Education*, Church Publications, Allahabad, 1993, p. 34.
2. Several female seers named *Ghora, Anbhrnivak, Visvavara, Romasa, Lopamudra, Apala* etc., were there.
3. Dr. A.S. Altekar, *Women in Hindu Civilization*, Motilal Banarsidas, Delhi, 1962, p. 342.

4. *Ibid.,* p. 344.
5. In the concluding half of the later Samhita period (1000 BC to 500 BC) the marriages of Aryan men with non-Aryan women were becoming common. It is important to note that the early Dharmasastra writers have no objection to an Aryan marrying a sudra woman. Provided he had another Aryan wife, it is only later writers who proceed to interdict such a procedure with a great vehemence. *Ibid.*, p. 345.
6. It is Aitisayana who is seen advocating this view by about 200 BC. It is however almost certain that he is merely a typical representative of a powerful school reaching back to a fairly great antiquity. It is not impossible that his school reaching back to a fairly great antiquity. It is not impossible that his school may be as old as 500 BC if not even earlier.
7. The Aryans had settled down in a rich and prosperous country and their political supremacy had become unquestioned. Naturally, they took to an easy and luxurious life and the marriageable age of boys and girls began to be lowered. In the Rigvedic age the father was anxious to have strong and numerous sons more for secular than for religious purposes. In the days of the later samhitas the son became a religious rather than a secular necessity. A man comes to this world saddled with a three-fold dept; the most important on of these was the debt to the manes which could be liquidated only by the birth of a son. Why then not marry as soon as she attains maturity and is in a position to present a son to her husband?
8. A.S. Altekar, *Women in Hindu Civilization*, p. 349.
9. Whenever there is social insecurity women's freedom becomes curtailed. Whenever there is violence and increase of crime in society women's freedom becomes imperiled. Swami Ranganathananda, *Women in the Modern Age*, Bharatiya Vidyabhavan, India, 1991, p. 26.
10. The widow in the care was persuaded to believe that her act of self-immolation was even more auspicious than the nuptial ceremony since it guaranteed the continual association with her husband in life after death. B.M. Sharma: Women and Education, Commonwealth Publishers, New Delhi, 1994, p. 192.
11. When the niyoga and widow remarriages were prohibited, society had to devise an honourable means to enable the widow maintain herself. The childless widow can stay separate from joint family and enjoy the husband's share of her life estate. As Altedar, *Women in Hindu Civilization*, p. 352.

12. The saints bore no ill will to woman as a person, for according to them, like man she is also creature of God, *Barthwal* from B.M. Sharma, *Women and Education*, p. 207.
13. The Smriti and Puranic ideal contemplated that they could secure Moksha only if they, as subservient wives (Pativrata) obeyed and ideally served their husbands. Now in contrast to this even a prostitute or a deserted woman could attain salvation through pure devotion to God, *Ibid.*, p. 207.
14. Even orthodox Smriti writers like Manu have recognised that a time might come when their rules would become obsolete, and have therefore declared that if any rule framed by them are found to be conducive to the welfare of the society, or against the spirit of the age, they should be unhesitantly abrogated or modified. Altekar, *Women in Hindu Civilization*, p. 368.
15. *Ibid.*, p. 361.

Chapter 24

Contribution of Sister Nivedita in Empowering the Women of Modern India

Rashmi Rekha

Miss Margaret Elizabeth Nobel, popularly known as Sister Nivedita, carved out a unique place for herself in the history of modern India. Although she was a foreigner, yet she lived, worked and died for the betterment of Indians. Her dedication and commitment to the cause of deprived Indians is unparalleled. She devoted her life energy to revitalize every aspect of Indian life, especially, education of women which was almost non existent then.

Nivedita had realised that male dominated Indian society had turned oppressor to their better halves due to their own ignorance and lack of proper education. Lack of education amongst women was more responsible for the deplorable condition of women as they themselves were not aware of their inherent power and potential. Lack of education meant lack of self-reliance and self-confidence. As a consequence, women were not able to even recognise their problems as problems, what to talk of overcoming them. She firmly believed that the Indian society as a whole has fallen in the trap of ignorance and are unable to realise their sufferings, leave alone planning for or making any efforts in the direction of ameliorating their sufferings. Women suffered more than men because of their precarious situation in the family as well as the society. So, she used education as a tool to empower the Indian society for ameliorating their social and economic problems. Her understanding of the social traditions and culture of India led her to believe that imparting education to a man means educating an individual only, while imparting education to a woman results in educating atleast a family, if not the society. Therefore, she focussed her attention more on the education of women.

For Sister Nivedita, empowerment of women meant development of skills and abilities in women which help them decide upon and to undertake actions which they believed were essential for their well being. To achieve this purpose, she stressed on the essentiality of 'Education'. She considered education that instruction or training by which women would learn to develop their power of thought, feeling and will as well as moral and physical power, thereby making their life more and more valuable and worthwhile to themselves and to society at large. Inspired by the spiritual radiance of her master Swami Vivekananda and guided by her own conscience and understanding of the Indian society Sister Nivedita moved to India in the year 1898 and started her campaign for education of women without wasting any time.

Nivedita did not want to follow any stereotyped method of work as one size does not fit all. First of all she wanted to study the enviroment, in which she had to work in this country, properly and then evolve an educational method that would be qualitatively true and universally applicable to the task of modern education for Indian women. After doing the spade work very meticulously, she organised a meeting at Balaram Bose's house on November 12, regarding the opening of a school. The very next day the school was inaugurated at 16 Bosepara lane, Baghbazar. Coincidently, it was the auspicious Kali Puja day also. It was indeed a red letter day in the history of Calcutta as it marked the beginning of a series of philanthropic, particularly, educational activities to be under taken by Sister Nivedita in years to come. Nivedita's vision about her school was clear. She wanted to use this institution of hers as a laboratory to demonstrate practically the ideas and ideals of women's education as propounded by Swami Vivekananda.

On that auspicious day, Sri Sarda Devi also came to grace the occasion and performed the opening ceremony herself. She, after opening the school, blessed it by saying, "I pray that the blessings of the Divine Mother may be upon the school and the girls, and the girls trained from the school may become ideal girls." Humbled by the blessings of Sri Sarada Devi and her keen desire educate women, Nivedita wrote thus, "I cannot imagine a grander omen than her blessing spoken over the educated hindu womanhood of the future."[1] Many members of the Ramakrishna Order were present on this auspicious occasion. It was not merely a school for girls, it was the humble beginning of a silent movement in the history of Indian education, particularly of women.

During these days Nivedita had to work in an extremely conservative society. The parents were not at all ready to educate their daughters. So, Nivedita had to walk from door to door to enlist her students. She used to teach the girls students History, Geography, Natural Sciences and a little bit of English. She would also teach them sewing, drawing and handicrafts. She also encouraged them to take up physical exercise because health and fitness is essential for realising one's full potential in life.

Vivekananda was very impressed by the attitude of renunciation and service exhibited by Sister Nivedita. He was also extremely appreciative of the efforts made by Nivedita in the field of women education. He always wanted the upliftment of women as it could easily be used as the stepping stone for the awakening of the masses. He used to say, "Educate your women first and leave them to themselves: then they will tell you what reforms are necessary for them". He had no hesitation in accepting that family or country, where there is no proper estimation of women or where they live in sadness, has no hope of rise, progress and prosperity. For this reason, he always advocated that they (women) have to be raised first and an ideal Math needs to be started for them. Vivekananda's dream of a Math for women was difficult to be fulfilled. Nivedita's small school came as an oasis in the desert for Swami Vivekananda and brought hope to him for the success of his dream of a Math. Knowing Sister Nivedita's capabilities and commitment, Swamiji was confident that her school would be successful, but at the same time he was also aware of the economic difficulty likely to come in the way of her persuit. The school had started with Nivedita's own savings and a small sum of money donated by the Raja of Kashmir. The school had no permanent source of income. It was impossible to meet the expenses of the school without any permanent source of income. There was no hope of raising adequate funds in India for this noble work. In order to ensure that their effort to educate

Indian women does not get aboted mid way she along with Swami Vivekananda left for the western countries to collect funds for her educational projects.

Nivedita visited many places, both in England and America, to collect funds for her educational projects in India but at the same time, she also used this opportunity to familiarise them with the Hindu ideals of womanhood. The response of the western world was mixed one, but she did not lose heart.

During her stay in western countries, Nivedita was shocked to learn the ill treatment given to Indians by the western countries. She felt that they dared to do so because India was not a free country. Many prominent persons like Vivekananda and Jagdish Chandra Bose also suffered humiliation because of this. The negative attitude of the British towards India compelled her to take interest in the activities of the Indian National Congress, which stood for satruggle for the end of colonial rule and freedom for India. She made her plans clear thus, "You must not think from all this that I cherish any idea of going out to tea with Brahmos, when I get back. Not at all. I belong to my work to the women and to the girls." A London correspondent described the part she played in London as 'a champion for India'. He wrote, "there has arisen a champion for India from an unexpected quarter, as was the way with champions of old, not from a far country, however, nor from a strange people, nor from masculine ranks, has this new champion come. She is a lady, belonging to the Ruling Power in India, a lady of exceptional ability, who had given up a promising career in England to devote herself to the service of women in India. Miss Margaret Noble is her name and though she has been only eighteen months in India, she has learned more of real Indian life during that time than have others who have passed as many years there".

After coming back to India she started her school with the help of her old nurse Miss Bet, who had come with her to help her in her objectives. Christine Greenstidel, who had met Vivekananda in Detroit on February 24, 1894, felt attracted to his Vedantic teaching and after taking his consent, also came to India in 1902 to help Nivedita.

Now in Calcutta, Nivedita turned her attention to the school which was started in February 1902. She took interest in all students and kept a detailed record of their progress. The curriculum of the school included Bengali, English, Arithmetic, Geography and History. As the school was founded on the kindergarten system in which all knowledge is supposed to receive a foundation in concrete experience and all work to appear to the child as play, drawing from observation, brushwork, clay modeling, mat weaving, paper cutting, sewing and games were introduced in the course of studies. Nivedita's record reveals that girls of all castes attended her school but two problems were obstructing their education-irregular attendance and child marriage. She felt that neither the pupils nor their parents considered regular attendance essential. As far as the second problem was concerned, she could do nothing immediately but remained hopeful that one day with the expansion of education the future of bright promising girls will not be nipped in the bud.

When Nivedita's educational work was making gradual progress, she received a shock in the form of Vivekananda's death. Although she lost her friend, philosopher and guide, it did not shake her determination to move on with her work. She felt more responsible than ever and wrote to her friend, "He is not dead. He is with us always. I cannot even grieve. I only want to work.'[12]

During this period Nivedita and Christine decided to open a women section in the school. For avoiding any possible embarrassment to the ladies it was decided to secure a carriage in which the ladies could be brought to the school and dropped back home. With initial reservation, both Swami Brahmananda and Saradananda accepted this suggestion, as they knew that ladies of the locality would come to school due to the reputation of Nivedita. Finally, the women's section was opened on November 2, 1903. The time of the school was between 12 PM to 4 PM. This school soon gained popularity. Nivedita wrote to Macleod, "It is unheard of that married zanana (ladies) should leave their homes and come to take lesson at the house of a European. But they do it and there never was a moment's difficulty."[13] This school got success because the Sisters proved by their deeds that they had no ulterior motive behind the facade of education. They only wanted well being of these ladies. Till that time, the experience was little bitter. Foreigners had worked in the educational field to convert Hindus into Christians. Common man felt relieved at the performance of her school and impressed with her well intended selfless service. In order to encourage Christine, Nivedita gave full credit for the success of the women's section to her. Nivedita wrote about her, "The women's work is a wonderful success but she is more wonderful. Her whole time is given up to study, work and visiting. She lives here, without fuss, with complexity. I look at her and feel that I never knew my own measureless inadequacy before."[4] Her praise for Christine is also indicative of her desire to build a team of dedicated persons to expand the work of women education.

The number of students increased in both section. So the old house at 16, Bosepara Lane was taken on rent. To attract the girls, she created a home like environment in her school. She would counsel, persuade and sometimes even fight with the family of her student for the continuation of their studies. Giribala Ghosh, a twenty two year old widow wanted to study in her school. She had a daughter also. She got admission in her school but had to leave the school because of social pressure. Again, she joined the school. But, she started skipping school because her family did not like the idea of walking down the lane to reach the carriage because the carriage was unable to enter the narrow lane Nivedita herself went to Giribala's house and convinced her maternal uncle to send her to school. She told him, "You may be displeased with me. Call me in whatever terms you may like to, but I beg of you to allow this girl from 11 am to 4 pm to go to my school. The women members of your family go to the Ganga for bath or to Kalighat. Why can you not send this girl for a few hours even?" While saying so Nivedita knelt down before that gentleman. Later on, Giribala's uncle allowed her to go to school. Nivedita took the girl to school herself on that day in her carriage and presented her a shawl and said "My Child, take this and come to school everyday, covering yourself thus".

The above incident shows Nivedita's concern for women's education. She tried her best to give them every possible facility in her school. She used to arrange food for the widow ladies on Ekadasis because they had to follow some rules regarding their food. One day on Ekadashi, she had some urgency to go to Jagadish

Chandra Bose's house. She forgot to feed a young widow student named Prafulla Devi. When Nivedita realised this, she immediately rushed to the school and apologized to her saying, "My child, I had forgotten, what a wrong! I haven't fed you while I took my meal. What a wrong!"

Nivedita's love for her students was unquestionable but she never liked indiscipline. Once she had made a rule that a girl to whom the question would be asked would only be permitted to answer. One day while teaching, Nivedita asked a question to a particular student but another student whose name was Nirjharini Sarkar answered that question. She did not like this and did not ask her any question for a few days. Later on, Nirjharini apologised for her behavior and Nivedita forgave her.

Apart from giving bookish knowledge, Nivedita taught her students to be clean and to maintain a high level of hygiene. She taught them to use their own clothing and bedding. She also did not like others using her. Once she found one of her students sleeping on her bed during the school hour. Nivedita showed her displeasure and got her instructed for not coming to school without taking a few days rest because it seemed that she was extremely tired. This incident shows her non compromising attitude towards cleanliness, hygiene and discipline.

Nivedita had unbounded love for her students. She always enjoyed feeding her students, especially, before the summer vacation. Nivedita had a huge number of students in her school but her economic condition was not so good to arrange good food for all of them regularly. So, she used to count the students well ahead of the vacation and buy some sweets and fruits for them according to her capacity. She used to wrap them in packets made of shal leaves and used to distribute them from a basket approaching each of her beloved students. She used to keep an empty basket in which her students used to throw the empty packets.

In order to teach her students about their culture, she used to take them to different places like Dakshineswar temple, museum etc. Apart from teaching them many things, Nivedita inculcated nationalistic values in the minds of the girl students through all their activities and behavior including language, dress, education, music and everything. She introduced singing of Vande Mataram in her school. Once the British Government set some political prisoners free from the Andaman jails Nivedita declared that day a holiday to show respect to the freedom fighters. She decorated the whole school and put mangal ghats, supported by plantain saplings at the entrance. She tried her best to make her students conscious of their national objects.

Once, the wife of the great scientist Abala Bose came to her school. On that occasion, Nivedita made her students sing the song "Banga Amar Janani Amar". She was very happy on that day when the girls were singing; her delight knew no bounds, tears of joy rolled down her cheeks. To inspire her students, Nivedita used to take them to hear the lectures of Surendra Nath Banerjee on national issue. One day she asked her students about the Queen of India, their answer was Queen Victoria. This made her very upset. She told them angrily that their queen is Queen Sita. She cried out thus, "You don't even appear to know who is the Queen of India!" Then she explained, "Look! The Empress of England, Queen Victoria, can never be the Queen of India. Your Queen is Queen Sita. Sita is the eternal queen of India." Nivedita, through her school tried to develop women into a traditional, spiritual as well as modern being.

Nivedita worked very hard for the all round development of her students. For the smooth running of her school, she tried to collect finances from all corners. Apart from getting help from England and America, she earned money by writing books. The name of Mrs Bull is prominent among them who helped her immensely. Praising Mrs Sara Bull's help, she wrote to her on August 11, 1910, thus," Don't you feel that it is a goodly array of things that you have made possible by your support?"[5]

In the starting, the school was not known by any particular name. Nivedita called it Ramakrishna School for girls in her project. Her western friends used to call it 'Vivekananda School' but for the people of that locality, it was simply Nivedita School. R.K. Mission took over it in 1918 after her death and named it Ramakrishna Mission Sister Nivedita Girls School. The School expanded rapidly and finally the management of the school was placed in the hands of the Ramakrishna Sarada Mission in 1963. At present this school is famous as 'Ramakrishna Sarada Mission Sister Nivedita Girls School'.

At the time, when sister Nivedita came to India, Indian education had lost its creativity and its direction due to adverse political situation that was why she paid more attention towards the development of education of women. She began her efforts in this direction even before Ranbindranath's Santiniketan School and before Gandhiji's experiments in educational reforms. Rabindranath added a section for girl in Shantiniketan eight years later in 1908 but it was to close down within two years because of social problems. It was again in the early twenties of the twentieth century that the Santiniketan School was opened again to admitting girls.

Nivedita wanted to impart education in India on pure Indian lines. She even refused Rabindranath to give his daughter English based education. She made it clear to him by saying, "what good is it to force education down the throat? For me real education is to draw out and develop the knowledge and skill which tradition has handed down and the aptitudes acquired by the child. Not to subject them to the steam roller of regimentation which goes by the name of English based education in India."

Nivedita wanted, firstly, education to be in a form which would help develop the faculties of mind and soul in harmony with one another. Secondly, it had to be national education, as well as nation making education by synthesizing the country and the family. Thirdly, this national education has to grow and to expand, in order to become universal and secular. In this connection, Nivedita said, "New ideals have to be approached through the old. The unfamiliar has to be reached through the familiar".

Nivedita not only advocated women education but also education for the common people. Without education neither man nor woman, whatever their social position, can work out their own destiny with self confidence and freedom. She knew it well that for the all round development of our nation the cooperation of whole country would be needed. So, she supported 'education for all'.

Nivedita fought the battle for India's identity and recognition in every field. Like an army doctor on the front lines, she rescued, gave first aid and lasting cures to the wounded self image of the nation. Not merely this, she fought hard for the reputation of India in the west".[6]

Nivedita used to visit different parts of India, still the school was running properly in her absence under the guidance of Sister Christine. For some time, she was helped by one Pusha Devi who left the school after her marriage. Later one, Sudhira Devi helped her who joined the school even before Nivedita's departure for the West in 1907. Sudhira Devi joined the school perhaps getting inspiration from her brother Debabrata who was a revolutionary but later on joined the Ramakrishna Mission. Sudhira Devi was not very familiar with Nivedita. So she kept some distance from her when she took charge of the school but later on Sudhira became her friend.

Nivedita faced economic problem, in running the school. She drastically cut down her expenses. She expressed her economic difficulty thus, "Rice and milk have both risen in price and the increasing poverty is something terrible to witness. We have gone into account and will have to cut down many expenses."[7] At Devamata's suggestion, she wrote to Olea and some other ladies for help but none helped her except Olea.

Nivedita had two branches of her school but one had to be closed down. Earlier she had taken on rent her old house 16, Bosepara lane, but had to leave that. Now the whole school was in her house. Though she faced financial crisis, but she did not leave her mission. Sara Bull left some money for her school at the time of her death. Many of her friends advised her to rent a house in the more spacious southern part of the city. But Nivedita refused to leave the lane. She told them frankly "It is a hard battle that has to be fought, but oh! It is so good to be once more in India."[8]

Nivedita was happy with the progress of the school but she was not happy with herself because she thought that she was not giving her best to the school. So, after coming back from the west, she tried to take over the school in 1909. She started teaching Geography, History and Needlework. There were some grown up girls in the school who used to teach in the school. Nivedita taught the girls drill in the small courtyard. She purchased a small plot adjacent to the building where a small garden with lawn and flower beds was laid out and where the girls used to play games. Nivedita used to decorate her small room with toys and paintings of the girls and showed them to all who came to meet her. One day, Ananda Coomaraswamy came to see her. She showed everything of her school to him. He was full of praise for the school. She also thought of introducing Sanskrit in her school. She used to teach historical personalities with keen interest, she also wanted to take her students to the historical places but her desire could not be fulfilled due to economic difficulty. However, she never missed an opportunity to take her students to short trips to Dakshineswar, zoo, museum etc. To instil nationalist feeling among his students, she used to take them to the Brahmo Girls School so that they listen to lectures given in the adjoining park. She employed a lady to teach students the technique of spinning. She was called as Charakha Ma.

By her continuous effort, Nivedita made her school a home of bliss. Students loved to be in the school with their caring teachers. Nivedita always looked forward to receiving her students in her school. Even in the midst of economic difficulty she continued to run the school imparting education to girls and women. She accept donations from willing donors who shared the mission and vision of Sister Nivedita but never accepted any help form the foreign government.

Nivedita had so much love for her school that even before her death on October 7, 1911 she bequeathed all her possessions and writings to the trustees of the Belur Math to be used for her school engaged in giving national education to the women of the country. Thus, she gave her all to India.

Inspite of being a foreigner, what ever Nivedita did for the education of Indian women is matchless. She worked tirelessly for their education only with the sole aim of empowering them so that they are able to realise their full potential and utilise them for their own well being as well as that of their society. Nivedita left her homeland, all comforts, powers etc and sacrificed her life for the upliftment of Indian women because she felt for them like a mother. That was why Rabindranath Tagore affectionately called her 'Lokmata'. Fraser Blair has rightly written about her thus, "By her birth in the West, and her life and death in India, she had enriched the world in twofold way. She brought to the exquisite ideals of Indian Womanhood the intellectual robustness and the modern outlook which are the heritage of Europe. She interpreted to the west the nobility and the sanctity which attend the Indian Woman in her home."[9]

From the above study, it is clear that quite long back, Nivedita had realised the importance of education in empowering the Indian women. Women have been considered equal partners in the development of any nation but without proper education they can not become an effective equal partner and contribute substantially in the all round development of the country. Realizing this truth after the dawn of independence and following the guidelines initiated by Nivedita and many other reformers, the government has made an elaborate plan for the education of women. All these programmes have pious motive, sufficient resources but the women are yet to be empowered in the true sense of the term. Thus, what is needed more today than the material resources is the spirit and commitment of Sister Nivedita to actually empower our women folk.

References

1. Complete Works of Nivedita, Vol-I, p. 112, Ramakrishna Sarada Mission. Sister Nivedita Girls School, Calcutta, 1967.
2. Letters of Sister Nivedita, Vol-I, p. 500, Nababharat Publisher, Calcutta, 1982.
3. Letters of Sister Nivedita, Vol-I, p. 660, Nababharat Publisher, Calcutta, 1982.
4. Ibid., p. 589.
5. Letters of Sister Nivedita, Vol-II, p. 1131, Nababharat Publishers, Calcutta, 1982.
6. Pravrajika Prabuddhaprana, Sister Nivedita Tells Americans their obligations to India, p. 571, Prabuddha Bharat, May, 1999.
7. The letters of Sister Nivedita, Vol-II, p. 990, Nababharat Publisher, Calcutta, 1982.
8. Ibid., p. 995.
9. The Modern Review, p. 451 April, 1912.

अध्याय 25

महिला सशक्तिकरण में शिक्षा एवं आर्थिक आत्मनिर्भरता की भूमिका

कमला कुमारी

युगों से 'स्वतंत्रता' स्त्रियों का सर्वोत्तम सुख रहा है, जिसकी प्राप्ति के लिए वे सतत् प्रयत्नशील एवं संघर्षशील रही हैं। गाँधी जी ने उनके भीतर की शक्ति को पहचान कर जगा दिया था। तभी तो भारत के आजाद होते ही उन्हें पुरुषों के साथ ही समान संवैधानिक अधिकार प्राप्त हो सके। किन्तु आजादी के बाद तमाम प्रगति के बावजूद समाज में परम्परागत पुरुष स्वाभिमान एवं पुरुष के अधीन रहने की नारी दासता की प्रवृत्ति के कारण भारतीय नारी को सहज ढंग से प्राप्त कानूनी अधिकार सामाजिक व्यवहार का अंग नहीं बन सका और नारी की स्थिति जैसी थी वैसी ही रह गई।

परिणामतः स्त्री-शोषण से जुड़े कई प्रश्न मुख हुए। आजादी के बाद के विभिन्न पंचवर्षीय योजनाओं में 'महिला विकास' की दृष्टि से कई कार्यक्रम एवं परियोजनाएँ प्रारम्भ हुईं। इस तरह सरकारी योजनाओं की सोच पहले 'महिला विकास' फिर 'महिला सहभाग' के रास्ते चलकर अब 'महिला सशक्तिकरण' तक आ पहुँची है। अब प्रश्न उठता है कि वस्तुतः 'महिला सशक्तिकरण' क्या है? मेरी राय में, भयमुक्त जीवनयापन, अपनी अस्मिता एवं आत्मसम्मान के साथ लक्ष्यों की प्राप्ति, आर्थिक आत्मनिर्भरता प्राप्त करने के पर्याप्त साधन की उपलब्धता के साथ-साथ परिवार, समाज एवं राष्ट्रीय स्तर पर उनकी इच्छा-अनिच्छा का सम्मान करना, देश की प्रगति एवं उत्थान में उनकी सहभागिता आदि कुछ ऐसे नियामक तत्त्व हैं जो महिला सशक्तिकरण के परिचायक हैं। दूसरे शब्दों में, समाजरूपी रथ के दो पहिए के रूप में यदि स्त्री एवं पुरुष को रखा जाए एवं पुरुष के अनुरूप ही स्त्री को भी सबल एवं सुयोग्य बनने का अवसर मिले तो यही सबलता एवं सुयोग्यता नारी के सशक्तिकरण की वास्तविक पहचान होगी।

वस्तुतः सशक्तिकरण एक मानसिक अवस्था है जो कुछ खास आंतरिक कुशलताओं और सामाजिक-आर्थिक परिस्थितियों पर निर्भर करती है। महिला सशक्तिकरण के विभिन्न आयामों में सर्वाधिक महत्वपूर्ण आयाम आर्थिक आत्मनिर्भरता को माना गया है। एक महिला तब तक पूर्णतः स्वतंत्र एवं सशक्त नहीं कही जा सकती जब तक कि वह सामाजिक दृष्टि से आर्थिक स्तर पर आत्मनिर्भर न हो।

स्वाधीनता की अर्द्धशताब्दी और महिला सशक्तिकरण प्रयासों की एक शताब्दी बीतने के पश्चात् भी जो चाहिए थे वे संतोषपूर्ण परिणाम हासिल नहीं हो सके हैं। महिलाओं को आर्थिक स्वतंत्रता तभी मिल सकती है, जब उन्हें समग्र सामाजिक परिदृश्य में अधिक भागीदारी प्राप्त हो। विभिन्न संगठनों द्वारा दिए गए आंकड़ों से जाहिर है कि आम भारतीय महिला के लिए आर्थिक सम्पन्नता अभी बहुत दूर की चीज है, आर्थिक स्वतंत्रता की तो बात ही बेकार है।

एक महिला को आर्थिक स्वतंत्रता प्राप्ति के लिए कई सीढ़ियों से गुजरना होगा जिसकी प्रथम सीढ़ी है—शिक्षा।

हमारे धर्मशास्त्रों के अनुसार महिलाओं का स्थान समाज में सर्वोपरि है। इतना ही नहीं, बल्कि वे राष्ट्र-निर्माण की प्रक्रिया में अहम भूमिका निभाती रही हैं। वे अपनी भूमिका के प्रति सचेत होने के बावजूद आज भी आर्थिक तथा सामाजिक अधिकारों से वंचित तथा उपेक्षित हैं। इसके मुख्य कारणों में एक है—महिलाओं का अशिक्षित होना। अतः अगर वास्तव में महिलाओं को विकास का केन्द्र-बिन्दु बनाना चाहते हैं, तो उन्हें जागरुक तथा राष्ट्रीय विकास की धारा में अपनी सक्रिय भूमिका और भागीदारी निभानी होगी और इसके लिए जरूरी है कि प्रत्येक महिला शिक्षित हो, तभी राष्ट्र का सर्वांगीण विकास संभव है।

जहाँ तक महिलाओं की शिक्षा का प्रश्न है, जिस परिवार में वे जन्म लेती हैं वहा। उनकी शिक्षा की जरूरत ही नहीं समझी जाती है। उनको शुरू से ही घर की देख-रेख करने में लगा दिया जाता है, जिसके लिए औपचारिक शिक्षा की जरूरत नहीं है। वे सब वे अभ्यास द्वारा सीख सकती हैं। ग्रामीण महिलाओं की स्थिति तो और भी खराब है। "भारत में प्राथमिक शिक्षा" की एक रिपोर्ट से पता चलता है कि ग्रामीण क्षेत्रों में हर सौ बालिकाओं में से, जिनका पहली कक्षा से दाखिला होता है, सिर्फ चालीस पांचवीं कक्षा तक, अठारह आठवीं कक्षा तक, नौ नौवीं कक्षा तक तथा सिर्फ एक बारहवीं कक्षा तक पहुँच पाती हैं। अर्थात् ग्रामीण क्षेत्रों में प्राथमिक स्तर पर ही बहुत सी बालिकाएँ पढ़ाई छोड़ देती हैं और कई परिवारों की बालिकाओं को तो प्राथमिक शिक्षा से भी वंचित रखा जाता है। यह स्थिति अनुसूचित जाति तथा अनुसूचित जनजाति में ज्यादा देखने को मिलती है। महिलाओं के अशिक्षित होने

के कई कारण हैं—माता-पिता का अशिक्षित होना, लड़का और लड़की में भेद, विद्यालयों का दूर स्थित होना, शिक्षा संबंधी सुविधाओं की कमी, छोटी उम्र में शादी होना, कम उम्र में लड़की का माँ बनना, स्वास्थ्य संबंधी समस्या, परिवार का रूढ़िवादी विचार, इत्यादि।

एक बालिका जब किसी परिवार में जन्म लेती है तो उस परिवार में अगर उसके माता-पिता अनपढ़ होते हैं तो वे यह जरूरी ही नहीं समझते हैं कि एक बालिका का शिक्षित होना जरूरी है। अगर बालिका की माँ अशिक्षित है तो वह सोचती है कि लड़की है, बचपन से ही घर के कार्यों में मदद मिलेगी। वह यह सोच ही नहीं पाती है कि एक बालिका के लिए शिक्षित होना कितना जरूरी है। ऐसी स्थिति में वह बालिका पुस्तकों की जगह घर के काम-काज में अपना समय व्यतीत करने लगती है। इसलिए जरूरी है कि माता-पिता एवं परिवार के अन्य सदस्य, जिस परिवार में बालिका जन्म लेती है उनका शिक्षित होना।

जब किसी बालिका के माता-पिता अशिक्षित होते हैं तो अशिक्षा के कारण उनके विचारों में संकीर्णता होती है, इसी कारण वे पुत्र एवं पुत्री में भेद करते हैं। जहाँ एक ओर पुत्र को पढ़ने की सारी सुविधाएँ दी जाती हैं वहीं लड़की की पढ़ाई पर कभी ध्यान नहीं दिया जाता। लड़की को बचपन से ही यह सुनना पड़ता है कि पढ़-लिख कर यह क्या करेगी? पुत्री के पढ़ाई पर खर्च करना माता-पिता व्यर्थ समझते हैं। परिवार में पुत्र एवं पुत्री के बीच इतना भेद-भाव रखा जाता है। पुनः हम देखते हैं कि आज भी अच्छे विद्यालयों की कमी है और कुछ अच्छे विद्यालय हैं भी तो बहुत से माता-पिता बहुत ज्यादा खर्च के कारण बच्ची को अच्छी शिक्षा नहीं दे पाते हैं। आज भी हमारे भारतीय परिवार में बालिकाओं का जल्दी विवाह कर देना ज्यादा श्रेयस्कर समझा जाता है। कम उम्र में विवाह कर देने के कारण बहुत-सी बालिकाओं की पारिवारिक जिम्मेवारियों के कारण पढ़ाई बन्द हो जाती है। जल्दी विवाह होने के कारण लड़कियाँ जल्दी ही माँ बन जाती हैं जिसके कारण उनका स्वास्थ्य भी ठीक नहीं रह पाता है।

इन सभी पहलूओं पर विचार करने के पश्चात् हम इस निष्कर्ष पर पहुँचते हैं कि एक नारी का सर्वांगीण विकास नहीं होने का मूल कारण अशिक्षा ही है।

एक अशिक्षित स्त्री न तो अपने लिए कुछ कर पाती है और न तो अपने आने वाली बच्ची के लिए ही कुछ कर पाती है। इसलिए शायद यह कहा गया है कि जब एक पुरुष शिक्षित होता है तब एक व्यक्ति शिक्षित होता है किंतु जब एक नारी शिक्षित होती है तब पूरा परिवार शिक्षित होता है। माता की गोद को प्रथम पाठशाला के रूप में स्वीकार किया गया है। अतः हर व्यक्ति को शिक्षा प्रापत करने का

अधिकार है। लिंग का भेद कोई भेद नहीं माना जा सकता। यदि पुरुषों को शिक्षा प्राप्ति का हक है तो औरतों को भी यह अधिकार मिलनरा चाहिए। प्राचीन भारत में वैदिक युग में औरतों को भी ठीक उसी प्रकार पढ़ाया जाता था जिस प्रकार पुरुषों को। मुगल शासनकाल से ही स्त्रियों को पर्दे के अन्दर रखा जाने लगा। उस समय स्त्रियों के लिए न तो पढ़ाई की उपयुक्त व्यवस्था ही थी और न अभिभावक ही अपनी बच्चियों को पढ़ने के लिए भेजते थे। अतः अनादिकाल से भारत में स्त्रियों को भी पुरुषों के समान शिक्षा प्रापित का समुचित अधिकार है। वैदिकयुग में स्त्रियों को सभी प्रकार की शिक्षा दी जाती थी। कुछ विदुषी स्त्रियों ने वैदिक-मंत्रों की रचना की और आध्यात्मिक विद्या पर शास्त्रार्थ भी किए, अतएव—जनक की राजसभा में 'गार्गी' ने याज्ञवल्क्य के साथ शास्त्रार्थ किया था, 'गन्धर्व-गृहीता' नामक एक अन्य स्त्री परम विदुषी व भाषण कला में निपुण थी तथा 'मैत्रीय' जैसी विदुषी महिला भी वैदिक युग में ही हुई हैं। फिर भी बालक और बालिका की शिक्षा में विभेद था—यदि बालकों की शिक्षा का उद्देश्य उन्हें श्रेष्ठ, सच्चरित्र और लौकिक जीवन में सफल बनाना था, तो बालिकाओं की शिक्षा का लक्ष्य उन्हें उत्तम गृहिणी और श्रेष्ठ माता बनाने का था। उस समय बालक-बालिकाओं की सहशिक्षा की प्रणाली नहीं थी, अपितु दोनों के लिए अलग-अलग शिक्षा केन्द्र होते थे। इसका प्रमाण भवभूति के नाटक 'उत्तररामचरित' में वर्णित कन्या गुरुकुल है। इसी प्रकार वात्स्यायन के कामशास्त्र से भी यह प्रकट होता है कि कन्याओं को अन्य विषयों के साथ-साथ विविध ललित कलाओं की शिक्षा भी दी जाती थी। मध्य युग में एवं आधुनिक युग के पूर्वार्द्ध में महिलाओं की स्थिति अत्यन्त दयनीय हो गयी। देश पर शक, हूण, पाषाणों आदि के आक्रमण के कारण महिलाओं की सामाजिक सुरक्षा कठिन हो गयी और उन्हें विभिन्न कुरीतियों का सामना करना पड़ा। इसी प्रकार आधुनिक युग के प्रारम्भ में विशेषतः मुगल आक्रमण के पश्चात् की स्थिति और भी ज्यादा दुभर बन गयी। तत्कालीन अक्षम शासकों के लिए अपने समाज एवं संस्कृति की रक्षा करना मुश्किल हो गया। यही कारण था कि इस समय में पर्दा प्रथा, सती-प्रथा, बाल-विवाह जैसी सामाजिक कुरीतियों का आर्विभाव हुआ। इन कुप्रथाओं का दुष्प्रभाव आज भी समाज में स्पष्टतः देखने को मिलता है। सही अर्थ में देखा जाए तो यह उन्नीसवीं सदी ही थी जब महिला समस्याओं की तरफ पुरुषों का ध्यान गया। राजा राममोहन राय ने सती-प्रथा के खिलाफ मुहिम चलाई। ईश्वर चन्द्र विद्यासागर ने महिला शिक्षा और विधवा-विवाह की वकालत की। गुजरात में दयानंद सरस्वती ने महिला के लिए अभियान छेड़ा। उसी तरह महाराष्ट्र में महादेव गोविंद रानाडे, गोपाल कृष्ण गोखले आदि ने महिला शिक्षा का जोरदार समर्थन किया। यद्यपि समाज सुधारकों के अपने अंतर्विरोध भी

कोई कम नहीं थे लेकिन नवजागरण काल को हम महिला पक्षधरता का काल भी कह सकते हैं। इसलिए साहित्य की कोटि में सिर्फ उपन्यास-कहानियों को न रखकर उन्नीसवीं सदी के समाज सुधारकों के लेखन को भी रखना चाहिए क्योंकि महिलाओं की आज की स्थिति के लिए पृष्ठभूमि उसी काल में तैयार की गई।

उन्नीसवीं सदी में ही भारत की महिलाओं के मन में वे प्रश्न उठने लगे थे जिनका जवाब पुरुष-प्रधान समाज के पास नहीं था। महिलाओं ने शिक्षा और राजनीतिक अधिकारों की मांग की। उधर सुधारवादी विचारक महिलाओं को कुछ अधिकार देना चाहते थे लेकिन महिलाओं की आजादी के संबंध में वे एकमत नहीं थे। 1858 से 1905 के नवजागरण काल में बहुत से पुरुष और महिला सुधारवादी उभरे। एक तरफ नवजागरण काल तो दूसरी ओर आजादी का संघर्ष। महात्मा गांधी ने आजादी की लड़ाई से महिलाओं को जोड़ा।

आजादी के बाद महिलाओं में साक्षरता बढ़ी है। 1961 में दहेज विरोधी कानून बना। बाल-विवाह पर रोक लगाने के लिए पहले ही 'शारदा एक्ट' बन चुका था। कल तक बलात्कार स्त्री के लिए सबसे बड़ा कलंक था। उसी की शिकार स्त्रिया। अब प्रतिरोध करने लगी हैं। मूल्यवृद्धि विरोध से लेकर 'पर्यावरण बचाओ' आंदोलन तक की अगुआई महिलाएँ करती हैं। एक तरफ महिलाएँ शिक्षित, साक्षर, आत्मनिर्भर बन रही हैं तो दूसरी तरफ उन्हें गर्भ में ही मारने के लिए अमीनोसेंटेसिस और अल्ट्रासाउन्ड ईजाद कर लिये गए हैं। वर्ष 1987 में रूपकंवर सती हो जाती है। उससे पहले शाहवानों को गुजारा भत्ता देने के नाम पर कट्टरपंथियों की विजय होती है। सरकार प्रगतिशीलता का मुखौटा ओढ़े उनके सामने घुटने टेक देती है। यह वह दौर है जब 1975 के अंतर्राष्ट्रीय महिला वर्ष के बाद अंतर्राष्ट्रीय स्तर पर ही महिला दशक मनाया जाता है। बहुत से महिला संगठन बनते हैं। महिला सशक्तिकरण का प्रश्न दुनिया भर के नेताओं और विवेकशील व्यक्तियों के लिए कई दशकों से चिंता का विषय रहा है। चीन के बीजिंग शहर में सितंबर 1995 में हुए चौथे विश्व महिला सम्मेलन में पुरुष के मुकाबले स्त्रियों को अवसरों और दर्जे की समानता देने की जरूरत पर जोर दिया गया था। स्त्रियों को स्वावलंबी बनाने और लक्ष्यप्राप्ति तथा अपने मनपसंद क्षेत्र में सफलता प्राप्ति के लिए उनमें आत्मविश्वास उत्पन्न करने में शिक्षा का अत्यन्त ही महत्वपूर्ण योगदान है। बीजिंग घोषणा में इस बात पर बल दिया गया कि भारत सहित अन्य सभी उपस्थित देशों की सरकारें विश्व स्तर पर स्त्री-पुरुष समानाधिकारों तथा संयुक्त राष्ट्र चार्टर में वर्णित सार्वभौमिक मानवाधिकार घोषणा तथा अन्य अन्तर्राष्ट्रीय मानवाधिकार दस्तावेजों, विशेषकर महिलाओं के विरुद्ध हर प्रकार के भेदभाव की समाप्ति संबंधी संधि और बाल अधिकार संधि तथा स्त्रियों के खिलाफ हिंसा मिटाने की घोषणा और विकास के अधिकार की घोषणा में

निर्दिष्ट अन्य उद्देश्यों व सिद्धान्तों के प्रति वचनबद्ध रहेंगी। इस सम्मेलन में कार्रवाई के लिए की गई राष्ट्रीय तथा अन्तर्राष्ट्रीय प्रतिबद्धताओं के जरिए सरकारों तथा अंतर्राष्ट्रीय बिरादरी में स्त्रियों के सशक्तिकरण और उन्नति के लिए प्राथमिकता के आधार पर कदम उठाने की जरूरत को स्वीकार किया। ऐसा महसूस किया गया कि एक बड़ा क्षेत्र जिसमें कार्रवाई की जरूरत है और वह है लड़कियों और औरतों की बुनियादी शिक्षा, जीवनपर्यन्त शिक्षा, साक्षरता व प्रशिक्षण तथा प्राथमिक स्वास्थ्य सुविधाओं के जरिए निरंतर आर्थिक उन्नति के साथ-साथ जन-केद्रित निरंतर विकास को बढ़ावा देना। इसलिए विश्व-स्तर पर यह स्वीकार किया गया है कि शिक्षा से व्यक्ति का सशक्तिकरण होता है तथा जीवनपर्यन्त वह निरंतर शिक्षा मानव जीवन के स्तर को उन्नत करती है। सदियों से स्त्रियों के प्रति भेदभाव किया जाता रहा है और उन्हें शिक्षा, उन्नति, विकास और निर्णयाधिकार से वंचित रखा गया है। भारत जैसे विकासशील देश के पारम्परिक समाजों के बारे में तो यह बात मुख्य रूप से सच है जहाँ 80 प्रतिशत जनसंख्या अभी भी गांव में रहती है। पारंपरिक रूप से औरत की भूमिका घर संभालने और बच्चों का पालन-पोषण करने तक सीमित है।

स्वतंत्रता-प्राप्ति के बाद से भारत में महिलाओं को शिक्षा की गारंटी देने के लिए कई पहलें हुई हैं, फिर भी संपूर्ण साक्षरता में कई रुकावटें आती हैं—कभी लिंग-भेद तो कभी जनसंख्या का बड़ा आकार तो कभी गरीबी। महिलाओं को शिक्षित करने के लिए जरूरी है कि हाईस्कूल और महाविद्यालयों के पाठ्यक्रमों में महिलाओं के संवैधानिक अधिकारों के बारे में जानकारी शामिल की जाए और उनके लिए सकारात्मक कार्य हेतु विशेष कानून बनाए जाएँ। केन्द्र सरकार के महिला और बाल विकास विभाग ने महिलाओं के अधिकारों और उनके हितों के संरक्षण-संवर्धन के लिए बनाए गए कानूनों की जानकारी के लिए 1990 के दशक में सरल भाषा में कई पुस्तिकाए प्रकाशित की थी। इनमें यह भी बताया गया था कि अनुपालक एजेंसियों के माध्यम से किस प्रकार इन अधिकारों को हासिल किया जा सकता है। यह भी महत्वपूर्ण है कि महिला अधिकार आयुक्त इस बात का निरीक्षण और निगरानी करें कि महिलाओं को न्याय व्यवस्था से न्याय किस प्रकार मिल रहा है। महिलाओं के व्यक्तिगत रूप से सहायता और उनके लिए कार्यरत स्वयंसेवी संगठनों को भी उपयुक्त कानूनी सहायता सुनिश्चित की जानी चाहिए। केन्द्र और राज्य सरकारों के विभागों तथा निकायों की शिकायत निवारण व्यवस्था के कामकाज की निगरानी करने वाले वरिष्ठ अधिकारियों को निरंतर यह देखते रहना चाहिए कि महिलाओं द्वारा लाई गई शिकायतों का निपटारा किस तरह होता है। इसके अलावा स्वयंसेवी संगठनों को सरकारी सहायता देते समय उन पर अपने कार्यक्रमों में महिल

जागृति और महिलाओं की विशेष आवश्यकताओं के बारे में लोगों को सचेत करने का दायित्व भी डाला जाना चाहिए, फिर चाहे ये संगठन, पुरुष, बच्चों या किसी भी क्षेत्र में कार्य कर रहे हों।

स्त्री-पुरुष अधिकारों में समानता और विकास के दृष्टिकोण के कारण भारत एवं अन्य विकासशील देशों में विगत दशक के दौरान आर्थिक अधिकारिता का महत्व बढ़ गया है। आर्थिक अधिकारिता के विभिन्न दृष्टिकोणों का सार इस परिभाषा में निहित है : आर्थिक परिवर्तन भौतिक लाभ और मोल-भाव की बढ़ी हुई शक्ति और या संरचनात्मक परिवर्तन जो महिलाओं को निरन्तर और नियमित आधार पर आर्थिक लाभ सुनिश्चित करने की योग्यता दिलाने में समर्थ हो।

समाज में सामान्य स्तर पर महिलाओं की आर्थिक भूमिका पुरुषों से भिन्न होती है। परिणामतः हम पाते हैं कि उनकी—

(क) आर्थिक गतिविधियों में कम भागीदारी,

(ख) कुछ सुनिश्चित कार्य-क्षेत्रों में अधिक जमाव और

(ग) अकुशल एवं अप्रशिक्षित एवं सीमान्त कार्यों तक ही सीमित रहना।

दूसरे शब्दों में, देश में उपलब्ध विभिन्न रोजगार अथवा कार्यक्षेत्रों का वितरण स्त्री-पुरुष के बीच एक समान नहीं है और न उनकी आय ही। साथ ही साथ वेतन में भी अन्तर विद्यमान है। विशेष तौर पर ग्रामीण रोजगार के मामले में यह असमानता सुस्पष्ट है।

आर्थिक एजेंट के रूप में बहुसंख्यक महिलाएँ (89% पुरुषों की तुलना में 95%) असंगठित क्षेत्र में रोजगार में लगी है। महिलाएँ प्राथमिक क्षेत्र एवं कुछ अन्य उद्योगों में बहुत अधिक संख्या में पायी जाती है (63% पुरुषों की तुलना में 81%)। ऐसे उद्योग या कार्य-क्षेत्र जिनमें पुरुषों की तुलना में महिलाए। अधिक हैं, वे हैं—मूँगफली की छटाई, बीड़ी निर्माण, नारियल जटा की कटाई, बुनाई एवं सफाई, चाय का बगान का कार्य, गृहिणी का कार्य, नर्स, आया, सेविका, घरेलू नौकरानी का काम आदि।

यद्यपि बहुसंख्याक महिलाएँ कुशल गृहिणी के रूप में महत्वपूर्ण आर्थिक योगदान करती हैं। इसके अतिरिक्त संतानोत्पत्ति, बच्चों का लालन-पालन जैसे अवैतनिक कार्य (इसमें वृद्धों एवं बीमारों की देखभाल भी शामिल है) का यथोचित आर्थिक मूल्यांकन अभी तक विश्व के अर्थशास्त्रियों के समझ से बाहर की चीज है और उनके लिए यह एक जटिल समस्या बनी हुई है।

उपर्युक्त विवेचन से स्पष्ट है कि आज के रूढ़िवादी सामाजिक व्यवस्था में 'लिंग-भेद' का परिणाम यह होता है कि नारी सामाजिक- आर्थिक रूप से पुरुष के

अधीन हो जाती है। सामान्यतः ऐसा माना जाता है कि नारी पुरुष द्वारा निर्देशित होने के कारण अपनी क्रमगत भूमिकाओं में पुरुष की प्रतिछाया बनकर रह जाती है तथा अपने वजूद को भूलने लगती है। लेकिन सत्यता यह है कि पुरुष किसी-न-किसी रूप में स्त्री पर निर्भर रहता है। इससे स्पष्ट है कि सामाजिक आर्थिक संरचना में स्त्री का विशिष्ट स्थान है तथा उसकी आर्थिक आजादी एवं आत्म-निर्भरता पर सामाजिक एवं नैतिक रूप से ध्यान देने की जरूरत है। औपचारिक आजादी के साथ अगर समाज के सभी सदस्यों के विकास के लिए भौतिक स्थितियों का पक्का एवं समान प्रबंधन किया जाए तो जाहिर है कि इससे सामाजिक स्तर पर 'लिंग-भेद' की असमानता दूर होगी तथा दोनों का सम्यक विकास होगा।

उपर्युक्त विवेचन के आधार पर हम कह सकते हैं कि महिला सशक्तिकरण का लक्ष्य तभी संभव हो पाएगा जब हमारी सामाजिक-नैतिक विचारधारा में परिवर्तन आये। इसके लिए आवश्यक है कि प्रत्येक स्तर पर परस्पर सामन्जस्य स्थापित कर समाज में गतिशीलता लायी जाये तथा राजनैतिक, आर्थिक, सामाजिक, सांस्कृतिक तस्तर को नैतिक मूल्यों के आधार पर निर्धारित किया जाए। पुरुष एवं विभिन्न क्षेत्रों में कार्यरत महिलाओं के लिए समान नैतिक मापदंड निर्धारित किए जाएँ ताकि समाज में बढ़ती अश्लीलता, विशेष रूप से आर्थिक उदारीकरण के नाम पर मॉडलिंग की होड़ में महिलाओं के शोषण पर अंकुश लगाया जा सके। हम महिला सशक्तिकरण को जितना टालेंगे, भावी पीढ़ियों के कमजोर होने का डर बढ़ता जाएगा। परवर्ती संतानें समाज की सामान्य भलाई के कठिन काम निपुणतापूर्वक नहीं कर पाएंगी। यह एक ऐसी स्थिति है जो अन्ततोगत्वा राष्ट्र के लिए अहितकर होगी। इस संदर्भ में स्वामी विवेकानंद के विचार उल्लेखनीय है कि औरतों की स्थिति में सुधार लाए बिना दुनिया का कल्याण संभव नहीं है। एक पंख से चिड़िया उड़ान नहीं भर सकती।

निष्कर्षतः महिलाओं की समस्याओं के निदान पर गहनतापूर्वक विचार करें तो हम पाते हैं कि सर्वप्रथम महिला को स्वतः अपनी मानसिक दासता के मुक्त होने की अनिवार्यता है। प्रत्येक व्यक्ति को अपनी लड़ाई स्वयं लड़नी पड़ती है। अतः शैशवावस्था से ही लड़कियों को अपने अधिकारों के प्रति नैतिकतापूर्ण ढंग से सचेत होने का संस्कार देने की जरूरत है। साथ ही उनमें इस आत्मबल की भावना को प्रस्फुटित करने की जरूरत है कि महिलाएँ तो स्वयं सशक्त हैं ही, केवल उनकी शक्ति को आत्मानुभूत करने की अनिवार्यता है ताकि महिलाएँ सशक्तिकरण से ऊपर उठकर सर्वशक्तिकरण की ओर अग्रसर हो सकें। यदि इस तथ्य की भवितव्यता पर गंभीरता से विचार किया जाए तो सही अर्थों में एक जागृत भारत, आधुनिक भारत एवं सर्वशक्ति-संपन्न भारत की आधारशिला रखने में सहायता मिलेगी।

अध्याय 26

मानसिक बदलाव : नारी समानता का प्रमुख कारक

इन्द्रा कुमारी

आज युगपरिवर्तन के इस महान क्षणों में हम नारी सशक्तिकरण की समस्याओं पर विचार कर रहे हैं। विश्व के प्रत्येक कोने में महिलाओं के विकास के अनुरूप वातावरण बनता जा रहा है। नारी शक्ति की प्रतिमूर्ति मानी जाती रही है इसलिए नारी में नये शिरे से शक्ति उत्पन्न करने की कोई आवश्यकता नहीं बल्कि भारत का नारी-समाज संकोच, भय छोड़कर महिला उत्कर्ष के महान अभियान में सम्मिलित हो, यही युग की पुकार है। त्याग-बलिदान की तो उसमें कमी ही नहीं। नारी का समस्त जीवन ही त्याग-बलिदान से ओतप्रोत है। अतः उसे लोभ, मोह छोड़ने की बात कहने, कष्ट सहने के लिए तैयार होने का उद्‌बोधन करने की तो आवश्यकता ही नहीं है। ये सारे गुण तो उसमें प्रकृति प्रदत्त है। उद्‌बोधन केवल संकोच और झिझक छोड़ने का है। यदि ऐसा किया जायेगा तो भारत भूमि हजारों इंदिरा गांधी, भण्डारनायके तथा गोल्डमेयर संसार को दे सकेगी।

नारी शक्ति अभियान प्रकारांतर से परिवारों को स्वर्ग समतुल्य बनाने का ऐसा सृजनात्मक काम है जिसके सत्परिणामों को सोचने की आवश्यकता है। आधुनिक काल का इतिहास साक्षी है कि पुनर्जागरण काल में समाज सुधारकों ने समाज को सशक्त बनाने में नारी जीवन की तत्कालीन स्थितियों में सुधार करना ही अपना लक्ष्य बनाया। उन विचारकों को स्त्री की दशा में सुधार लाने के लिए किसी दूसरे समाज से नीतिनियम या व्यवहार उधार लेने की जरूरत नहीं पड़ी। वैदिक युग में भारतीय समाज व्यवस्था की धुरी स्त्री थी। शास्त्रों के सृजन से लेकर महत्वपूर्ण निर्णय लेने सम्बन्धी प्रक्रिया में वह हर मोड़ पर मौजूद थी। नारियों का व्यक्तित्व पूर्ण रूप से सुरक्षित था। वे अपना जीवन-साथी अपनी इच्छा से चुनती थीं, उनमें इतनी योग्यता

थी कि वे अपना हानि-लाभ, उचित-अनुचित समझ सकती थीं। अपनी योग्यता, विद्वता और विवेकपूर्ण बुद्धि के बल से द्रौपदी की भांति अपने पतियों को भी सत्परामर्श एवं शिक्षा देने को प्रस्तुत रहती थीं। लेकिन इस विकास प्रक्रिया में कहीं चूक हुई और स्त्री धुरी से परिधि में आ गई। मिथ्या धारणाओं और अप्रासंगिक रूढ़ियों के बल पर उसे मात्र गृहिणी बना दिया गया। गृहिणी के रूप में भी उसके केवल कर्त्तव्य ही निर्धारित किए गए। अधिकार के रूप में उसके पास सिर्फ "जननी" बनना शेष रहा। प्रेम और बलिदान की भावना कालान्तर में विष बन गई। उनका पुरातन सेवाभाव उन्हीं के लिए घातक बन गया। उसने प्रेमवश अपने को समर्पित किया था, परन्तु निर्दयी पुरुष ने उसे बन्धनों में जकड़ लिए। तिरस्कार और उपेक्षा उत्तरोत्तर बढ़ती गई।

इस भयावह स्थिति के कारणों का एहसास आधुनिक युग के समाज सुधारकों को होते ही इन कुरीतियों से स्त्री-समाज को मुक्त करने के प्रयास प्रारम्भ किए गए। स्वामी दयान्द सरस्वती, राजा राम मोहन राय, महर्षि करवे, महात्मा फुले जैसे समाज सुधारकों ने इस तथ्य को प्रस्तावित किया कि जब तक नारियों में अपनी स्थिति के प्रति सजगता का विकास नहीं होता, तब तक देश में बुनियादी बदलाव नहीं आयेगा। आज भी नारियों में अन्धविश्वास, अशिक्षा, अस्वच्छता आदि सामाजिक दोष घर किये हुए हैं। यही कारण है कि स्त्रियों की समस्यायें दुरूह होती जा रही है और वे पतन के कगार की ओर बढ़ती जा रही है।

आज नारियों की दशा ऐसी विभत्स है जिसे सुनकर रोंगटे खड़े हो जाते हैं। मनुष्यता करबद्ध विनीत वाणी में पूछती है—मनुष्यों! नारी के उपकार का क्या यही प्रतिफल है? जन्मदात्री के ऋण को क्या इसी तरह चुकाया जा सकता है। इसलिए आवश्यकता है उसे मुक्तकर सम्मानप्रद जीवन प्रदान करें। देशभर में प्रतिवर्ष बहुत सारी महिलाएँ आत्महत्या करती हैं। सिर्फ दहेज लालच में किये गये दुष्कर्मों के कारण अपने निर्धन माता-पिता को धन के अभाव में दर-दर भटकते देखकर भावनाशील कन्याओं के हृदय टूट जाते हैं। दहेज के लिए प्रताड़ित किए जाने और भीषण यंत्रणाएँ भुगतने के कारण वे अपने आपको असहाय, अनाश्रित अनुभव करने लगती है। प्रताड़ना की स्थिति में उस नारी के सामने घोर अंधकार छा जाता है। हमारे समाज में जहाँ एक ओर आदर्श प्रणाली चली आ रही है, वहीं सास द्वारा बहुओं पर शासन करने की अन्धमान्यता ने भी न जाने कब से स्थान ग्रहण कर लिया है। इस संकीर्ण मनोवृत्ति के कारण दोनों में टकराव होता है, जिसमें जीत प्रायः सास की ही होती है। बहू को हमेशा दुधारू गाय समझने वाले, हर आर्थिक जरूरत की पूर्ति के लिए उसके मायके वालों पर आँखें गड़ाये रखने वाले और माँग पूरी न होने पर उसके

साथ हिंसक व्यवहार करने वाले ससुरालवालों के खिलाफ हर सम्भव सख्त कार्यवाही होनी चाहिए और दहेज उत्पीड़न के खिलाफ महिलाओं को कानूनी संरक्षण मिलना चाहिए। दहेज से जुड़े मुद्दे और तमाम उप मुद्दों को आज भावना के कोरे दृष्टिकोणों से देखने के बजाय यथार्थ के धरातल पर रख कर देखने की जरूरत है।

अब प्रश्न है कि नारी जागृति के लिए बदलाव कैसे आए? क्या यह स्वयमेव घटित होगा? कोई दैवी शक्ति इस घृणित विचारधारा को बदलेगी? नहीं, ऐसी बात नहीं है। परिवर्तन जहाँ कहीं, जिस स्तर पर भी होता है वहाँ उसके पीछे कोई न कोई निमित्त कारण की आवश्यकता होती है। दुनियाँ परिवर्तनशील है। एक जैसी कभी नहीं रहती। समाज गतिशीलता है। जीवधारियों में भी ऐसी गति है। जीवन के सभी क्षेत्रों में पुरुषों से प्रतिद्वंदिता चाहते हैं तो नारी शक्ति को अधिक सबल बनाने के लिए नारी शिक्षा आवश्यक है। अभी भी ऐसे लोग हैं जो बेटी को पढ़ने में व्यर्थ खर्च समझते हैं। नारी शिक्षा समाज में शांतिपूर्ण क्रांति ला सकती है। शिक्षित नारी अपने देश के विकास में महत्वपूर्ण सहयोग दे सकती है जीवन के सभी क्षेत्रों में पुरुषों के काम में हाथ बँटा सकती है। यहाँ तक की युद्ध के क्षेत्र में भी महत्वपूर्ण काम कर सकती है। देवासुर संग्राम में कैकेयी ने अपने अद्वितीय कौशल से महाराजा दशरथ को चकित कर दिया था। अपनी योग्यता, विद्वता और विवेकपूर्ण बुद्धि के बल पर ही द्रौपदी अपने पतियों को सत्परामर्श देती थी। मैत्रेयी, शकुन्तला, सीता, अनुसूईया, दमयन्ती, सावित्री आदि स्त्रियाँ इनके ज्वलन्त उदाहरण है। नारी की शिक्षा के लिए उनके मानसिक धरातल के अनुकूल तथा गृहविज्ञान की शिक्षा आवश्यक है।

अवनति का एक कारण बाल विवाह एवं अनमेल विवाह है। छोटी अवस्था में माता-पिता का स्नेहपूर्ण घर छोड़कर बालिकाओं को अपरिचित के घर जाना पड़ता है। अपरिपक्व अवस्था में माता बन जाना अकाल मृत्यु को दस्तक देना होता है। किसी प्रलोभन में आकर कम उम्र की लड़की का ब्याह अधेड़ आदमी के साथ किया जाता है। वह अधेड़ आदमी न तो उसके जीवन का साथ ही निभा सकता है और न उसे संतुष्ट कर सकता है। बेमेल ब्याह का तात्पर्य अवस्था से ही नहीं है, स्वभाव, गुण और कर्म से भी मेल होना आवश्यक है। विवाह के सम्बन्ध में पर्याप्त छानबीन करनी चाहिए। लड़कियों को अपना वर चुनने की स्वतंत्रता मिलनी चाहिए। सम्पत्ति के उत्तराधिकार का कानून लागू होना चाहिए। अधिकार सिर्फ कागज पर अंकित करने मात्र से ही नहीं मिल सकता बल्कि व्यावहारिक जीवन में उन अधिकारों के प्रयोग की पूर्ण सुविधा मिलनी चाहिए। इसके लिए उचित साहित्य तैयार करना चाहिए और उस साहित्य का स्त्री समाज में पूर्ण प्रचार-प्रसार होना चाहिए जिससे उनके मानसिक क्षितिज पर प्रभाव पड़े। शिक्षा से ही मनुष्य की बुद्धि का परिमार्जन

होता है। जीवन का वास्तविक मूल्य शिक्षित नारी ही समझ सकती है। नारी जाति को समुचित प्रतिष्ठा, मनोबल, स्वाभिमानपूर्ण जीवन प्रदान करने की आवश्यकता है। यदि हम सभ्य समाज के नागरिक हैं, एक महान संस्कृति के अनुयायी हैं और नए विश्व का नेतृत्व करना है तो नारी को मान-सम्मान देना होगा।

जब तक मनुष्य की मूलसत्ता में आमूलचूल परिवर्तन नहीं होता, तब तक बदलाव स्थायी नहीं हो सकता है। मनुष्य के समग्र परिवर्तन के लिए मानवी अंतराल का सम्पूर्ण बदलाव जरूरी है। चाहे जिस भी काल में यह पूर्ण बदलाव आए, वहाँ मानवी अन्तःकरण में क्रान्ति अवश्य घटित होगी। इसके लिए उत्कर्ष की दिशा में कदम बढ़ाने की आवश्यकता है। हमें स्वयं से संघर्ष करना होगा। आत्म परिष्कार की साधना किसी महाभारत से कम नहीं है उसमें क्षण-क्षण में मनोभूमि में आनेवाली बुराइयों और दुष्प्रवृत्तियों से लोहा लेना होगा। हम सभी नारियों को एक सैनिक की भूमिका निभानी होगी और कुविचारों एवं दुर्भावनाओं के आते ही उसे धर दबोचना होगा ताकि उनकी मलिनता मानस पटल पर हावी न हो पाए। यदि हमारी अन्तरात्मा जीवित है तो नारी के प्रति समाज का जो अनुदार, संकीर्ण अहंकार भरा दृष्टिकोण है उसे हटाना होगा। नारी ने पति के आगे आत्मसमर्पण का जो अनुपम आदर्श रखा है उसका यह अर्थ नहीं होना चाहिए कि उसका मूल्य कुछ भी नहीं है। आखिर नारी की आत्मा भी पूछती है कि—उसे अपने मनोवांछित सम्मान और स्वातंत्र्य से कब तक वंचित रहना होगा? कब उसे वह अवसर प्राप्त होगा कि पिंजड़े में बंद पक्षी एवं खूँटे से बंधे पशु से ऊपर समझा जाए। उसे भी उन्नति एवं प्रगति का अवसर मिलना चाहिए। इस स्थिति को लाने के लिए हमें रूढ़िवादी विचार को बदलना होगा और नैतिक दृष्टि अपनानी होगी। इसी आधार पर पति-पत्नी एक दूसरे के प्रति प्रेम, विश्वास, आदर, त्याग, सेवा, क्षमा, उदारता एवं समानता का व्यवहार कर दाम्पत्य जीवन की सुदृढ़ आधारशिला रख सकेगी।

अब समय की पुकार है कि हम अपनी उस भूल को सुधारें, नारी के विकास की आवश्यकता को अनुभव करें और इसके लिए सच्चे मन से प्रयत्नशील रहें। सारे समाज को कुकृत्यों के प्रायश्चित के लिए तैयार होना पड़ेगा, भूल सुधार करना होगा तभी नारी का उत्थान सम्भव है। इस परिवर्तन के लिए प्रयास एवं पुरुषार्थ को सदैव ध्यान में रखना होगा। वैसे मान्यताए बदल रही है। बेटे की अपेक्षा बेटियों की लालसा बढ़ रही है। लिंग भेद की रूढ़िवादी मान्यताएं नव दम्पतियों में बदल रही हैं। ऐसे दम्पतियों की संख्या में तेजी से वृद्धि हो रही है जो पहली सन्तान के रूप में बेटी को ज्यादा पसन्द करते हैं। यहाँ तक की एक सन्तान के रूप में सिर्फ एक बेटी को ही पसन्द किया जा रहा है। अब बेटी के जन्म पर सन्नाटा, मायूसी एवं

चिन्ताएं नहीं है। यह नारी के प्रति मानसिक बदलाव का ही परिणाम है कि बेटियाँ बेटों से एक कदम आगे हैं। इसका मुख्य कारण है कि बेटियाँ बुनियादी तौर पर ईमानदार एवं स्नेही होती हैं। मनोवैज्ञानिकों की नजर में भी लड़कियाँ प्रायः अपने लक्ष्य के प्रति दृढ़ रहती हैं। यूनिसेफ की रिपोर्ट में स्पष्ट हो गया है कि 1981 में भारत में लड़के की आबादी में लड़कियों की भागीदारी का अनुपात एक हजार के मुकाबले 915 था जो बढ़कर 2001 में 938 तक पहुँचा है। यह परिवर्तन मामुली नहीं है। इंदिरा गांधी से आज राबड़ी देवी तक, मेघा पाटेकर से शीला दीक्षित तक तथा अरूंधती राय से ऐश्वर्या राय तक एक लम्बी कतार है जिन्होंने अपनी योग्यता से हवा का रुख मोड़ा है।

स्पष्ट है कि मानवीय गरिमा अच्छे विचार को धारण करने में है। इसके लिए प्रबल पराक्रम करना होगा जिससे चेतना की गति ऊर्ध्वमुखी हो। धरती पर सतयुगी वातावरण की सम्भावना को साकार करने के लिए एकमात्र आधार यही है कि मनुष्य अपनी क्षुद्रता को त्यागे, काम-क्रोध, ईर्ष्या-द्वेष को तिलांजलि दे और उच्च आदर्शवादिता को अपनाये। महिलाएं भी अपनी दिमागी सोच-बदलें। जब पारिवारिक व्यवस्था को संतुलित करने में वह सफल हो सकती है तो दुनियाँ का कोई काम उससे अछूता नहीं। पुरुष समाज उसपर विश्वास करे, उसकी योग्यता को भी समझे तो आशातीत परिणाम सामने आ सकता है। आज समाज में अपनी खोई प्रतिष्ठा और शांति पाने के लिए आधुनिकता के साथ अपनी सांस्कृतिक परम्पराओं की रक्षा करने की आवश्यकता है। स्त्रियों को हर मोर्चे पर परिवार से सहानुभूति, संवेदना और समर्थन चाहिए। व्यावहारिक रूप से यह प्रयास हो कि स्त्री-पुरुष एक दूसरे के स्पर्धी नहीं बल्कि पूरक हैं।

अध्याय 27

स्त्री सशक्तिकरण : भारतीय संदर्भ

सरोज कुमार वर्मा

स्त्री सशक्तिकरण वर्तमान दुनिया का बेहद जरूरी विमर्श है। चूँकि यह स्त्री की स्वतंत्रता, समानता, मजबूती और महत्ता का हिमायती है, इसलिये इसे संपूर्ण मानव जाति के आधे हिस्से की बेहतरी से जुड़ा विमर्श कहा जा सकता है। यूरोप में इसकी शुरुआत कोई दो शताब्दी पहले हुई, जब मेरी वोल्सटन क्राफ्ट की पुस्तक 'ए विन्डिक्शन ऑफ द राइट्स ऑफ विमेन' का प्रकाशन 1792 में हुआ। इसमें पहली बार मेरी ने फ्रांस से प्रभावित होकर 'स्वतंत्रता-समानता-भ्रातृत्व' के सिद्धान्त को स्त्री समुदाय पर भी लागू करने की माँग की। उन्होंने[1] स्पष्ट रूप से कहा कि कोई भी समतावादी सामाजिक दर्शन तब तक वास्तविक अर्थों में समतावादी नहीं हो सकता जब तक कि वह स्त्रियों को समान अधिकार और अवसर देने तथा उनकी हिफाजत करने की हिमायत नहीं करता। इसीलिये मेरी वोल्सटन क्राफ्ट को स्त्री-मुक्ति का आदि-सिद्धान्तकार माना जाता है। बाद में स्त्री की इस मुक्ति की वकालत जॉन स्टुअर्ट मिल ने 1869 में प्रकाशित अपनी पुस्तक 'द सब्जेक्शन ऑफ विमेन' में की, जिसे और मजबूत स्वर मिला सिमोन द बोउवार की 1949 में प्रकाशित पुस्तक 'द सेकेण्ड सेक्स' से। इनके अतिरिक्त जाँ आँतुआँ कोन्दोर्से, ओलिम्पी द गूजे, चेर्नीशेव्स्की, अलेक्सान्द्रा कोल्लोन्ताई तथा जर्मेन ग्रीयर आदि ने भी स्त्रीवादी विचारों को स्थापित और विकसित करने में महत्वपूर्ण भूमिका निभाई। इस सबके सम्मिलित एवं निरंतर प्रयास से ही यूरोप में फ्रांसीसी क्रांति के दौरान शुरू हुआ संगठित स्त्रीवादी आंदोलन सघन और व्यापक रूप ले सका।

भारत में स्त्री के हित और अधिकारों से जुड़े आंदोलन की शुरूआत उन्नीसवीं सदी के पूर्वार्द्ध में हुई तब न्याय, नैतिकता, आचार और परंपरा से संबंधित विमर्श भी हुये। परंतु इन सब पर कहीं-न-कहीं राष्ट्रीय गुलामी की छाया पड़ी रही। बीसवीं सदी के राष्ट्रीय जागरण काल में यद्यपि स्त्री-मुक्ति की चिन्ता भी शामिल थी, लेकिन

राष्ट्रीय स्वाधीनता आंदोलन की तीव्रता के कारण यह चिन्ता कोई स्पष्ट आकार ग्रहण नहीं कर सकी। आकार की यह स्पष्टता कोई ढाई-तीन दशक पहले के स्त्रीवादी आंदोलनों में प्रकट होनी शुरू हुई, जब वैचारिक स्तर पर स्त्री-मुक्ति की नई लहर उठी। स्त्री सशक्तिकरण इसी लहर की तार्किक परिणति है। इसलिये इसे वक्त के कैनवस पर स्त्री के भविष्य का स्केच कहा जा सकता है। यह स्केच भारत सहित पूरी दुनिया में खींचा जा रहा हैश और यह प्रयास किये जा रहे हैं कि स्त्री इसमें अपनी इच्छानुसार रंग भर सके।

भारतीय इतिहास के वैदिक युग में स्त्रियों की स्थिति सुदृढ़ थी। उन्हें कुलदेवी का स्थान प्राप्त था। शिक्षा का समान अधिकार मिला था। तभी तो वे ज्ञानी, विद्वान, पंडित और विचारिका हुआ करती थीं। स्त्रियों द्वारा रची गई वेद की कई ऋचायें इसके प्रमाण हैं। संपत्ति पर भी उनका समान हक था। इसका उल्लेख आपस्तम्ब-धर्म-सूत्र (2/29/3) में मिलता है। घर की स्वामिनी होने के बावजूद उनका कार्य क्षेत्र घर तक सीमित नहीं था। वे घर के बारह भी निकलती थी। क्षत्रिय स्त्रियों को तो युद्ध में सारथ्य करने का अधिकार प्राप्त था। परंतु बाद में उनकी स्थिति बदतर होती चली गई। उनके अधिकार छीनते चले गये। पुरुषों ने अपने लिये जो नियम-कानून बनाये, स्त्रियों को उनसे वंचित कर दिया। पति की सेवा, बच्चे का जन्म तथा गृहकार्य तक उनकी जिन्दगी सिमट गई। पुरुषों ने उन्हें पराधीन, हेय और अशिक्षित करके घर में कैद कर दिया। उनकी हर सांस पर अपना अधिकार जमा लिया। वे एक निर्जीव पदार्थ के समान हो गईं जो अपने ऊपर होने वाले अत्याचारों के विरुद्ध उफ् भी नहीं कर सकतीं थी।

स्त्रियों की यह दारुण स्थिति भारत समेत पूरी दुनिया में थी। सब जगह उनको पुरुषों के अत्याचार सहन करने पड़ रहे थे। उनके शोषण से रू-ब-रू होना पड़ रहा था। और इसका आधार लिंग-भेद था। जबकि लिंग के आधार पर ऐसा होना नहीं चाहिए। लिंग की भिन्नता शरीर की भिन्नता से तय होती है और शरीर की भिन्नता किसी को दोयम दर्जे की नहीं बनाती। शरीर के कारण कोई ऊँच-नीच, शिक्षित-अशिक्षित, मूर्ख-बुद्धिमान, स्वतंत्र-परतंत्र, समान-असमान तथा अधिकारयुक्त अथवा अधिकारच्युत नहीं होता। नहीं होना चाहिए। इसलिए सिमोन ने इसका प्रतिवाद करते हुए कहा—"......शारीरिक भिन्नता के बावजूद ये सीमायें औरत की अनिवार्य और स्थायी नियति के रूप में नहीं स्वीकारी जा सकती। शारीरिक भिन्नता यह नहीं स्थापित करती कि औरत अन्या, गौण या यौनजाति सोपानीकरण में नीचे की सीढ़ी पर बैठी हुई है। ये जैविक परिस्थितियाँ औरत को अधीनस्थ भूमिका स्वीकारने के लिए मेरी समझ में बाध्य नहीं कर सकतीं।"[2]

ऐसी ही समझ जब भारत में विकसित हुई तो यहाँ भी स्त्रियों की बेहतरी के प्रयास शुरू हुये। स्वतंत्रता, समानता, शिक्षा और स्वास्थ्य के उनके अधिकारों पर बल लिये गये। उन्हें घर से बाहर निकलने की सुविधा दी गई। अर्थोपार्जन के अवसर उपलब्ध कराये गये। उनके दायित्वों का संकुचित दायरा टूटा। सामाजिक और राजनैतिक क्षेत्रों में भागीदारी के मौके मिले। उन पर लगी कई प्रकार की पाबंदियाँ और वर्जनायें खत्म हुईं। इनमें कुछ तो स्त्रियों ने अपने संघर्ष से हासिल किये परन्तु अधिकांश पुरुषों द्वारा राजनैतिक और वैधानिक प्रावधानों के अंतर्गत दिये गये, जो अब तक पर्याप्त नहीं है।

परन्तु इससे बंद दीवार में एक खिड़की खुली, जिससे स्त्री को बाहर झांकने का मौका मिला। उसने सुनहरी धूप और ताजा हवा के बारे में जाना। उसके भीतर दीवार से बाहर आने की ललक पैदा हुई। खुले आकाश में उड़ने की आकांक्षा ने पंख फैलाये। ऐसा इसलिये हुआ कि यद्यपि किसी भी तरह के राजनैतिक और वैधानिक प्रावधान सहजता से तत्काल समाज में स्वीकृत नहीं हो पाते, परन्तु एक शुरुआत जरूर होती है जिसे धीरे-धीरे स्वीकृति मिलने लगती है, यद्यपि कि इसमें एक लंबा वक्त लगता है। स्त्री की समानता और स्वतंत्रता को लेकर भी ऐसा ही हुआ है। उसने इस दिशा में अतीत से लेकर अब तक एक लंबी यात्रा की है। फलस्वरूप उसके स्त्रीत्व की छुई-मुई वाली मानक छवि में एक तब्दीली आई है और उस तब्दीली को समाज में स्वीकृति भी मिलने लगी है। बावजूद इसके अभी वह इतनी समर्थ नहीं हुई है कि इस बदली छवि को मनचाहे ढंग से सजा सके। स्त्री सशक्तिकरण इसी संपूर्ण सामर्थ्य के लिए किया गया प्रतिबद्ध और प्रामाणिक प्रयास है। इसका प्रस्थान बिन्दु स्त्रियों द्वारा अपनी छवि और अपना कार्य दोनों के निर्धारण संबंधी अपना निर्णय स्वयं लेने का अधिकार है, जिसकी सार्थकता किसी के दे देने में नहीं, स्वयं आगे बढ़कर ले लेने में है। दरअसल स्त्रियों को भी अपनी स्वतंत्रता लेनी पड़ेगी। लेकिन स्वतंत्रता बहुत जोखिम भरी होती है, क्योंकि उसके साथ जिम्मेवारी भी अवियोज्य रूप से जुड़ी रहती है। अतः स्त्रियों को सशक्तिकरण का दस्तावेज लिये ठहर कर सावधानीपूर्वक यह तय करना पड़ेगा कि उनकी स्वतंत्रता और समानता का स्वरूप कैसा हो और उन्हें प्राप्त करने की प्रक्रिया क्या हो?

सावधानीपूर्वक इसलिये कि अक्सर ऐसा होता है कि शोषक वर्ग के विरुद्ध जब शोषित वर्ग संघर्ष करता है तो उसे अपनी मुक्ति शोषित वर्ग का प्रतिरूप बन जाने में ही दिखाई देती है। स्त्रीवादी आंदोलन भी इससे वंचित नहीं है। दुनिया भर में पुरुष वर्चस्व के खिलाफ जब स्त्रियों ने विद्रोह किये तो अपनी आजादी पाने के बदले अपनी पहचान ही गँवा बैठीं। प्रतिरूप को मूल का पर्याय मानने के कारण वे एक

हास्यास्पद अनुकरण की शिकार हो गईं। वे एक मौलिक स्त्री बनने के बजाये नकली पुरुष बनने लगीं। पुरुष जैसे कपड़े पहनने, बाल कटाने, चलने-बोलने तथा शराब-सिगरेट पीने आदि को ही अपनी आजादी समझने लगी, जबकि यह आजादी नहीं, पुरुषों की श्रेष्ठता स्वीकार लेने जैसी गुलामी ही है। इसीलिए चर्चित दार्शनिक ओशो (भगवान श्री रजनीश) इस अनुकरण से बचने की हिदायत देते हुये कहते हैं—"यह ध्यान रहे स्त्री के पास एक अपने तरह का व्यक्तित्व है। जो पुरुष से बहुत भिन्न है, बहुत विरोधी, बहुत अलग, बहुत दूसरा है। उसका सारा आकर्षण उसके जीवन की सारी सुगंध, उसके अपने होने में है, उसके निज होने में है। अगर वह अपनी निजता के बिन्दु से च्युत होती है और पुरुष जैसे होने की दौड़ में लग जाती है तो यह बात इतनी बेहूदी होगी जैसे कोई पुरुष स्त्रियों के कपड़े पहन के दाढ़ी मूंछ घुटा के स्त्रियों जैसा बनके घूमने लगता है तो वह बेहूदा हो जाता है। यह बात इतनी ही गलत है।"[3] इसलिये स्त्री, स्त्री की तरह बची रहे तभी वह स्वतंत्र, समान, सशक्त तथा सम्माननीय हो सकती है। पुरुष की नकल तो उसे और दोयम दर्जे की स्थिति में लाकर गुलाम और कमजोर बना देगी। यह बात स्त्रियों को गंभीरता से महसूसनी होगी।

इसी तरह उन्हें आज के बाजारवाद और उपभोक्तावाद के शिकंजे से भी अपनी आजादी और अस्मिता को बचाये रखने की जरूरत हैं। वैज्ञानिक आविष्कारों के बाद औद्योगिक प्रगति के क्रम में जो नई सभ्यता विकसित हुई है उसके केन्द्र में बाजार है। बाजार का दबाव आज हर क्षेत्र में है। आदमी की सोच, शैली, गति और दिशा सब बाजार तय कर रहा है। जो देश आर्थिक उन्नति के शीर्ष पर हैं, उनका मुख्य काम नये-नये उत्पाद निर्मित कर पूरी दुनिया में बेचना है। उनके नक्शे-कदम पर चलते हुये बाकि के देश भी यही कर रहे हैं। अब उत्पादों को खरीदने के लिए उपभोक्ता भी चाहिए। उपभोक्ता को आकर्षित करने के लिए विज्ञापन का सहारा लिया जाता है। स्त्रियाँ इसका माध्यम बन रही हैं। वे अपने रंग-रूप, नाज-नखरे के सहारे इन उत्पादों को बेचने में लगी हैं और प्रकारान्तर से खुद बिक रही हैं। जब कोई स्त्री विज्ञापन में चप्पल, टायर, ठंडा पेय, अथवा मजबूत सिमेंट बेच रही होती है तो इन सबके साथ वह स्वयं भी बिक रही होती है और इसके लिए अपने वस्त्र उतारने से भी परहेज नहीं करती। इस प्रकार विज्ञापन इस नयी सभ्यता द्वारा स्त्रियों के लिए निर्मित किया हुआ नया बंधन है, जो आकर्षक और खूबसूरत होने के कारण उन्हें सहज स्वीकार्य लगता है।

मगर इसके पीछे भी पुरुष की चालाकी और कुटिलता है। आज के अर्थ युग में अपने अधिकाधिक लाभ के लिए वह स्त्री का उपयोग कर लेना चाहता है। इसके

लिए स्त्री का गुलाम रहना जरूरी है। इसीलिए वह गुलामी के ज्यादा मोहक और नफीस तरीके निर्मित कर रहा है, जो पहले से ज्यादा ठोस और सख्त हैं। दिलचस्प बात यह है कि स्त्रियाँ भी इसे अपनी मुक्ति का पर्याय मान रही हैं। परन्तु यह कितनी बड़ी विडंबना है कि स्त्री की मुक्ति और अधिकार की लड़ाई को देह की नग्नता और उपभोग की स्वच्छंदता से परिभाषित किया जाये? उसे वर्जनाओं से मुक्ति मिलने के बदले वस्त्रों से मुक्ति मिले। स्त्रियों ने अपने पुराने गहने, बंधन के प्रतीक मानकर, इसलिए नहीं उतारे थे कि अपने बाल को काले-घने रखने तथा अंग-अनुपात का सौष्ठव बनाये रखने जैसे शरीर के रख-रखाव संबंधी नये गहनों से सज-संवर कर बाजार में बिकने के लिए बैठ जाए। ख्यातिप्राप्त साहित्यकार प्रभाकर श्रोत्रिय इस पर विस्तार से विचार करते हुए कहते हैं—"यह सूक्ष्म और वायवीय कैद पहले की कैदों से ज्यादा मजबूत है।...यह अधिक चुनौती पूर्ण इसलिए हो उठा है कि स्वयं स्त्रियों का एक वर्ग नये भ्रमजाल में फँसकर स्त्री मात्र को फँसा रहा है, बिना यह सोचे कि साबुन के सान्निध्य में प्रेमिका जैसी लाज; घोड़ा, साबुन और हवाखोरी के रिश्ते; सांसों की खुशबू से प्रेम संबंध का निर्धारण, असंख्य स्त्रियों को क्या संदेश दे रहा है? स्त्री क्यों इन्कार नहीं करती कि वह बाजार का माध्यम नहीं बनेगी। अपनी व्यावसायिक आत्म-निर्भरता के बदले लाखों-करोड़ों स्त्रियों को वस्तुओं का दास नहीं बनायेगी।"[4] अपनी स्वतंत्रता और समानता के लिए संघर्ष करने वाली दुनिया की तमाम स्त्रियों और स्त्रीवादी आंदोलनों को इस साजिश को समझते हुये इससे सचेत रहना पड़ेगा।

फिर भारतीय स्त्रियों को एक अतिरिक्त सावधानी यह भी बरतनी पड़ेगी कि वे पश्चिमी स्त्रीवादी विमर्श को अपना आदर्श न मानें। कोई भी व्यक्ति वहीं के चौखटे तोड़ सकता है, जहाँ वह रहता है। इसलिए भारतीय स्त्री को भी यहाँ के चौखटों को पहचान कर उन्हें ही तोड़ने का प्रयास करना चाहिए। चूँकि भारतीय स्त्रीवादी आंदोलनों के विकास में पश्चिमी स्त्रीवादी आंदोलनों की महती भूमिका रही है, इसलिए भारतीय आंदोलनों पर पश्चिम का पर्याप्त प्रभाव रहा है और यहाँ के आंदोलन अपना उपजीव्य भी वहीं से प्राप्त करते रहें हैं। इसीलिए यहाँ के व्यावहारिक कार्यक्रमों में भी वहाँ के आदर्शों और योजनाओं का समावेश रहा है। यहाँ के स्त्रीवादी आंदोलनों की बागडोर यहाँ के अभिजात वर्गों के हाथ में रही है और यहाँ अभिजात होने का अर्थ पश्चिमी शैली का जीवन जीना है। इसलिए इस वर्ग के द्वारा यहाँ के स्त्रियों के लिए जिस आजादी की वकालत की गई उसमें पश्चिम के तर्ज पर ही एकल जीवन की सुरक्षा, बिना विवाह के पुरुष के साथ रहने की स्वीकृति, कुँवारी माँ बनने का अधिकार, विवाह करके भी माँ नहीं बनने की छूट, तलाक की सुविधा,

विवाहेत्तर यौन-संबंधों की इजाजत, एक से अधिक विवाह का हक, इच्छानुसार प्रेम-संबंधों की अनुमति आदि मिलने की स्वच्छंदता शामिल है। कुल मिलाकर यह एक ऐसी जीवन शैली की वकालत है, जिसमें जो मन में आये वही करने की आजादी हासिल हो। इसीलिए यहाँ भी स्त्री-समलैंगिकता के चर्चे हैं और एक छोटा स्त्री-वर्ग उसका पक्षधर भी है। यद्यपि पश्चिम से प्रभावित अभिजात वर्ग की स्त्रियों ने ऐसी आजादी के लिए ईमानदार प्रयास किये परंतु उन्हें सफलता नहीं मिली। इसलिए कि उनके तमाम व्यावहारिक कार्यक्रम स्थानीयता से कटे रहे। यद्यपि इन्होंने न्याय, समानता, मानवीयता, स्वतंत्रता जैसे कई आधारभूत प्रश्न खड़े किये, जो पश्चिमी स्त्रीवादी विमर्श से इन्हें मिला है, परन्तु यहाँ के लिये भी प्रासंगिक और जरूरी होने के बावजूद ये सारे प्रश्न बेमानी हो गये, क्योंकि इनका व्यावहारिक कार्यान्वयन भारतीयता के संदर्भ में नहीं किया जा सका।

इसलिये भारतीय स्त्रियों की स्वतंत्रता और समानता की रूपरेखा यहाँ की नैतिकता, परम्परा, संस्कृति और सभ्यता को ध्यान में रखकर तय करनी होगी, क्योंकि ये सब देश-काल सापेक्ष होती हैं, निरपेक्ष नहीं। इसीलिए पश्चिमी समाज की परंपरा और नैतिकता भारतीय समाज के लिए स्वीकृत नहीं हो सकतीं, न वहाँ की सभ्यता और संस्कृति यहाँ के लिए अणुकरणीय। यही वजह है कि पश्चिम से आयातीत यौन-उन्मुक्तता, शरीर-उद्योग, अनब्याही पत्नी तथा कुँवारी माँ जैसे आदर्श थोड़े अपवादों के अतिरिक्त भारत के शेष स्त्री समुदाय का अभीष्ट नहीं हैं। वह इनके बिना ही स्वतंत्रता और समानता प्राप्त करना चाहती है। यह बात भारतीय स्त्री के लिए सुखद दाम्पत्य और किलकते बच्चों की तुलना में शरीर और यौन संबंधी जरूरतें गौण महत्व की होती हैं। यहाँ की परम्परा भी ऐसी ही रही है। यहाँ वैयक्तिक तुष्टि के लिए अनियंत्रित यौन-संबंधों की वकालत कभी नहीं की गई बल्कि संतानोत्पत्ति के लिए मर्यादित यौन-संबंध की स्वीकृति दी गई है और उसका आधार एकनिष्ठ दाम्पत्य को माना गया है। इसलिये यहाँ की स्त्री यह जानती है कि परिवार और नैतिकता के संदर्भ में यौन-स्वच्छंदता के बगैर भी वह समान और स्वतंत्र हो सकती है। इसलिए उसकी मुक्ति और समानता का अर्थ उसके साथ किया जाने वाला मानवीय व्यवहार है, जिसके अंतर्गत उसके लिए शिक्षा, स्वास्थ्य, रोजगार तथा निर्णय के समान अवसर उपलब्ध हों। उसका दाम्पत्य जीवन सुखद तथा स्थायी हो तथा बांझ होने अथवा बेटे की माँ न बन पाने की स्थिति में भी उसे अपमानित न होना पड़े। अतः उसके सशक्त होने का तात्पर्य पुरुष से सर्वथा विलग होकर कोई स्वायत्त स्त्री-समाज निर्मित कर लेना नहीं है, अपितु पुरुष के साथ रहते हुए उसका

दृष्टिकोण बदल पाना है ताकि वह उसके साथ समान और सम्मानित व्यवहार कर सके। स्त्री विमर्श की प्रामाणिक लेखिका अर्चना वर्मा के शब्दों में—"प्रश्न पुरुष पर निर्भरता से मुक्ति का नहीं, पुरुष का दृष्टिकोण बदल पाने का है जिससे कि निर्भरता में भी सम्मानीय रहा जा सके...।"[5]

यह इसलिये भी जरूरी है कि स्त्री पुरुष के पार्थक्य से परिवार टूटता है, जिसका सर्वाधिक खामियाजा बच्चे को भुगतना पड़ता है। बच्चे भविष्य होते हैं, इसलिए उन्हें हाशिये पर रखकर किसी भी भविष्य के बारे में कोई भी सार्थक विचार संभव नहीं हो सकता। बेहतर भविष्य के लिए बच्चों का स्वस्थ और संतुलित विकास जरूरी है, जो सुखमय परिवार में ही संभव हो सकता है। एक अमेरिकी सर्वेक्षण में यह बात स्पष्ट हुई है कि वहाँ के भारतीय बच्चे अमेरिकी बच्चे की तुलना में विद्यालय तथा अन्य क्षेत्रों में इसलिए अधिक सफल हो पाते हैं कि उनका पालन-पोषण सुखी परिवार में होता है जबकि अमेरिकी बच्चे इससे वंचित रह जाते हैं। ऐसा सुखी परिवार स्त्री-पुरुष की आपसी समझ और पारस्परिक सहयोग से बनता है।

इसके लिए स्त्री का आर्थिक रूप से स्वतंत्र होना जरूरी नहीं है। यद्यपि आर्थिक स्वतंत्रता किसी के लिए भी स्वतंत्र होने की अनिवार्य शर्त है, परन्तु इतने मात्र से कोई स्त्री स्वतंत्र हो जायेगी, ऐसा नहीं है। कई बार ऐसा होता है कि आर्थिक रूप से स्वतंत्र होने के बावजूद पत्नी का अपनी कमाई पर अधिकार नहीं होता। पति जोर-जबर्दस्ती से उसे छीनकर अपने हिसाब से खर्च अथवा दुरुपयोग करता है। इसलिए वास्तविक स्वतंत्रता तो निर्णय की स्वतंत्रता है। अतः भारतीय पारिवारिक संरचना में यदि स्त्री का दाम्पत्य जीवन सुखी और अनुकूल है तो आर्थिक स्वतंत्रता के बगैर भी वह स्वतंत्र हो सकती है। बच्चों के बेहतर विकास के लिए यह और भी जरूरी होता है। अर्थोपार्जन के लिए घर से बाहर निकलने वाली स्त्रियों के बच्चे उपेक्षा और अकेलेपन के शिकार हो जाते हैं जो उनमें हीनता और कुंठा पैदा करती हैं। फलतः उनका संतुलित विकास नहीं हो पाता। इसलिए आदर्श स्थिति तो यही होगी कि पति अर्थोपार्जन करे और घर तथा बच्चे का पूरा दायित्व पत्नी पर रहे और उसके इस कार्य को हर ढंग से पति के बराबर समझा जाये। इससे सहमत होते हुए मिल भी कहते हैं—"अगर घर या दाम्पत्य जीवन की आर्थिक स्थिति असंतोषजनक नहीं है, तो मेरे विचार में पत्नी को अपनी खुद की आय अर्जित करने की जरूरत नहीं महसूस होनी चाहिए।"[6] मिल की इस सहमति से यह सिद्ध होता है कि यद्यपि यह भारतीय समाज का अभीष्ट है, परन्तु पश्चिमी समाज के लिए भी उपयोगी है। हाँ अगर परिवार की आर्थिक स्थिति संतोषप्रद नहीं है तब पत्नी का अर्थोपार्जन करना जरूरी हो जाता है लेकिन तब पति का भी दायित्व हो जाता है कि वह पत्नी का

सहयोग करते हुये घर और बच्चों के काम में उसका हाथ बँटाये। ऐसी स्थिति में, जब अर्थोपार्जन के लिए स्त्री का घर से बाहर निकलना जरूरी हो, उसके काम के घंटे, काम का समय, नौकरी की आयुसीमा, छुट्टियों का प्रावधान आदि पुरुषों से भिन्न होने चाहिए। इससे वह अपने बच्चे का पालन-पोषण सही ढंग से कर पायेगी। मगर किसी भी हाल में सुखी परिवार और संतुष्ट दाम्पत्य में कोई बिखराव नहीं आना चाहिए ताकि बच्चे, जो पति-पत्नी दोनों की अमूल्य निधि और भविष्य हैं, का संतुलित और समुचित विकास हो सके। फिर बच्चों के साथ-साथ परिवार से स्त्री-पुरुष दोनों के हित भी जुड़े होते हैं।

इसलिए स्त्री सशक्तिकरण के लिए चलाये जाने वाले आंदोलन को स्त्री बनाम पुरुष की लड़ाई की जरूरत नहीं है, क्योंकि यदि स्त्रीवादी विमर्श की इस बुनियादी स्थापना को स्वीकार लिया जाये कि स्त्री कोई बनी-बनाई चीज नहीं होती, बना दी जाती है तो फिर यह भी स्वीकारना पड़ेगा कि पुरुष भी कोई बनी-बनाई वस्तु नहीं होता, बना दिया जाता है और इन दोनों के बनने में परम्परा, इतिहास समाज और शिक्षा आदि की महत्वपूर्ण भूमिका होती है। इसलिए स्त्रीत्व और पुरुषत्व के अब तक जो प्रतिमान गढ़े गये हैं, जैसे कोमलता, समर्पण आदि स्त्रियों के गुण हैं और कठोरता, आक्रामकता आदि पुरुषों के गुण इत्यादि, उन पर फिर से विचार करने की जरूरत है और दोनों अपने इन रूढ़ हो गये प्रतिमानों के खोल से बाहर निकलकर एक-दूसरे को अंतरंगता में जानना-समझना है ताकि उनके संबंध द्वन्द्वात्मक न होकर सहयोगात्मक बने। स्त्री तभी सशक्त हो सकती है।

और स्त्री का सशक्त होना केवल उसके हित में नहीं, बल्कि पुरुष के हित में भी है, और न केवल पुरुष के बल्कि सारे समाज और राष्ट्र के हित में है। कोई भी समाज और राष्ट्र अपने आधे अंग, स्त्री की मुक्ति और मजबूती उन्नति नहीं कर सकता। फिर स्त्रियों के सहयोग के बिना पुरुषों ने अकेले जो दुनिया बनाई है वह असंतुलित और अराजक है। इस हद तक हिंसक और आक्रामक कि तीन हजार वर्षों में पन्द्रह हजार युद्ध लड़े गये। यह पूरी मानवता के विक्षिप्त होने का प्रमाण है। ऐसा इसलिए हुआ कि अपनी कमजोर स्थिति के कारण स्त्रियों ने मनुष्यता के विकास में कोई योगदान नहीं दिया। सारा विकास अधूरा और एकांगी रहा। स्त्री मजबूत होकर इसे पूरा और सर्वांगीण बना सकती है। वह समाज, सभ्यता, संस्कृति, शिक्षा आदि तमाम क्षेत्रों में बढ़कर योगदान कर सकती है। हिंसा मुक्त अहिंसक दुनिया की संरचना कर सकती है। एक ऐसी मानवता निर्मित कर सकती है जो प्रेम सहयोग, करुणा और सहिष्णुता आदि सद्गुणों पर आधारित हो। ऐसी तभी हो सकता है जब स्त्री मजबत हो। परंतु उसे ऐसी मजबूती पुरुष से अलग होकर नहीं

उसे साथ लेकर ही मिल सकती है। इसलिए स्त्री सशक्तिकरण कोई पुरुष निरपेक्ष नहीं बल्कि सापेक्ष विमर्श है। और इसके लिए पुरुष को भी लचीला और उदार होना पड़ेगा। चूँकि किसी दूसरे को गुलाम और कमजोर बनाकर कोई स्वयं मुक्त और मजबूत नहीं हो सकता, इसलिए उसे समझना पड़ेगा कि स्त्री की मुक्ति और मजबूती में ही उसकी भी मुक्ति और मजबूती निहित है। ऐसी मुक्ति और मजबूती के साथ जब स्त्री-पुरुष एक-दूसरे का सहयोग करेंगे तभी उन दोनों के साथ-साथ बच्चे, समाज, देश और दुनिया का भी हित संभव हो सकता है।

संदर्भ

1. मेरी वोल्सटन क्राफ्ट, "स्त्री-अधिकारों का औचित्य-साधन" (संपादकीय प्रस्तावना), ('ए विन्डिक्शन ऑफ द राइट्स ऑफ विमेन' का हिन्दी अनुवाद, अनुवाद-मीनाक्षी), पृष्ठ-19, राजकमल प्रकाशन प्रा0 लि0, 1 बी, नेताजी सुभाष मार्ग, नई दिल्ली-110002, 2003
2. सीमोन द बोउवार, "स्त्री : उपेक्षिता" ('द सेकेन्ड सेक्स' का हिन्दी रूपान्तर, रूपान्तरकार-डा0 प्रभा खेतान), पृष्ठ-36, हिन्दी पाकेट बुक्स प्राइवेट लिमिटेड, जी0 टी0 रोड, शाहदरा, दिल्ली-110022, 1994
3. भगवान श्री रजनीश, "संभोग से समाधि की ओर", पृष्ठ-270, रजनीश धाम, 17, कोरे गांव पार्क, पूना-411001, महाराष्ट्र, 1983
4. प्रभाकर श्रोत्रिय, 'स्त्री : युद्ध का मोर्चा' (संपादकीय), "वागर्थ", अंक-32, नवम्बर 1997, पृष्ठ-7, भारतीय भाषा परिषद्, 36 ए, शेक्सपीयर सरणी, कलकत्ता-700017
5. अर्चना वर्मा, 'सशक्तीकरण पिछली सदी के स्वप्न का आगामी यथार्थ', "वागर्थ", (इक्कीसवीं शती का भविष्य विशेषांक), अंक-75, सितंबर 2001, पृष्ठ-164, भारतीय भाषा परिषद, 36 ए, शेक्सपीयर सरणी, कलकत्ता-700017
6. जॉन स्टुअर्ट मिल, "स्त्री और पराधीनता" ('द सब्जेक्शन ऑफ विमेन' का हिन्दी अनुवाद, अनुवादक-युगांक धीर), पृष्ठ-58, संवाद प्रकाशन, आई-499, शास्त्रीनगर, मेरठ-250004 (उ0 प्र0), 2002

Chapter 28

Woman Elite Today

Yogini G. Nighoskar

An Abstract

This is an age of awakening, especially for woman-force. After dark ages of suppression, a woman at last has found her voice, thanks to education and mass media. Problems and plights of women world over may differ due to many factors, but at core, they reflect a common fulcrum. An elite woman is no exception, but of course, she can make her point with a difference, due to her privileged and superior disposition

Woman Elite Today

Since time immemorial, woman has remained the subject of natural interest for mankind in general and men in particular. Woman has her own share of strength and weakness as any other living being on this earth. Her strength lies in her very biological structure. She brings forth a new life. It is she who exemplifies the basic and natural instincts (or values?) of loving and protecting her issues. She has been bestowed with the unanimous status of 'Teacher of all Teachers' almost by all civilization especially due to her selfless role as mother.[1] It is impossible to list her contribution to society in this capacity. (Let us not remember her weakness if any because it is the outcome of her physical disposition by and large.)

The versatile woman of today's elite world is a honourable species which should be well noticed and appreciated. Her role is multifarious, and if carried out effectively, is capable of changing the face of the world.

Problems faced by an educated woman, who also enjoys a respectable status in society are quite different from those with lesser deals. It is customary in Indian Society to accept woman as the sole controller of the family affairs related to home life. In West, this trend of India is highly appreciated for its stabilizing value, though not practiced in general. Hardly there is any field where woman power has not showed its splendors. The past may have produced women of eternal charms and unearthly beauty, and men, with special physique and velour boasting male chauvinism. We may be regaled by the rich heritage and intricate cultural ethos that shaped our woman-folk of yester years. No doubt this royal reminiscence is spotted in life and narration of various forms. But they have ceased to influence society by and large. One in a while, they shine out as a noble politician or a devout social worker. The latter expression of woman power, if tapped fully will work wonders. Graced and wedded to etiquette, knowledge and means, she has brought back the lost smiles on many faces. Mother Teressa has inspired many a woman of high breed to take after charity, not as something just done and forgotten, but a deed done with a respect for human dignity without humiliating the receiver. A 'Maharani' of Yore is a benefactor of many an institutions of social welfare in many places of our knowledge. A Royalty may choose to analyze the social structure of the slum-life rather than delve into the other world of self-forgetting. A woman, thus dedicated to the cause of humanity, is by far superior to one who chooses some such areas of service because of some other reasons. If a woman elite serves or sacrifices or loves or does some worthwhile odd jobs, then her work will surely bear her trademark. Problems faced by woman in different stratas of society will differ and at the same time may appear to be similar.

Problems of working women which may belong to any socio-economic group almost wear the same technical garb of boss-colleague relationship, colleague to colleague relationship, exploitation, and so on; where as elite woman is spared some such ignominies, she may be targeted on other fronts like a 'hot-favourite' of the authorities. The easiest way to furnish a woman's caricature is the private character assassination which unfortunately, is difficult to sue in Court of Law, much less to prove it.[2]

Elite woman has to undergo a mental exercise of accepting mediocrity at almost all levels of interaction. In the process, she has to stoop down, lest her vitalities suffer a set back. Else, she stands up to be counted as a person with a mind of her own, and then face the social trauma of being an autocrat. Under the circumstances, the elite woman often takes to the second recourse and as a consequence, there has emerged an image of a "tyrant woman" who often is looked upon as having a hen-packed husband.[3] The problem is enlarged if she happens to be single. All possible diseases belonging to the mental, ate conveniently transferred to her. Often there is a not of sympathy (apathy) unwanted, uncalled for. It runs thus: Oh! that's the psychology of such women! Unhappy, dissatisfied, incomplete as they are, they give their vent to suppressed feelings through acts of arrogance. More often than not, such a group of sympathizers belong to social strata of deficit class, socially, economically and even dream to be in the shoes of elite woman—a fact of which they are painfully aware. The woman, in all her maturity, overlooks such overtures as pathetically misplaced and miscalculated.

Status of urban woman elite is definitely meaningful in city locale. It is difficult to identify such a force in urban locality, even if one exists there. Woman—elite's work area may be a corporate or an academic field. Everywhere she faces more or les similar man-made restraints basically having roots in man dominated social structure; they are too well known to be narrated here.

Let us be square and even with the fact the there are some sections of work areas where woman force is outnumbered by man force. Even quality-wise, a woman's performance is treated to be inferior due to sheer biological reasons, especially in acts which call in for velour.

Woman elite is the sole "agent of excellence" where social and moral issues are at stake. It is an awakened woman after all who brings to fore-front the woes of suppressed class of woman. At the same time, it is because of such organized woman power which brings a moral pressure on men who wield power, that men suffer a setback. This theme has been advantageously exploited by stage, cinema and novels.

Earlier, women elites were in the garb of poetess or artists. To-day, they have entered into every field of our complex society with all its contradictions. One such contradiction a woman faces in her own home. While her domestic life demands everything that a wife, a mother, a sister, a daughter or likewise relations can offer, her office looks upon her as a mere entity who is expected to discharge all official duties efficiently. Striking a balance between the two roles is often tiring, and sometimes, it cuts through the very fiber of her womanhood. And when it ultimately happens, there emerges a dangerous species, which the society calls 'a tyrant woman, a ruthless person,' who ill-treats or insults her colleagues of a lower social strata. The remedy of this malady lies with the woman herself. More often than not, she uses her good senses to see reason; the point is to make her realize through an appropriate authority whom she recognizes as accepted. Such an authority can be in the form of a moral preceptor, a guru, an elderly respectable member of society or even her own immediate relative. Else, an elite woman possesses a wonderful self-correcting mechanism in-built in her personality which she can tap in the moments of crisis and tensions.

With the double attack from mediocre male, groupism and female inferiority-complex mentality, her task of regulating the routine office or academic work, suffers from lethargy. In her zeal to achieve efficiency, she takes normal steps and even these may be disproportionately represented to the social groups.

Much has been written and deliberated upon women, from psychological, cynical, psycho analytical, religious and other feministic points of view.

Feminism[4] may appear 'modern' because of the involvement of elite woman in this sphere. Many authors have written books on historical and contemporary situation in western culture. It is at once scientifically accurate in matters of biology and comprehensiveness; and it is frank in disclosing a woman's individual development and social relations, founded upon a broadly generous and consistent philosophy.

A woman elite is the constant resistance to the man-oriented and man dominated world of yester years of to-day and of years to come. It is truly said, that educate a woman if you want to educate the society.

References

1. Feminism holds equality central, and any special reference to a gender could land us in the zones that are slippery. With advanced technical age, men and women no longer are confined to their traditional, will-cared roles of one, as the bread-winner and the other as the bread maker.
2. Womanhood is a biological phenomenon and everything that goes with it should be taken in the stride of the games of hormone.
3. Most woman-related problems are because of their insecure economical status. A working woman therefore, and an elite at that, may be spared the trauma and tortures of the materialistic in-laws.
4. Simone de Bealevair, in his book *The Second Sex*, (Penguin, 1979, p. 7) remarks that feminine literature in our days is animated less by our wish to demand our rights by effort to wards clarity and understanding.

अध्याय 29

अमरकांत के कथासाहित्य में नारी संघर्ष

पूनम सिंह

सृजन स्वयं में एक सामाजिक दायित्व का कार्य है। सृजन का क्षेत्र है जीवन और जीवन संघर्षों एवं द्वन्द्वों से युक्त है, इन संघर्षों एवं द्वन्द्वों के बीच से ही नारी सशक्तीकरण को ऊर्जा प्राप्त होती है। प्रस्तुत लेख में 'अमरकांत के कथा साहित्य में नारी संघर्ष' को विषय बनाया गया है।

अमरकांत एक प्रगतिशील कथाकार हैं और प्रगतिशील रचनाएँ मनुष्य की संघर्षशीलता को उजागर करती हैं। उनके सम्पूर्ण कथा साहित्य का अनुशीलन करने पर उसमें उद्घाटित संघर्षशीलता के तत्व का साक्षात्कार जीवन के विविध स्तरों पर होता है। उनके कथासाहित्य में संघर्षशीलता का यह तत्व कहीं भी आरोपित या कल्पित नहीं है। हाँ, यह बात सत्य है कि जहाँ एक ओर उनकी कहानियों में संघर्षशीलता, प्रगतिशीलता के जीवंत वस्तुशिला पर अभिव्यक्त हुई है वहीं दूसरी ओर उनके उपन्यासों में संघर्षशीलता का यह तत्व रोमानी धरातल पर है। स्वयं अमरकांत संघर्षशीलता के इस तत्व को रचना का प्राण मानते हैं। उन्हीं के शब्दों में "द्वन्द्व जीवन की आवश्यक शर्त है, क्योंकि जीवन स्थिर नहीं है। द्वन्द्व ही जीवन की गति एवं प्रगति के सूचक हैं। द्वन्द्व ही यथार्थ के सही आकलन में सहायक होते हैं और उसे ऐतिहासिकता से आलोकित करते हैं। जो रचना द्वन्द्व से शून्य है, वह शिल्प की बनावट व पच्चीकारी अथवा आत्मगत 'सत्यों' के प्रक्षेपण अथवा रोमांटिक काल्पनिकता के बल पर खड़ा होने का नाटक करती है, पर वस्तुतः वह जीवन शून्य होती है"।[1]

अमरकांत ने अपने कथा साहित्य में नारी-संघर्ष के विविधायामों का सजीव एवं सूक्ष्म वर्णन किया है। उनकी कहानियों की अपेक्षा उपन्यासों में नारी-संघर्ष का विस्तृत फलक प्राप्त होता है किन्तु फिर भी उनकी जिन कहानियों में नारी-संघर्ष के विविध स्वरूपों की प्राप्ति होती है, वह है—'असमर्थ हिलता हाथ', 'प्रिय मेहमान',

'लाखों', 'तूफान', 'स्वामी' आदि। यह बात सच है कि 'अमरकांत' ने अपने उपन्यासों में प्रेम-प्रसंगों का बड़ा चटकारा लेकर वर्णन किया है किन्तु उन प्रेम-प्रसंगों के पीछे नारी-संघर्ष की चेतना भी ध्वनित हुई है। वस्तुतः अपने कथा साहित्य में उन्होंने नारी के संबंध में मध्यवर्गीय मानसिकता के अनेक दुष्प्रवृत्तियों का पर्दाफाश किया है। सामाजिक रूढ़ियों, कुप्रथाओं, संकीर्ण विचारधाराओं, अंधविश्वासों, कट्टर धार्मिक भावना, छुआ-छूत, नारी के प्रति संकीर्ण दृष्टिकोण तथा सामाजिक विसंगतियों आदि ने नारी-संघर्ष को और जटिल एवं तीव्रतर बना दिया है। उनके कथा साहित्य में नारी कई रूपों में संघर्ष करती हुई परिलक्षित होती है—कभी पत्नी के रूप में, कभी माँ के रूप में या परित्यक्ता, या शोषिता के रूप में। नारी-संघर्ष को निम्नलिखित बिंदुओं में रखकर समझा जा सकता है।

नारी-संघर्ष भारत में केवल वैवाहिक संबंध के पश्चात् ही नहीं शुरू होता बल्कि उसकी शुरूआत तो तभी हो जाती है जब वह यौवन की दहलीज पर पैर रखती है। मध्यवर्गीय परिवारों में अविवाहित लड़कियों को कठोर अनुशासन में रखा जाता है, ताकि उनके चरित्र पर किसी प्रकार का लांछन न लगे। अपनी जवान लड़कियों को सचरित्र बनाये रखने के लिए वे इतने चिंतित होते हैं कि चरित्र बिगड़ने की संभावना मात्र से ही उन पर अनेक प्रतिबंध एवं अंकुश लगा दिये जाते हैं अमरकांत ने अपनी कहानी 'असमर्थ हिलता हाथ'[2] की नायिका लक्ष्मी एवं उसकी पुत्री मीना के माध्यम से नारी संघर्ष की बेलौस तस्वीर प्रस्तुत की है। यह एक असफल प्रेम कहानी है, जिसमें युवावस्था में हुए प्रेम को माता-पिता तथा समाज के हाथों बलि चढ़नी पड़ती है, लेकिन यहाँ मीना की माता के दो रूप मिलते हैं। पहला माँ का शाश्वत रूप है, दूसरा अपने प्रेम की असफलता पर पश्चाताप करने वाली नारी। उसके प्रायश्चित का क्षण तब आता है जब वह लकवे से पीड़ित होती है और अपना असमर्थ हाथ हिलाकर स्वीकृति प्रदान करती है, लेकिन तब तक बहुत देर को चुकी होती है और पुनः एक बार उसी असफल प्रेम-कहानी की पुनरावृत्ति होती है और उसकी बेटी भी अपने प्रेम को पाने में असफल रहती है।

इस कहानी में कहानीकार ने एक ऐसी मध्यवर्गीय नारी की मानसिकता को उभारा है जो अपने यौवन काल के प्रथम प्रेम में सामाजिक-धार्मिक रूढ़ियों के चलते असफल होकर असामान्य सी बन जाती है और समाज से बदला नहीं ले सकने के कारण अपने पारिवारिक आत्मीय जनों पर ही तरह-तरह के अत्याचार कर अपना बदला लेती है। 'असमर्थ हिलता हाथ' में मध्यवर्गीय यथार्थ को गहरी संवेदना के साथ प्रस्तुत किया गया है। इस कहानी में परम्परागत संस्कारों के संघर्ष से उत्पन्न

भयावह पारिवारिक स्थिति को चित्रित किया गया है। माँ के रूप में लक्ष्मी का संरक्षण और आज के परिवेश को देखते हुए मीना का विद्रोह आज के यथार्थ को सशक्त रूप में प्रकट करता है। इस प्रकार इस कहानी में अमरकांत ने असफल प्रेम की मानसिकता की खरी और बेलौस तस्वीर पेश की है।

अमरकांत की एक अन्य कहानी 'लड़का-लड़की'[3] में निम्न मध्यवर्गीय परिवार की 'तारा व चन्दर' के बीच आदर्श एवं यथार्थ के अंतर्द्वन्द्व को कथाकार ने अपनी लेखनी से ऊर्जा देने का कार्य किया है। चन्दर लाड़-प्यार में पला, हवाई किले बनाने वाला युवक है, वह परिश्रम, कर्त्तव्य, स्वावलम्बन पर बल देता है पर इनमें से एक का भी अपने जीवन में पालन नहीं करता, वह दूसरों की बातें नहीं सुनता बल्कि अपने सिद्धान्तों को दूसरों पर जबरन लादने का प्रयास करता है–'उसकी बात', 'मेरे विचार में' या 'मैं यह सोचता हूँ' से शुरू होती थी। उसको पूरा विश्वास था कि वह एक महान क्रान्तिकारी और परोपकार का कार्य कर रहा है।' जिसमें अपनी पूर्ण विजय और सर्वोच्चता की बात सोचकर वह सारे समाज को अपने शत्रु के रूप में कल्पना करने लगता। अपने प्यार को लेकर वह निरंतर संघर्ष और लड़ाई की बात सोचता था और इसी के लिए तारा को तैयार करना चाहता था।[4]

चन्दर-तारा के प्रेम प्रसंग का तारा के घर में पता चलता है तो तारा की माँ उसे बुरी तरह पीटती हैं माँ से मार खाने पर भी वह अपने विचारों पर भूखी रहकर भी कायम रहती है। पिता से स्पष्ट शब्दों में सब कुछ कह देती है। तारा के पिता अपनी बेटी का निश्चय व अपनी हैसियत देखकर चन्दर से विवाह करने को तैयार हो जाते हैं। प्रसन्न तारा जब यह खबर चन्दर को सुनाती है तो वह कहता है कि–'तुमने धोखा दिया, तुम संघर्ष नहीं कर सकती'[5] तो तारा अपने ही व्यक्तित्व को स्वयं उभार कर रख देती है–'मैंने तो जीवन के आरम्भ से ही संघर्ष किया है, आपने क्या किया है, आप भूख जानते हैं? आपको गरीबी, जलालत, घुटन, ऊब, निराशा का पता है? साफ बात तो यह है कि आपको एक नारी-देह की जरूरत है और जरूरत है अपने अहंकार की तृप्ति की'। और अंत में वह स्पष्ट कह देती है–'खैर आप यह गाँठ बाँधकर रख लीजिए कि मैं किसी भी दया पर निर्भर नहीं रहना चाहती'।[6] तारा के चरित्र में प्रारम्भ से लेकर अंत तक संघर्ष दिखायी देता है और संघर्ष पर अपने परिश्रम से विजय दिखायी देती है। जबकि चन्दर फिल्में देखकर, उपन्यास पढ़कर आदर्शवाद का ढोंग रचता है और आदर्शवाद के झूठे किले में जीवन के सुख का उपभोग नहीं कर पाता। प्रेम की सफलता का निर्विकार रूप सामने खड़ा होता है और व्यर्थ में त्याग और बलिदान की बातें करता है।

अमरकांत के उपन्यासों में प्रेम-प्रसंगों को लेकर नारी-संघर्ष की चरम सीमा प्राप्त होती है, जिसे वे उलट-पलट कर खरापन प्रदान करते हैं। 'सूखा पत्ता'[7] में कृष्ण कुमार और उर्मिला, 'ग्रामसेविका'[8] में दमयंती और हरचरण 'कँटीली राह के फूल'[9] में अनूप और कामिनी, 'काले उजले दिन'[10] में नायक और रजनी, 'दीवार और आँगन' में दीप्ति और मोहन एक दूसरे के प्यार को प्राप्त करने के लिए संघर्ष करते हैं। उक्त उपन्यासों की परिस्थितियाँ एवं संदर्भ भले ही भिनन हों किन्तु उनकी संघर्षरत जिन्दगी में भिन्नता नहीं है। अमरकांत के उपन्यासों का सूक्ष्मतापूर्वक अवलोकन करने के बाद यह ज्ञात होता है कि वस्तुतः नारी-संघर्ष को उभारने के लिए ही उन्होंने अपने उपन्यासों की पृष्ठभूमि वैसी चुनी है जिसमें नारी जीवन-संघर्षों के विभिन्न आयामों का उद्घाटन हो सके। 'सूखा पत्ता' के तीसरे भाग, 'उर्मिला' में कृष्ण कुमार और उर्मिला का प्रेम वर्णित है। कृष्ण कुमार उर्मिला से अंतर्जातीय विवाह करना चाहता है। वह उर्मिला से कहता है–'यह सही है कि हम एक जाति के नहीं हैं, पर हमारे दिल एक हैं। सच कहता हूँ, मैं जातिवाद को अपनी सारी शक्ति से घृणा करता हूँ। तुम स्वीकार कर लो, मैं सारे समाज से लड़ूँगा और अगर वे नहीं मानेंगे तो हम समाज से अलग होकर रहेंगे।' दोनों विवाह की प्रतिज्ञा करते हैं परन्तु अंतर्जातीय विवाह की स्वीकृति इन्हें नहीं मिलती। अंत में जब उर्मिला का बाप कृष्ण कुमार के चरणों पर गिर पड़ता है तब वह अपनी एक साथ जीन-मरने की प्रतिज्ञा से अलग हो जाता है और उर्मिला को किसी दूसरे से विवाह करने की सलाह देकर दूर हट जाता है और आत्महत्या का निर्णय लेता है। नायक में इतना साहस नहीं कि तमाम वर्जनाओं को तोड़कर वह उर्मिला को अपना ले। वह अपने प्रेम को प्राप्त करने की प्रतिज्ञा करता तो है किन्तु कायरतावश उसे पूरा नहीं कर पाता जबकि संघर्ष के लिए पूरी तरह से तैयार होते हुए भी नायक के पीछे हट जाने से वह भी हताश हो जाती है। वस्तुतः मध्यवर्ग की यही नियति है और इसी नियति का यथार्थ चित्रण अमरकांत यहाँ करते हैं।

अमरकांत की दूसरी उपन्यास 'ग्राम सेविका' में एक ऐसी नारी के जीवन संघर्ष की कथा वर्णित है जो ग्राम सेविका के रूप में गाँव-गाँव में शिक्षा के प्रचार-प्रसार हेतु विभिन्न ग्रामों में ग्राम सेविकाओं की नियुक्तियाँ की थी। इन्हीं ग्राम सेविकाओं में दमयंती भी है। जो इस उपन्यास की नायिका है। दमयंती गाँव के अशिक्षित बच्चों, स्त्रियों को एक स्थान पर इकट्ठा कर उन्हें प्रारम्भिक स्तर की शिक्षा देती थी। 1950 के आस-पास स्त्रियों का ग्राम सेविका जैसी नौकरी करना जिसमें घूम-घूमकर अपने कार्य को संपादित करना होता था, अशिक्षित गाँव वालों के गले नहीं उतरता था। वे ऐसी औरत को जो घर से बाहर रहकर नौकरी करती हों, हेय दृष्टि से देखते थे।

ऐसी औरत उनकी निगाह में बदचलन और व्यभिचारिणी अवश्य होती थी। वे ऐसी औरत से पढ़ना-लिखना तो दूर अपने बच्चों को पास तक नहीं फटकने देते थे। वैसे जहाँ तक पढ़ाई-लिखाई की बात रही, 1950 के आस-पास वज्र देहाती इलाके में पढ़ना-लिखना अच्छी बात नहीं समझी जाती थी। पढ़ लिखकर बच्चे बिगड़ जाते हैं, वे अपने माँ-बाप से दूर हो जाते हैं। ग्रामीणों की यह विकृत मानसिकता उनके अशिक्षित होने का विशेष कारण थी। ऐसी ही मानसिकता के बीच एक ग्राम सेविका का गाँव में पाठशाला चलाना कितने संघर्ष और साहस का कार्य था, सोचा जा सकता है। गाँव वाले दमयंती जैसी पढ़ी-लिखी लड़की के बारे में यही सोचते हैं कि दमयंती पढ़ लिखकर बदचलन हो गयी है। गाँव वालों की ऐसी ही सोच के खिलाफ दमयंती संघर्ष करती है और किसी प्रकार कुछ बच्चों और स्त्रियों को जंगी जैसे एक गाँधीवादी गँवार की दालान में इकट्ठा कर पढ़ाती है। गाँव में हैजा फैल जाने पर लोगों की सहायता करती है और उनके अंधविश्वासों को दूर करती है। एक स्थान पर दमयंती जमुना से कहती है—'भूत-प्रेत कुछ नहीं है। जमाना तेजी से बदल रहा है। बड़े-बड़े रोगों की दवायें तैयार हो गयी हैं। पहले दवाओं की सुविधा नहीं थी तो लोग झाड़फूक से संतोष कर लेते थे।...अनगिनत बच्चे हर वर्ष अंधविश्वासों के कारण मर जाते हैं। कोई भी बात होने पर फौरन डॉक्टर के यहाँ जाना चाहिए।'[11] इन सब कामों के लिए हरचरण, जंगी और जमुना आदि दमयंती की सहायता करते हैं। दमयंती इन सबों की सहायता से संघर्ष करते हुए अपने उद्देश्य को पूरा करती है।

अमरकांत अपनी कहानियों से विवाह पश्चात् पति-पत्नी के संबंधों में उठने वाले अंतर्द्वन्द्वों का बड़ा ही सजीव चित्रण किया है। इस अंतर्द्वन्द्व के प्रायः दो कारण हैं—पहला कारण पति-पत्नी की रूचि भिन्नता, व्यक्तिगत सत्ता की चेतना की महत्वाकांक्षा और जीवन स्तर में असमानता। इससे एक दूसरे के बीच संघर्ष होना स्वाभाविक होता है। पति-पत्नी के संबंधों में अंतर्द्वन्द्व का दूसरा कारण तीसरे व्यक्ति का प्रवेश होता है। यह तीसरा व्यक्ति या तो पत्नी का प्रेमी होता है या पति की प्रेमिका। पति-पत्नी के बीच इस तीसरे व्यक्ति के प्रवेश से परिवार की शांति भंग हो जाती है। अमरकांत की कहानी 'स्वामी' ऐसी ही कहानी है जिसमें मनोहर लाल को अपनी पत्नी नीलिमा पर संदेह है कि उनके नौकर हरिया के साथ नीलिमा का अनैतिक रूप से संबंध है। निःसंदेह वह अपनी पत्नी से पूर्ण समर्पण और वफादारी की आशा करता है जैसा कि सभी मर्द करते हैं।

दाम्पत्य संबंधों के परिप्रेक्ष्य में अगर हम पति-पत्नी के परस्पर प्रेम का रूप देखें तो ज्ञात होगा कि आज का प्रेम पूर्णरूपेण यथार्थ के धरातल पर आधारित है। नारी चेतना की जागृति के कारण स्त्री-पुरुष समान अहं वाले हैं तथा उनका व्यक्तित्व भी

समान है। इस कारण प्रेम संबंधों में अपने अस्तित्व का संघर्ष भी है तो बचाव भी। अब दाम्पत्य प्रेम मानसिक विलास की अनुभूति मात्र नहीं वह समग्र व्यक्ति की एक यथार्थ प्रक्रिया के रूप में अभिव्यक्त है। 'वह भीतर चले आये और कमरे के सामने ओसारे में खड़े होकर बंदर की भाँति आँखें मटका कर उन्होंने रसोई घर की ओर देखा। उनकी पत्नी जमुना पीढ़े पर बैठी, होंठ पर होंठ दबाकर मुँह फुलाए तरकारी काट रही थी। वह मंद-मंद मुस्कराते हुए अपनी पत्नी के पास चले गये। उनके मुँह पर असाधारण संतोष, विश्वास और उत्साह का भाव अंकित था।'[12]

इस प्रकार पति की यह प्रक्रिया प्रेम-संबंधों को उसी मर्यादित रूप में प्रस्तुत कर रही है। इस दृष्टि से प्रेम ने सामाजिक, नैतिक मूल्यों का मान रखा और परंपरागत मूल्यों के साथ निष्ठावान् रहा है। इस प्रकार अमरक़ांत की इस प्रसिद्ध कहानी 'डिप्टी कलक्टरी' में सच्चे दाम्पत्य प्रेम को प्रदर्शित किया गया है, जो मात्र वासनात्मक न होकर मानवीय संबंधों पर आधारित है।

अमरकांत ने पारिवारिक परिवेश में नारी की जो कभी-कभी दुर्गति होती है, उसका भी अच्छा चित्रण किया है। कभी बेवजह पत्नियों पर शक करना परिवार में अनेक समस्याओं को जन्म देता है। उनकी 'स्वामी' नामक कहानी इसी प्रकार की है। परिवार के प्रति गहरी आस्था एवं आदर्शवादी भावना और संबंधों के पारम्परिक रूप को लेकर इस कहानी की रचना की गई है। कहानीकार ने अपनी इस कहानी में स्त्री-पुरुष को पाम्परिक आदर्शों और नैतिक मूल्यों के परिप्रेक्ष्य में देखा है। 'नीलिमा' एक कुलीन, पतिव्रता, सुदृढ़ और हँसमुख स्त्री थी, उसके पति मनोहरलाल को अपनी पत्नी के हाव-भाव पर शक होता था, उसकी निश्छल हँसी भी उसे रास नहीं आती थी।' मनोहरलाल जैसे लोगों की खास लतें, निष्ठा, प्रेम और समर्पण के नाम एवं रूप को घिनौना कर दिया है–'बार-बार पूछते', तुम क्यों हँसती हो? तुम खानदान को कलंकित करने पर तुली हो। तुम्हारे दिल में जरूर कोई खोट है'।[13]

अमरकांत की कहानियों में नारी शोषण अपने विविध आयामों में उद्घाटित हुआ है–शारीरिक, मानसिक, आर्थिक एवं सामाजिक सभी प्रकार के शोषण 'पलाश के फूल', 'प्रिय मेहमान', 'हत्या', 'मूस' आदि कहानियों में ऐसे ही प्रसंगों का वर्णन हुआ है।

नारी शोषण के पीछे पुरुष की अहंकारी विचारधारा, नारी के प्रति हीन दृष्टि तथा उसे पुरुष की भोग्या समझने की मानसिकता विशेष कार्य करती है। सदियों से नारी का शोषण विभिन्न रूपों में समाज में पुरुषों द्वारा होता आया है। विवाहोपरान्त अन्य स्त्री के साथ संबंध और पूर्व पत्नी को त्यागकर अलग जीने की प्रवृत्ति भी सामाजिक परिप्रेक्ष्य में एक समस्या के रूप में उभरी है। आधुनिक समाज में एक ओर जहाँ

समस्त यौन-वर्जनाओं का निषेध मिलता है तो दूसरी ओर जीवन को पूरी ईमानदारी से जीने की सहज दृष्टि का विकास मिलता है। अमरकांत की सशक्त रचना 'पलाश के फूल' सामंती शोषण से ओत-प्रोत रचना है, जिसमें लाठी तिकड़म या पैसे के बल पर रायसाहब कच्ची उम्र की अजोरिया को वासना के कीचड़ में घसीटते हैं और फिर बड़ी आसानी से उससे छुटकारा पाकर अपनी पीठ ठोकते हैं और भगवान की कृपा पर गद्गद होते हैं। इस कहानी का पात्र रायसाहब जैसे लोगों के कारण नारी का शोषण अंतिम सांसें ले रहा है। ऐसे लोग अपनी हुकूमत के बल पर सब कुछ वसूल करना चाहते हैं फिर चाहे वह नारी की अस्मत ही क्यों ना हो। अमरकांत की 'प्रिय मेहमान'[14] और 'हत्यारे'[15] इसी कोटि की कहानी है।

भारतीय समाज में परित्यक्ता, विधवा या घर-परिवार से विस्थापित नारी, पति द्वारा छोड़ी गयी स्त्री प्रायः अत्यंत दुर्दशा को प्राप्त होती है। विधवा होने पर जहाँ वह परिवार की क्रूर यातनाओं का शिकार बनती है, सभी सुख-सुविधाओं से वंचित कर दी जाती है वहीं परित्यक्ता या विस्थापिता होने पर समाज के कुत्सित एवं नीच व्यक्तियों की काम-पिपासा का केन्द्र बिन्दु बन जाती हैं वह सम्मान पूर्ण जीवन जीने की इच्छा रखते हुए भी नहीं जी पाती। अमरकांत की महत्वपूर्ण उपन्यास 'सुन्नर पांडे की पतोह' की नायिका राजलक्ष्मी इस स्थिति से जीवन पर्यन्त संघर्ष करती है और वह इस संघर्ष में अंततः विजयी होती है।

भारतीय नारियों के जीवन की अनेक समस्याओं को परत-दर-परत उघाड़ते हुए कथाकार ने उनके कुछ महत्वपूर्ण पहलुओं को भी स्पर्श किया है जिनके आधार पर भारतीय हिन्दू नारी विश्व की अन्य नारियों से अपनी अलग पहचान बनाती है, सौभाग्यवती हिन्दू नारी अपनी माँग में सिन्दूर भरती है। यह लाल सिन्दूर जहाँ एक ओर पति के प्रति उसके हृदय में अनुराग को प्रकट करता है वहीं वह उसे समाज से लड़ने का आत्मबल देता है, सामाजिक सुरक्षा प्रदान करता है और जीवन को भरपूर जीने की ललक पैदा करता है। सिन्दूर विहिन हिन्दू नारी अपने को मुर्दा समझती है, उसकी सभी लालसाएँ मर जाती है। सुन्नर पांडे की पतोह अपने पति झुल्लन पांडे के घर से चले जाने के बाद भी वृद्धावस्था तक सिन्दूर पहनती है। उसका सिन्दूर ही उसे भरोसा दिलाता है कि उसका पति जिंदा है और वह कभी न कभी उसके समीप अवश्य आयेगा। यह भारतीय आशावादिता ही उसे लंबा जीवन जीने की प्रेरणा देता है। सुन्नर पांडे की पतोह के माथे के सिन्दूर के विषय में कथाकार कहता है—'झुल्लन पांडे चले गये और सिन्दूर छोड़ गये। बूँदी, पाला, गर्मी—बरसात, होली-दिवाली, तीज-त्योहार हर दिन सिन्दूर उसी तरह चमकता रहा।... पहले सिन्दूर का मतलब था पति, बाद में पति का मतलब सिन्दूर हो गया। अब सिन्दूर ही उसका

पति बन गया। सिन्दूर ही उसकी आशा, आकांक्षा, आत्मा और परमात्मका था। सिन्दूर ही ऐसा तिनका भी था जिसके सहारे वह भयावह तरंगों से भरपूर संसार रूपी महानदी में धारा के विपरीत तैरती रही। औरत की इच्छाओं, हौसलों और अधिकारों से वंचित होने पर भी उसे सिन्दूर ही औरत होने का गर्व और गरिमा देता है और सिन्दूर ने ही दी थी उसे मन को जोड़ने, अपने से और दूसरों से लड़ने और अपनी ही शर्तों पर खड़ा रहने की अद्भुत आत्मिक शक्ति।[16]

नारी जहाँ पुरुष शोषण का शिकार हुई वहीं वह समाज में अपना स्थान पाने के लिए प्रयत्नशील भी है। उसके सम्मुख अनगिनत बाधाएँ हैं, परन्तु वह आगे बढ़ने के लिए निरंतर तत्पर है। अपनी इस निरंतर संघर्षशील प्रवृत्ति के कारण आज नारी प्रत्येक क्षेत्र में पुरुष के मुकाबले आ रही है। शिक्षा के क्षेत्रों में भी नारी बहुत प्रगति कर गई है। शिक्षित नारी अपनी लड़ाई स्वयं लड़ने की सामर्थ्य रखती है। अमरकांत की कहानी 'तूफान' में सुमन अपने पिता से स्पष्ट शब्दों में कहती है—'मैं जवान हूँ, अपनी लड़ाई मैं खुद लड़ सकती हूँ, उस लड़ाई में खुशी-खुशी अपना बलिदान दे सकती हूँ, दूसरे के लिए आप गलत लड़ाई और गलत ढंग से जो लड़ाई लड़ रहे हैं, उससे मैं आपको रोक सकती हूँ, मुक्त कर सकती हूँ...।'17

मध्यवर्गीय पुरुष भी अपनी पत्नी को शिक्षित व सलीकेदार देखने का आकांक्षी है। अपनी पत्नी को प्रभावशाली व्यक्तित्व प्रदान करने का लोभ मध्यवर्गीय पुरुष की मानसिकता की एक कड़ी है। कथाकार स्वयं स्त्रियों को समान अधिकार प्रदान करने के पक्षधर हैं। अमरकांत ने अपनी कहानी 'पेड़-पौधे' में इसी व्यापकता को नायक प्रशान्त के माध्यम से अभिव्यक्त किया है, जहाँ नायक नायिका से कहता है कि 'सीमा, मैं उन लोगों में नहीं हूँ जो स्त्रियों को कोई अधिकार देना नहीं चाहते। मैं पुरुष और स्त्री में कोई फर्क नहीं समझता। तुम आगे बढ़ो, लोगों से मिलो-जुलो बहस करो, बात-चीत करो...। पूरी तरह आजाद हो तुम...।[18]

वस्तुतः अमरकांत ने अपने समय और परिवेश के जिन व्यापक नारी-संघर्षों का साक्षात्कार किया उन्हें ही अपनी कहानियों एवं उपन्यासों में घटनाओं, स्थितियों, पात्रों के रूप में मूर्त करके यथार्थ को परिभाषित करने का श्लाघनीय प्रयास किया है उनकी सम्पूर्ण कथा यात्रा में नारी-संबंधी इतिहास की विसंगतियों एवं असफलताओं पर गंभीर चिंता व्यक्त की गयी है, प्रगतिशील शक्तियों का पक्ष लिया गया है तथा बदलाव की व्याकुलता ध्वनित हुयी है।

संदर्भ

1. अमरकांत वर्ष 1, संपादक–रविन्द्र कालिया, 1977, पृष्ठ-114
2. अमरकांत की संपूर्ण कहानियाँ, भाग-2, पृष्ठ-3, प्र. स.-1998
3. अमरकांत की संपूर्ण कहानियाँ, भाग-2, पृष्ठ-64 प्र. स.-1998
4. वही, पृष्ठ-67
5. वही, पृष्ठ-70
6. वही, पृष्ठ-71
7. अमरकांत : 'सूखा पत्ता', राजकमल पेपरबैक्स प्रकाशन, नई दिल्ली, प्र. सं.-1984
8. अमरकांत : 'ग्राम सेविका', लोकभारती प्रकाश, इलाहाबाद, प्र. सं.-1962
9. अमरकांत : 'कँटीली राह के फूल'
10. अमरकांत : 'काले उजले दिन', वोरा एण्ड कंपनी, पब्लिशर्स प्रा. लि., इलाहाबाद, प्र. सं. -1969
11. अमरकांत : 'ग्राम सेविका', पृष्ठ -43
12. अमरकांत : 'डिप्टी कलक्टरी', अमरकांत की संपूर्ण कहानियाँ, भाग-1, प्र. स.-1998
13. अमरकांत : 'स्वामी', अमरकांत की संपूर्ण कहानियाँ, भाग-1, पृष्ठ-303, प्र. स.-1998
14. अमरकांत : 'प्रिय मेहमान', अमरकांत की संपूर्ण कहानियाँ, भाग-1, पृष्ठ-58, प्र. सं. -1998
15. अमरकांत : 'हत्यारे', अमरकांत की संपूर्ण कहानियाँ, भाग-1, पृष्ठ-182
16. अमरकांत : 'सुन्नर पांडे की पतोह', पृष्ठ-34, कृतिकार प्रकाशन इलाहाबाद, प्र. सं. -1993
17. अमरकांत : 'तूफान', अमरकांत की संपूर्ण कहानियाँ, भाग-2, पृष्ठ 212, प्र. स.-1998
18. अमरकांत : 'पेड़-पौधे', अमरकांत की संपूर्ण कहानियाँ, भाग-1, पृष्ठ-288, प्र. स.-1998

Sub-section (b)

Political Issues

Chapter 30

Situating Women in Early Nationalist Discourse: Problems and Prospects

Prabhakar Prasad Singh

The abolition of *Sati Pratha* in 1829 marks a striking moment in the history of women in modern India. Since then major social reform movements in the 19th century began to dominantly focus women issues that helped not only in ameliorating their conditions but also in developing a kind of women consciousness that lies at the root of our present day concern for women empowerment. What began as a liberal reform movement under the auspices of patriarchal ideology subsequently graduated into a gender consciousness according centrality to a feminine identity. Not only the women began to demand their commands but attempted to command their demands. The reform movement that took up women issues was a major constituent of our nationalist struggle. Keeping this in perspective, the present paper seeks to address the interaction between social reform and women movement in the background of a broader nationalist ideology in colonial India. Historically thus probing the trajectory of the women movement my be useful to development strategists, policy planners and social activists in their exercise of conceptualising and formulating the problematics of women empowerment.

Of late, women issues have come to prominently figure in historical debates. We come across two genres of historical representation of women issues. One is the feminist, while the other is known as women studies carried under the rubric of social history. The distinction between the two approaches remains blurred, a deliberately maintained obfuscation,'[1] however, it seems difficult to erase the marks of perspicuous differences underlying their basic assumptions. Declaring the entire system of knowledge as suffering from male bias the feminists believe that sex differentiation is not biological, rather a symbolic cultural construct of social inequality. Biology, in fact, is used to perpetuate such differentiations.[2] As any reality is really gendered, in history too gender metaphors have freely been used in favour of male domination. The feminist basic formulation implies that women have always had a history different from men. Historian are said to have 'subsumed women and included them in a generalized and unified conception that was at once represented in the idea of Man, but was always different from and subordinate to it.[3] The feminists even object to the use of the word history itself, because the first syllable of the word 'his' in the pronoun form represents something belonging to man, and instead they advocate the use of the term 'her-story'.[4]

Different from feminism, the social history treats gender discriminations or inequalities as outcomes of socio-economic causes and processes; its explanations of changing socio-economic structures may be with or without gender differentiations. It seems contextually relevant to briefly discuss how the women could find their place in the newly emerging trends of social historiography in the last century. The *Annales* school in France[5] in the 1930s sincerely sought to closely associate historical researches with other social sciences like economics, sociology, anthropology etc. that world produce the picture of past societies in their totality. The distinguished *Annalist*, Fernand Braudel more firmly echoed the views of his predecessors in treating the relationship between history and social sciences as 'an exchange of services'.[6] After the World War II the process of cross-fertilisation of history with other social sciences, especially sociology and anthropology, began to grow in proportion and dimension as is evident from the writings of British social historians.[7] If E.E. Evans Pritchard on the one hand clearly said. 'Anthropology must choose between being history and being nothing,[8] Eric Hobsbawm, following the paradigm of Fernand Braudel on the other hand unhesitatingly pleaded to erase the marks of differentiation between sociological explanations of historical events and historical explanations of sociological phenomena.[9] From 1960s onwards American scholarship also began to accept the sociological perspectives of historical researches.[10]

The developing trends of interdisciplinary orientations in historiography led to the diversifications of the objects of its study. The historical focus was 'shifted from the individual to the collective, from political to social history, from description to analysis, from monocausal to multidimensional explanation'.[11] The historian now began to give attention to groups hitherto marginalised in the central storyline of history. As such, like ethnic minorities, peasants and workers, women too came to be included in the historical project. Backed by the eruption of the feminist movement in the 1970s the new wave of women history expanded further the horizons of social history.[12] Some historians with socialist leanings started taking special interests in women history. For example, Raphael Samuel, a member of the editorial board of *New Left Review*, founded in 1976 *History Workshop: A Journal of Social Historians*, whose subtitle, just after four years was expanded to *A Journal of Socialist and Feminist Historians.*[13] The paradigm of 'new social history' in spite of its limitations on other theoretical fronts[14] did make seminal and substantial contributions in the growth of women history. As a result, themes such as, the role of family, the relationship of the rise of industry to marriage patterns, late marriage sexual frustration, hysteria, witchcraft, contraception, birth-rates etc. began to be included in historical projects.[15] The popularity of the subject may be measured from the fact that any major bookseller in England is supposed to have a separate shelf either on women history or women studies in his shop.[16]

Compared to that of the west, the picture of modern Indian historiography appears not so encouraging in context of women history. Different historical versions regarding modern India such as imperialist, nationalist, Marxist, neo-Cambridge and others hardly present a living debate on the role of women as a group in the dynamics of modern India. We only come across casual discussions either on the lives and achievements of few distinguished women or on the exploitations and sufferings of womankind in the hours of social reformations. Even most of the *subaltern* historians failed to pay proper attention to women issues in their historical works.

Relying on the basic premise of dialectical relationship between the ruler and the ruled, these historians largely focussed on themes like riots, rebellions and other organised political movements. The 'history from below' approach, though liberating historiography from elitist biases, seems rather silent on forms of social resistance in everyday life, especially in the context of male-female dialectical relationship.[17] A noted *subaltern* scholar, Gayatri, Spivak, herself accepts the unwelcome situation of women history still roping in darkness in *subaltern* studies.[18] However, during the last two decades some worth noticing words on women history have appeared. The works, apart from adding a new dimension to the conceptual-analytical framework, have come to seriously challenge the earlier historical conclusions about changing patterns of gender relationship in colonial India.[19] From standard research works down to school textbooks, 19th century social awakening is usually projected as the precursor and promoter of women liberation and their modernisation. The projection is not without justification. Though the colonial regime occasionally took up some measures with a view to ameliorate women suffering and its judiciary is supposed to 'have silently promoted the cause of female emancipation and progress,[20] its attitude towards women was not altogether sympathetic. The British society in India did not appreciate 'unconventional behaviour in women', and a careless English woman was branded as 'going jungli'.[21] The 19th century English society itself failed to make a commendable advance towards gender equality. Even a noted English woman writer like Mary Shelly has to work under 'social and psychological pressures', because publishing by a woman was in itself a 'subversive act', because it exploded the common assumption of female passivity.[22] The colonial masters could not be expected to do something better in Indian context. That is why the colonial rule remained unconcerned about female education. In such an unfavourable situation, it seems really revolutionary on the part of reformers like Ram Mohun Roy, Ishwar Chandra Vidyasagar, Dayanand Saraswati, M.G. Ranade and several others to have taken up women issues such as the abolition of *Sati Pratha*, women education, widow remarriage, child marriage, polygamy and so on. The ongoing debates on gender problems led to the legislative enactments related to the abolition of

Sati practice, widow remarriage, the age of consent bill etc., which clearly indicate that women issues began to influence the decision-making processes of the colonial state. Reviewing the 19ht century scene in this context, a renowned scholar comments:[23]

For the first time since Manu, perhaps, and in a very different sense from him, family life and womanhood directly and explicitly emerged as a central area of problematisation.

The reformers, in spite of their ideological differences on several other social problems were perhaps unanimous in their resolutions of disabilities faced by women. It is interesting to note that even Radha Kant Dev who strongly opposed the abolition of the practice of widow burning enthusiastically favoured the promotion of women education.[24] In this respect, 19th century India presents a picture more advanced than 19th century France where women education became one of the most bitterly contested issues in the struggle between clericals and anti-clericals.[25]

The seeds of social reform did not fall on a barren land. The vast expansion of education among women, *inter alia*, considerably transformed their role, status and self-perception that enabled them to effectively articulate themselves and participate in contemporary social dynamics.[26] More importantly, a social practice, i.e., child marriage, when affecting even an individual woman, involved cross-section of the people in controversies that got a wide coverage in journals and periodicals across the subcontinent. Interestingly same religious texts were put to opposite interpretations by both the proponents and the opponents in context of a particular social reform. Consequently, a critical cultural outlook began to catalyse the process of nationalism. The case against Rakhmabai by her husband for the restilution of conjugal rights seems the most befitting example to be cited here[27] without going into its details.

While highlighting the positive impacts of social awakening, historical scholarship need not gloss over the hidden agenda of reforms. In order to critically evaluate the working of complex social mechanism, we must take into account the priority given to culture over other social issues in the early nationalist discourse. Taking nationalism as 'primarily a cultural doctrine, or more accurately, a political ideology with a cultural doctrine at its core'[28] we can easily trace the roots of Indian nationalist consciousness in its cultural awakening. The mind-set of educated Indian middle classes, which played a pioneering and leading role in national movement clearly reflected a belief-system which, having conceded to the west superiority in 'the realm of material culture', preserved for itself, superiority of the East 'in the domain of spiritual accomplishments'. A combination of western material advancements with the eastern spiritual greatness was thought to be the basis of India's modernity.[29] As the evidences of the acclaimed spiritual superiority were available in the cultural arte-facts of the past with their authentic representations in Sanskrit-written ancient Hindu texts, a process of sanskritisation of Indian culture became the 'hallmark of India's modernity' in the 19th century. That is why the important journals and leading intellectuals supported the cause of Sanskrit.[30] What was urgently needed in national interest was to re-interpret and reorder the cultural values that would serve as a powerful means in defining India's independent identity as a nation on the lines of the West, but not like the West.

The overriding cultural concern of early nationalism becomes more apparent even during the debates on *sati*. Rights and status of women began to be discussed; however, the debates were not 'primarily' about women, rather about authentic scriptural interpretations. Women in fact became the site on which tradition was debated and reformulated.[31] Both the supporters and opponents of *Sati pratha* sought the authority of textual origins of their belief, and 'caught in the context over whether tradition did or did not sanction *sati*, the colonized subaltern women disappeared.'[32]

It is to be added that social reformers became active promoters of women education, because they took it as essential for spiritual upliftment. Moreover, the concern for female education was not with women as individuals, but their development as able companions to men, and as members of civil society. The purpose of education was to bridge the communication gap between a literate husband and his illiterate wife. The removal of women illiteracy was seen not in terms of social progress rather it was an attempt to remove a possible inconvenience to the newly emerging family structure of Indian middle classes.[33] It needs to be added that 'whereas education for males was directly related to the pursuit of employment, female education had no economic function' nor was it related to the development of professional expertise among women.[34] Education was a moral project in terms of male domination. A young Bengal radical observed in 1856:[35]

Females are required not to be educated by the standard which is adapted to men...........The end and aim in her life is to cultivate the domestic affection, to minister to the comfort and happiness of her husband, to look after and tend her children, and exercise her little supervision over domestic economies............

Thus the idea of an educative mother-figure began to gain currency. Women came to be treated as remaining unpolluted by western influences; they were supposed to have preserved the purity of the country and all kinds of virtues in themselves. In course of time, the image of an educative mother-figure, coupled with the idea of womanhood as repository of high traditional values began to influence 19th century nationalist discourse. From the last quarter of the19th century, woman appeared as a dominant theme in Bengali literature. Ideal patriotism and female qualities became synonyms. Nationalist discourse began to be feminised at least in terms of cultural symbols.

In order to counter imperialism, which spoke in masculine terms, nationalism in Bengal developed an oppositional ideology, which glorified feminine principles. Such a theme appears in the literary masterpieces of Bengal, particularly Bankim Chandra's *Anand Math*.[36] The Bengali model was later on followed in literary works of other regions. As the nationalist language, while singing the political lore, began to use the vocabulary of kinship, it led to the crystallisation of matriarchal connection where again the mother-figure became dominant. The agonies, frustrations and exploitations to the present drove the Indian intelligentsia back to take an imagined resort in their past, which declared: 'Mother and motherland are important than the heaven'.

The middle class projection of women in the background of national cultural regeneration soon became popular. The appearance of new techniques in art-forms in the 9th century began to produce pictorial bazar images of mythological feminine characters that played a crucial role in 'negotiating and reconstructing' the notions of tradition and national ethos. Among other things 'accretion of religious, mythic, aesthetic, social and political values transformed the same images into icons' and popularised them.[37]

Though the deification of feminine cults came to be inextricably wedded to the nationalist discourse, the inherent tendency of male domination remained as strong as ever. Even triumphant *Mahisasurmardini*, the most popularly worshipped Mother Goddess in Bengal, was transformed into an ideal mother-figure. To quote the famous nationalist Bepin Chandra pal:[38]

This is nothing but a mother's beauty..........My mother is not Sanyasini, but is hungry for affection tirelessly serving others..........the hair piled up on the top of the head does not denote the state of yogini but that of busy cook about her business. The heavy breasts indicate a plentitude of milk awaiting the infant. The parted lips denote the ecstasy experienced at the moment of suckling child.

Such an interpretation amounted to domesticating the role of women in society. The nationalist discourse carried within it 'the seeds of colonial assumption about gender' that depicted women as being 'dependent' upon their husbands and not as 'political' subjects.[39] Once the mother awakens the sons, the leadership passes into the hands of her sons. Moreover, the woman is the mother, but the child is always a son. The spiritualisation of womanhood was evolved as a form of symbolic cultural representation in order to contest colonial hegemony[40] in other spheres of social activities, however, gender equality was not so worth-cherishing. Even Bankim Chandra, who so powerfully pictures the female divinity of the motherland in *Anand Math*, speaks differently in his another historical novel, *Devi Chaudharani*. In this novel, after the battle is over, the heroine lays down the glorious garb of robber queen and turns to dishwashing.

Facing the odds of male domination women reformers like Ramabai, Swarna Kumari Devi and several others sought to make their space in the social discourse. As pointed out earlier, women themselves began to evaluate their role and status in the background of contesting ideologies of nationalism and colonialism. Journals and magazines such as *Bharati, Antahpur, Sahitya, Mukul, Sakha, Pradip* and others began to be published under the editorship of educated women. Consequently, in these magazines women issues began to be discussed by the women themselves. The women reformers attacked the new kind of patriarchy which redefined male-female relationship. They developed an ambivalent attitude towards their newly assigned role.[41] Krishnababhini Das, in an essay entitled 'What will happen to us?' pointed out that in terms of freedom her mothers and grandmothers lived in a better state.' Complaining about the little or half-education, in the same essay she strongly pleaded for the advanced education of women, which would enable them perform their high calling.[42] The women produced literature held men responsible for their deplorable conditions and began to question male domination. Another woman reformer, Ramabai wrote a book in America in 1886, entitled *The High Caste Hindu Women* with a view to raise funds and propagate the cause of women reform. Its ten thousand copies were sold in America. In this book, she was critical of many aspects of gender discrimination. She pointed out that subject womanhood could produce nothing 'better than a subject nation'. The growing feminine consciousness was bitterly critical of the social forces that combined to go against the interests of womankind. Reacting upon the judicial pronouncement against Rakhmabai in the already referred case for the restitution of conjugal rights, Ramabai remarkably observed;[43]

Taught by the experience of the past, we are not all surprised at this decision of the Bombay Court. Our only wonder is that a defenceless woman like Rakhmabai dared to raise her voice in the face of the powerful Hindu Laws, the mighty British Government, the one Hundred and twenty nine million men and three hundred thirty million gods to crush her to nothingness.................

In the light of above discussion, we may conclude that India represents multiple social formations in terms of religion, region, caste, community, sex and so on. The strings of social differentiations are so interwoven that movement in one is supposed to advantageously or adversely affect the movement in other. The more dominant ideology of the time overshadows the other kinds of ideological formations. That is why due to primacy given to culture in the 19th century nationalist agenda, the women issues, in general, remained largely ignored. The trends in pre-colonial India may be found continuing, though in different context in post-colonial India. For example, two decades ago, the Shah Bano case became more an issue of acrimonious debates between Hindu and Muslim fundamentalists, rather than an issue of women equality. Similarly, the implementation of Mandal Commission Report divided woman community into forward and backward castes.[44] It is one of the ironies of history that as women have always been used by dominant ideological forces not as an end in itself rather as a means to achieve some other ends, they have till date failed to be assertive as a homogenous social group in the true sense of the term.

References

1. Michelle Perrot et al, 'Women's Culture and Power.' A Historiographical Essay' in Maurice Aymard & Harbans Mukhia, eds. *French Studies in History: The Departures*, vol. II, Orient Longman, New Delhi, 1990, p. 456 .
2. Janet Sayers, *Biological Politics, Feminist and Anti-Feminist Perspectives*, Tavistock Publication, London, 1982, pp. 1-2, Kate Millett, Sexual Politics, Abacus Publication, rept. 1972, pp. 26-27.
3. Jona Wallach Scott, *Gender And The Politics of History*, Columbia University Press , New York , 1988, p. 183.
4. *Ibid*., pp. 21-22.
5. The *Annales* group does not represent a school of thought in the strict sense of the term; it simply stands for non-traditional approaches in methodology and analysis in historical researches published in the articles of the journal *Annales* started in 1929 under the title *Annales d' Historie Economique et sociale*. The journal periodically changed its name. For *Annales* paradigm, see Maurice Aymard and Harbans Mukhia, eds., *The French studies in History*; vol. I and vol. II, Orient Longman, New Delhi, 1989 & 1990 respectively. For a critical understanding, see Stuart Clark, ed. *The Annales School : Critical Assessments* in four vols., Routledge, London, 1999.
6. F. Braudel, quoted in Colin Lucas, 'Introduction' in J. Le Goff and P. Nora, eds. *Constructing the Past: Essays in Historical Methodology*, Cambridge University Press, Cambridge, 1985, pp. 4-5.

7. Craig Calhoum, 'History and Sociology in Britain', *Comparative Studies in Society and History*, 1987, vol. 29, pp. 615-25
8. E. E. Evans Pritchard, *Anthropology and History*, p. 20, quoted in Hans Medick,' "Missionaries in the Row Boat", Ethnological Ways of Knowing as a Challenge to Social History', *Comparative Studies in Society and History*, 1987 vol. 29, pp. 76-98, reference on p. 78. Also see Bernand S. Cohn, 'History and Anthropology: The State of Play,' *ibid*, 1987, vol. 22, pp. 198-224.
9. F. Braudel, *On History*, Weidenfield and Nicolson, London, 1980, p. 69. Eric Hobsbawm, From Social History to the History of Society' in M. W. Flinn and T. C. Smout, eds. Oxfod University Press, Oxford, 1974. Also see P. Burke, *Sociology and History*, George Allen and Unwin, London, 1980; Sumit Sarkar, 'Social History: Predicaments and Possibilities', *Proceedings* of The 45th session of the Indian History Congress, pp. 480-502.
10. Victoria E. Bonnell, 'The Uses of Theory, Concepts and Comparisons in Historical Sociology' in*Comparative Studies in Society and History*, 1980, vol. 22, pp. 156-173.
11. Colin Lucas in J. Le Goff and P. Nura, *op. cit*, p. 4.
12. James F. McMillan, 'Social History, "New Cultural History", and the Rediscovery of Politics: Some Recent Works on Modern France', *The Journal of Modern History*, 1994, vol. 66, pp. 755-758.
13. Susan Magarey, 'The Hoary Old Chestnut, Free Will and Determinism: Culture Vs structure, or History Vs. Theory in Britain', *Comparative Studies in Society and History*, 1987, vol. 29, p. 636.
14. Christopher Lloyd, 'Methodologies of Social History: A Critical Survey And Defence of Structurism', *History and Theory*, 1991, vol. 30, pp. 180-219.
15. Susan Mosher Stuard, 'The *Annales* School and Feminist History: Opening Dialogue with the American Stepchild'; in Stuart Clark, *op. cit,* vol. II, pp. 14-22.
16. Jane Rendall, 'Women's History: Beyond the Cage', *History*, 1990, vol. 75. pp. 63-65.
17. Douglas Haynes and Gyan Prakash, eds., *Contesting Power: Resistance and Everyday Social Relations in South Asia*, Oxford University Press, Delhi, 1991, pp. 1-22.
18. Gayatri C. Spivak, 'Can the Subaltern Speak', in Carry Nelson and Lawrence Crossberg, eds., *Marxism and the Interpretation of Culture*, University of llinois Press, Chichago, 1988, p. 287.

19. For example, see G. Murshid, *Reluctant Debutante: Response of Bengali Women to Modernisation 1849-1905*, Rajshahi University Press, Rajshahi, 1983; Meredith Borthwick, *The Changing Role of Women in Bengal, 1849-1905*, Princeton University Press, Princeton, 1984; Kumkum Sangari and Sudesh Vaid, eds., *Recasting Women: Essays in Colonial History*, Kali for Women, New Delhi, 1989, Geraldine Forbes, *Cambridge History of India: Women in Modern India*, Cambridge University Press, Cambridge, 1996.

20. Kunal M. Parker, 'A Corporation of Superior Prostitues': Anglo-Indian Legal Conceptions of Temple Dancing Girls, 1800-1914', *Modern Asian Studies* 1998, vol. 32, pp. 559-561.

21. Margaret Macmillan, *Women of the Raj*, Thames and Hudson, London, 1988, p. 200.

22. Jane Aron, 'The Return of the Repressed: Reading Mary Shelly's The Last Man' in Susan Seller, ed., *Feminist Criticism: Theory and Practice*, Harvester Wheatsheaf, New York, 1991, pp. 9-22.

23. Tanika Sarkar, quoted in Himani Bannerji 'Fashioning a self: Educational Proposal for and by Women in Popular Magazines in Colonial Bengal', *Economic and Political Weekly*, 26 October 1991, p. 52.

24. Geraldine Forbes, *op. cit*, p. 39.

25. James F. MacMillan, 'Clericals, Anti-clericals and Women's Movement in France under the Third Republic; *Historical Journal*' 1981, vol. 24. pp. 361-376.

26. G. Murshid, *op. cit.*, p. 13.

27. For details see Sudhir Chandra, 'The Problem of Social Reform in India', in S. C. Mallik, ed., *Dissent , Protest And Reform In Indian Civilization*, IIAS, Shimla, 1977, pp. 250-267.

28. Anthony D. Smith, *National Identity*, Penguin, Harmondsworth, 1991, p. 74.

29. Partha Chatterjee, *Nationalist Thought and the Colonial World: Derivative Discourse,* Zed Books, London, 1986, pp. 38-51.

30. For example, journals like *Calcutta Review, Indian Mirror, Theosophist* and reformers like Swami Dayanand, Vivekanand, Annie Beasant and others supported the cause of Sanskrit. Respect for Sanskrit was found in 20th century leaders like Gandhi and Nehru. See Sumathi Ramaswami, 'Sanskrit for the Nation', *Modern Asian Studies*, 1999, vol. 33, pp. 339-381.

31. Lata Mani, 'Contentious Traditions: The Debates on Sati in Colonial India' in Kumkum Sangari and Sudesh Vaid, *op. cit.*, pp. 88-126.

32. Gayatri C. Spivak in Carry Nelson and Lawrence Grossberg, *op. cit.*, pp. 299-307.
33. For details, see G. Murshid, *op. cit.*
34. Himani Bannerji, *op. cit.*, p. 51.
35. Quoted in Sumanta Banerjee, 'Marginalisation of Women's Popular Culture in Nineteenth Century Bengal' in Kumkum Sangari and Sudesh Vaid *op. cit.*, p. 162.
36. Tanika asarkar, 'Nationalist Iconography in 19th Century Bengali Literature', *Economic and Political Weekly*, 21st November, 1987, pp. 2011-2015.
37. Tapati Guha Thakurta, 'Women as 'Calendar Art' Icons: Emergence of pictorial Stereotypes in Colonial India', *Economic and Political Weekly*, 26 October 1991, pp. 91-99.
38. B.C. Pal, quoted in Tanika Sarkar *op. cit.*, p. 2012.
39. Kamala Visweswaran, 'Small Speeches, Subaltern Gender: Nationalist Ideology and its Historiography in Shahid Amin & Dipesh Chakrabarty, eds., *Subaltern Studies*, Vol. IX, Oxford University Press, Delhi, 1996, pp. 83-84.
40. Tanika Sarkar, *op. cit.*
41. For female criticism of gender discrimination, see Himani Bannerji, *op. cit.*, pp. 50-62. Also see Uma Chakravarti, 'Whatever Happened to the Vedic Past? Orientalism, Nationalism, and a Script for the Past' and Sumanta Banerjee [already referred] in Kumkum Sangari and SudeshVaid, *op. cit.*, pp. 27-87 and 127-179 respectively.
42. Himani Bannerji , *op. cit.*, p.57.
43. Ramabai quoted in Uma Chakravarti in Kumkum Sangari and Sudesh Vaid, *op. cit.*, p. 74.
44. Susie Tharu and Tejaswini Niranjana, 'Problems for a Contemporary Theory of Gender', in Shahid Amin and Dipesh Chakraborty, *op. cit.*, pp. 232-239.

Chapter 31

Gender Difference and Participation of Women in Political Process

Y.V. Satyanarayana

The title of the paper itself suggests that the "difference" in gender does not necessarily imply "inequality" between male and female. In this paper, I have made an attempt to show that—"man and woman are equal"—and they should be treated equally in all matters of their social life. This argument is based on—if a "difference" within a same gender does not imply "inequality", then, how can the "difference" between two genders imply "inequality"? The argument that—"differences in gender implies gender inequality"—contradicts the principles of equality and freedom.

The principle of "equality" or "inequality" refers to the functional aspects of human beings such as ability, efficiency, capacity, capability and so on; but not to the gender aspects of male and female. In fact, within one gender, neither two men nor two women are "same or identical". Therefore, "sameness" and "difference" cannot make man and woman as equal or unequal. The differences in gender may be understood as "gender disadvantage" rather than "gender inequality".

I

Meaning of Equality

It is said in the American Declaration of Independence, that—"All men are born equal". Human beings are unequal in bodily proportions, physical strength, intellectual abilities and moral capacities. The statement—"all men are born equal"—is not a statement of 'fact' but it is a statement of 'right'. That is to say, all human beings have a right to equal consideration, equal opportunity and equal treatment in matters of their social life.

The principle of equality emerged as a protest against the gross inequalities that prevailed in ancient societies. The idea of equality has thus grown out of the idea of privilege. Inspite of many natural inequalities between human beings, they are equally endowed with certain basic capacities and needs that are radically different from animals. Hence all human beings should be treated a like in respect of certain human traits that are common to all, such as dignity and worth as human beings. Every human being has been endowed with some natural rights such as - right to freedom, right to equality and so on, and without these rights it would be difficult for men to realize their true human nature.

The idea of equality has two sides—positive and negative. In the positive sense it means provision of adequate opportunities to all and in the negative sense it means absence of special privileges. Equality does not mean to treat everyone equally; but it implies that equals should be treated as equals and unequal should be treated unequally, in proportion to their difference.

Inequality is of two types—1. Natural inequality which is based on the law of nature, 2. Social or conventional inequalities are alterable; whereas natural inequalities cannot be alterable. We have to find ways to remove or at least diminish certain inequalities. The moral law demands that all man-made social inequalities, which are unnecessary and unjustifiable ought to be eliminated

Equality of Sex: A Philosophical Approach

What does equality of sex mean? In what sense a man and a woman are equal? What constitutes equality or inequality? Does difference in gender imply gender inequality? These questions are Philosophical in nature. Philosophical approach seems to be more appropriate for a proper understanding and appreciation of the relation between man and woman.

Man and woman are basically human beings. They are gifts of nature (secular) or of God (religious). A man without a woman or a woman without a man is inconceivable, Man is born of woman; he is flesh of her flesh and bone of her bone; they are one not only in flesh, but also in spirit; the soul in both is the same; both are fundamentally one; each is an absolute equal of the other; they are two sides of the same reality; they are inseparable and interdependent; no existence to one apart from the other; neither is a complete being without the other; both have the same life; have the same feelings and aspirations; have the same aims and goals of life; they are equally necessary for the survival of the human race and to keep the creation going on. It is the law of nature and the law of love that make them held together to discharge their moral duty to nature.

Since the origin of man and woman is same, that is, the same Substance (Matter or God), to conceive them as unequal on the basis of gender is a conceptual mistake. For instance, the law of creation suggests that—no two men or no two women—are equal either from the standpoint of physical strength and physical features or from the standpoint of mental abilities and capacities. If it is so, the difference in gender need not necessarily make male and female as unequal. We may say at best men and women are different; but we should not say they are unequal.

Nature has created man and woman in a different form, with a different purpose and they are bound to discharge their moral duties to nature. The differences we conceive between a man and a woman are just like any other difference between one individual and the other, with reference to their functional aspects. Therefore, to differentiate male and a female on the basis of gender or on gender based functions and treat them unequally in matters of their social functions, is not morally justifiable. The unequal treatment between man and woman, in most of the societies, is not based on natural inequality existing between them. Rather, we can say, they are man-made inequalities or socially induced inequalities, which exclude woman from their rightful role in social, political, economic and other related spheres of activity. The sexual division of labour which does not bring disadvantage to one sex in relation to the other might be morally acceptable.

II

Participation of Women in Political Process

Political participation does not mean merely exercising of political rights like franchise. It also means involvement of woman in a wide range of political activities such as membership in political parties, living in contact and communication with political leaders and legislators, propagation of political ideas and programs of the political parties among the electorate, extension of voluntary services to the people, contesting in elections, involvement in the decision-making bodies of the government and other related activities. These activities are very crucial because they provide an opportunity to the women to acquire the necessary political experience, knowledge, skills, and recognition, which are essential for public life.

Factors Restricting Participation of Women in Politics

Traditional thinking and social conditioning have marginalised the participation of women in political process. The traditional gender based division of labour in the family mostly limits the activities of women to the generation of children, their care and nurture and household duties. The role of woman, as a wife and as a mother, progressively confines her to the home and withdraws her participation from the wider aspects of socio-political and economic fields. She has no leisure time even to contemplate on these issues and problems. These constraints are more or less common to all sections of women irrespective of their class or community.

Socialization is the process by which society prepares children for adulthood. We see much difference in the socialization process among the preadolescent boys and girls. The younger girls and boy, during the formative period of their life, learn societal values and norm as at home. In the socialization process, the older women and mothers play an important role in our families. They usually aim to inculcate respect for traditional social norms, into the minds of the young.

The restrictions imposed on movement of girls and their engagement in domestic works obstruct the girls' exposure to the outside world. In most of our families, the voice of a daughter counts less when compared to the son in matters of decision-making and this creates a sense of ineffectiveness in the girl rights from their childhood. Even after marriage, a woman does not have much important role in decision- making in her in- laws' family. In many families, we find, a difference of treatment between sons and daughter in their day-to-day activities. The parents give less importance to the education of their daughters in comparison to their sons for various reasons. This type of differential treatment prevailing between sons and daughters in a family creates a sense of inferiority in the minds of girls and this will continue in their later life also.

Age is an important factor for participation of women into politics. The attitude of traditional thinking prevents entry of young and unmarried women in politics because they become an object of public attention. Women, in general, prefer to play a "two-role" function-the traditional house-wife-mother functions, and socio-political functions simultaneously. Many women believe that the ideal age for them to enter the political arena is 35 or 40, because the women of this age group are relatively free from gender responsibilities; mentally more matured and experienced; possibly less prone to the pitfalls of scandals and character assassination. The choice of political parties is also in favour of elderly women with less family responsibilities. The electorate are also having strong reservation to elect young and unmarried women.

Moral support of husband and other family members constitutes a crucial factor for the active participation of women in politics. The husband and other members of the family have to bear the prolonged absence of her at home due to her long hours of political activity and sometimes her preoccupation of legislative business etc. In such a situation, they have to forego the services generally they expect from her.

Women's entry into politics is severally restrained by the contemporary political atmosphere in the country. Threats of political violence, criminalisation of politics and character assassination are preventing women to enter into political arena in large numbers. Under these conditions, many men are reluctant to encourage their women to participate in politics. The unmarried educated girls are also not allowed by their parents to enter into polities or hold any political post.

The financial status of women in the society is another impediment for women's participation in politics. Money plays an important role in politics. Most of the women in our society are neither economically independent nor having sufficient financial resources. Because of high cost of electioneering, the choice of political parties is always in favour of women with good financial background, at the time of selection of candidates to contest in elections.

Illiteracy is also a factor for non-participation of women in politics. An uneducated woman has generally less self-confidence and less control over external enviornment. An educated woman feels herself as politically more competent than less educated woman.

Keeping woman in purdah or seclusion, is also a notable factor, which hampers women's public life. It is an evil relic of a barbarous custom, which imprisons the body and mind of many women and restricts their free movement in the society. For whatever purpose it might have been introduced in the beginning, it is doing great harm to women and to the nation.

Freedom Struggle and Liberation of women

The freedom struggle, under the leadership of Gandhi, and the legacy of freedom movement have brought a radical change in the status and position of women in India

1. It provided an opportunity to women to play an active role in the freedom movement which include—processions, protests, shouting slogans, singing patriotic songs, courting arrest, going to jail, facing, lathi-charge, police firing etc.
2. It contributed for the liberation of women by themselves from many inherited customs that enchained her and dragged her down.
3. The legacy of freedom struggle enabled women to achieve equal rights at par with men and these rights ate guaranteed by the Indian constitution.
4. It helped women to prove their organizational abilities, moral courage and intellectual capacities and potentialities. All the political leaders of freedom movement recognized these qualities of women and as a consequence of this, many women held high positions like Governors, Chief Ministers, Ambassadors etc. in Independent India.

5. It created political awareness among Indian women; minimized the inferiority complex that developed in them through ages and raised their dignity and status.

Referring to the participation of women in civil disobedience movement in 1930, Jawharlal Nehru observed;

> 'Most of us menflock were in prison....our women came to the front and took charge of the struggle....Not only the British Government but by their own menflock by surprise....It was not only that display of courage and daring, but what was even more surprising was the organised power they showed.....We could hardly talk about all this among ourselves, for our hearts were full and our eyes were dim with tears'[1]

Remedial Measures Suggested for Improvement of Women's Position in Politics

1. Education is an essential factor for an effective and meaningful participation of women in politics. It enables women to assert their rights, to exercise them wisely and to work for their liberation from social evils and age-old customs. It provides political awareness, political commitment and involvement in political activities. It also makes them to be able to act independently and take autonomous political and administrative decisions. Compulsory education upto high school level and free education to all girls upto degree course may be helpful to them.
2. The political parties can play a crucial role in motivation, training and involvement of women in political process. They should motivate and attract more number of women into the party and allot a reasonable number of positions in the party organization at all levels. The political parties must evolve a policy, to allot more number of seats to women to contest in the elections at the state and national level.
3. The media, both print and electronic, can play a very potential role in bringing out the inherent qualities and potentialities of women. Because women are less mobile and less exposed to the contemporary problems and issues, media can play educative as well as conscious-raising role for women. It can create socio-political consciousness among women for a better use of their rights. The media should give wider coverage to various activities of women, highlight their problems, and motivate them for an active participation in politics.

4. Economic Independence makes women to feel more secured, more independent and more free. The rights of a wife in husband's property and daughter's right of inheritance along with the sons must be admitted. The government should bear the total expenditure of electioneering of women, contesting in elections on a party ticket (recognized political parties), to the legislative bodies at the state and national level.
5. The local bodies, like Panchayat Raj institutions and Municipal Corporations, constitute an important ground to have political training for women. The 73rd and 74th constitutional amendments, which reserve one third of the seats to women in local bodies, provides a good opportunity to women for direct participation in self-rule at the local level. These institutions may help women as training grounds for the emergence of leadership.
6. As time is an important factor for women to play a double role-domestic and socio-political, the husband and other family members should cooperate and share some of her burden in discharging her duties. Of course, the modern electronic and other home appliances, professional child-care centers and old-age homes etc. have relieved her burden to some extent at home and gave her some leisure time to participate in the socio-political activities.
7. The women should be given proper representation in all decision-making bodies of the government. They should have a rightful place in all important committees, commissions and delegations constituted by the government from time to time.
8. The women should actively participate in protests, demonstration—against the evils, like child marriages, dowry deaths, molestation of women, price-rise and other such related activities, which make them aware of the social problems and also help them to develop leadership qualities.
9. The evil customs of child-marriages and purdah or seclusion may be curtailed through legislative measures and by the pressure of public opinion. Compulsory registration of marriages may check the evil practice of child-marriage to a considerable extent.
10. Is one third reservation of seats in legislative bodies necessary for women? It is true that the current rate of women's

representation is quite less, both at the state and central level, when compared to their population. But, reservation of one third seats in the state legislative Assemblies and Parliament through constitutional amendment may not solve this problem and it may lead to more problems which are detrimental to the interests of women due to the following reasons:

1. This practice is contrary to the principle of equality.
2. It is an interference and encroachment on the rights of man.
3. This reservation may be misused to bring wrong women by traditional power brokers, which is already in practice in local bodies.
4. Unless the women are politically conscious, and actively participate in large number in politics, it is neither good to them nor desirable to send them to legislative bodies, because they cannot function in an effective and meaningful way.
5. As an alternative to the constitutional amendment for the reservation of seats for women, we may suggest, a different measure to enhance the representation of women. The election commission may amend its law and make it mandatory for all recognized political parties to allot a minimum of 20 per cent of seats to women taking each state as a unit, and this percentage may be increased in the course of time. The election commission's formula of reservation of particular constituencies may not be suitable for the choice of political parties to select deserving and efficient women candidates among their party workers. Therefore, it is better to leave the choice of the constituencies as well as the choice of the women candidates to the political parties so that they can select suitable and efficient candidates to contest in the elections. The political parties can select women belonging to different sections of the society depending on the local situation.

III

Conclusion

The "man-woman" relation should not be conceived or understood as a relation existing between—master and servant or exploiter and exploited or suppressor and suppressed or a relation between a slave-owner and a slave. These relations are not based on the principles of equality and freedom; but of subordination and subjugation. Such a distorted exposition of man-woman relation is far from truth; contrary to the law of nature; counter to the law of love and hostile to the purpose of human life. This type of destructive interpretation of man-woman relation is neither good for the future of man, of woman because "anything that will impair the status of either of them will involve the equal ruin of both".[2]

The Unity between a man and a woman is not merely a physical unity, but a unity of both mind and heart. It is the law of love that binds them together. Love is the attraction of one human being to another under the guidance of the highest sentiments. Husband and wife constitute one whole; each as absolute equal of the other; each master of the other; each helpmate of the other; each is the companion of the other; each cooperating with the other in the performance of life's tasks and duties. This is the vision and the ideal towards which both men and women should strive.

We cannot live entirely to ourselves. Apart from the biological side, we need a life-partner with whom we can communicate and exchange our deepest ideas; with whom we can share our inner most thoughts and feelings; with whom we can share intellectual sorrows and pleasures, in short, "for completeness of our experiences".[3]

The Indian constitution guarantees equality between men and women and a number of laws have been enacted from time to time to implement these guarantees. Many legislative measures have been taken by the government in matter of inheritance of the property, employment, marriage, maternity benefits, crimes against women and so on. However, the legislation of equal rights itself cannot ensure gender equality as long as majority of women do not claim their entitlement.

Women cannot achieve true liberation without the participation and cooperation of men. The main obstacle to the realization of equality was pervasiveness of social attitude deep rooted in tradition. We have to bring a change in the attitude of men and women; bring change in their "mind-set" or in thinking process, through education or by the pressure of public opinion. Legal rights can never ensure social practice. Legislation by itself fails to offer a complete solution to the problems of women. The Indian women "have to free themselves from the tyranny of man-made customs and laws; they have to carry on this struggle by themselves".[4]

Thus the government, the political parties, the public in general, and the family members in particular, should encourage and cooperate for an effective and meaningful participation of women in the political process.

References

1. Jawaharlal Nehru; *Discovery of India*, pp.41-42.
2. M.K. Gandhi, *Women and Social Injustice*, p. 5.
3. S. Radhakrishan, *Religion and Society*, p. 152.
4. S. Gopal, *Jawaharlal Nehru: An Anthology*, p. 247.

Chapter 32

A Response to Our Politics For the 'Better Half'

D.N. Mallik

It is the question of politically bettering the lot of the 'better half' of the Indian populace. It does involve a very complex task in view of the highly petrified socio-economic realities of our anciently traditional society in its transition to modernity. The task is deeply and sharply challengingly confronting. What is called for is perseverance with patience with reference to an atmosphere of vitiating over politicization.

Political dynamism does need hue and cry. But it is served much better by advocacies based, as much as possible, on prudence kept off agitative allegations and counter-allegations. Apparently, all among the players of our politics for women—opinion leaders, media, academia intelligentsia, women's fora and political parties—stand for empowering women and doing away with their inequality, having no public voice of dissent as yet. Nevertheless there has been the recent empowerment of women in the Panchayat system. Underlining why it is so has to be a primary concern of any serious thought on the matter.

How is it that our ancient society throwing up the saying that gods abide where reverance for women prevails and having the poise that no major performance is complete if it is unpartnered by the performer's better half grew ruthlessly patriarchal and denied gender equality to the half of its members not only in the basics of social growth, in running its economy and in pursuing its politics but, very considerably, also in managing the family.

The malaise has been an ugly outcome of millennia. How is it that our womenfolk were led (in fact mesmerized) to take the husband as God? It must have been a craft par excellence to attitudinally enslave them through some unique kind of indoctrination backed by uninterrupted family training and social conditioning of ages. They were made to observe severely ascetic widowhood full of deprivations. In fact, the Sati practice was glorified to deification. Not that these beliefs and practices passed in *toto* to all sections of the populace. They could be enforced only in relatively smaller numerical sections, other sections only marginally abiding by them or even ignoring them almost altogether. But the adhering sections were made to matter as social superiors.

Whenever foreigners subscribing to non-Indian religions captured power in India, the natives were led to act more and more resolutely in self-preservation through tightened control of our women with greater severities.

But all this passed as long as society, as a whole, remained traditional. Its transitional passage to modernity for about a century and a half has been slowly, yet gradually progressively, bringing about changes more in the high-urban and, to some extent, even in the middle-urban and sub-urban social strata. Thus it has continued to be signaled that modernity has its own consequences to be hopefully banked on. But that developmental process has been eclectic and sporadic. What is obviously warranted is a major social engineering of which political efforts have to be the most important part.

Impediments to our politics for ensuring women's enhanced and in depth participation in decision-making basic to governance and socio-economic management, for capacitating them to keep up their rights and dignity and enabling the nation to deploy them, the half of our population, as better and better human resources have been basically three (1) the inertia of patriarchal male dominance, (2) the perpetual ignorance and passivity of our womenfolk and (3) the socially fragmented psyche of our national politics.

The first two are attitudinal problems accounting for the continuing incapacitation of our women. But the third impediment has been somewhat inherent in the democratic-participatory evolution of our national politics, more particularly since the fourth general elections, against the background of millennia's social unevenness.

The success of our politics in at least formally empowering our women at the tertiary, local-democratic level, though marginal, has not been mean. Even if our women, so empowered, at times appear acting in their husbands' care, signaling that the progress may yet take time to gain substance, that should not cause much worry. Substance may come to the progress sooner than we can guess. News reports nationally surfacing have brought forth instances of appreciably sensible handling of local-democratic governance by female representatives as also of female entrepreneurial achievements.

What has been holding up such progress at the state and national levels of governance? Enactments have continued to be obstructed principally on account of the difference of stands between those who view our women as a single category for the purpose and those who ask for quotas of reservation in terms of their social subcategories. What is the real import of this difference? Are those, who differ on either side, guided by an essential difference may be, by even hostility to the cause? Or are they being guided by their respective political calculus of losses and gains in political power?

If former is the case, it is sinister. Women's fora, backed nationally by all other upholders of the cause, must become much more tenacious than they have been so far in exposing the game and twarting it. If the case is latter, it is, first, a matter of all-women and all-party consensus. If the consensus does not appear emerging, our women will be well-counseled to be guided by liberal realism and to act unitedly for their quota-based enhanced representation in the legislature. They would thus compel the difference between the two sides of political parties to became irrelevant. Quotas carry substance with reference to the given social realities conditioning our politics. Gains and losses in terms of power for political parties cannot be permanent as, in fact, political lineaments and affiliations cannot be permanent.

There is absolutely no reason why our women should show more patience for getting their nationally acknowledged due. They have to rise up in every nook and corner of the country to ensure that they get it. With the tenacity and numerical strength they are in a position to muster and mobilize and they may stun not only this nation, but the whole world. They do have a stock of powerful, talented and courageous elements in their midst in dozens of national fora and important walks of our national life. Now they have a readily available soldiery of representatives in the local self-governing bodies in a kind of firm national network.

Women in political parties ought to have the courage to cut across their party lines if necessary. Soft-pedallers may be identified and ignored as self-servers with despise. Their struggle, if pitched to 'do-or-die' tempo and kept frantically time-bound, will not be long-drawn and will deliver the good shortly.

Chapter 33

Cross-Currents in Ongoing Process for Political Empowerment of Women in India

Anil Kumar Ojha

Since 1990s the question of reservation of one-third seats for women in the Lok Sabha and State Vidhan Sabhas has occupied the centre-stage of public debate in India. This issue was portrayed as a significant step towards women's empowerment. Three constitution Amendment Bills—81st, 84th and 85th moved between 1996 and 1999 failed, having lapsed with the Eleventh, Twelfth and Thirteenth Lok Sabhas. The table below indicates thin representation of women in politics.

Table 1: Number of Women elected into Lok Sabha since 1952

Yrs. of Election	Nos. of Seats	Nos. of Elected Women	Percent of Women
1952	489	22	4.5
1957	494	27	5.5
1962	494	35	7
1967	520	30	5.8
1971	520	21	4
1977	542	19	3.5
1980	542	28	5.2
1984	542	42	7.7
1989	529	27	5.1
1991	521	39	7.5

1996	543	40	7.2
1998	543	43	7.5
1999	543	49	8.6
2004	543	44	8

[Source: *Economic and Political Weekly (EPW),* 36 (17), April 28, 2001, p.1438 and *EPW,* 49 (51) December 18 , 2004, p. 5433.]

I

Origin

73rd and 74th Amendment Acts

It all began with the passage of the Constitution 73rd and 74th Amendment Acts during 1992-1993. Then the Congress party was in power at the Centre with P.V. Narsimha Rao as the prime Minister (P.M.). These Acts inserted Part IX and Part IX A in the Constitution that respectively came into force with effect from April 24, 1993 and June 1, 1993. These Acts provided constitutional status to the rural and urban local self-governing institutions (LSGIs) and made elaborate arrangements about their structures, functions and finances. Till then, being a subject in the State List under Schedule VII of the Constitution, the existence, autonomy, periodic elections, etc. of these bodies depended on the mercy of the state governments. Even relevant state legislations were scantly respected and implemented.

Besides strengthening LSGIs, these Acts made an innovation by reserving one-third elective seats and posts in these bodies for women. Article 243 (D) (2) states that not less than one-third seats reserved for the Scheduled Castes (SCs) and the Scheduled Tribes (STs) shall be reserved for women belonging to these communities. Further, Article 243 (D) (3) sates that, 'Not less than one-third (including the number of seats reserved for the SCs and STs) of the total number of seats to be filled by direct election in every panchayat shall be reserved for women and such seats maybe allotted by rotation to different panchayat (at district, intermediate and village levels)'. As regards the office of the chairpersons at different levels, Article 243 (D) (4) made similat provisions. The same scheme of reservation for women in urban LSGIs was introduced through Article 243(T). This step was characterized as a revolutionary move, which would herald a new era of women's empowerment.

Demand

Thereafter the demand in favour of such reservation in state Assemblies and the Parliament were raised and thus started a debate over it. Earlier, the National Perspective Plan for Women, a document prepared under the Rajiv Gandhi government, recommended that (i) 33 per cent of seats in elected assemblies, from the village to the union level, be reserved for women, and that (ii) political parties promote women's political representation by giving at least 33 per cent tickets to women candidates,[1] which had become the starting point of the above scheme.

II

Genesis

Historical Background

Pre-Independence

The issue of reservation of women had come up in the Constituent Assembly but had been rejected by women representatives as it was felt unnecessary, since the working of democracy in natural course would ensure the representation of all sections of Indian Society.[2]

Separate Electorates and Women's Suffrage

Earlier, the questions of separate electorates and women's political representation had engaged much attention during early 1900s. A Muslim delegation met Lord Minto in 1906.[3] In 1909 Muslim League was formed. Through the establishment of separate electorates in 1909 and their expansion under the constitutional reforms of 1919 and in 1935, the colonial state constructed political identity along religious lines.[4] So far is the women's movement for political representation is concerned, the All India Women's Conference (AIWC) became the movement's centre. It was formed in 1927 with 5,492 members and grew to 25,000 members in 1945.[5] In its early phase, this was a small movement composed of urban, educated, middle-class women. Later on, Provincial and national organizations were formed. The movement regarded itself as including and representing women of all religious communities castes and classes.

The first phase of Hindu-Muslim tensions played out within the women's movement during the deliberations on constitutional reforms in 1930s. Congress took a strong position against separate electorates, while the Muslim League continued to support. Many scholars argue that while Congress claimed a secular anti-communal identity, its nationalist rhetoric relied on Hindu imagery to rally mass support.[6] The Muslim League went on record as supporting women's suffrage and representation in June 1932 in testimony before the Lothian Committee in 1933. They defended separate electorates, women's seats reserved on communal basis and same qualifications for women electors as men, as they believed that literacy and wifehood qualifications being proposed by the British would enfranchise more Hindu women.[7] The Muslim League Spokesman Mohammed Yakub had stated, "women do not belong to a separate community; they belong to the community to which their men belong and there can be......no conflicts of interests between men and women".[8] The Muslim legislators elected under separate electorates tended to identify their political survival with the continuation of the electoral system. Two Muslim women leaders—Begum Shah Nawaz and Begum Hamid Ali took contradictory positions on women's representation in Muslim seats. The AIWC insisted on unity of women, which led to the formation of a women's wing in the Muslim League by 1938. Ayesha Jalal notes these positions were defined by dominant values and, political preoccupations of Muslim men.[9]

In the elections for provincial assemblies held after the Government of India Act 1935, approximately 41 per cent of the adult males and 9 per cent of the adult females were enfranchised. Can any analogy be drawn between these debates and one going on currently over women's reservation?

Post-Independence

The suggestion was also seen to underestimate the strength of women to compete as equals. Committee on Status of Women in India (CSWI) considered the question in 1974 and rejected the idea for such a reservation. Arguments made against reservations were mainly that (a) this would run counter to the principle of equality in the Constitution; (b) women cannot be equated to socially backward communities as they are not a socially homogeneous group; (c) women's interests cannot be isolated from those of other economic, social and political strata; (d) such a system would give rise to similar demands from other groups and communities, thus posing a threat to national integration. Finally the CSWI by a majority decided to uphold the position taken in the Constituent Assembly and rejected the reservation of seats in parliament and state assemblies[10] Veena Majumdar, who was member secretary of the CSWI, points out how 'as daughters of independence' her generation had been critical of special representation, but 'we have found our understanding of nation-building radically changing'.[11] This marks a radical change of perspective because ever since 1930s even as recently as the 1970s, most women's organizations and their supporters resisted and openly rejected proposals for reserved seats. Major sections of the women's movement have been campaigning actively with considerable public support, to get the measure approved.

Scenario in Europe During 1990s

Prominent first world nations have had to contend with very low levels of women's political representation[12] as evident from the tables given below. Even British and French legislatures had 7.4 and 5.9 per cent women members in 1990s.

Table 2: Women in the Parliaments of European Union

Country	Election Yrs.	Lower House	Upper House	Total Parliament
Sweden	1994	40.4		40.4
Finland	1995	33.5		33.5
Denmark	1994	33.0		33.0
Netherlands	1994-1991	31.3	28.0	30.2
Germany	1994	26.3	19.1	25.7
Austria	1994	25.0	21.9	22.7
Luxembourg	1994	16.6		16.6
Belgium	1995	11.3	23.6	15.3
Spain	1993	16.0	12.6	14.6
Ireland	1992	12.0	13.3	12.4
Italy	1994	13.9	8.3	12.0

Portugal	1995	11.7		11.7
U.K./ U.Kingdom	1992	9.2	6.5	7.4
France	1993-95	6.0	5.6	5.9
Greece	1993		5.3	5.3

(Source: Danille Haase-Dubosc, Movement for Parity in France, EPW35 (43&44), October 28, 2000, pp. 3855-3860).

Table 3: Number of Women Ministers and European Deputies in the countries of the European Union, 1995

Country	Date of formation of Last Govt.	% of Women in the Govt.	% of Women in the European Govt.
Sweden	1994	50.0	45.5
Finland	1995	38.9	62.5
Denmark	1994	35.0	43.8
Netherlands	1994	34.6	32.2
France	1995	Juppe I: 27.9 Juppe II: 12.5	29.9
Austria	1994	23.8	33.3
Ireland	1992	16.7	26.7
Spain	1994	16.6	32.8
Luxembourg	1994	16.6	33.3
Germany	1994	15.6	34.3
Belgium	1995	11.7	32.0
Portugal	1995	8.9	8.0
Italy	1994	7.8	10.3
UK	1992	7.0	18.3
Greece	1994	5.6	16.0

(Source: *Ibid*)

III
Progress in India

By the time of general elections of 1996, women's organizations put forward a joint demand to all political parties supported for reservation for women in state assemblies and in Parliament.[13] The major parties supported the demand, although they themselves gave less than 15 per cent of their total number of tickets to women. The manifestoes of all major political parties emphasized the need to ensure a strong presence of women in elected assemblies. The Common Minimum Programme of the United Front (UF) Government, which assumed office after the elections, included the women's reservation issue. The women's Reservation Bill (WRB) first came as the 81st Amendment Bill in 1996. It had proposed to reserve 33 per cent seats in parliament and state assemblies for women.

Argument in Support

On the question of reservations for women in Parliament and State Legislatures, the argument in favour of reservation were mainly that (i) political parties because of their generally patriarchal character were reluctant to sponsor women candidates, and therefore reservation were necessary; (ii) reservations would increase the number of women in Parliament at once and they would be able to act as strong lobby. At present, their being in a small minority inhibits their effective participation in their interests of women; (iii) the presence of more women in Parliament would lead to a change in the direction of debates and policy.

These arguments put forth in favour of the WRB may be briefly discussed. Firstly, since women constitute half the population, it is only just that some affirmative action be taken to ensure a fair place for them in politics. "[Reservation for women].....will definitely right the wrong and change the imbalance in legislative representation overnight [....] we must have more women if we want democracy to flourish",[14] declared Najma Heptullah, the deputy chairperson of the Rajya Sabha.

Secondly, a strong presence of women would ensure that issues concerning women would be more adequately dealt with. [Women's] concern—rich or poor—is for an environment of security, free of criminals, free of violence, for raising families; their domestic responsibilities generate primary concerns for access to water, healthcare, schools for children and in the case of the masses, for income and assets, for shelter and for cooking energy. These would give a direction to the development agenda, drawing attention to basic amenities, wrote Devaki Jain.[15] Another assertion in the same vein is worth quoting, "Women's participation in politics is necessary for holistic development......[Women] are bound to have a better perspective on vital issues such as environment, healthcare and education, particularly of the girl-child, as these affect them directly".[16]

Thirdly, a massive presence of women in political assemblies would automatically transform the function of the political life and make it more peaceful, more honest, more sincerely devoted to the common good. "Women will definitely help to end corruption", said Girija Vyas,[17] the then president of the Mahila Congress and presently the chairperson of the National Commission for Women. Even the former Chief Election Commissioner, T.N. Seshan, said, "Everybody knows that women are less easily carried away and are more objective [than men]. They will make politics more sober".[18] There appeared a consensus between people of very different ideological backgrounds.

Arguments in Opposition

Even then it could not be passed and had to be referred to a Joint Select Committee (JPC). Opposition to the Bill came mainly from within the ruling coalition itself. One of the UF constituents—the Janata Dal (JD), from which the P.M himself belonged, opposed it tooth and nail. The PM H.D. Deve Gowda remained a silent spectator, when Sharad Yadav, a very senior JD member and party's Working President; vociferously protesting snatched the copy of the Bill from the hands of the Minister tabling it and literally tore it into pieces. Samajwadi Party, another important UF constituent whose leaders were holding important cabinet berths including Defence, was equally opposed to the intended measure. In the face of such a strong opposition, it was sent to a JPC. The Eleventh Lok Sabha was dissolved in December 1997 and the WRB lapsed with it.

During the 12th Lok Sabha, the Bill numbered as 84th Amendment Bill was reintroduced by the Bhartiya Janata Party (BJP) led National Democratic Alliance (NDA) government in 1998.It faced strong opposition from within the ruling coalition as well as from outside. NDA constituent—Samata Party members opposed the Bill at the introduction stage itself in the House. The JD and its breakaway faction—Rashtriya Janta Dal, having stronghold in Bihar, and also the Samajwadi Party opposed it.

Arguments made by political parties against reservations were mainly that (i) if it were passed Other Backward Castes (OBC) women would actually be further marginalised; (ii) in any electoral contest OBC women—who are largely uneducated—would stand little chance against women from more privileged castes/ classes; (iii) OBC leaders saw it as a weapon to deprive them of the political gains they have made since 1980s and claimed that a third sub quota be defined within the 33 per cent for OBC women. Some analysts suggest that the emergence of women as a significant grouping in Indian politics is only one of the factors shifting the consensus on women's reservation. The other factor—an equally significant development, is the transformation of caste composition of parliament through successive elections. It is underlined that two very different set of concerns—feminists and upper caste produce this sudden general acceptability of women's reservations.[19]

Quota within Quota

In 1998, five political parties—the Rashtriya Janata Dal, the Samajwadi Party, the Bahujan Samaj Party, the Indian Union Muslim League and the National Conference joined forces to demand that a sub quota for Muslim women be also devised within the WRB, in addition to the sub quota for OBC women.[20] This claim amounted to stalling the bill in three respects. From a legal angle, the sub quota for OBC and Muslim women would require beforehand the implementation of quotas for OBCs and Muslims as a whole in political assemblies. If OBCs and Muslims women were granted a sub quota, the 'other more' backward communities could also demand specific provisions for their women. Lastly, the very mention of quotas for Muslim women makes the whole scheme appear as a potential Pandora box of division of the electorates on communal grounds rendering it as a taboo. And the WRB was derailed once again. However, some analysts view this demand of 'quota within quota' as an 'opportunity to link women's rights to rights based on caste, or minority status in the broader context of a common democratic struggle'.[21]

After the 13th Lok Sabha elections in 1999, the BJP-led NDA coalition returned to power with an altered configuration of allies. Its Agenda for Governance proclaimed, 'we will make law for reservation of thirty three per cent seats in Parliament and State Vidhan Sabhas for women'.[22] The WRB was again introduced in December 1999 as the 85th Amendment Bill. Its fate remained uncertain throughout the period (1999-2004) as it faced opposition from the same parties having roots in North India's countryside. However, the main opposition—the Congress party and the Left block of parties—CPI (M), CPI, RSP and Forward Block had expressed their support to the scheme. Efforts to form political consensus failed and the government facing dissension within the ruling coalition could not muster requisite majority to get the constitution amendment measure passed. And the 85th Constitution Amendment Bill met the fate of the previous 81st and 84th Amendment Bills.

An Alternative Women's Bill was drafted by the Forum for Democratic Reforms, proposing to make it mandatory for political parties to give 33 per cent of tickets to women candidates. This sought to shift women's quota to the party level.[23] This was also supported by the Election Commission. Madhu Kishwar, a member of the above forum, wrote an article 'Equality of Opportunities vs. Equality of Results' explaining the scheme.[24]

IV

Present Position

The United Progressive Alliance (UPA) coalition governmen led by the Congress leader Dr. Man Mohan Singh took office ir May 2004 after the elections for the 14th Lok Sabha. The UPA i a coalition of 14 parties and is supported by the Left parties fron outside.[25] The UPA coordination committee under th chairpersonship of Congress President Sonia Gandhi provides th institutional mechanism for inter-party deliberations within the UP and between the UPA and the Left parties. The UPA issued a Common Minimum Programme (CMP). The CMP of the UPA has this to say on the women's reservation issue: 'The UPA Government will take the lead to introduce legislation for one-third reservation for women in Vidhan Sabha and the Lok Sabha'. On women's issues it has other commitments also. The CMP, further, states, 'Legislation on domestic violence and against gender discrimination will be enacted'.[26]

Hermeneutically speaking, the two expressions: first as regards women's reservation that 'the government will take the lead to introduce legislation', and second on domestic violence and against gender discrimination its emphatic statement that 'legislation will be enacted' make the priorities, constraints and compulsions of the UPA coalition clear. Since, the second largest constituent of the ruling UPA coalition—RJD does not hide its opposition to the women's reservation without a provision of 'quota within quota'. In June 2005 the government decided to enact legislation against domestic violence and gender discrimination during the monsoon session 2005.

Prospects

The subject of reservations- that is the creation of special quotas for specific groups in the legislatures, public services and institutions of higher education—has repeatedly emerged as a critical issue in the political history of 20th century India, There appears no respite from the quagmire. No other policy measure has raised so many fundamental questions about the nature and composition of our society, and how the structures of modern governance may promote citizenship and equality[27] In view of the fact that ever since 1996; the WRB is opposed by the OBCs lobby composed of OBC parliamentarians cutting across party lines, there appears a very dim chance of its passage, particularly during the present coalition era. Further, the same vested interest of entrenched politicians is capable enough to stall it, which has repeatedly obstructed delimitation of constituencies. The stalemate proves that gender has become legitimate as a political category; it remains less legitimate than caste, class and tribe.[28]

Summing up, the cross-currents delineated above—demands in favour by women's organizations having overt support from the

Congress, BJP and the Left parties and opposition to it in its present form overtly from the OBC lobby and covertly from the patriarchal political culture make its passage difficult.

References

1. Government of India (1988): The National Perspective Plan for Women, 1988-2000, Delhi.
2. Nivedita Menon, 'Elusive 'Women': Feminism and Women's Reservation Bill', *Economic and Politics weekly EPW 35(*43&44), October 28, 2000, p. 3835.
3. Kooiman, Dick (1995): "Communalism and Indian Princely States: A comparison with British India", *EPW,* 30(34), pp. 2123-33.
4. Jana Everett, 'All the Women Were Hindu and All the Muslims Were Men': State, Identity Politics and Gender, 1917-1951, *EPW,* 36(23), July 9, 2001, p. 2072.
5. Cousins, James H. and Margaret E. Cousins (1950): *We Two Together,* Ganesh and Company, Madras, p. 448.
6. Wolpert, Stanley (1988): "The Indian National Congress in Nationalist Perspective in Richard Sisson and Stanley Wolpert (eds.), Congress and Indian Nationalism: The Pre-Independence Phase, University of California Press, Berkley, pp. 21-44.
7. Jana Everett, 'All the Women Were Hindu and All the Muslims Were Men': State, Identity Politics and Gender, 1917-1951, EPW 36(23), 9 June, 2001,p. 2073.
8. UK (1932-33): Parliamentary Papers, Indian Franchise Committee, (112) VII quoted in N. 9, pp. 2071-80.
9. Ayesha Jalal (1991): "The Convenience of Subservience: Women, State and Ideology and the state of Pakistan" in Deniz Kandiyoti (ed.), *Women, Islam and State,* Temple University Press, Philadelphia, pp. 77-114.
10. No. 8 above.
11. Veena Majumdar, 'Historical Soundings', Seminar, 457, September 1997, pp. 15-16.
12. Anne Phillips, *The Politics of Presence: The Political Representation of Gender, Ethnicity and Race,* Clarendon Press, Oxford, 1995 (reissued in paperback 1998).
13. Veena Majumdar, 'Historical Soundings', Seminar, 457, September 1997, pp. 15-16.
14. The Economic Times, New Delhi, March 16,1997.

15. The Telegraph, Calcutta, March 22, 1997.
16. Ashok Chelly in the pioneer, Delhi, April 24, 1997.
17. The Sunday Observer, New Delhi, November 3-9, 1996.
18. India Today, October 15, 1996.
19. Nivedita Menon, 'Elusive 'women': Feminism and women's Reservation Bill', *Economic and Political Weekly EPW* 35 (43&44), October 28, 2000, p. 3836.
20. Stephanie Tawa Lama-Rewal, 'Fluctuating, Ambivalent Legitimacy of Gender as a Political Category' *EPW* 36 (17) April 28, 2001, p. 1435-40.
21. Mary E. John, 'Alternate Modernities: Reservations and Women's Movement in Twentieth Century India', *EPW,* 35 (43&44), October 21-27 October— 28, November 3, 2000, p. 3822.
22. NDA's Agenda for Governance, *Election Manifesto: 1999,* BJP Publication, New Delhi, 1999, p. 6(*emphasis added).*
23. The Hindu, Delhi, April 28, 2000.
24. See. *EPW,* 35 (47), 18 November, 2000.
25. The UPA is a coalition of the Congress (138) and its pre-poll allies that include the RJD (24), DMK (16), NCP (9), PMK (6), TRS (5), JMM (5), LIP (4), MDMK (4), AIMIM (1), PDP (1), IUML (1), RPI (A) (1), RPI (G) and Kerala Congress (J) (1). The Left Parties (61) support it from outside—CPI (M) (43), CPI (10), RSP (3) and Forward Bloc (3) and two Independents. Some Other Parties—Samajwadi Party (36), Bahujan Samaj Party (BSP)(19), Janata Dal (Secular) (4), and Rashtriya Lok Dal (3) also extend outside support to it. (Figures in brackets indicate the number of seats held by parties in the 14th Lok Sabha).
26. Common Minimum Programme, The Hindu, Delhi, May 28, 2004, p.12.
27. Mary E. John, 'Alternate Modernities: Reservations and Women's Movement in Twentieth Century India', *EPW,* 35 (43&44), October 21-27 October 28—November 3, 2000, p. 3822.
28. Stephanie Tawa Lama-Rewal, 'Fluctuating, Ambivalent Legitimacy of Gender as a Political Category' *EPW* 36(17), April 28, 2001, pp. 1435-40.

Part III

Social Thought Perspectives

Chapter 34

Women's Empowerment: The Vedantic Perspective

S.B.P. Sinha

The problem of women's empowerment presupposes that they are less powerful or subject to various infirmities due to factors for which their counterparts may be said to be responsible. This predicament also implies that women are not regarded at par with their male counterparts. So obviously this problem involves inequality or something like this between men and women. To further explain and explicate this point, it may be observed that women though theoretically equal partners have been subjected to various forms of exploitations, unjust treatment and this also implies that they have been made to suffer in various ways. To further illustrate this point, it may be observed that they have been harassed in various ways and have been also deprived of their rightful and just position and place. The story of their weal and woe is further seen in various kinds of exploitations and tortures including maltreatment and even deaths due to dowry problems. The department has done quite well to organize a seminar on this burning problem and deserves congratulations and credits for selecting this subject, which is really quite important in the domain of applied philosophy. Really, it is high time that philosophers should not only confine themselves to studies of speculative and to logical analysis and discussion but should also come forward to such pursuits which aim at socio-spiritual reformation. Perhaps this is more befitting and is in consonance with the spirit of Indian Philosophy, which is said to be more practical in comparison to mere intellectual pursuits.

Having made these prefatory observations, now it is proposed to make a few brief and critical observations in this context. At the very outset, it may be observed that in our land such discrimination on the ground of gender has not been conceived right from the ancient era. It is needless to remind us that Maitreyi, Gargi and such other ladies participated even in philosophical discussions. Women were accorded equal status. Not only this, our ancient scriptures highlighted the adorable position of women in society. Besides this, the conception of God as divine mother also eulogises and elevates the status of women. This cult of shaktism, which can be traced back to the Vedas and which has been more pronouncedly advocated in the Puranas is also quite popular during the present times. It is not necessary to dwell on this point in more details but it would be interesting to quote Ramakrishna Paramhansa who is said to have remarked, "Women are but so many forms of my Divine Mother. I cannot bear to see them suffer. They are all images of the Mother of the Universe".[1]

So, obviously women have been given their important and equal place in our traditional scheme, but at the same time this fact of various atrocities, unjust and inhuman treatment and allied forms of meted out to them cannot be denied exploitations. We all hear about dowry deaths and other forms of maltreatment done to the female sex who is regarded to be the personification of universal motherhood. No doubt, there are social and economic factors, which have contributed to this great malady. Economic factors have been rectified by various laws, which purport to give equal rights to women in matters of property. Everybody knows that the Hindu law has been effectively modified and daughters are to be treated on par with sons. Laws banning dowry have not been improved considerably. No doubt our constitution has guaranteed equality to them. It is also seen that our government is doing a lot for better position of the female sex. Various commissions like "Mahila Ayoga etc." have been entrusted with this task. Moreover the position of women has been also tried to be strengthened by provisions of reservations in different spheres. But it appears that this predicament can be better solved perhaps and in more enduring way not only by these above mentioned means.

That is why, it is proposed to briefly and critically study Vedantic approach, so that it maybe seen whether this can be regarded to be more effective and lasting. Here, it would be better to see at the very outset what we mean by Vedantic approach. Of course, it is neither possible nor desirable to discuss the meaning and development of the schools of Vedanta. But our intention can be explained clearly by pointing out that the advait schools of Vedanta is regarded to be the most prominent school of Indian Philosophy. Let us quote following lines in this context. "The Sutras of aphorisms of Vyasa are the basis of the Vedanta philosophy. These Sutras have been variously explained by different commentators. From these interpretations have arisen several schools of philosophy, viz., Kevala Advaita philosophy of Shri Shankaracharya, the philosophy of qualified Monism or Vishishtadvaita of Sri Ramanujacharya, the Dvaita philosophy of Sri Madhvacharya, the Bhedabheda philosophy of Shri Nimbarkacharya, the Shuddha Advaita philosophy of Shri Vallabhacharya, the Achintya Bhedabheda philosophy of Shri Chaitanya and the Siddhanta philosophy of Sri Meykander".[2]

Literally also Vedanta means the end of the Vedas and it is rightly considered to be the culmination of ancient Vedic knowledge. Although, Upanishads are regarded to be the fountainhead of Vedanta. But it is well known that Vadarayana systematises this in his 'Brahmasutra'. Further it is seen that Shankar, Ramanuja and others developed this through their different learned commentaries. Of course, they also took into account Upanishads, Gita besides 'Brahmasutra'. Here, we are mainly concerned with Shankara's approach to Vedanta, which is known as Advaita. Without going into minute details, it would suffice to observe here that Shankar's Advaita is rightly regarded to be the paragon of all monistic systems, Maxmuller, Frazer, Radhakrishnan, T.M.P. Mahadevan have naturally highlighted the profound philosophical importance of Shankar's approach.

Before coming to the present context, it may be clarified that contemporary Indian thinkers, both technical philosophers as well as non-technical creative thinkers have been naturally inspired by this ancient lofty philosophy. In this context, it may be added here that generally speaking non-dualism signifies that philosophical doctrine which upholds the reality of Brahman alone and believes in the identity of Atman and Brahman. It is also further seen that the plurality is regarded to be phantasmgoric production of nescience. Now instead of studying these concepts relating to Maya etc., it would be more pertinent to observe here that modern Vedantins, who are also known as neo-Vedantins, tried to develop what may be considered to be more constructive and affirmative approach. In this context it would be interesting to refer to the approach of Swami Vivekananda, the dynamic counterpart of Ramakrishna Paramhansa and Swami Sivananda. This is because they have explicitly added practical dimension to the philosophy of advaita. This does not mean refuting or contradicting Shankar's positions but this only shows that they tried to universalize the teachings of Vedanta by adding practical implications, which they involve. We may quote Swamijee, "The Vedanta, therefore, as a religion must be intensely practical. We must be able to carry it out in every part of our lives. And not only this, the fictitious differentiation between religion and the life of the world must vanish, for the Vedanta teaches oneness-one life throughout. The ideals of religion must cover the whole field of life, they must enter into all our thoughts, and more into practice".[3]

To further explain and expound this approach, Swamijee tries to emphasize the fact of essential unity of existence besides laying stress on the innate divinity of every being, the 'Jiva' is 'Shiva'. This has to be realized through different spiritual paths like Jnanayoga, Bhaktiyoga, Karma Yoga and Rajayoga. This is religion according to him. It is needless to say that he does not attach much importance to ritualistic and theistic approach.

Again, coming to Swami Sivananda, it would suffice to mention here that he also tries to add realistic and dynamic dimension to the philosophy of Advaita. To illustrate this point clearly, we may quote him, "One soul abides in all. There is one humanity. There is one brotherhood. There is one atmahood. None is high. None is low. All are equal. Vain are the distinctions. Man-made barriers should be ruthlessly broken down. Then alone there will be peace in this world. There is only one caste, the caste of humanity. There is only one religion, the religion of love. There is only one commandment, the commandment of truthfulness. There is only one law, the law of cause and effect. There is only one God, the omnipresent, omnipotent, omniscient Lord. There is only language, the language of the heart or the language of silence".[4]

So, it is obvious that both Swami Vivekananda and Swami Sivananda and such others have tried to lay stress on the fact of unity of existence and naturally in this scheme all distinctions are not real in the ultimate sense. It is needless to observe here that distinctions, differences and other mattes relating to discord find no place in this scheme of practical Vedanta. So naturally it can be observed that distinctions made on the ground of gender or sex can not be justified ultimately speaking and other factors of distinctions and disintegration also need to be dismissed from this point of view.

But at the same time, as indicated earlier the facts of injustice of maltreatment to women cannot be denied. Swami is conscious of this fact. Swami Jitatmananda rightly refers to this aspect of Swami's profound concern for women. It would be interesting to quote following lines in this context. "Vivekananda repeatedly told the India's downfall was largely due to the negligence of the women. The great image of Gargi of the Upanishadic age, the great image of Sanghamitra, the woman Missionary carrying Buddha's message to Syria and Macedonia, all were lying buried deep due to a millennium of foreign domination. The mid-nineteenth century India saw women, the great mother power, shackled and degenerated to more 'child-producing machines', as Vivekananda saw it. A bird that seeks to fly on one wing crashes down on the ground. India had suffered the same fate".[5]

It may be further observed that Swami Vivekananda the great dynamic Saint, travelled to different parts of the world and tried to observe things. In this context he tried to realize that Indian women are primarly mothers. Perhaps this means that according to him and other Vedantins and spiritualists motherhood is the consummation of womanhood. Perhaps this is unlike the approach, which is found in west and other countries, where women are regarded to be important as wives. To quote Swamijee, "The very peculiarity of Hindu women, which they have developed and which is the idea of their life, is that of the mother. If you enter a Hindu's home, you will not find the wife to be the same equal companion of the husband as you find her here. But when you find the mother, she is the pillar of the Hindu home. The wife must wait to become the mother, and then she will be everything".[6]

Besides this uniqueness, it has been already seen that the important uniqueness of women in India is also corroborated by the fact that they are regarded to be the personification of Shakti. Besides these points, it is evident to realize that from Advaitic point of view, any kind of distinction and discrimination between men and women is unacceptable and untenable. They have to be treated on equal basis and so any kind of maltreatment, exploitation and such other vices and crimes meted out to them, need to be discouraged and eliminated. Perhaps in this context Swamijee would suggest proper education for women so that they may realize their real nature and strength. We may quote again Swami Jitatmananda relevantly here, "If in Ramakrishna Vivekananda saw the saviour of the masses and the women, in Holy Mother Sarada Devi he saw the rising of the Great Mother Power that will purify society by inspiring the rise of countless Gargis, Maitreyis, and such other Brahmavadins—the women-knowers of God of the Upanishadic age".[7]

To make these observations more intelligible, it may be observed here that women of our country are also partly responsible for this pitiable plight. Perhaps western culture and ways of life, which may be suitable in a different context have been ignorantly emulated by some women. They have ceased to realize their ancient position. Further, they have also allowed themselves to be used as object and commodities and are oblivious of their equality and identity with men. So it may be reiterated that they need to be educated in the real sense of the term and should act not under the sway of materialistic and consumeristic culture and should shun forces of exhibitionism and such other commercial devices due to which they are exploited. This is desirable and possible in this background of practical Vedanta and our ancient spiritual wisdom. Instead of going into further details, it would be desirable to refer to Swami Sivananda also. He also exhorts the modern woman to realize her purity and potentiality. He says, "woman is Chaitanya Maya. She is the energy aspect of the Lord. She is the child of Adi Sakti. She holds the key of this world. She controls the destiny of children. She is the mother of Sankaras, Buddhas and Janakas".[8] He further highlights the importance of Indian womanhood. To quote him again, "If a woman be pure, she can save and purify man. Women can purify the race. Women can make a home a sacred temple. The Hindu women have been the custodians of the Hindu race. The Hindu religion, the Hindu culture and civilization, still survives in spite of the many foreign invasions, when other civilizations have come and gone, on account of the purity of Hindu women".[9]

He also warns them against modern pitfalls. So he also in his own way advocates gospel of spiritualism and moralism in consonance with our ancient Vedantic wisdom for improving the lot of suffering women. He would also support Swami Vivekananda and other Vedantins, who advise women to take recourse to spiritualism for treating and curing the various ills and maladies to which women have been subjected.

Before concluding our observations here, it would be interesting to refer to the views of Manjula Bordia, who has studied this problem perhaps quite holistically and rightly holds that Indian women should not blindly follow western women to remedy the various problems which they are subjected to. She rightly favours spirituality as panacea for misplaced feminism. She naturally refers to Swami Vivekananda and such others in this context. It would be interesting and illuminating to quote her few following observations, "when the Indian women woke up to the feminist storm raised by their western sisters they committed the grave folly of following those glamorous leaders without giving enough thought to its relevance to their own culture and the problems which are of a very different nature............Women have to realize that they will get empowerment by spiritual awakening only, as it is spirituality that strengthens the inner self. The constitutional provisions are external to the self and fail to give inner strength or real empowerment".[10]

Conclusively, it can be observed that other means of women empowerment need not be underrated. They can also be used effectively and can mitigate the problem at hand. But at the same time, it would be advisible to develop this type of spiritualistic approach on the basis of our Vedantic wisdom. Modern women and others should not think that this is something, which is not practical. In fact, what is needed is that women and all of us should try to develop more holistic approach. Women should therefore try to realize their real nature as well as their tremendous power and potentiality. Initially this may appear to be difficult but they can indeed march on this path quite successfully. We can be inspired by the clarion call of Swamiji here, "You are the pure one; awake and arise, mighty one, this sleep does not become you. Awake and arise, it does not befit you. Think not that you are weak and miserable. Almighty, arise and awake and manifest your own nature".[11]

References

1. Sri Ramakrishna Paramhansa, *Prabuddha Bharat*, vol. 107, April, 2002, p. 235.
2. Sri Swami Sivananda, *All about Hinduism*. Divine Life Society, India, 1977, p. 276.
3. *The Complete Works of Swami Vivekananda,* vol. 2, Ashrama, 5, Dehi Entally Road, Calcutta, 1989, p. 291.
4. Sri Swami Shivananda, Bliss Divine, The Divine Life Society. P.O. Shivannadanagar, Distt. Tehri—Garhwal, U.P., Himalayas, India, 1974, p. XXXV.
5. Swami Jitatmananda, Swami Vivekananda, Prophet and Pathfinder, Sri Ramkrishna Math 16, Ramakrishna Math Road, Mylapore, Madras, 1985, p. 118.
6. *The Complete Works of Swami Vivekananda*, vol. 9, 1977, p. 201.
7. Swami Jitatmananda Vivekananda Prophet and Pathfinder, 1985, p. 119.
8. Swami Sivananda, Bliss Divine, 1974, p. 647.
9. *Ibid.*
10. Manjula Bordia, The Vedanta Kesari, January 2002, p. 25.
11. Swami Vivekananda, Vivekananda, His call to the Nation, Advaita Ashrama (Publication Department) 5, Dehi Entally Road, Calcutta, 1999, p. 101.

Chapter 35

Women's Empowerment and Swami Vivekananda

Swami Brahmeshananda

A hundred years ago, Swami Vivekananda had said, *"India's two national sins are the neglect of the masses and the neglect of the women"*. India has suffered foreign subjugation for centuries due to these two great sins and it is regretted that even today they are persisting in one form or the other. The former President of India, Sri Narayanan, has pointed this out in his address to the nation this year on the eve of the Republic Day. Although something has been done in the sphere of women's education and other means of their upliftment, the gender-based crimes on women are increasing.

Swami Vivekananda has further said that just as a bird cannot fly with only one wing; its both wings must be intact and equally strong, similarly, no nation can rise without the equal and harmonious development of both its men and women. As a matter of fact, Swami Vivekananda laid greater stress on the education and uplift of women than of men. He would say, *"First there be monastery for the mother, her daughters (i.e. Holy Mother Sri Sarada Devi and her women disciples) and then father and sons (i.e., Sri Ramakrishna and his male disciples)."*

Swami Vivekananda was of the firm opinion that women can solve their own problems without the intervention of men; only they must get proper education. Once, when some one asked him about the solution of the problems of Indian widows he had replied," Am I a widow that you are asking me this question?

There is a touching little incident in the life of Swami Vivekananda, while in the U.S.A., to attend Parliament of Religions at Chicago in 1893. Swamiji was put up with one Mr. Leon. Mr. Leon's grand-daughter, a little girl of 5-6 years, would play with Swami Vivekananda, who used to tell her Indian folk tales. Once, Swamiji asked her to show him her school books. The little girl ran to her room and brought the books, and showed them with great enthusiasm to Swamiji. But she was taken aback when she saw Swamiji's face becoming sad on looking at the books. She asked why was he sad. Did he not like the books? Swamiji consoled her and said that the books are indeed good. Unfortunately such books for the education of Indian girls were not there in India, and this was the cause of Swamiji's sadness. Indeed, so keen Swamiji was for the education of Indian women that he inspired Miss Margaret Noble who later became known as Sister Nivedita and started a school in Calcutta for the education of girls.

Empowerment of Women by Sri Ramakrishna

It is likely that Swami Vivekananda got a hint, at least, of the need for women's empowerment, from his great teacher and Guru Sri Ramakrishna. Sri Ramakrishna always gave the greatest respect to the women. He, for example, chose a feminine deity, the Goddess Kali as his adored chosen deity and accepted a lady of exceptional spiritual attainments, Bhairavi Brahamani, as his spiritual guide.

Sri Ramakrishna's empowerment of his wife and spiritual consort, Sri Sarada Devi, who is worshipped and adored all over the world today, was unique. He never even once in his life hurt her, even by words! He even worshipped her as the Divine Goddess herself. He gave detailed spiritual as well as secular instructions so that she could grow into an able guide to the people. Before passing away, he commissioned her to help the people of the world groveling in the world as worms. The result was that Sri Sarda Devi continued to live for 34 years after the passing away of Sri Ramakrishna and not only provided succour, peace and guidance to the many householders who thronged to her for peace, but also guided the monastic brotherhood of the Ramakrishna Mission, in its early period of doubt and uncertainty.

The Holy Mother and Women's Empowerment

The Holy Mother was extremely bashful. She never appeared in public and was so soft-spoken that it was difficult to listen to what she said. She was illiterate as well; and yet her spiritual attainments were so great and her common senses so sharp that she became virtually the uncrowned queen of the Ramakrishna Mission. The great Swami Vivekananda, and Swami Saradananda, the General Secretary of the Ramakrishana Mission consulted her for major problems and never went against her wishes. Her commands were final and were obeyed implicitly. Swami Vivekananda wanted to introduce animal sacrifice during Durga Puja at the Belur Math, but it was the Holy Mother, who ruled that this must not be done. Again Swami Vivekananda wanted to sell away the newly acquired land and buildings at Belur Math for meeting the expenditure of relief works then in progress. It was the Holy Mother, who prevented it by saying that Swamiji had no legal or moral authority to do so, since the Math belonged to Sri Ramakrishna. Besides, the Math was not meant to be expended only in carrying out one relief work. Hundreds of such welfare activities would be carried out in future. This cannot be done if Math was sold.

Those days were the days of struggle for Indian independence. Some revolutionaries, however, had given up their earlier associations and inspired by the teachings of Swami Vivekananda, joined the Ramakrishna Mission. This gave wrong signals that the mission was supporting and protecting the revolutionaries. The then Viceroy of India, Lord Carmichael, in his Durbar speech at Dhaka, once made some derogatory remarks against the Ramakrishna Mission, which created a crisis-situation for the Mission. It was proposed that the revolutionaries, who had joined the mission, must be expelled to prevent the ire of the British Government. Swami Saradananda, the General Secretary, consulted the Holy Mother on this issue, who said that those who have joined the Mission have given up all terrorist activities and must not be expelled. She further advised Swami Saradananda to personally meet the Viceroy and explain the whole situation. This was done with favourable results. The Viceroy withdrew his derogatory remarks officially.

Though illiterate herself the Holy Mother was extremely enthusiastic about girl's education and took keen interest in the activities of the Nivedita School. She even encouraged girls to remain unmarried and devote to education and to higher pursuits in life, rather than getting caught in wedlock and family life .

Women's Empowerment as Motherhood

In India women have always been honoured as mothers. In Chandi it is said that the "Divine Mother Goddess resides in all beings as Mother" It is also said there that all women are the embodiment of the Goddess herself.

In spite of such lofty sentiments, India neglected the women and did injustice to them. This is not the case in India alone, but all over the world. It is but natural that as a reaction a feministic movement and demand for greater empowerment of women must arise.

The present Feminist Movement, however, pits women against men in a confrontation, with deleterious effects for the society in general and mental health of the children in particular. Divorces, breaking down of families, one-parent families etc. cause great shock and trauma to the children. Even the exponents of Feminist Movement have been disillusioned by the direction it has taken. The only solution is the Indian—that of honouring and empowering women as mothers. Swami Vivekananda has said that the West has risen to the height of success and glory by worshipping women as mistress; to what greater glory would India attain if she worshipped women as mother? But for this, first of all we must stop treating women badly and learn to respect them. Once, Hari (later Swami Turiyananda) a monastic disciple in making, said to his guru, Sri Ramakrishna that he hated women. This attitude on the part of monks-in-the making in India is not unusual, for they must be very vigilant in observing their basic vow of celibacy. In the other orthodox monastic circles the saying is prevalent that a woman is the gateway to hell. However, when Sri Ramakrishna heard Hari's statement, he rebuked him and said that he wouldn't be able to escape the snares of women if he hated them. He must respect them as the embodiments of the Divine Mother.

Indian culture has always maintained that a woman attains highest fulfillment in being a mother. Once late Indira Gandhi, the Ex Prime-Minister of India, was asked when she was at the height of her glory, what was the happiest moment in her life. Indira Gandhi replied it was the day she became a mother!

Let us conclude with the Benediction, which Swami Vivekananda has for Indian women:

The mother's heart, the hero's will
The sweetness of the southern breeze,
The sacred charm and strength that dwell
On Aryan altars, flaming free;
All these be yours and many more
No ancient soul could dream before—
Be thou to India's future son
The mistress, servant, friend in one.

Chapter 36

The Gandhian Approach to Women's Empowerment

Anima Kumari

An attempt has been made in this article to study briefly and critically Mahatma Gandhi's approach to the various problems with which modern women are confronted with and see what Mahatmajee has to say in respect of these maladies and social evils. At the very outset, it may be observed here that Mahatma Gandhi is really more interested in social, moral and political matters and he is generally more conspicuous for his practical approach. Though he is not an academic philosopher in the technical sense of the term, yet his contributions as a creative thinker are of profound philosophical importance. Like the ancient Indian philosophers, philosophy is not merely a way of thought but also a way of life for him. Indeed he lived philosophy in the real sense of the term. Professor P.T. Raju has rightly observed, "Professor Radhakrishnan rediscovered our philosophical concepts and infused life and vigour into their petrified forms by approaching them from the living philosophers of the west and comparing them with the concepts of the latter. Mahatma Gandhi infused life into some of them by coming across them in the very course of his life, which is a struggle for the discovery of truth."[1] Again, it would be interesting to quote here Professor Margaret Chatterjee whose following observations appear to be quite relevant in this context, "Gandhi was, above all, a man of action. But it would be a mistake to underestimate the intellectual sinews of his thought, not only in the sphere of ethics and religion but also in the socio-economic and political fields".[2]

Having thus highlighted the role of Mahatmajee as a philosopher, now, it would be in the fitness of things to study his approach to the burning problems of women. But before coming to this, it would be desirable to mention here that he is a great theist and a moralist. As has been relevantly observed by Professor D.M. Datta, "The nuclear element of Gandhi's thought was his idea of God".[3] Of course, he has unique conception of God as he finally holds that Truth is God. He also clearly upholds the ideals of truth and non-violence. Besides these, he is well known for his celebrated gospel of 'Satyagraha'. It is also important to remember that he tries to moralize and spiritualize politics and other domains of human life. It is not necessary to discuss all such concepts in detail here, but it may be observed that his approach to the present problem concerning women naturally appears to be influenced by his theistic and moralistic approach. Besides this, we can also see that he is also inspired by ancient Indian approach to women. To make this point more clear, it may be stated that according to our ancient Indian tradition women are treated to be quite respectable and adorable. It is believed that Gods reside in the house where women are properly respected. It is also noteworthy that during the ancient period, women got equal position and prestige. We are all aware of the names of Maitriya, Gargi and many such others. Besides this, the cult of Divine Mother worship clearly testifies to the fact of importance and equality of women and men. Even in the present period, women have been granted equality and dignity on par with men. The great indologist rightly says, "The constitution invested women with a new status of equality and dignity: they participate in most spheres of life along with men. The enthusiasm with which hundreds of thousands of women went to the polling booths at the General Elections indicate that they have become conscious of their new status".[4]

But it is really sad to see that women have been deprived of this dignity and equality in actual practice. They are confronted with several problems like various kinds of exploitations and oppressions. Dowry system, tortures/trials and tribulations of widows, exploitation of working women are some of these pitiable and serious events which the females are subjected to. It appears that people have forgotten old ideals and traditional wisdom and consequently half of society is not happy in various ways. So, obviously, there is the urgent need to empower women in face of all these trials and tribulations. No doubt, laws have been enacted to rectify these malpractices but unfortunately, these laws of the land have not proved to be quite effective and have not fully checked these ugly and ignoble practices like dowry deaths, various kinds of molestations and exploitations. No doubt, besides these civil laws, there are voluntary semi-governmental organizations like 'Mahila Ayoga'. But these are also not full proof security against these terrible and horrible crimes pertaining to harassment and other allied problems relating to women.

So, it is necessary and befitting to see how Gandhi handles these problems. It is well known that he is the great spiritualist and moralist. It is also noteworthy that he has championed the gospel of various moral principles like those of Satya, Ahimsa, Satyagraha, Brahmacharya, Aparigraha, Asteya and Abhaya. So Gandhi's remedy for these maladies are naturally on the basis of his moralistic and spiritualistic attitude. To begin with, it may be mentioned here that Gandhi clearly and categorically holds that women should not be considered to be the weaker sex. For him, they are equal if not more in comparison to the male sex. He despises and deplores all kinds of injustice and malpractice to women. He says, "Of all the evils for which man has made himself responsible, none is so degrading, so shocking or so brutal as his abuse of the better half of humanity. To me, the female sex is not the weaker sex. It is the nobler of the two, for it is even today the embodiment of sacrifice, silent suffering, humility, faith and knowledge".[5]

Again, it would be interesting to note here that Gandhi is naturally influenced and inspired by our ancient wisdom and culture. So he does not feel happy with recent developments of consumerism and such other allied ramifications. Perhaps, he would not feel happy with various tendencies with which modern women in this nation have been inspired. Perhaps this problem is also aggravated because modern women of India have conveniently become oblivious of their ancient culture and feel attracted towards western culture. They have forgotten their pristine position and are swayed by hedonistic and consumeristic approach. So naturally, Gandhi exhorts these women to realize their position as well as their ancient role.

He is also for the path of self-help and self-suffering. This is quite in tune with his ideal of Satyagraha. So, he says clearly, "Women must cease to consider herself the object of man's lust. She must refuse to adorn herself for men, including her husband, if she will be an equal partner with man. I cannot imagine Sita even wasting a single moment on pleasing Rama by physical charms".[6]

So, it is seen that Gandhi exhorts women to be bold, fearless and conscious of their place in the society. They should not feel that they are inferior to men in any way. Like Swami Vivekananda, Gandhi says that women should realize their power and potentiality and should play their part in accordance with this ancient spiritual and moral background. Naturally, he clearly advises them to realize that they are not inferior to their male counterparts. We may quote Mahatmajee relevantly, "To call woman the weaker sex is a libel, it is man's injustice to woman. If by strength is meant brute strength, then, indeed, is woman less brute than man. If by strength is meant moral power, then woman is immeasurably man's superior. Has she not greater intuition, is she not more self-sacrificing, has she not greater powers of endurance, has she not greater courage? Without her man could not be. If non-violence is the law of our being, the future is with women.......who can make a more effective appeal to the heart than men".[7]

So, Gandhijee directly and indirectly suggests that women alone can empower themselves in the true sense of the term. What is needed is that they should be conscious of their important and equal position. They should further take recourse to the method of Satyagraha in their own way. They should be bold enough to resist all kinds of exploitations, injustice and maltreatment. They should be bold enough to refuse to marry if there is dowry and such other conditions. They should also refuse to be exploited by their husbands and bosses or their 'in-laws'. Further, they should refuse to be just a tool of exploitation and enjoyment. They should clearly know that they are equal partners and have equal rights in various domains of life. They should also realize that they are personification of the ideal of Ahimsa and sacrifice and so they can effectively empower themselves by following the noble ideals of Ahimsa, Satya, sacrifice etc. So, Gandhi clearly observes, ".......The woman who knows and fulfils her duty realizes her dignified status. She is the queen, not the slave, of the household over which she presides".[8] Gandhi further observes to highlight the importance of Ahimsa as follows: "I have suggested...........that woman is the incarnation of ahimsa. Ahimsa means infinite love, which again means infinite capacity for suffering. Who but woman, the mother of man, shows this capacity in the largest measure? She shows it as she carries the infant and feeds it during nine months and derives joy in the suffering involved. What can beat the suffering caused by the pangs of labour? But she forgets them in the joy of creation".[9]

Further it would be interesting to see that Gandhijee advocates clearly and categorically equality of men and women and so naturally he believes that both should enjoy equal rights and privileges. To quote him again, "My own opinion is that, just as fundamentally man and woman are one, their problem must be one in essence. The soul in both is the same. The two live the same life, have the same feelings. Each is a complement of the other. The one cannot live without the other's active help."[10]

He makes this point more clear and conspicuous at another place, "I am uncompromising in the matter of women's rights. In my opinion, she should labour under no legal disability not suffered by men. I should treat the daughters and sons on a footing of perfect equality".[11]

So, Gandhi laid stress on proper education of women so that they may be aware of their rightful position. It is also to be noted here that he naturally talks about Satyagraha for remedying these vices and allied problems related to them. He says thus, "Therefore, I advise women to resort to civil rebellion against all undesirable and unworthy restraints. All restraints to be beneficial must be voluntary. There is no possibility of harm resulting from civil rebellion. It presupposes purity and reasoned resistance".[12]

Now, instead of going into more minute details, it would be better to observe here that he also takes into account problems like marriage, divorce, dowry system and tries to champion the cause of Satyagraha for solving ills and vices, which are rampant in various walks of life due to social, economic and other factors. Gandhijee would say that crime and injustice against women can be solved in more enduring way on the basis of the technique of Satyagraha and such other moral maxims. Sometimes Gandhi's approach in this context may be dubbed as utopian and unpractical. But this is becoming blind to history. History testifies to the facts that Gandhi's methods of non-violence worked quite effectively in South Africa as well as in our national struggle for Independence. So there is no reason why this technique should not be successful in the problem of women's empowerment. Of course, this does not imply that other means for empowering women are not effective. They can also be quite effective to undo this evil and injustice but at the same time it has to be borne in mind that Gandhian approach has its own importance and effectiveness. Undoubtedly his views in this context are of profound theoretical and practical importance and as such this needs to be taken quite seriously and sincerely by all concerned.

References

1. P.T. Raju, *Idealist Thought of India*, George Allen & Unwin, London, 1953, p. 292.
2. Margaret Chatterjee, *Mahatma Gandhi, Essays in Social and Political Philosophy*, General Editor D.P. Chattopadhyaya, ICPR Series, New Delhi, 1989, p. 329.
3. D.M. Datta, *The Philosophy of Mahatma Gandhi*, Madison, The University of Wisconsin Press, 1953, p. 22
4. Kulapati Vani, *Women With New Status, Bhawan's Journal*, vol. 47, No. 15, March 15, 2001, p. 7.
5. *Young India*, 15-9-1921, p. 292.
6. *Young India*, 21-7-1921, p. 229.
7. *Young India*, 10-4-1930, p. 121.
8. *Harijan*, 12-10-1034, pp. 267-277.
9. *Ibid.*, pp. 13-14.
10. *Harijan*, 24-4-1940, p. 13.
11. *Harijan*, 17-10-1929, p. 340.
12. *Ibid.*, 23-3-1947, p. 80.

Part IV

Ethical Perspectives

Chapter 37

Empowerment of Women and Gender Equality: A Critique of Issues in Applied Ethics

Sadanand Prasad Singh

Introduction

Woman is the mother of the race and serves as the link between one generation to the other. Indian culture attaches much importance to this section of society, which constitutes nearly half of our country's total population. India has rightly been symbolized as the Mother India. Keeping in view the exemplary qualities of women i.e. patience, endurance, love and affection, sacrifice, sympathy and generosity Pt. Jawaharlal Nehru, the maker of Modern India, once said, "To awaken the people it is the woman who must awaken. Once she is on the move, the family moves, the village moves, the nation moves".

The Indian woman has passed through various phases of civilization like women in other countries. But her condition became pitiable since the 17th century because of certain historical reasons.

With the advent of the British rule in India a new social era emerged, and particularly after independence, all round efforts have been made to promote the welfare of women in the country. In spite of the constitutional guarantee of equality for men and women and various social reforms meant for the protection of women's interest, they lag behind men in different spheres.

The studies on women in India were scant upto the declaration of International Women's Year 1975. This declaration gave impetus to governments, academic bodies and individual researchers to take up the issues regarding women and as a result a number of studies of women appeared. An attempt is made in this paper to analyse some of the critical issues pertaining to the empowerment of women and gender equality from the point of view of Applied Ethics.

Issues Involved

Indian women are today at the cross-roads of their destiny. There is a great upsurge in consciousness about their rights among all sections and classes of society in all regions of the country. There has been a tremendous increase in development activity for women since the eighties with a great leap forward in the nineties. The country has entered the new millennium with the hope that we will achieve even greater equity in the 21st century.

Traditionally the woman earned her maximum respect as a mother, where she was compared to the earth, which upholds everything, the dawn that brings hope and the night, which gives comfort. There are also regional differences between the heartland of the Indo-Gangetic plain, the centre of India and the north-west having gained less from the development process than the south and the north-east. Where the Indo -Aryans came and settled down first, there the society is more male dominated than in the deep south of Dravidian culture.

In Indian society class barriers exist even today. Those born in more privileged circumstances have generally done better. The old class barriers had given higher caste women, or those belonging to aristocracies, greater opportunities in education and political empowerment. The old classes are seeing bad days in our society, along with the rest of the world. The fall of these barriers has not meant the elimination of class barriers, as new types of classes have come into existence based on political power, money, merit and glamour. Women coming from these classes have achieved higher development than the rest in terms of higher education, high positions in government, business and higher profile jobs. As in the past, like in all traditional societies, women who do not care about social norms cross all barriers of class as seen from the empowered women in fine arts and cinema.

The effort of development has been both in the social and economic spheres although it is clear that more emphasis has been placed on improving women's social status. When we assess this situation one basic and glaring cultural norm stares us in the face and that is the continuing preference for a son over the birth of a girl child. This preference has become stronger than even before and is present in all communities and classes. The hold of this preference has strengthened rather than weakened in our society.

As social development is basic to raising the status of women and giving her a more equitable share of development benefits we have to see how women are faring in this field. Here, the government's strategy, as well as that of most reformers, has been to secure women better rights through the process of legislation. The constitutional provisions of equality in employment along with labour legislation have not benefited women in the unorganized sector to any significant extent although they are mostly concentrated there. In the formal sector too, there is a great difference between legislative rights and actual practice but still women have acquired many rights, which were unheard of before.

The legislation, which affects women the most is their situation in marriage and inheritance. If we take the status of women in marriage there are certain common civil laws like the Special Marriage Act, 1927, given to us by the British to which all women have access. In the case of Muslims and Christians the status of women is governed by their customary law. The Muslim women cannot complain against polygamous marriages (limited to four) against husbands and the Christian customary law does not recognize a second marriage. Although the Hindu Marriage Act, 1956, has enjoined monogamous marriage for Hindu men and the wife can prosecute the husband if he undertakes a bigamous union with another women, in practice this is not being done even by women in economically empowered sectors of society, due to the danger of being stigmatised as prosecutors of their husbands, traditionally believed to be gods and protectors of women. In spite of repeated efforts of voluntary organizations and even the Department of Women and Child Development, it has not become a cognizable offence against which a complaint for prosecution can be registered by anyone, or any organization—voluntary or government. Law has created a psychological fear in the minds of men against such unions and the overwhelming majority of Hindu marriages continue to be monogamous and polygamy has been generally eliminated. The practice of taking a second wife has not been completely eradicated in spite of legislation. The Anthropological Survey for India (1992) states that the percentage of Hindu men having more than one wife living is more than the Muslims who are legally allowed to have four wives.

The right to divorce given to the Hindu women is very rarely resorted to. It is practised by the elite class but it is still rare among the middle and poor classes. Among all communities and classes, many women would rather continue in humiliating marriages than break their marital vows. However, the legal situation of the Hindu women is better than those of the Muslim women.

A social evil affecting women of all communities, religions, castes, classes and regions of the country which is now practised in a prenicious form is dahej (dowry). This custom wherein there is provision of gifts at the time of marriage rituals, by the parents of the girls, is now negotiated, demanded and insisted upon everywhere with few dignified exceptions where again it may not be demanded but is expected. The expectation of these gifts or dowry at the time of marriage is so acute that marriages sometimes actually break just before the performance of rituals and more commonly after the ceremony. The Dowry Prohibition Act has been an absolute failure. On the other hand, though this was a cancerous growth in Hindu society it has spread to Muslims and Christians also. The level of expectation for dowry is so high that the worst forms of crimes against women are perpetrated due to frustration of expectations. It is also the most important reason for lowering the social status of women.

As far as rights of inheritance are concerned, the Muslims and Christians continue to be governed by their customary laws whereas the Hindu Succession Act, 1956, has legally given Hindu women inheritance rights as daughters, wives and mothers to an extent which they never had before. In fact, it was a revolutionary legislation, which should have had an overwhelming empowering impact for the great majority of Indian women. We find that the rights to property, which were meant to give them economic empowerment have been rarely invoked especially, as far as their inheritance as daughters and mothers is concerned. The actualization of rights as daughters is very tardy to say the least. In practice, it would be correct to say that by and large they have not tried to inherit land left by their parents in case brothers were present. This has been done by women on most occasions voluntarily, in order not to have a break in relations with their brothers, especially if they happen to come from the rural areas and land is located in natal villages. The traditional make belief that land should not go outside the patriarchal family continues to operate and we find very few mutations under Land Revenue Acts of the states taking place in the name of women.

The Anthropological Survey of India states that among 3,680 out of a total of 4,635 communities in India, property is shared equally among sons. In 570 communities equal shares are allowed to sons and daughters. In twenty-five communities, daughters inherit the property equally, while in thirteen communities property goes to the youngest daughter. It is obvious from this that the daughters' inheritance from their natal family is very limited. Whether there are any class, creed or regional differences have not been indicated by a national level survey. Moreover several years after this significant legislation, there is still a certain stigma attached to women inheriting the paternal lands as it is believed that with that they would be cutting away from relations with the paternal family, as brothers are supposed to inherit the land and provide protection and sustenance to sisters when they are in need or on special occasions like the sisters' marriages, the death of her husband or her children's marriages. In Punjab, Haryana, Uttar Pradesh, Rajasthan and Bihar many women continue to voluntarily abnegate their rights to paternal land in order to maintain customary friendly social relations with their brothers.

Remedial Measures

The provision of the inheritance laws governing Hindu women which have loopholes need to be plugged. It is also imperative that these rights are also made available to women belonging to the minorities. It is extremely important that the government gives serious consideration in a time-bound fashion to the amendments suggested in existing laws by the National Commission for Women and the Department of Women and Child Development.

The success of legislative measures available to women of all religions and communities in the forms of the Child Marriage Restraint Act, 1930, the Suppression of Immoral Traffic in Women, 1987 and the Indecent Exposure of Women Act has not led to the suppression of practices indicated in them. Of these three, the Child Marriage Restraint Act, though not completely successful in banning child marriages, has helped in raising the mean age of marriage to over 20 years. The incidence of immoral traffic in women has not significantly come down. The Indecent Exposure of Women Act has been the most disastrous failure as the indecent exposure of women in all forms of media has increased beyond all measure, with hardly any prosecution.

Though legal measures create an enabling atmosphere, they have not been successful in giving women great empowerment. They are also definitely not the most important remedy for every social disease. Here the role of government's implementing agencies for these laws and what we can do ourselves for getting out rights through these laws is most important. All development schemes relating to women, whether implemented by government agencies themselves or through voluntary organizations, should carry a component of gender awareness, literacy, family welfare and skill training so that the quality of development is sustainable and lasting. The efficacy of purely administrative agencies cannot be totally depended upon. There has been a gearing up of these agencies in most cases by widespread efforts of voluntary organizations. Here the contribution of the voluntary sector has been significant in sensitizing police machinery on the need for greater efforts in the prevention of crimes against women. They have also powerfully contributed in sensitizing women by spreading knowledge about their legal rights.

What is left to be done requires Herculean efforts. The contribution of individual educated middle class women singly and through associations for voluntary action in rural and urban areas has to be much more than it has been. It is their duty to lead as they have a more privileged existence. They should spread awareness about women's legal rights, the desirability of having a girl child and above all build a national movement against the giving of dowry in all communities. That is the basic social evil as a result of which parents prefer sons. It is a cancer that is eating into our vitals and dragging down the self-esteem and status of women. This custom has to be fought in every village and city. The main energy for fight has to come from women themselves. Every woman has to take part in this great endeavour with all her resources and might. Success will certainly come to them if they mobilize and organize themselves with skill and awareness. This will lead to the building of a great social determination that this evil has to be eradicated. They have to set personal examples by not accepting or giving dowry, and sensitizing their families, their communities, residential areas, governments and their men.

Ever since the very inception of planned development in our country, a quantum jump in enrolment of girls at primary, secondary high schools and university level has been achieved. What is more important than this is that a great upsurge for getting educated has occurred among the girl children themselves. Parents' views on the desirability of girls' child education have also radically changed over the years. Having said this, in all areas of education the male-female gender gaps persist. Our efforts at raising literacy rates have been so low as to have proved disastrous not only for family welfare programmes but also for economic development. In fact, we have to ensure that girls get educated at least up to the high school level. The resource constraint for closing these gaps has not been as significant as the lack of determination for diverting the existing resources to give women their rightful share. Unless the light of knowledge dawns on the women of our country, we can never join the community of developed nations. Good quality education has to be the foundation of every developmental nation-building activity.

For effecting social change through social development the most powerful instrument besides social awareness and voluntary community action would be economic empowerment. This economic empowerment will basically be achieved through the instrumentality of education and employment. After years of development efforts, women constitute only 28.58 per cent of the work force and among these also only 26.43 per cent of them are main workers and 25.49 per cent are marginal workers. They are mostly concentrated in rural areas and in the private sector. A vast majority of them are unskilled and the number of the educated unemployed women continues to be high. We have to get all girls up to the age of eighteen into schools. Till universal enrolment is achieved, we have to impart training to girls in life survival skills in schools, girls who are drop-outs from the school system and those who have never been to school. Young women, deserted women, widows, women who head households in the absence of husbands and those who are below the poverty line have to be covered at an accelerated rate under the government's rural employment schemcs.

Ultimately, the success of empowerment through employment which goes against Indian cultural norms of home-based industry and agriculture for women, would require a tremendous awareness generation effort among young girls and their parents about making them self-reliant and self-dependent through the capacity of earning their own livelihood. This will give them the wherewithal of leading a life of dignity by contributing their own self-earned resources to the family. This awareness has already risen among middle class families. It is extremely important that this awakening is generated among all classes of people. This message has to be spread through the school system and its textbooks and through voluntary organizations and most importantly the media, which should portray women as having great potential for achievement in all spheres of life.

Women have to realize that their strength in social situations and economic empowerment will also accelerate their political empowerment. In this case, they have to be seen as a positive force for development. There is traditionally great respect for women as a cultural norm. When women combine and insist on any change male bastions usually crumble. It is their lack of awareness, motivation and mobilization that has created the gender gaps. Women should adopt the strategy of demanding the cleaning up of our public life. They have to agitate for civic consciousness, people's rights and functioning of all government and local agencies by setting examples of greater honesty and efficiency when opportunity comes to them. This challenge has come to them through the Panchayat Raj and Local Bodies Amendment Act. They must act as the conscience keepers of the nation for the promotion of child welfare for which they are eminently suited. As traditional family cooks, they have to be watchdogs for the implementation of the National Nutrition Policy. The national immunization and child survival programmes and enrolment of children in primary schools and the proper functioning of health and education infrastructures should be monitored by them.

Concluding Remarks

Women and their organizations can play a very important role in the reduction of crimes against women by assisting police in tracking down criminals. They can also play a powerful and positive role in confidence-building in their daughters and other women to promote self-reliance and the strength to resist crimes.

Women can be the harbingers of communal harmony. Any disharmony and civil disturbance affects women much more than men. Women's organizations should mobilize public opinion against those who provoke communal sentiments by completely exposing them.

Women have a great role to play in projecting Indian culture, the Indian way of life and promoting international understanding through networking with women's organizations all over the world. The Indian women's voice should always be for peace and harmony in international relations.

In these challenging times leadership will go automatically to positive leaders and women have to emerge as agents of social, political and economic change in our society. If they continue to indulge in complaining, pleading agitators asking more for themselves, they arouse resistance and confrontation among men who perceive them as a menacing force. Women themselves do not want confrontation but justice. They have to play their cards subtly and with determination to make the 21st century a century of women.

Chapter 38

An Analysis of Women's Right to Maternity in the Biological, Social and Ethical Perspectives

S.K. Singh

Genderwise females and males are mutually dependent beings. Females are biological necessity of men and vice-versa. They are made for each other. They are biological partners in the process of evolution and they have equal indispensable importance. They fulfil their sexual urge and in the mating process, the females conceive and in due course give birth to their offspring. This way process of biological evolution goes on. This is true of all living species.

In this process of biological evolution, females and males are not inferior or superior to one another. They are just equals and complementary to each other. Males are strong and sturdier than females as they have to face hard and difficult task outside whereas females are fragile, tender, loving and sacrificing by nature because they have to foster the foetuses in their wombs and take care of the babies after birth till they grow and gradually become self-dependent. It is the nature that has made them what they are.

What is true of all living creatures in this particular context also holds good for the *homo-sapiens*. With the passage of time and development of human civilization, the institutions of marriage and family have gradually evolved. For regulating sex and having a stable family, women and men live together under the bond of monogamous or any other type of marriage. Thus we see that institutions of marriage and family are the result of human intellect and creativity. But sex is instinctive and motherhood is the byproduct of this instinct. Motherhood is one of the most important instinctive feelings of women. This is why girls play with dolls and caress and hug them with motherly affections and sentiments. After marriage when they become pregnant, they have the sense of completeness and fullness. Womanhood culminates into its zenith and perfection with the achievement of motherhood.

This is due to the reasons delineated above that women are by nature averse to the idea of abortion of their first conception whether it is the result of socially unauthorized sex before marriage or authorized and acceptable one after wedding. They are disinclined to the idea of termination of pregnancy because it spoils their maiden opportunity of achieving completeness and significance of their womanhood. They resist and also fight in occasional cases against the dictates of their lovers/ husbands who thrust removal of pregnancy on them. But they have to succumb to the pressures most unwillingly keeping in view the plight and prospect that await them after giving birth to the foetuses, the result of their first love. So not allowing the women to become mother is to eclipse her womanhood. In one of her stories Mahadevi Verma, the renowned novelist and litterateur, has beautifully portrayed this psychological aspect of a woman. A young lady married in her childhood was widowed while in her teens. The unfortunate young woman, who was parentless, was passing her days of distress with her old and poor grandfather and her father's sister who was also a window. While passing her bad days, she was attracted to a young man of her age. They developed intimacy to the extent of physical contact as a result of which she became pregnant. When her family members came to know about this state of affair, she was already deserted by her paramour. Under the prevailing social conditions, she was advised abortion by her guardians. The young lady boldly refused to accept the advice and insisted on giving birth to foetus growing in her womb. Then her grandfather and aunt devised a planning. They migrated to a new town where nobody knew them. In course of time the young lady gave birth to a baby. Thereafter she was pressurized to abandon the newly born baby. Here again she vehemently protested against this abandonment and resolved to foster the baby inspite of the impending opposition of the society. At this point of time, Mahadevi Verma came to her help by firmly standing by her, as she was no way responsible either for her widowhood or desertion by her lover. The young widow was advised to assert her right to maternity by looking after baby resolutely amidst all oppositions.

There should be no infringement upon women's right to maternity. Their this right should be safeguarded also because all women and men want to perpetuate their remembrance and continuance through procreation. This is possible when women play their part as mothers with all protection, care and cooperation of the society. Women's right to maternity should be ensured and safeguarded in the democratic and egalitarian society of the new millennium.

There are physical, social, economic and religious factors that contribute to the denial of this fundamental right to them. Women are dependent on others, both physically and physiologically, for giving birth to the foetuses and for the upbringing of the children. The factors of physiology and dependence force them to obey what they rebel from the core of their hearts. The society also is against women who assert their right to maternity. It regards such women with contempt and the persons cast aspersions both overtly and covertly on them. Even women folks do not lag behind in this tirade. Instead of giving emotional support and protection, they take lead in criticism and condemnation.

Apart from physical and social factors, economic dependence and religious restrictions and taboos are the greatest impediments of women's liberation from shackles of tradition and subjugation. Generally, women are dependent for their livelihood and subsistence on parents, husbands and in-laws. So long they are not made self-dependent, they cannot dare to go against oppressive social traditions and discriminations. By and large, religions also do not allow women such freedom. Women opting for such alternative are looked upon with contempt and hatred. They are threatened with condemnation in hell. Some religions do not permit women to have pre-marital sex and widow marriage. They are exhorted to be loyal to their husbands and are forced to obey the dictates of religion. We have recently seen that women during Taliban regime in Afghanistan were coerced to wear *burqua* to cover themselves from toe to head. Girls were prevented from prosecuting their studies and were compelled to confine themselves to hearth and home. Women are the worst victims of religious fundamentalism and terrorism. On August 6, 2001 two unidentified terrorists splashed acid on the faces of two school girls (*Kulsooma* and *Fowzia)* in Jammu & Kashmir for not kow-towing to the dictates of the Muslim Militant Organization (Lashkar-e-Jabbar) to wear *burqua*. There is no tradition of wearing *burqua* in the state of Jammu & Kashmir nor is there any reference in *Quran* making covering of face mandatory for women, then why should the whimsical and Un-Islamic directions of the said fundamentalist and militant organization be observed by women? Can we imagine the innocent girls whose faces have been disfigured in this so-called civilized society of the 21st century?

In India, females are subjected to discrimination from and before their birth. Due to the advent of the ultrasound technology, gender of the foetuses is known much before they are born and women are forced to undergo the process of abortion if they have female foetuses in their wombs. Due to alarming growth of female foeticide and decrease in women's population, these days the government seems to have risen from slumber and determination of sex in the ultrasound clinics has been made a punishable offence. If somehow female foetus survives in mother's womb, all members of a family become sad on getting the information that a female infant has been born. The lady members of the family are more shocked than their male counterparts. The mother is cursed for giving birth to a female child when she has no role to play in the determination of sex of the foetus in her womb. There is no dearth of examples where in the hope of a male child, over a half dozen of girls are born. In such cases, the girls are not only discriminated in food, cloth, medication, education etc. but are also deprived of love and affection of their parents. They are brought up in hardship and discrimination. They are not given proper opportunity to prosecute their studies. They have to share the household responsibilities from their childhood. They are married to the persons of the liking of their guardians who normally do not care to take consent of the girls.

The second part of their life is spent with their husbands and in-laws. Here again, they have to face discrimination and harassment due to dowry problem. Greedy in-laws and husbands of the young ladies directly and indirectly torture them to pressurize their parents to fulfil the chain of unending demands. The number of dowry harassment cases are shooting up at a rapid pace. Despite all the noise women's organizations are making about dowry deaths, the conviction rate for this heinous crime is very low. Even educated women are harassed for getting dowry. There are examples of Medicine and Management degree holders committing suicide because of growing torture by the in-laws. The officers of administrative and police services do not lag behind in making enormous dowry demands. The Judges and lawyers are also involved in receiving and giving dowry when they know that it is unethical and also illegal to be associated with it.

If we analyse the situation objectively and impartially, we find that dowry, though condemned in public, is condoned and practiced in private by the cross sections of society. There are persons who feel elevated in the public display of dowry and marriage extravaganzas. We have seen some unscrupulous politicians spending crores of rupees in the wedding of their sons and daughters. Two such marriages in Chennai and Patna had caught the attentions of both media persons and public in not a very distant past. The parents and relatives of the girls do not have will, courage and resources to fight against the oppression at the hands of the husbands and in-laws of the victims. A lot of cases are dismissed on grounds of insufficient evidence. There are appeals by the accused in the higher courts and final verdict takes years and decades. In some cases, the accused persons are convicted after long drawn legal battle of 15-20 years. But then only a few complainants have that kind of tenacity. Normally, existing laws are not implemented. Medical reports are manipulated by the accused. The police investigation is not thorough for public prosecutions and justice is either delayed or lost in the highways of lengthy and faulty legal systems.

In this pathetic background, women's right to maternity remains a wishful thinking. The women may aspire for this natural and fundamental right but under the present socio-economic and ethical conditions prevalent in India, it seems to be a distant dream unless mass awareness programmes to allay all discriminations and biases against women are launched and mobilized and the society extends them moral, emotional and physical support. The government is also required to come in a big way by framing necessary statutes to provide legal, financial and insurance cover and security to those women who want to avail of their right to maternity. Their sons and daughters should also be protected against being teased and harassed for being without fathers. The women should also rise to the occasion by becoming economically self-dependent and mentally and morally strong in order to shield themselves from any disdain and onslaught. By-and-by this would change our male-oriented mindset both ethically and otherwise.

Chapter 39

Female Foeticide: An Ethical Issue

M.P. Chaurasia

The Indian women are the victim of male dominated Indian societies on the ground of gender and sex. The gender is a social and grammatical category while sex is a biological dichotomy.[1] The Indian women experience the negative effects of race, class and gender operations simultaneously. All differences between male and female are due to the constructionalism of our society. The centre of construction of our society is the power that may be wealth-power, Knowledge-power or political-power. The Indian women always have to pay the cost to save the centre of the society. The Gujrat during recent violence is the burning example of the above facts.

Now we shall consider the problem in the above light in Indian perspective, especially in the context of female infanticide. In Indian society 'political power' and 'wealth power' have played a vital role. Michel Foucault has argued that the rises of parliamentary institutions and of new conception of political liberty were accompanied by a darker counter-movement, by the emergence of a new unprecedented discipline directed against the body. Every body has been born either male or female, but not masculine or feminine. Femininity is an artifice or an achievement. Foucault further argued that the transition from traditional to modern societies has been characterized by a profound transformation in the exercise of power, what he calls "a reversal of the political axis of *individuation*".[2]

Now in the light of power and individuality we shall consider the condition of Indian femininity. In Indian society there are 4 *Varnas;*

Brahmins, Kshatriya, Vaishya and *Shudras,* but I think , our society has also a fifth *Varna,* i.e. female. The gents of every *varna* have oppressed women equally. From the very dawn of the Indian civilization we find an apathetic attitude towards our female members. Grammarian like Yaska used the term *duhita/durehita* in a peculiar sense which means daughter must live on a far distance. According to Durgacharya *Sahityataraiva deyate ttraiva durhia bhavati*[3] that means where she goes there she has been upbraided. The term *duhita signifies* the nature of daughter i.e. always a tendency to borrow something from her father. In some old mythological books girls are not much respected. In *Aitreya Brahman,* it is mentioned that *Kripann hi duhita, jyotirhi putrah.* All these references belong to the Brahman books and old Vaiyakarana period, which is historically regarded as post-Vedic era. Even in Manusmriti we find contradictory views regarding women. Manu restricted the status of women and suggested that a woman should be regarded as a goddess.

So is the case in mediveval period. Hatred towards the female of post-Vedic era developed in the form of girls killing. Such practice came into existence during the Turkish and Persian invasions.[4] It is said that one of the early muslim invaders of Jharja dominated areas, who were experiencing tough resistance sought to consolidate their vested interest in that particular region by demanding the beautiful daughters of King in marriage. The high-spirited Jadeja aristocrats could not brook the disgrace. And they pretended that they did not preserve their daughters. But as they were fearful of the consequences that force, would be resorted to, they listened to their Rajguru in this extremity and put their daughters to death. When the king showed aversion to the murder of a woman, the Rajguru deluded the king by the "fictitious" responsibility, which he accepted and the practice of female infanticide had since then originated.[5] And till 11th century and onwards, the repeated muslim invasions and their rule led to further deterioration in the position of women. Now the killing of girl child expanded to the entire royal Rajputa family. Orthodox Hindu society was constantly threatened by the fear of the invader's attacks on women. All the elite Hindu family began to hide their daughters behind the curtains. The birth of a daughter was unwelcome because she was considered to be a cause of expense, troubles and anxiety to her parents, since they were merely a custodian till her marriage.[6] Here, we find that the cause of female infanticide was power and wealth.

The Britishers first located female infanticide in India in 1789 in the Varanasi division of the northwestern provinces. Jonathan Duncan found during his official tour of Jaunpur district that the Raj Kumar Rajputs killed their female infants.[7] Subsequently, in early 19th century the Britishers found female infanticide to be prevalent among Jadeja Rajputs of Kutch and Katiaward.[8] By 1850, several castes in north India such as the Jata, Ahirs, Gujars and Khatris, and the Lewapatidar, Kanbis in central Gujarat were found to practice female infanticide.[9]

In the light of above discussed facts we can understand that female infanticide, in India, has its origin in the history of foreign invasions and their rules in India. Certain ruling and warrior communities[10] who were also ruling communities in maximum number in northwestern provinces of India from where invasions were invasions were forced to practice this inhuman and cruel act in order to protect the honour of their female counterparts and also humiliation arising out of this situation. The lust of foreign invaders and some Muslim rulers for beautiful Hindu girls and women, especially queens and princesses, were increasing day by day. The story of Padmavati and several acts of Jauhar committed in India very well support the facts as analyzed above. All martyrdoms of women were committed under the compulsion of our society to save the power, prestige and wealth.

So far the question regarding the origin of female infanticide in India is concerned, there may be lot of controversial opinions. But we cannot deny the fact that it has become a real phenomenon for the whole of the country due to many reasons, which have developed over a period of time. Now prevalent alarming situation compels us to think over the problem.

It is significant to note that though female infanticide was outlawed more than a century ago, its detection and prevention are virtually impossible despite reports from across the country which testify to its continued prevalence. Some new-born girls still have poisonous berry juice trickled down their throat, others still choke on when a larger than usual 'laddoo' is forced into their mouths.[11] As per one report: "They (villagers) let the baby starve, or make it lie on the stomach as soon as she is born or to cover the face with wet towel."[12] But more sinister, and perhaps more widespread than the murder of a baby girl is the newest form of violence against her killing even before she is born. Amniocentesis, originally intended as pre-natal test to detect certain genital abnormalities, is now widely used across the country to determine the sex of fetus and abort it if it happens to be a female. In a study of 8,000 abortions after Amniocentesis in Bombay it was reported that 799 of the aborted fetuses were female.[13] It is also estimated that 1.20 crore girls are born in India every year. About one fourth of them die before their fifteenth birth day because of female infaniticide, malnutrition, discrimination in health care and material morality and as victim of rape and molestation.[14]

Now such practice has reached middle class urban families especially in metropolitan and district towns in India. Perhaps this is the latest form of violence against girl child. Many reports of this sense have been highlighted in several newspapers by different non-government organizations. There are several clinics in every town, which are running on the name of maternity care centres or family health centres. Many reports of this fact were published in a national daily that in 1991 approximately one thousand fetuses were destroyed in India of which nearly 995 were female fetuses. The people, who were indulged in this misdeed, belonged mostly to the educated and well to do family.[15] According to Sanjeeva Kulkarni of the Foundation Research in Community Health 5,000 amniocentesis tests are carried out in Bombay annually to detect the fetus, Mostly pregnancies were aborted after sex determination of the fetuses in which the number of the female was greater than that of the male. In *India Today,* a report of Anna M.S. Veticad and Ramesh Vinayak was published last year under the title "Maada Bhrun Hatya ka Jaari Hai Dhanda". The report says that more than lac of female fetuses are killed every year in Punjab, Haryana, Chandigarh, U.P. and Uttranchal.[16]

This situation has further taken alarming proportions after the new researches that provide possibility of pre-conception sex-selection technologies. Cashing in on son-preference, a value that is entrenched in Indian society, this new sex-selection procedure has entered the market and 'Gender Selection' is now a reality. As a result of the new techniques the genetic determination has taken an ugly turn. It blocks the path of coming of a female child on the earth in a most sophisticated manner. Several reports reveal this aspect. The status of the girl child is reflected in the juvenile sex ratio, which has registered a sharp decline over the last decade from 945 female per 1000 male in 1991 census to 927: 1000 and now in certain parts of India this ratio is 703:1000 in 2001.[17] Arvind Jain has mentioned in his report in *Hindustan* " Kaun sunta hai stri ki cheekh" presented a horrible fact about female foetecides.[18] In India every year 40,000 new girls, due to poverty, are coming in the job of prostitution.

Many arguments can be forwarded either in favour of such act or against it. Jill and Scott Sweazy, the promoters of a U.S. based 'Gen-select' company which provides 'Gen-select-kit' to have a child of desired sex by parents with the help of preconception sex-selection technology have argued that question of genetic determination is related only to the parents of an incoming child, because it is the liberty of the parents to choose the desired child. They further argued that, "with our product, the *freedom to choose the gender of* your next child is preserved, while the moral, ethical and legal issues of foeticide are put to ease".[19] In the same way, various arguments have been advanced by many intellectuals on the basis of utilitarian philosophy. According to this theory human beings are supposed to be guided only by pleasure-pain principle and the only criterion of determination of what is good or bad is the amount of pleasure or pain it gives. So, if the arrival of a male child proves a source of pleasure, the parents should have the freedom to enjoy it. But in Indian context such is not the case. Here the freedom of mother is overpowered by father's desire. Here, utilitarian principle of ethics has not been enjoyed in its true spirit. Parents ignored the freedom of the incoming child. We cannot ask for freedom outside the state and society. So only socially sanctioned freedom must be entertained. Recently the Human Rights Commission has declared the right to life. And this right is ignored in case of a girl child, if she is not allowed to see the world either by abortion of female foeticide or by not allowing her to take shape with the help of pre-conception sex-selection techniques. Several ethical objections have been raised when the misuse of some techniques has already taken place. Ultra-sound is one of those techniques through which such act is performed and this event has taken a form of 'menace' in India. Moral philosopher J.S. Mill also holds that liberty does not mean the liberty of will, it has to work within the framework of society and state. The liberty of the individual must thus far be limited, he must not make himself a nuisance to other people.[20] From my point of view no freedom is possible in the absence of authority and the authority is state, which must be legitimate and not be absolute. I don't want to raise the pros and cons of abortions but I want to attract the attention of learned people towards those abortions, which are based on sex-determination. Such abortion is committed only when the incoming child is girl. So it is an ethical issue. One cannot discriminate a people on the basis of caste, sex and race, as it is related to biology, it is a gift of nature.

In India, the government has exercised a few laws. The Sansad of India has legislated certain laws to stop this misdeed in which some are under consideration. Recently, apex court of India has passed a judgement against pre-natal sex-determination test. In it, the Court has decided to impose seven years' rigorous imprisonment. In previous Panchayat and District Board elections certain electoral constituencies were reserved for women and they were elected too. But so far the exercising of power is concerned, they all have authorized their male relatives to enjoy the power. Just I remember Hillary Clinton's address in Beijing on the eve of Fourth World Conference on Women, sponsored by U.N.O. In Indian context she told, "It is a violation of human rights when individual women are doused with gasoline, set on fire and burnt to death because their marriage dowries are deemed too small, it is a violation of human rights when babies are killed because they are girls, when women are sold into prostitution or raped as prizes in war or subjected to violation in their houses". She further said, "If there is one message that echoes from this conference, let it be that human rights are women's rights and women's rights are human rights once and for all.[21]

We have already discussed all the mishappenings with Indian women from pregnancy to marriage and also some legal remedies related to it. We have also seen that political and legal advantages are unable to stop such injustice. There are certain states in India of which Chief Ministers are women, but even then such heinous crime is going on. If one opens the daily newspapers of Bihar, one will find that in Saran range 80% abortion cases are happening due to pre-natal sex-determination test and brides are burnt to death even for a buffalo or a motorcycle. But it is good for the sake of women that a few women of our society have dared to knock the door of the court. But it is not enough.

For the sake of remedy, only the state and court interventions are not sufficient. There must be some proper ethical consciousness. The women should be empowered with certain rights that can stop these activities successfully. The right of maternity and the right of marriage should be wholly granted to the women. But to provide with rights is not the proper treatment of this evil. We should also create an ethical environment in which all those reformations may flourish.

So far the ethical consideration is concerned professional philosophy and ethics have equally ignored this problem. Moral philosopher like Kant has aparted it to say simply' fair sex'. But Kant in his theory of knowledge has emphasised the cause of this separation. According to him knowledge is actively constructed rather than passively received. Time, space, self and other, as well as the categories of developmental theory, all arise out of the active interchange between the individual and the physical and social world in which we live and of which we strive to make sense. The moral judgment is a statement of priority, an attempt at rational resolution in a situation where, from a different point of view, the choice itself seems to do violence to justice. For the sake of moral evaluation two conditions are necessary: an individual and his relationship with others. Only a true individual can judge the action properly. The other condition is the capacity to take responsibility as an individual. Actually what Kant meant to say is the above fact. Only taking of one's responsibility and obligation makes his action right or wrong. For the sake of one's personality development, the capacity of mature judging is necessary. But Indian feminine lots still are passively accepting the events rather than making the events according to their choice. The essence of the moral decision is the exercise of choice and the willingness to accept responsibility for that choice. In this course women have no choices and they correspondingly excuse themselves from the responsibility that decision implied.[22] The conflict between self and other thus constitutes the central moral problem for women, which can only be resolved by a reconciliation between femininity and adulthood. Indian women are always ready to take obligations of others like wives and mothers but never as an individual themselves though from the moral point of view only individual's decisions are relevant. Self-realization is the first step of morality and the second level is known as responsibility and obligation. Women should prefer existing by themselves to move around others. In this course the transition from selfishness to responsibility is a move towards social participation. The morality of men is based on rights till date while the morality of women is based on duty in India, i.e. duty of sacrifice and nothing else.

Terms like power, control, distribution and their forms have a significant place in modern moral philosophy.[23] In the same way Carol Gilligan emphasises that power and attachment are two ways of defining relationship, two ways of defining responsibilities.[24] Morality is a perception, it is a thing to follow, and the idea of having a concept of morality is to try to figure out what it is that people can do in order to make life worth living and make for a kind of balance, a kind of equilibrium, a harmony in which every body feels he has a place and an equal share in things and doings. It is woman and only woman who bears the responsibility of other individual's coming in the world. If she herself is ready to take her own responsibility, she does not need the approval of a man at all. She is harassed and exploited everywhere not for herself but for others.

Now a day the updated people have changed the meanings of the terms 'right' and 'wrong' silently 'right' is rooted in law, the world of rights. Good in the relevant sense suggests commerce, the world of goods. So, every kind of ethical theory depends on a special kind of relationship that is responsible to the situations. The term friendship is vague one. Sometimes it implies the meaning of sexual intimacy, Kinship and a variety of networks loosely dubbed and sometimes personal relationship and informal practices. Indian women need theories of ethics of informal and personal relationships. The informal and the personal relations are the same. An informal agreement need not be personal. An interpersonal relationship is personal when it matters to either of the parties and its importance depends on the natural of the relationship. "Personal" suggests closeness and intimacy.[25] A relation is formal to the extent that it is well defined, limited, in a way that are publicly understood and publicly sanctioned. Formality is not the same as legality. Public life relationships are formal while official relationships are informal. So women should take the responsibility as per the importance of the relationship but they must be always aware of their own status. Every path is open, but no other people can lead them to their goal. Only women have to cross the road and attain the goal. Recently, in a personal talk, M.N. Sinha has told me that in Hariyana, society has provided the right of marriage to the girls and there mostly cases of dowry practices have come to a halt.[26]

References

1. Douglas, A Gentile, "Just What Are Sex and Gender, Anyway? A Call for a New Terminological Standard," *Questions of Gender: Perspectives and Paradoxes,* ed. Dina L. Anselmi & Anne L. Law, McGraw-Hill, 1998, p. 14.
2. Michel Foucault, *Discipline and Punish* Vintage Books, New York, 1979, p. 44.
3. Yaska, Nirukta, 3.4.4.
4. See Pandit Satantee Pelladrah, " Women in Ancient India", in Bhudev Sharma *Revisiting Indus-Sarsvati Age and Ancient India,* Unashi Press, Meerut, 1998, p. 257.
5. Now Jhareja is known as Jadeja, see *Sulochana Krishnamurti, "Discovery and Suppression of Female Infanticide in Western India (1800-1885)" in proceeding of he Indian History Congress,* 60th Session, Kalilat, 1999, p. 592.
6. Shashi Tiwari, "The Status of Women in the Rgveda", In Bhudev Sharma, *op. cit.*, pp. 233-34.
7. See J. Duncan to Carnwallis, Dec.1789, in J.W. Kaye, *The Administration of the East India Company, 1966,* p.554.

8. John Wilson, *History of Suppression of Infanticide in* Western India, 1855, in *the proceeding of the Indian History Congress, 55th* Session, Aligarh, 1994, 1995, p. 606.
9. J.C. Brown, India Infanticide: Its Origin, Progress and suppression, 1857, and also H.R. Cooke, "Repression of female infanticide in Bombay Presidency, 1875" *Selection from the Records of the Bombay Government,* No CXIVII, p. 13.
10. See Adarsh Sharma, et. al. "Girl Child in India: A quest for equality", in Mitra Badra (ed.) *Girls Child in Indian Society,* Rawat Publication, New Delhi, 1999, p. 123.
11. See Gauri Srivastava, "The Indian Girl: A Situational Analysis", in *Ibid.*, p. 24
12. See Vaasomthi, "Salem: The Klling Goes on", *India Today,* Sept. 30, 1995, p. 83.
13. Gauri Srivastava, *op. cit.*, p. 94.
14. *Ibid.*, p. 71.
15. *India Today, (*Hindi), July 18, 2001, pp. 50-53, also see, Mrinal Pandey, "Stri Aur Garib Virodhi Juaara Jaamat".
16. *Hindustan* (Hindi), Dec. 30, 2001, p. 8.
17. Parvathi, "Dubious Choice", *Front line,* January, 4, 2002, pp. 118-19.
18. *Hindustan,* (Hindi), July 10, 2002, p. 8.
20. J.S. Mill, *Utilitarianism, Liberty, Representative Government*, Everyman's Library, London, 1968, p. 65.
21. "Hillary hiteout China", *The Time of India,* New Delhi, Sept. 6, 1995, p. 1.
22. Corol, Gilligam, "In a different Voice", Women's Conceptions of Selfad of Marality", *Feminist Social Thought: A Reader,* (ed.) Diana Tietions Meyers, Routledge, New York, 1997, p. 555.
23. See Hogland, S.L., *Lesbian Ethics,* Palo Alto, Calif: Institute for Lesbian Studies, 1988.
24. Gilligan, *Ibid.*
25. Clandia, Carel, "Gender and Moral Luck" in *Feminist Social Thought,* p. 655.
26. M.N. Sinha, Professor and Head, Department of Philosophy, B.R.A., B.U., Muzaffarpur conveyed me at Chapra.

Part V

Existential Perspectives

Chapter 40

Gender Inequality: An Existential Analysis With special reference to Simone de Beauvoir

Shiva Bhanu Singh

In his illuminating book 'The pleasures of Philosophy,' great contemporary philosopher, writer and historian will Durant comments that if asked about the outstanding feature of human events in the first quarter of the twentieth century, we shall perceive that it was not the great war, nor the Russian Revolution, but the change in the status of woman. History has seldom seen so startling a transformation in so short a time. The "sacred home" that was the basis of our social order, the marriage system that was our barrier against human passion and instability, the complex moral code that lifted us from brutality to civilization and courtesy, are visibly caught in that turbulent transition which has come upon all our institutions, all our modes of life and thought, since factories out wooed the fields, and cities absorbed the natural and human resources of the country side.[1]

Earlier in past centuries woman was treated as house hole slave, a social ornament or a sexual convenience. The roots of sexual discrimination and prejudiced outlook towards woman can be traced in ancient theology where Eve is depicted as made from what Bossuet called 'a supernumerary bone of Adam.[2] Thus humanity is male and man defines woman not in herself but as relative to him; she is not regarded as autonomous being. Male supremacy and prejudices towards woman are not common only in ordinary persons rather some great philosophers and theologians also had such kind of evil tendency. For instance, Aristotle said, the female is a female by virtue of certain lack of qualities. We should regard the female nature as afflicted with a natural defectiveness'. The medieval theologian St. Thomas pronounced woman to be an imperfect man', an 'incidental being'.[3] In 'Pleasures of Philosophy', Will Durant quotes, 'Gorki and Chekov were walking in the crimea. They came upon Tolstoy as he sat on the beach, his great head bent in meditation, his beard sweeping the sand. They squatted down beside him and began to talk about women. For a long time Tolstoy listened in silence. Then suddenly he said, "And I will tell the truth about woman only when I have one foot in the grave. I shall tell it, jump into my coffin, pull the lid over me and say, 'Do what you like with me now".[4] Will Durant again cites an example by saying that when Bernard Shaw was invited by Count Keyserling to contribute an essay to "The Book of Marriage, Shaw refused by saying', No man dare write the truth about marriage while his wife lives."[5] Even in contemporary age some philosophers and psychologists have observed major psychological and biological differences between females and males. It has been argued that while social conditioning plays some role in respect of determining psychological differences between the sexes, biological factors are also at work. The evidence for this view is particularly strong in respect of aggression. In '*The Psychology of Sex Differences*' Eleanor Emmons Maccoby and Corol Nagy Jacklin give four grounds for their belief that the greater aggression of males has a biological component.

1. Males are more aggressive than females in all human societies in which the difference has been studied.
2. Similar differences are found in humans and in apes and other closely related animals.
3. The differences are found in very young children, at an age when there is no evidence of any social conditioning in this direction.
4. Aggression has been shown to vary according to the level of sex hormones, and females become more aggressive if they receive male hormones.[6]

Besides above mentioned differences, some moral and mental differences between females and males have also been advocated but latest studies and feminist analyses have demonstrated that none of the moral and intellectual differences are innate or hereditary rather these are due to social conditioning and environmental influences. H.B. Thompson in *'Mental Traits of Sex'* "Boys are encouraged to individuality. They are trained to be independent in thought and action...........They are encouraged to experiment and make things for themselves. Girls are taught obedience, dependence and deference. They are made to feel that too much independence of opinion or action is a drawback to them not becoming or womanly. A boy is made to feel that his success in life..........will depend upon his ability to accomplish some thing new............ No such social spur is applied to girls."[7] It has been advocated that industrial revolution and feminist movements have bridged the moral and mental gap between the sexes. It has been argued that given equal opportunity female can rival male in all walks of life more than half a century after the publication of the 'Second sex' in 1949, Simon de Beauoir is still recognized as the first philosophical thinker to have systematically raised the issue of 'sexual difference'. Her work has inspired many subsequent developments in feminist theory as well as shaping the gender critique within the discipline of philosophy itself. While it is true that Beauvoir position has often been criticized for some of its existentialist assumption, it is equally true that even her most trenchant critics credit her with having the courage and tenacity to systemize a topic ignored by western philosophy for over two millenia. Simon de Beauvoir is one of the leading exponent of a Philosophy of existence that privileged freedom, transcendence and authenticity. She was of the opinion that the ideal of freedom, as expressed by being for itself could be seriously impeded by the sociocultural structures and institutions limiting individual development. For de Beauvoir, the oppression of women through out history represented the paradigm, case of this constraint. She maintained that 'man' has consistently defined himself as pure 'being-for-itself, leaving only the role of an inessential and objectified other' for 'woman' to fill. Moreover, this attitude had been internalized by women themselves, thereby reinforcing the invisibility of this oppression. Simone de Beauvoir has attempted to unpack the geneology of women's peripheral status as well as to suggest how status could be actively and historically changed.

De Beauvoir vigorously rejected as too simplistic, the commonly accepted biological, psychological and economic explanation for women's marginal condition. While she acknowledged that the reproduction facts of sexual difference did perhaps burden women more than men, she claimed that the context of social values and attitudes counted for more than the physical facts themselves. She did not support Freudian explanation of woman's oppression. In the same manner she remained sceptic of Marxist attitude of explaining women's oppression due to capitalist tendency. However Beauvoir located the site of women's continuing oppression in patriarchal institutions and myths. The 'essential feminine' qualities of sacrifice and narcissism promoted by these myths were targeted by Beauvoir as particularly detrimental to women's identity. All of women's efforts towards freedom and transcendence would face insurmountable odds as long as they remained passive and accommodating in their social roles. She suggested that women seek their economic independence through work outside the home, while simultaneously challenging themselves intellectually to understand their own history and prospects for the future.

Simone de Beauvior observes that man defines woman not in herself but as relative to him, because she is not regarded as an autonomous being. It is said, 'The body of man makes sense in it quite apart from that of woman where as the latter seems wanting in significance by itself...........Man can think of himself without woman. She cannot think of herself without man'.[8] Beauvoir observes that woman is simply what man decrees, thus she is called 'The Sex', by which is meant that she appears essentially to the male as a sexual being. For man woman is sex-absolute sex, no less; she is defined and differentiated with references to man and not he with reference to woman; she is the incidental, the inessential as opposed to the essential. He is the Subject, he is the Absolute, she is the other. Men deprived women of their subjectivity, individuality and treated them as object. Beauvoir observes that it is unfortunate that women have accepted the position given by men. They did not resist against it nor did they revolt. They do not authentically assume a subjective attitude. They have gained only what men have been willing to grant. They have taken nothing, they have only received.

Demonstrating the above prejudiced and biased attitude towards woman, Dorothy Parker, "I can not be just to books which treat of woman as woman, may idea is that all of us, men as well as women, should be regarded as human beings".[9] Pointing out the main reasons of woman's marginal condition in human being, Beauvoir observes that women lack concrete means for organizing themselves into a unit which can stand face to face with the correlative unit. They have no past, no history, no religion of their own and they have no such solidarity of work and interest as that of the other oppressed class like proletariat. They live dispersed among the males attached through residence, house work, economic condition and social standing to certain men-fathers or husbands, more firmly than they are to other women. Woman has always been man's dependent if not slave. These two sexes have never shared the world in equality and even today a woman is heavily handicapped, though her status has changed a lot. She is gaining almost equal legal status but still long standing customs and traditions prevent the full expression of legal rights. In economic sphere too women are competing men in getting all kinds of jobs. However in industry and politics men are still occupying better positions and key posts.

Simon de Beauvoir observes that change in women's condition began in eighteenth century when genuinely democratic man began to view the matter objectively. Diderot for instance strove to show that woman is like man, a human being. Later John stuart mill came frequently to her defense. But these philosophers displayed no usual impartiality. In the nineteenth century the feminist quarrel became again a quarrel of partisans. One of the consequences of the industrial revolution was the entrance of woman into productive labour and it was due to this that the claims of the feminists emerged from the realm of theory and acquired an economic basis, while their opponents became more aggressive. Even within the working class the men endeavoured to restrain woman's liberation because they began to see the women as dangerous competitors. In proving women's inferiority the antifeminists then began to draw upon not only on religion, philosophy and theology as before, but also on science, biology, experimental psychology etc. At most they were willing to grant equality in difference to the other sex.

In 21st century women are achieving their lost identity and are enjoying autonomous and independent status. They are giving their valuable contribution in all walks of life. However, women have still to fight for their complete subjectivity and individual identity. By their ability, merit and competence women have proved all psychological, moral and mental differences as false and baseless. The existentialist approach towards women has demonstrated them as free, autonomous and independent human being. Women are successfully fighting for their individuality, subjectivity, freedom and autonomy. She is not an 'object,' or 'other sex' rather a conscious human being, an individual like a man. All kinds of sexual discrimination are baseless. Beauvoir emphatically observes that this status will be established only by the efforts of women, men will not give this status by themselves.

References

1. Will Durant, *The Pleasures of Philosophy,* Simon & Schuster, 1953, p. 128.
2. Simone de Beauvoir, The Second Sex (Introduction) London: Cape, 1953, trans, D Baired. H.M. Parshley, p. 97.
3. *Ibid.*
4. Gorki, *Reminiscences of Tolstoy*, p. 65, Will Durant *op. cit.*, p. 115.
5. *Ibid.*
6. Quoted from *Practical Ethics* by Peter Singer, p. 34, Cambridge University Press, 1993.
7. Will Durant, *op. cit.*, p. 127.
8. Simone de Beauvoir, *ibid.*, p. 97.
9. *Ibid.*, p. 96.

Part VI

Feminist Perspectives

Chapter 41

Feminist Ethics and Empowerment of Women

Asha Mukherjee

Feminism sometimes takes reflective side of the movement and takes the shape of understanding social reality of gender relations and tries to get rid of the patriarchal of male dominated culture. When feminists regard ending of sexual oppression and injustice as a moral imperative at the level of thought and practices it is called "Feminist ethics". There is no unitary view of ethics that can be identified as "feminist ethics." Feminist approaches to ethics share a commitment to "rethinking ethics with a view to correction whatever forms of male bias it may contain." (Alision M. Jaggar, "Feminist Ethics: Some Issues For The Nineties" *Journal of Social Philosophy,* 20, 1989, p. 91) While those who develop these approaches are "united by a shared project, they diverge widely in their views as to how this project is to be accomplished. Not all feminists agree that there are distinctive feminist virtues, values. Some are even skeptical regarding the traditional positive virtues such as willingness to nurture or an affinity with caring. Still, I think it is possible to get some important focal points evident in current feminist attempts to transform 'ethics' into 'feminist ethics'.

Feminism rejects a *priori* premise of male superiority. It argues that if women perceive the normative structures of ethical theory as inadequately grounded in their own experience, then the fault lies with the theory and not with the women. There is distinctive women's social experience, which is worthy of exploration. Feminist ethics has opened up a wealth of issues, which were on periphery such as issues of sexuality, the bodily self, moral connectedness, care, trust, friendship, mothering, nurturing, emotions, psychological fluidity and finitude. Feminist thinkers about ethics have to discuss all this within the boundaries of socio-cultural reality. Thus there is a kind of delicate balancing on the hand the social reality of feminity which is a part of our own social being and on the other we must 'avoid any naive celebration of "feminine" characteristics which may be regarded as effects of oppression'.

What features of 'normal' female experience are in question here? Within the phenomenon of gender difference the central point is the contrasting relation of men and women to the fact of embodiment. But the proposition that moral autonomy is more difficult to women than to men, or women cannot be full moral subjects, strikes most of us as self-evidently absurd. Women are obviously as capable as men of taking up the subjective viewpoint, of making moral judgments and exercising will and controlling desire. The adult women must all be competent of making life and death decisions about conception, birth, abortion, the care of the dying etc. Yet there is massive contrast between male and female subjectivity in respect of the empirical conditions under which each is constructed. Male subjectivity enjoys the support of social institutions "which generate a sense of selfhood and personal importance and which do so-in part at least-by positioning women as the excluded 'other.'" (M. Griffiths & M. Whitford ed. *Feminist Perspectives in Philosophy,* Macmillan, 1988, p. 122). But, by contrast, men's absence from women's (traditional) grouping tends to be experienced, precisely, as an *absence*. Now the question arises how do the facts of gender affect the meaning for women of central ethical concepts such as rights, justice, duty, virtue, pleasure, guilt, shame, etc.? Is it possible to sustain a 'normal' female identity while trying to conceive of one's own relation to other persons as suggested by liberal democratic thinkers? Thus 'otherness' becomes very important in Feminist Ethics. On the one hand, there is a rejection of 'masculine' values as an ideal, 'successful' man as role model, and on the other a refusal to be treated as *second sex*. There is dissatisfaction in the modern society over the formal 'equality' between man and woman. They have challenged the idea of 'equality' that prevails in liberal theory as well as in feminism.

The difference in affirmation also leads to many problems. The main risk remains that we may be back with the same sort of qualities and roles, associated with traditional male conservatives. The other risk is of any idea of a universal 'feminity' which would generate solidarity between women. Gender difference is central to our social experience, but it is only one of many systems of difference around which that experience is organized. Perhaps the most hopeful outcome of these difficult debates would be an appreciation that 'otherness' extends beyond the phenomenon of gender, and there is a more generous conception of the ideal of *unity in difference.*

It is often suggested that in recent past a qualitatively new level of acceptance in the male world of business and government has emerged. This view is also questioned by the feminist ethics because it underestimates the continuing direct oppression of women by men. The real target of feminist critique has never been simply the empirical fact that various sorts of goods have been unequally distributed between sexes. Rather, it has been the very existence of the social system by which male and female individuals are assigned from birth to distinct classes whose identity is determined by their *relation to one another*—the relation of dominance in case of 'men' and the relation of subordination in case of 'women'. This hierarchical relation cuts to the depth of our social being.

From a feminist point of view, moral theory along with almost all theories will have to be transformed to take adequate account of the experience of women. What are the fundamental aspects of the history of ethics, which have not been gender-neutral? What are the issues where feminist rethinking is transforming moral concepts and theories? Let us try to answer these questions one by one.

The split between reason and emotion is one of the most familiar of philosophical conceptions. Reason has been associated with male endeavor and emotion with female weakness and of course this is not an accidental association. Maleness was aligned with active, determinate, and defining form; femaleness with mere passive, indeterminate, and inferior matter. (Lloyed, G. *The man of Reason: Male and Female in Western Philosophy,* Uni. of Minnesota Press, 1984, p. 104) Feminists repeatedly show, if the concept of "human" were built on what we think about "woman" rather than what we think about "man" it would be very different concept. Ethics, thus has not been a search for universal, or truly human guidance but a gender-biased enterprise.

The other conceptual distinction between public/private as usually formulated, has been to privilege the point of view of men in the public domain of state and law, and later in the market place, and to discount the experience of women, relegation of the private to the natural and the concept of the self as construed from a male point of view. Mothering has been conceptualized as a primary biological activity, even when performed by humans, and virtually no moral theory in the history of ethics has taken mothering, as experienced by women, seriously as a source of insight, until recently feminists have begun to. (Ed. Joyce Trebilcoe, *Mothering: Essays in Feminist Theory,* New Jersy: Rowman and Allanheld, 1984) Women were seen as emotional rather than rational beings, and thus were not granted full moral personhood. Women's behavior was regarded as "natural" and driven by instinct and so was irrelevant to morality and moral principles. (It is worth nothing that Rousseau, Kant, Hegel all have ignored the reality of women, although they paid homage to the emotional power and aesthetic sensibility). Annette Baier recently speculated about why it is that moral philosophy has so seriously overlooked the trust between human beings that in her view is an utterly central in moral life. She noted that "the great moral theorists in our tradition not only are men, they are mostly men who had minimal adult dealings with women. ("Trust and Anti-Trust," Annette Baier, *Ethics*, 96 (1986), pp. 247-48).

Now the question arises how to get away with this situation or how to change this traditional way of doing moral philosophy? To simply bring women into public and male domain of the polis will leave no one to speak for the household, will leave no one involved in the nurturance of children and cultivation of social relations Nurturance and cultivation of social relations can be of greatest moral import. Therefore there are very good reasons for women not to want simply to be accorded entry as equals into the enterprise of morality as so far developed. Women should certainly not agree, as the price of admission to the masculine realm of traditiona morality, to abandon our own moral concerns as women. Althoug we do not have any feminist moral theory to offer as yet, we ca suggest some directions to develop such theory. They may not be such "star" feminist moral theorists such as Rawls and Nozick are; we are in principle, as feminists, against self-presupposed star-centered male-dominated theory. "We experience it as a common labor, a common task" (Kathryn Morgan, "Women and Moral Madness" in *Science, Morality and Feminist Theory,* ed. Hanen and Nielsen, p. 223).

These are some of the questions about which every one has to think for her. All this is done as Enquirer and not as 'expert'.

Now let us try to see how it is related with women empowerment.

The reflective side of feminist ethics when gets translated into action, one of the major forms it takes is women empowerment.

Since United Nations Conference on Population & Development (ICPD, 1994) the concept of women's empowerment has drawn attention of the world over and a commitment to women empowerment is pervasive throughout. There is necessary relationship between development and women empowerment. What is the nature of this relationship. Is it necessary or it is necessary and sufficient both are the issues, which need to be explored. Concept of 'women empowerment' is also not very well defined; its relationship with development process has not been well defined either theoretically or empirically.

Very recently, the issue of empowering women has been a focal of discussion at different levels. And obviously one tries to understand what these issues are and the difference in different groups of women becomes the prime concern of such discussions. The diversities in women condition whether they are cultural, social, religious or simply due to their educational background, play a very important role in the program of empowerment. At the same time, when women groups are treated at par with other different cultural groups specially when human rights of a particular tribe or community are treated at par with women rights of a particular group although women form almost half of the population of the world if not more, things become all the more complicated. If we insist upon this dichotomy then we will clearly strengthen the other hierarchies of the society in general and this would consequently hurt the real cause of the women in general. The question still remains what is the "real cause of most women"?

What is meant by empowerment of women? Is it different from the empowerment of Schedule Caste/tribe and other backward classes? If it is different, in what sense it is different? At least in Indian context, we have tried many ways to empower the SC/ST and other backward classes by making reservations and by implementing other Govt. programs and many NGOs have helped them to empower. One important program was Barga system in West Bengal. The other program that is specially meant for women is the Panchayati Raj reservation for women very much similar to the reservation for SC/ST.

According to Kant "Treat humanity as an end and never as means only"; women or men being humans have to be treated equally. Thus the concept of 'equality becomes very much significant in this respect. In what sense men and women both are equal? It is in the sense of 'equality with difference'. Equality does not mean 'sameness'. 'Equality could only be interpreted as having equal opportunity to decide and live according to their own choice but unless one is aware of the opportunity to decide and live according to their own choice but unless one is aware of the options available to her one would not be able to exercise one's choice. Thus the need to make them aware of the choices is felt. The choice has to be a free choice. It does not mean that there is no 'cause' of the choice but there are 'reasons' which are rational only for the choice. Some choices could be rational and some may not be but it would be sufficient for a woman to be able to decide to choose certain way of living or action due to her own choice after due deliberations.

Empowerment just by being financially or economically strong, politically strong (by making Panchayat Pradhan) would not be sufficient. As it is possible that woman is economically and politically empowered, still she is mentally dependent on other men or her family. This is not to deny the emotional attachment with the other members of her family or society but to emphasize on the rational choice of women is very important.

The other question which is also important is "what are the special features of being a woman'? Women are also a bundle of possibilities. She may have emotions, motherhood and nurturing nature inbuilt in her personality but she is equally strong, sometimes even stronger than her male counterparts. Strong are her decisions, she is strong in her commitments and determination and above all strong in resistance power. She makes her way with all odds even before she is born. Birth of a female child itself is enough proof of her being strong. Now the question is how and why the social and environmental pressure weakens this strong element gradually? Can't we nurture the female child in such a way that she fully blooms into a fully strong personality? This is what is meant by empowerment of women- woman as a free human being exercising her choice in a rational way, ability to assert herself, striving for upward mobility or attaining the psychological state of being powerful. But ability to do things is dependent on cultural norms and institutional arrangements that regulate their lives. The social rules and roles keep women's needs and achievements outside the purview of the public world. The emphasis on women's rights to move around freely, work outside the home, to bodily integrity and freedom from violence, rising from the rules and roles which govern everyday lives of women, right to vote and access to education are all crucial for women empowerment. Emphasis is lead on equal rights in practical sphere and also challenging patriarchal structure. The idea of empowerment through gaining equal right has been challenged by radical feminists who feel that a separate set of rights are required for the full empowerment of women (Gilligan 1982). According to this view equal rights simply allow women the right to compete for masculine achievements. Equal rights do not attend to the rights necessary for attending to activities, which is traditionally associated with women's roles. It can only enable to get the same education, can apply for the same jobs and vote but 'family' issues such as child birth, child care, support, nurturing and sustenance of less able members of the family were all left outside the purview of 'real" work and 'real' social needs. Thus 'Women rights' need to be redefined as 'human rights', which are specifically women's concerns.

There are two alternative approaches and answer to these two questions. The question is are 'Women rights' equal to men or 'women rights are the rights specifically attending to the needs of women? Answer of these questions will lead us to different directions of women empowerment. Since it is a global issue the debate continues about the meaning and scope of the term such as women empowerment. Can woman be treated as an individual or she is always as an individual a cultural entity? Or are women rights just like any other cultural group rights?

Liberation of womanhood to gain her personhood is a fundamental of humanity's right. That idea is indefeasible and meant to gain new height of battle-readiness with each passing day. We need to blend the practical measures with ideas, we need the institutions to translate the promises and ideas to real life and empower the women. The progress of world is integrally linked with the advance of women, commissions are set up to empower women to fight against women injustices.

Social roles in social situations are dependent on the culture of the society in question, which is the result of a historical process. At some point they must be taken as universally valid roles. But as Margaret Mead argues that these so called universally valid roles rest on an ethnocentric illusion. The male and female roles are defined by any physiological difference of sex as such. The change of women in the family and the change of status of women in public life apart from their family functions both are desired under the empowerment of women. Modern education and modern economic life are compelling Indian women to come out of the narrow sphere of the family and work side by side with men and this is giving rise to completely new problems for women. To understand these we have to know the change, which regulates the status of women in public.

In ancient times, women were treated as movable property and she was reduced to her sex function only. Women were kept away from public life and *purdah* became the symbol of the "protected" respectable, 'well-to-do-' women. The *Purdah* system in a broader sense has even today considerable influence on the relationship between the sexes in the middle classes. The norms that regulate the appearance of women in the extremely masculine public sphere are after all was derived form the *purdah* complex of the ruling classes. Even today it is considered normal that the 'society' has to protect the chastity of women, since they themselves are incapable of doing it.

The process of social change and empowerment also relates essentially to the value change. The nuclear family system is an unavoidable consequence of urbanization and industrialization. The family ideology of educated Indian middle class is combined with the mechanism of "Sanskritization and Westernization" due to the family conception of the dominant Brahmanic ideals as well as the impact of TV culture. It is paradoxical that the western educated elite women try to liberate themselves from the hands of patriarchal ideal of womanhood but at the same time maintains "Hindu ideal of womanhood", the pativrata ideal of women, completely dependent of the husbands as a sign of a higher stage of culture. In this induced process of empowerment there is a kind of internal colonization through which the culture of the dominant group and with it their conceptions of marriage and family are imposed upon non-conforming minorities in the name of "higher morality" exactly as before was done in the name of the colonial administration. The middle class women are facing a conflict due to women's double role in the home and at work. Women are not defined any more by her biological function.

In Indian context, the village women think that they are very happy with their life, they do not need anything to be empowered about, it could be lack of awareness of other alternative way of life or it could be due to ignorance. Many times their thinking faculties are so moulded or conditioned that they hardly can think of any alternatives but the moment they would be aware of such choices they may choose to remain in their original position. After all it is their considered decision and we must respect it. Thus any kind of empowerment which is imposed from the 'above' could not be desirable

Empowerment can be defined as "the process by which the powerless gain greater control over the circumstances of their own lives; control relating to both resources and ideology." The power relation that has to be transformed includes women's lives at multiple interlinked levels; the house hold/family, the community, the market, and the state. Empowering women is important to securing their reproductive and sexual rights which are universally valid. Paula England offers a model where women empowerment is based on social and economic conditions. Women's empowerment is the actor's self-interest (defining as 'anything a woman might want food, medical care, shelter, income, respectful treatment for herself, a job, property, freedom from violence, sexual pleasure, the family size she desires and so on. Acting in one's self-interest is influenced by the use of power, which in turn has two interacting components: objective power (economic resources, laws and institutional rules and norms held by others) and subjective power (self-efficacy and entitlement).

Social dimension of a woman is interesting starting point for ethical discussion of women empowerment. Taking on a particular role such as "mother", "teacher" or "friend", "employer" or "employee", "citizen", "member of society" is often thought to involve a change in one's moral status. Social roles create obligations or expand our responsibilities. Social roles may conflict with intuitions, and worse yet, the different roles each person assumes may again offer conflicting guidance about what is right and wrong in particular cases. So, we cannot regard social rules of women as unimpeachable sources of ethics. We need to consider intuitions, rules, of women as unimpeachable sources of ethics. We need to consider institutions, rules, codes and social roles as each providing input into a process of ethical deliberation. Amartya Sen and Martha Nessbaum have motivated a discussion in this direction. in this direction. They have suggested models for betterment of the society, specially the women, on the basis of the economic and political developments. A society, which will be right based, utility based would take deontic considerations seriously. The practical issues such as rights, justice, liberty, utility, Responsibility, care etc. are the key concepts that need to be discussed in detail under this approach.

Govt. organizations translate women's empowerment into policies and programs and are creating new models for the future, and the available data regarding the status of women, such as education and empowerment provide useful information. But very often they are not sensitive enough to capture the nuances of gender power relations. We need to move beyond the traditional variables of women's status although we agree that status variables are necessary first step leading to more complex task of conceptualizing meaning and analyzing women's empowerment.

Chapter 42

Women's Empowerment and Gender Justice

S. Shyam Kishore Singh

Man and woman are inseparable biological partners. The inalienable relation between them is the subject of legends and mythologies. It has also been the theme of great literary works. In the Šaiva Daršana, Lord Šiva who is the creator of the universe is known as *Ardhanârišvra*. He is the divine embodiment of the male and the female principles of creation. Creation is regarded as the harmonious play of Šiva and Šakti. In the ancient Chinese thought, two primary elements, viz., *yin* and *yâng*, the male and female elements, are regarded as essential to the composition of all the things.

In the *Symposium*, which is one of the famous Dialogues of the Greek philosopher Plato, Aristophanes narrated that in the beginning the human body was bi-sexual. Mankind had a unique physical constitution because the human body was half male and half female. They were very strong and intelligent too. In course of time, their population multiplied and they became a formidable rival to the gods. Zeus, the king of the gods, decided that unless these people were split into two physical halves, they will dominate the heaven and the earth. He realized that the strength of these people lay in the combination of man and woman in one body. So Zeus bifurcated their bodies vertically into two halves—one half into man, another half into woman. Since then, man and woman remained half-complete and each half yearned for re-union with the other half. Love is regarded by Aristophanes as the desire on the part of man and woman for re-union. Considered from the above accounts, it is quite appropriate that woman is regarded as "ardhângini", the "better half" of man.

It is interesting to note that there are scientific evidences for the bi-sexual nature of the human body. Recent scientific researches in the fields of genetics and cell-biology have pointed to the bi-sexuality of the human brain. Traces of bi-sexuality have also been found in the cells of various organisms right from the simple cell of amoeba to the complex human cells. These evidences have shown that there is inalienable relationship between the two sexes for the sake of biological continuity and joint functioning for survival. However, it may be noted that in human society, since time immemorial, the male members have played leading and dominant role. There were several reasons for male dominance in the past. The need for the protection of woman against the hostile environment and wars, the need for care during the period of childbirth, etc., have necessitated the dependence of woman on man for centuries, thereby generating a domineering mentality in man's psyche. In several societies in the past, women have been subjugated and marginalized. Even in the present days, male dominance is prevalent in many parts of the world, particularly in the underdeveloped and developing countries. In spite of the legal safeguards of the rights of women, introduced by the modern governments, the socio-economic and political status of woman still remains lower than that of man.

At the international and national levels, a number of plans, policies and projects have been taken up for improving the social status of woman. The U.N.O. has launched programmes for the education and healthcare of woman throughout the world. The U.N. Charter has given due importance to the protection of the rights of women and respect of their human dignity. The U.N.O. has observed the Decade for Women in 1975-1985 with the objective of developing and uplifting the condition and status of woman. The Government of India have constituted National Commission for Women in 1970 for safeguarding the rights and interests of women and for monitoring the implementation of various legislations and development works for gender justice and improvement of social, political and economic conditions of women.

Recently, there has been a strong move for the amendment of the Constitution of India for 33% reservation of seats for women members in the parliament and the state legislative assemblies. Already under the National Perspective Plan (NPP), the reservation of one third of the seats for women in the local bodies, such as Panchayats and Nagar Palikas, has been implemented in partial phases (under the Constitution 73rd and 74th amendment, 1993). For the present, women play minor role in the law making function in the parliament and state legislatures due to the low percentage of women's representation in these law-making bodies. Hence, there is a serious need for taking up due measures for the empowerment of women so that women may take equal share with men in all activities of nation building. Of course, different policy approaches have been introduced over the last thirty years. Attempts have been made to translate into action the concepts of "women's welfare" in the 70s, "Women's Development" in the 80s and "Women's Empowerment" in the 90s. The empowerment of women and other weaker sections of the society is one of the priority areas of the 9th Five Year Plan (1997-2002).

The Constitution of India enjoins on every citizen the obligation "to renounce practices derogatory to the dignity of women" [Article 51-A(c)]. It has provided equal rights for the protection of the interests of women. Several other legislations for the special protection of women have been enacted. Mention may be made of the Hindu Marriage Act (1955), the Hindu Succession Act (1956), the Suppression of Immoral Traffic Act (1956), the Dowry Prohibition Act (1976), etc., as examples of the legal safeguards of women. Besides, there are special provisions in the I.P.C. and Cr. P.C. for the deterrence, punishment and speedy trial of sexual crimes against women. These legal provisions not only aim at gender equity but also guarantee gender justice.

It is very unfortunate that inspite of these legal provisions for the protection of women against exploitation, the incidence of violence and crime against women remain unabated. Women have been subjected to humiliating sexual violations not only by the anti-social elements but even sometimes by the keepers of law. Many young brides lose their lives in the dowry related atrocities. There are many other crimes committed against women, and discriminations are still there against the girl child. A recent survey shows that 97 lakh girl children faced pre-natal elimination during the last three years as a result of pre-natal sex determination through Ultra-Sound screening.

There are many stumbling blocks on the way of the development of women in the economic, social and political spheres. Women's education has faced a number of acute problems even after fifty years of independence in India. Although 52.2% of the country's adult population as a whole is now counted as literate, 67.83 per cent of its female population remains illiterate. Despite the transformation that is taking place in India, there is still discrimination against the girl child in respect of education and upbringing.

The Indian Education Commission (1964-66) has recommended that the education of girls should receive emphasis not only on grounds of social justice but also on grounds of accelerated social transformation, and the National Policy on Education (1986) has endorsed this recommendation. The NPE has strongly stated that the educational system must play a "positive interventionist role" in changing social values and attitudes that obstruct women's rights and equal participation not merely in all respects of development but even in education. The NPE has devoted a separate section (Part IV, 4.2 and 3) called "Education for Women's Equality" to drive home the urgent need for action in that direction. The policy statement runs as follows:—

"Education will be used as an agent of basic change in the status of women. In order to neutralize the accumulated distortions of the past, there will be a well-conceived edge in favour of woman. The National Education System will play a positive interventionist role in the empowerment of women. It will foster the development of new values through re-designed curricula, text books, the training and orientation of teachers, decision makers and administrators and the active involvement of educational institutions. This will be an act of faith and social engineering. Women's studies will be promoted as a part of various courses and educational institutions encouraged to take up active programmes to further women's development".

The National Policy on Education and the Programmes of Action are the endeavours in the right direction. Giving the right type of education to all sections of the society is one of the steps for solving problems relating to gender inequality and the maladies that confront women in the society.

Indian women, mostly in the rural areas are engaged in the tiresome drudgery of farming, forestry, handloom, handicraft and other small industries, construction works, etc., besides looking after the family by rearing children, cooking, fetching firewood and water, cleaning, washing and other domestic chores. In return many of them get ill treatment and atrocities from their husbands and in-laws. Although the condition of the working women in the urban societies are comparatively better than that of women in the rural areas, they face another sort of problem. Many of the working women (even some of the career women) have to work for extra hours, because in addition to their routine duties in the work places, they have to work at home also, since they have to play their roles as wives, mothers, and daughter-in-laws doing household chores of cooking, washing, child-rearing, etc. Hence, the daily routine of the working women is really taxing and burdensome.

In order to alleviate the woes of different sections of women in the Indian society, there is a great need for concerted efforts at various levels-at the individual level, at the level of family and the society at large-besides the measures taken up by the government at the provincial and the national levels. The social workers and the non-governmental organizations have a big role to play for bringing about awareness among the people for gender equality and gender justice, as well as for taking up timely and effective steps for checking violence and injustice against women. Moreover, there is a great need for the establishment of good understanding between man and woman because most of the problems have arisen from lack of appraisal and understanding of their roles in the family and the society. Only when man and woman work in tandem with the sense of equality, there will be peace and progress in the family and the society. The time has come for men-folk to share extra-workload of women in the family wherever possible since the compulsions of modern life have made both man and woman busy. Men should, therefore, look at women as equal partners on the path to progress and development. Besides this, proper measures should be taken up for the empowerment of women for the upliftment of their status through legislations and social understanding. For the translation of these measures into action, we should accept gender equality as the social reality. Man and woman should work together as equal partners for the realization of the good life without malice towards none.

Part VII

Medico-Technical Perspectives

Chapter 43

Sri Sarada Devi: A Symbol of Women Empowerment Through Spirituality

Rashmi Rekha

Empowerment has several connotations in common parlance. Most generally it means investing legally or formally authority in someone to enable one to take decision about one self according to one's wisdom and will. The need of empowerment arises because someone is either denied or deprived of one's power. Empowerment essentially implies existence of 'disempowerment' or 'unempowerment'. Empowerment as a concept is quite similar to the concept of 'light' in the Indian Philosophy. In essence, 'light' is nothing but absence of 'darkness'. Similarly empowerment is nothing but absence of disempowerment or unempowerment .Whenever or wherever there is darkness, one has to kindle light to dispel the darkness. Analogously, whenever or wherever there is disempowerment of someone in the society, one has to empower that individual or group in the interest of better health and strength of the society.

Traditionally, Indian society is patriarchal in nature. Patriarchy as a system rests on division of labour on sexual basis and strongly believes that the tasks performed by men are more 'productive', more 'serious' and more 'skilled' than the tasks performed by women. This notion leads men to believe that they are responsible for looking after, protecting and controlling women. Unlike men, women are looked upon as members of the family rather than as individuals. As a result of this patriarchy and practice of male dominance, the status of women got relegated to that of subjugation and surrender to the whims and fancies of men. This is basically the perversion of the age old Indian system of recognizing the 'division of labour' amongst various groups in the society according to their respective abilities as the most rational system of organizing the functional needs of the society. But perversion crept into our society because 'division of labour' was not simultaneously supported by recognizing and respecting the 'dignity of labour'. Thus equality of man and man, and man and woman as preached by the 'Vedanta' through the concept of 'Unity of Existence' has been totally belied in actual practice in our society. Ignorance of the traditional Vedic System as well as the egalitarian modern teachings of 'equality and justice to all' in our social, political and economic life had led to alarmingly rapid decline in the status of women all around during the time Sri Sarada Devi lived on this planet earth.

During the time of Sri Sarada Devi a girl child was an unwelcome burden in the parental home, she would be ill treated and abused within the domestic fold vis a vis her brothers, she would be married to an unknown person against her wishes at a tender age and quite often to an old man, she would be denied education and other human rights, she would be either sold or tortured for dowry, she would not be allowed to remarry if her husband died early where as men could practice polygamy, sometimes she would be forced to become even a sati, she would not get equal wage for equal work and so on. The list of their miseries was endless. They would remain confined to the four walls of their houses. Involving them in outdoor activities or in developmental processes was just unthinkable. In a nut shell, the condition of women was really pathetic and deplorable vis a vis men. Indian Society was paying heavily for the disempowerment of their women folk through total deprivation of their basic human rights and continued exploitation. So, there was a need to empower women in India if it had to really move on the path of peace, progress and prosperity.

Any scheme or step towards empowerment of women often views women as a target, whereas they should be an important and active participant in the process of empowerment. There has been a lot of debate on the content as well as ways and means of empowering women. A plethora of literature is available on the subject but the sum and substance of all these are more or less the same. Therefore, I will focus on only few of them which broadly reflect the representative view on the subject. Henrietta Moore is one of them who define women empowerment as power to make decision or resist decisions made by others which affect women.[1] According to Margaret Stacey and Marion Price the notion undoubtedly has to do with the ability of an individual or group to influence the course of events in the direction they desire even against resistance by others.[2] Women's empowerment thus refers to development of skills and abilities in women to decide upon and to undertake actions which they believe are essential for their well being. Thus, empowerment of women emphasizes on creation of an environment which will enable them to realize their full potential and promote equality between women and men. In this context, women empowerment means economic independence, possession of knowledge, self image and autonomy for decision making.

Sri Sarada Devi was an illiterate and simple housewife belonging to a poor rural family of Bengal. She was far away from anything and everything that could have been understood as 'power' in the material sense of the term by a common man. In other words, she was a totally disempowered women in the eyes of a normal material human being who could have deserved 'empowerment'. She had no material resource or support system to empower herself in the material sense of the term. But she was fully aware of the transient nature of all material acquisitions and attainments, so instead of wasting her vital life energy in accumulating them she turned inward to her consciousness for empowering herself with the inexhaustible source of Divine Power and Eternal Bliss. Under the able guidance and companionship of her husband Sri Ramakrishna Pramhansa, she undertook inner journey for full development of her spiritual potential and used the same for the empowerment of those individual or group, who were disempowered by the circumstances. In order to understand this unique process, a journey to the life of Sri Sarada Devi is imperative.

Sri Sarada Devi, the divine consort of Sri Ramakrishna was born of very pious brahmin parents in the obscure village of Jayrambati in West Bengal on December 22, 1853.[3] She was brought up in the pure and simple village atmosphere. She started her initial life like an ordinary girl child but by virtue of her lovable and caring nature, devotion to domestic work and spiritual inclination , she became the apple of everyone's eyes. She gradually grew up to be an asset to the family. In May 1859, at the age of five, she was married to Sri Ramakrishna because child marriage was not uncommon then in Bengal in particular and India in general. After, her marriage, she continued to stay in Jayarambati and played the 0role of an ideal daughter and a sister. By her service, she made herself indispensible in the family. In other words, she carved out a position of power in her family.

She occasionally went to Kamarpukur, the native village of Sri Ramakrishna, although he himself mainly stayed at the temple of Dakshineshwar engaged in his intense sadhana. People considered his god intoxication as madness. With mock sympathy they would say, "Shyama (Sarada's mother) has married her daughter to a mad man. Alas, how unlucky poor Sarada is, what a hapless girl". But even in this complex and depressing situation, she did not get discouraged. In order to know the truth, she herself went to Dakshineshwar to find out the reality about the madness of her husband. Describing this Swami Pavitrananda has written thus, "Saradamani could hardly believe her eyes when she found her husband, who was reported to have gone mad, feeling so much anxiety at her illness and showing so much kindness and affection. Was there any women in this world so blessed as to receive such loving care from her husband? Saradamani knew for certain that whatever might be peoples' opinion, her divine husband was perfectly sane; not only that, but there had also not been the least change in his attitude towards her".[4]

Contrary to all rumours about his insanity, she found him to be a perfectly normal human being having full love, affection, concern and care for all people around him including herself . She was particularly impressed with his care and concern about her illness and exhibition of so much kindness and affection for her. Thereafter, she lived with her husband for about ten years, except for short visits to her native village, Jayarambati. On the other hand, Ramakrishna was also equally impressed by her simplicity and high spiritual qualities. Leaving no scope for any doubt she made it clear to him that she had not come to Dakshineswar to drag him in the sensual worldly life. Declaring her intention very clearly and firmly she asserted thus, "Why should I desire to drag your mind down to the worldly plane? I have come only to help you in your chosen path. I desire only to live with you and serve you and to learn of you".[5] Her determination to discharge her worldly responsibilities by serving her husband and simultaneously desiring to pursue spiritual goals in his guidance gave satisfaction to him. Soon he found her progressing rapidly on the spiritual path. He was impressed with her spiritual power gained in a short span of time. She secured for herself a great place in the heart of her husband and guru Ramakrishna.

Nothing would have made her happier than to give her husband all kinds of services that was possible for her to give. She also said that as long as Sri Ramakrishna was alive, the 'pitcher of her heart' was always full of bliss. This joy she got out of only 'giving' and not 'receiving'. In ordinary marriages the 'give me' factor prevails between spouses causing disharmony and the breakup of marriages.

Sri Sarada Devi did not have any biological child, she considered every one coming to her as her own child. She was a universal mother of all children. She was for everyone whether good or bad, rich or poor, man or woman. Her motherly love didn't recognize boundaries of caste, sex, income, race, nation or culture etc. She was the mother of all and that was her power.

After the death of her husband in 1886, this woman behind the curtain of conventional orthodoxy emerged as an empowered 'Sangha Janani'. The followers of Sri Ramakrishna, scholar sannyasins , considered her not only a source of moral and spiritual inspiration but also an advisor, the operative source of authority in moments of crisis. Although she was not learned, yet her spiritual attainments were so great and her common sense so sharp that she became virtually the head of the Ramakrishna Mission. Vivekananda, Saradananda, and other Swamis used to cousult her on major problems and they never went against her wishes. Vivekananda wanted to introduce animal sacrifice during Durga Puja at the Belur Math and indeed, once at Kali Puja goat sacrifice was done. But later the 'Holy Mother' ordered that this must not be done. Once Vivekananda wanted to sell away the newly acquired land at Belur for meeting the expenditure of the relief works. Sri Sarada Devi did not allow him to do so because hundreds of such welfare activities were to be carried out in future through the Math. She could guide them with firmness because she considered herself to be their mother. She used to say, "I am Mother in the true sense of the term. I am not just the wife of your Guru, not a surrogate or make believe mother. I am your genuine Mother".[6] Thus, Sri Sarada Devi demonstrated empowerment through motherhood.

Many revolutionaries had given up their earlier association and joined the Ramakrishna Mission. The then Viceroy of India, made some remarks regarding this and it was proposed to expel them from the Mission to avoid the anger of the British Government. Swami Saradananda consulted her on this issue. She advised him not to expel those persons who had given up all revolutionary activities. She advised him to meet the Viceroy personally to explain the whole situation. This was done with favourable results. The Viceroy withdrew his derogatory remarks officially. Praising Sri Sarada Devi's insight, Swami Nirvedananda has rightly remarked thus, "Her quick penetrating insight into the core of any problem placed before her and her extraordinary power of passing large and generous judgment on matters however new or complex, all these were no less impressive than her motherly tendency".[7]

She demonstrated to the world that she kept her promise and commitment given to her husband. She had assured her husband at such an early age that she had come to stay with him not to drag him back to domesticity, but to help him in his spiritual mission. At that time, she was in teens only, but even then she was aware of her both spiritual and physical power and turned her promise into a reality. This is really unique of her. This aspect of her personality shows her inner strength to overcome the sensual and material desire and sets an example for the women of future generation.

Sri Sarada Devi nurtured the Ramakrishna Mission since its early days. If she had not protected and guided it, it would not have such a grand beginning on a firm footing. She successfully helped in making 'The Ramakrishna Order' stronger. Sri Sarada Devi's efforts to groom this institution made her the supreme authority. Nobody handed over power to her to be the key functionary in the institution but by virtue of her continuous hard work and sincere efforts she gained that position and prominence for herself. Thus her journey from 'underpowered' to 'empowered' proceeded through the phases of awakening, dawning of self awareness, gaining a clear idea of what she could be and what she could do. This inner realization made her worthy of the power she enjoyed. She never misused her power. She demonstrated the true meaning of 'Democracy' and the concept of human rights in which there is no giver and no taker. Sri Sarada Devi proved that 'empowerment' meant power to do and power to excel. Empowered women should shoulder the responsibilities, offer services and support, encourage both material and moral advancement, not necessarily competing with men but as an independent, self sufficient, self possessed section of the community. This aspect of Sri Sarada Devi's life can be an inspiration for the women of present era who are desperate to empower themselves without understanding its meaning properly. That is why on many occasions even empowered women fail to contribute substantially towards their own well being as well as the well being of others.

Sri Sarada Devi showed interest in imparting education to women. Though she herself was illiterate, but she knew the importance of education in empowering the women of India. That was why she always showed interest in Nivedita's educational activities. When Nivedita's school was inaugurated on November 13, she went to attend the opening ceremony. She, after inaugarating the school, blessed it by saying, "I pray that the blessing of the Divine Mother may be upon the school and the girls, and the girls trained from the school may become ideal girls."Along with her, many members of the Ramakrishna Order were present on the occasion. She used to visit the school frequently to encourage Nivedita in her educational endeavour. She used to be very happy to see the girls engaged in constructive activities. She knew it well that this would lead them to a life of independent nature. Dr Barnali Das has written that she often inspired Sister Christine, Sudhira Devi and Sarala Devi for their works and selfless dedication in Nivedita's School.

Sri Sarada Devi did not approve early marriage of girls. Once a mother approached her to counsel and convince her daughter to agree to the proposal of her family to marry her early. She replied, "Is it not a misery to remain in lifelong slavery to another man and always dance to his tune?" She advised the mother that her daughter should not be forced to marry against her wish. She advised another woman to admit her daughter in the school of Sister Nivedita for making her future bright. She advocated for the spread of women education. When a grown up girl of an orthodox Brahmin family was asked not to attend the school, she made it clear that education would make the girl more useful not only to the family but also to the society. Though she advocated modern education for women, she also made them conscious that the only ornament of a woman is her modesty.[8]

Sri Sarada Devi showed much interest in the welfare activities of women. Three institutions can be mentioned whose inauguration and working were deeply influenced by her -the Ramakrishna Sarada Math, the Saradeswari Ashram of Gauri Ma and Sister Nivedita's School for girls. The latter two were started during her life time. The very name of the Saradeswari Ashram started by Gauri Ma at the instance of Ramakrishna Mission testifies to the influence of the Holy Mother on it. She often visited the Ashram and was virtually worshipped by Gauri Ma and the inmates of the Ashram. A prominent figure of this Ashram, Durga Puri Devi was also an ardent disciple of Sri Sarada Devi. 'The Ramakrishna Sarada Math' was started much later but it is based on the ideals of Sri Sarada Devi. Sarala Devi, who later became the first president of the Sarada Math with the name Pravrajika Bharatiprana was a disciple of the Holy Mother. Sri Sarada Devi was the main inspiration behind this movement.

Sri Sarada Devi considered English language as a tool to preach the ideas of Sri Ramakrishna among foreigners, both in their own land as well as when they visited India. That was why she expressed great joy at the knowledge of English of the south Indian girls whom she met at the Nivedita's Girls High School, Calcutta.

There are many instances in which she protested against the ill treatment of women by men. Jogy was very close to her as the head of the group of palanquin bearers and often carried the holy mother in his palanquin when she used to travel. He was physically strong and at times used to beat his wife in a drunken state.Once his wife complained to the Holy mother about his beatings. She instantly called him and instructed him in clear words never to beat his wife again in future. She did not bother for the consequence of being deprived of the services of Jogy and his men in case he became annoyed with her because of her advice.

One summer evening, when mother was at Udbodhan overlooking an open space across the road where some labourers lived in huts. In one of them, a man was beating his wife mercilessly. She scolded the man who was out of control due to extreme anger but a look at the Holy Mother acted like a charm on him. He felt ashamed and stopped beating his wife.

Sindhubala's case also proves Sri Sarada devi's concern for the ill treatment of women . There were two Sindhubalas. The Police wanted to arrest one Sindhubala due to her involvement in subversive activities but due to some confusion, they took into custody the wrong Sindhubala with one more woman. She was in family way. The Police treated the woman badly. When Sri Sarada Devi heard this incident, she was deeply hurt and reacted sharply against the British government. She felt relieved only after the news of her release came.

The heart of Sri Sarada Devi always bled for the poor. She was deeply concerned with the extreme poverty which women in the villages had to face due to the exploitative nature of the British Rule. They did not have means to meet their basic needs. She used to weep bitterly for their miserable condition and pray for the exit of the British whom she held responsible for their bad condition. She did whatever she could do to mitigate their miseries.

Ramakrishna loved and respected her a lot. She also had great love and respect for him but sometimes she would resist and refuse to dance to the tune of her husband. When Ramakrishna asked her not to send his food through a woman of low repute, Sri Sarada Devi refused to listen to him and gave him a very sublime reply, "It is impossible for me to refuse someone who calls me 'mother', moreover, you are not simply God to me, you are God to all." On another occasion when Ramakrishan did not approve of her distributing food with generosity, she showed her objection vehemently for which Ramakrishna had to apologize to her. Sri Ramakrishna was very strict with his young disciples as regards their diet, spiritual practices, etc. One day he learnt that Baburam (afterwards became Swami Premananda) took five or six chapattis at night. That was too much; he thought and asked why he took such a large quantity at night. The young boy replied that the Holy Mother served meal to him. Thereupon Sri Ramakrishna went to the Holy Mother and took her to task for thus spoiling the spiritual prospects of the boy. At this the holy Mother replied thus, "you need not worry about their welfare. I will look to that".[9] The master saw the sentiment behind these words and simply laughed. Sri Sarada Devi at times dared to stand against the wishes of her husband which was unusual during those days.

Sri Sarada Devi also did not hesitate in breaking the traditional conventions established for the widows. After the death of her husband, she was about to put off her bracelets but she had a vision of Ramakrishna appearing before her and requesting her not to do so because he had not gone away. So she neither shaved her head nor accepted any symbol of widowhood. She continued to wear her trade mark white sari with the red border, of course the border became little thinner. Her continuance to wear a cloth with coloured borders and some ornaments was in recognition of the Master's assurance that there was no death for him and therefore, no widowhood for her. She considered her husband eternal and undying spirit. She faced criticism from her villagers for this but she never relented to them. By going against the established custom, she showed her inner strength and power to stand against all odds.

Besides sense-pleasure, the greatest traps for human beings are the desire for name and fame, the desire for honour and the desire for power but she had no such desire either. During his lifetime, Sri Ramakrishna's name began to spread all over the world and he was held in high regard. The well-known saint Pavhari Baba of Ghazipur kept a photo of Ramakrishna in his cave. And in London the renowned scholar and Indologist Max Muller became fascinated simply by hearing about Sri Ramkrishna's life, and he immediately wanted to write a book about him. After Swami Vivekananda's success at the Parliament of Religions in Chicago, Ramakrishna's name spread even faster. With all this, Holy Mother could have easily occupied the centre stage of an international religious movement. She could have been adored and honoured by millions during her lifetime. Instead, she preferred to spend most of her time in a remote village of India, cooking and cleaning, wearing simple clothes, and living a simple life in a mud hut. Preference to an austere life over the glittery luxurious life is a testimony to her enlightened existence. Swami Gambhirananda gives us a glimpse of her routine in Jayarambati: "At Jayarambati she tirelessly went through her daily routine. Looking to the comforts of the devotees, dressing vegetables in the morning for about two hours, taking out stores for the kitchen, arranging for the worship (of the Master) and then worshipping with her own hands, distributing the prasada, making at least a hundred betal rolls, kneading flour and preparing chapatti and luchi, boiling milk, cleaning lamps, and such other works followed one another without intermission and without anybody else's help as if they were her duty alone".[10]

Sri Sarada Devi's life is an open book for all. Her rise to the highest place in human culture from a poor uneducated background shows how empowerment can be achieved through the tool of spirituality.It is a ray of hope for all disempowered in general and women in particular. She affirmed that the soul has no sex and it stands for no discrimination. It suffers no discrimination either. Everyone irrespective of sex, caste, creed, race etc is eligible to empowerment through spiritual development. Her rise to the high peaks of power, prestige and attainments both spiritual and material without any compromise with her modesty chastity, dignity, honesty, purity, common sense, intelligence, wisdom, sympathy, kindness, contentment and broadmindedness acts as a source of inspiration for all women and will continue to do so in future also.

It is true that through the spiritual path Sri Sarada Devi was able to empower herself in the most odd circumstances and work for the empowerment of women and other disempowered groups. After a gap of a full century and a half between her time and the present time almost everything has changed, even the society, pattern of life, ways of looking at things have changed but a lot remains to be changed in respect of our women folk. There is also an apparent change between the position of Sri Sarada Devi and the militant position assumed by the women activists . This study clearly reveals that the strategy adopted by Sri Sarada Devi for her own empowerment as well as that of other disempowered groups can act as a role model for empowering the Indian women of modern times. She became the guiding force of the "Ramakrishna Mission" which is still serving both for the spiritual elevation and worldly welfare of the society.

References

1. Henrietta Moore, Divided We stand : Sex, Gender and Sexual Difference, Feminist Review, No. 47, Summer, p. 85, 1994.
2. Margaret Stacey and Marion Price, Women, Power and Politices, p. 3, London & New York : Tavistock, 1981.
3. Swami Pavitrananda, A short life of the Holy Mother, p. 4, Advaita Ashrama, Mayavati, Champawat, Himalayas, 1998.
4. Ibid., p. 16.
5. Swami Nirvedananda, The Holy Mother in Great women of India, p. 482, Advaita Ashrama, Third Impression, September, 1993.
6. Swami Gambhirananda, Sri Ma Sarada Devi, p. 170, Udbodhan, 1989.
7. Swami Nirvedananda, the Holy Mother, p. 66, Sarada Math, Calcutta, 1983.
8. The Message of the Holy Mother, p. 1, Advaita Ashrama, Mayavati, Pithoragarh, Himalayas, 1992.
9. Swami Pavitrananda, A short life of the Holy Mother , p. 39, Advaita Ashrama, Mayavati, Champawat, Himalayas, 1998.
10. Swami Budhananda, Studies on the Holy Mother, in Sri Sarada Devi the Great wonder, p. 428, Advaita Ashrama, Calcutta, 1994.

Chapter 44

Violence Against Women from Womb to Tomb

Rangila Sinha

Women are subject to violence throughout their lives starting from mother's womb (Uterus) in the form of prenatal sex determination and abortion of a female child to abuse and forced suicide even murder of elderly widows. They face violence as follows:—

Table No. I

Phase	Type of violence
Pre-Birth	Sex selective abortion; effects of battering during pregnancy on birth outcome.
Infancy	Female infanticide; physical, sexual & psychological abuse.
Girlhood	Malnutrition, Child marriage; Discriminatory health care. Child prostitution.
Adolescence/Adulthood	Dating and courtship violence (e.g., acid throwing and date rape); dowry abuse & murders; neglect during pregnancy & child birth, forced pregnancy leading to high maternal mortality, psychological & sexual abuse in work place, partner violence, partner homicide.

Elderly	Forced "suicide" or homicide of widows for economic reasons; sexual, physical & psychological abuse.
Domestic Violence	Women suffer maximum violence in family, in intimate relationship, in many countries 25% to 50% women report having been abused by current or ex-partner and in-laws. In India 18% to 45% of married men (6902) from five districts of Uttar-Pradesh accepted physically abusing their wives. Women undergoing domestic violence are at higher risk of contracting severe gynecological and obstetrical complications apart from other physical and psychological trauma.

Among all above mentioned violence against women the most heinous crime is infanticide and its recent version feticide, which has altered the female to male ratio in recent census. (1991)

Female Feticide & Infanticide

Female feticide is abortion of a pregnancy after sex determination of unborn female fetus. It is modern version of female infanticide and an abuse of high technology developed for prenatal diagnosis and detection of fetal anomalies. *Female Infanticide* is intentional killing of a baby girl, which is most brutal and destructive manifestation of bias against women in patriarchal society of India, China and some other neighbouring countries.

One has to pause and think why is it happening?

Why a mother wants to kill her own female child after knowing the sex of the baby? Is she doing it willingly? No, she is a helpless and dependent person, forced by family tradition and wishes of her husband and in-laws she commits this crime of getting a female fetus aborted. Many women have confessed to me that they do not want to give birth to a female child because her birth will bring many miseries in family and the girl child will be an unwanted child. The fear of dowry and allied expenses on one hand and losing property inheritance on the other makes a girl child as a loosing proposition.

Apart from this, finding a suitable match for marriage of a girl within certain age limit, which is a must in Indian culture, involves lots of physical and mental burden on the family. All these are considered as negative points of a girl child. Hence a girl in the family is a liability whereas a boy is an asset.

In spite of all these negative aspects there was no way out to get rid of a girl child except in extreme step like infanticide, which is still practiced in many parts of India.

In a female bias society of India the prenatal diagnostic tests like *chorionic villus biopsy, amniocentesis* and *ultrasonography* are misused simply. These tests are only meant for diagnosis of different diseases and abnormalities including sex linked diseases of the fetus while in utero, but they are being used in India to eliminate female children before birth.

Chorionic villous biopsy

It was introduced in the year 1971 as prenatal diagnostic test and can be performed as early as 8-10 weeks of pregnancy. In this test a portion of developing placenta is aspirated through a special type of catheter under the guidance of ultrasound probe. After chromosomal analysis of the cells, the sex of the embryo can be detected with 99% accuracy. There is 1% -2% chance of abortion after this procedure.

Amniocentesis

This is another method of prenatal sex determination. In this method a needle is inserted in uterus through maternal abdominal wall and fluid in which the fetus is floating in the uterine cavity is aspirated and fetal cells are collected for chromosomal analysis and sex determination. The above-mentioned tests take only a few hours to do sex determination.

Ultrasonography

It has surpassed all the previous technologies available for the detection of fetal sex. In this procedure, it takes only a few minutes to correctly diagnose the sex of the fetus in almost 96% to 98% cases in the hands of expert sonologist after 16 weeks of pregnancy.

It is the gravest abuse of an unique technology, which is the most useful diagnostic tool developed in the recent years. It has opened so many closed doors of diagnosis and treatment in all branches of medicine and it has greatest beneficial impact on the practice of Obstetrics and Gynaecology. But its abuse in prenatal sex determination and then female feticide has posed a big question before right thinking people of all walks of life.

After knowing the sex of the fetus by above-mentioned tests, request is made for termination of pregnancy. According to medical termination of pregnancy (MTP) Acts 1972—a pregnancy can be terminated up to 20 weeks on certain valid grounds e.g., health of the women and health of her existing children, pregnancy after rape, pregnancy after failure of contraceptive methods and pregnancy in mentally retarded women. Currently medical termination of pregnancy is being projected by government as a method of family planning; hence MTP services are given almost in all government hospitals and in private sector health facilities on demand. Medical termination of pregnancy is hazardous after 10 weeks of pregnancy but these women are desperate to get rid of their female fetuses and are ready to take any risk for that matter.

There is a mushroom growth of sex determination and pregnancy termination clinics all over India where with the connivance of the doctors lakhs of parents are getting rid of their unborn daughters. Some doctors are even taking their mobile ultrasound machines in rural areas for sex determination of unborn children. The practice of selective Feticides and Infanticides have assumed an alarming proportion which is reflected in female to male ratio at age group (0-6) of 1991 census.

Table 2

Female to Male Sex Ratio in India

Year	Female	Male
1901	972	1000
1981	934	1000
According to census 1991(0-6 age group)		
1991	929	1000

(International Family planning perspective; June (1993 p. 42)

Orissa, Bihar, M.P., U.P. have shown maximum decline in female to male sex ratio.

Haryana has lowest sex ratio	875 (female)	1000 (male)
Punjab	882 (female)	1000 (male)

Venkatesh Athriya, Head of Economics department of the Bharathidasan University in Tamil Nadu, thinks that this decline in female to male ratio is a result of a combination of both Inganticide and Feticide, because the technology for Feticide has been introduced in India only recently.

Consequences

The probable consequences of Female Foeticide, Female Infanticide and reduction in Female to Male Sex will be a further increase in atrocities on women, sexual crime and sex related diseases. There will be fewer women to live with men and whole social order will be changed for its worst. A problem of this magnitude can be tackled only by combined efforts of government, private sector doctors, hospitals and non-government organizations (NGO) and religious leaders.

This matter was raised from time to time by different social and professional associations engaged in welfare of women and children. The federation of Obstetrics and Gynaecological Societies of India (FOGSI), which is a strong body of 14000 Obstetricians and Gyneacologists practicing all over India, has directed all its members not to get themselves indulged in sex selective abortions.

The directive is that even the membership of the society can be terminated if a member is found guilty of performing sex selective abortions.

The association of ultrasonologists of India has taken similar steps against pre-natal sex detection of fetus. But it is difficult to prove a crime if both parties (consumer and provider of a service) are equally interested. It is only with the co-operation of all doctors who are engaged in the well-being of the mankind in general and women and children in particular that this evil practiced for performing MTP are suggested to take in writing from the couple who requests for termination of pregnancy that the *sex of the fetus has not been detected or determined.*

NGO has valuable role in creating awareness in society regarding adverse consequences of prenatal sex determination, female feticide and its legal aspect.

To highlight these matters a special leave petition was filed in Supreme Court by the Center for Enquiry into Health and Allied Themes (CEHST) and the Mahila Sarvangeen Vikash Mandal (MASUM). This petition draws attention to the gross misuse of diagnostic technologies in a society with a bias against female children where female Infanticide is still in practice. Misuse of these technologies will create further gap in already low female to male sex ratio.

In response to this public interest litigation Supreme Court, vide its order dated May 4, 2001 pulled up center and all state governments for failing to check female Feticide. It directed all the state governments to constitute appropriate authority to check female Feticide and implement prenatal Diagnostic Techniques (regulation, prevention and misuse Act 1994 (PNDT Act) with all vigour and zeal.

Illegal sex determination is a punishable offence. The pregnant women, her relatives and doctors involved in illegal sex determination of fetus have to undergo imprisonment for 3 years and pay a fine of Rs. 10,000/. Persons found guilty of doing it for the second time will get 5 years imprisonment and a fine of Rs. 50,000/. The point is that the PNDT Act 1994 and MTP Act 1972 are on paper but making law on paper is something and implementation of the law is something else.

Previously this evil practice of sex selective feticide was more prevalent in North India but it is a matter of great concern that this evil practice of sex selective feticide is spreading fast in almost all the districts of South India as well. This is reflected in decline of Female to Male ratio in South except in Kerala. (*Times of India* November 6th 2000).

Action taken by the State Governments

The first step taken in this direction by all state governments is to constitute state and district level supervisory committee to insure that all centers possessing prenatal diagnostic equipments, mostly ultrasound machines, are registered with the government. Prenatal diagnostic centers were served notices for strict compliance with the PNDT Act 1994 in their day-to-day practice.

Role of religious Leaders

The religious bodies have to come forward in rooting out this evil practice from society in a big way. In this direction the step taken by Sikh community is highly praiseworthy. A Hukumnama command has been issued by the AKAL TAKHT the highest order for Sikh Community on 18th April 2001—the land mark directive from the highest religious and temporal seat of Sikh states that any one indulging in female feticide would be declared a *Tankhaiya* (guilty of religious misconduct and would be ex-communicated from the community).

Other religious leaders should act in same direction and exhort their community members to stop this evil practice or face the consequences of expulsion from the community. Such action should be taken by Kanchi Shakara Charya Jee, the Arch Bishop of Delhi and Shahi Imam of Jama Masjid Syed Abdul Bukhari, as years of propaganda against Foeticide, Infanticide and other violence against women have failed. (The Hindu June 22-2001).

Conclusion

The violence against women and Female Infanticide are an age-old evil practice of patriarchal society of India, and some other countries. But its recent version Female Feticide is one step forward to eliminate the female fetuses while in utero after diagnosing its sex. The reduction in female to male ratio in 1991 census is a matter of great anxiety. Education at grass root level, raising the status of women, economic and other incentives for girl child, special recognition of girls who live with their parents, social security for elderly people, women empowerment and all such steps will help in attitudinal change of the society.

Government, Non Government Organizations, Private Sectors and religious leaders all have to contribute their might to rot out this extreme and reprehensible form of violence against women, which is female infanticide and female foeticide.

References

1. Female Infanticide continues unchecked unhurt (Times of India November 06-2000).
2. "IMA plans religious leaders meet to Fight Female Feticde" (The Hindu June 22, 2001).
3. Protecting the girl child challenge before society. (Dr. Mrs. Vir Bala Agarwal) (Employment News 01-07 June 2002)
4. Gender Side Watch-Case Study Female Infanticide (www.genderside.org).
5. Women and Gobal Human Right (www.webster.edu).
6. Female Feticide in Karnataka (Times of India August 24, 2001).

Chapter 45

Gender Discrimination: A Socio-Medical Problem

Ram Udaya Sinha

Inter-disciplinary approach for social problem is need of the day and it should be encouraged. Science and Humanity can together deliver more goods than either can do independently.

I would like to place certain basic facts so that one is able to differentiate facts form fiction. My endeavour would be to place the information in easily understandable words.

The Emergence of The planet Earth and Life on it

It may be a matter of dispute when and how the planet earth came in existence, but it is a fact that life on it is a much later development. First life started in sea in form of amoeba.

Transition from Amoeba to Homo Sapiens

The first life form was a unicellular organism, "Amoeba". The single cell of amoeba was versatile and was able to perform all functions of living being. For its propagation it needed to be divided simply in two parts. This type of propagation is called Asexual Reproduction.

Asexual reproduction is prevalent in primitive animals and plants. For example, when we cut a part of plant and put it in earth, which subsequently develops in another plant, it is asexual growth, when plant comes in existence by way of implanting fruit (seeds) this is example of sexual growth. Homo sapiens are the most advanced life form on the earth. They propagate by sexual way. Herein lays the problem of sexual discrimination by nature. In fact, the most developed "Human Brain" is the root cause of most of the ills of the society.

It is different

It is an essential function of Nature to sustain and propagate life form. If the propagation is by asexual method, then there is no scope of sexual discrimination. However, as earlier stated, the asexual method is available in primitive organization only.

For sexual propagation, the male and female are made differently. Thus gender equality in theory is a misnomer. Still there must be equality among the unequals for healthy society and nation.

XX /XY

Each individual should understand the riddle of XX / XY, whether he is illiterate or well read intellectual. This knowledge is essential for every mother in-law (SAAS) and to every daughter-in law (BAHU).

As we know, there are specific genetic codes for every species of life form and Chromosomes are its carrier. For convenience, the Chromosomes are numbered as 1, 2, 3 etc. This number system is applied for the Chromosomes responsible for all the body functions except the sexual functions.

The names of Sex Chromosomes are 'XX' for female and 'XY' for male. A female human being has 44XX Chromosomes i.e., 22 pairs of Somatic Chromosomes and a pair of Chromosome designated as 'XX'. Male individuals have 22 pair of Somatic Chromosomes as in females one 'X' chromosome as in females, and one 'Y' chromosome distinctive foe male Sex. So, every male is "*Ardha Narishwar*".

As we know that when a small new born ultimately develops as adult, lots of new cells are constantly added. There is always loss and repair of the Chromosome i.e. "22X" Chromosome. Thus all the Ova in any female will contain "22X" Chromosome. In male, it is different. The sperm (the seed cell of male) may contain either "22X" or "22Y" Chromosome.

When Ovum (with 22X Chromosome) meets the sperm within '22X' Chromosome the resultant life form is female, when ovum meets sperm with "22Y" Chromosome male life is male.

Thus, it is apparent that sex of the offsprings depends on the sperm of male partner and the female partner no way is responsible if a female child is born, if at all, the blame should be on husband.

Cloning

I would like to inform about human cloning at this stage. This is an asexual type of propagation and when it becomes scientifically feasible it will bring about all sorts of medical and social problems. At that time one can order, thousand of "Duryodhans" at a time and one can't imagine what would happen to "Draupadis" of tomorrow. Social scientists and philosophers should ponder on this point in right earnest before hand.

Embryo/Fetus

After mating of ovum with sperm, the embryo comes into existence. Embryo is named fetus, after twelve weeks of gestation.

It is a medical fact that female embryo is more agile and it is a positive gender discrimination practiced by nature.

Advanced medical technology and sophisticated machines and equipments have given the present day medical men great powers. Now it is possible to detect diseases in embryo or fetus and to treat and cure it *in situ.*

However, the same technology can be misused to differentiate the sex of fetus and for selective feticide.

Science is a two edged weapon and it can be either used or misused. The nuclear technology used for making weapon of mass destruction is also used to treat cases of cancer and other diseases.

Full term normal delivery of healthy baby

Whenever there is pregnancy, everybody desires for uneventful delivery of a healthy baby. However, in actual practice, we do it differently. It is a common knowledge that a pregnant woman will require much more food for herself and her baby in womb. However, the woman receives less and less of food with lesser nutritive value. This leads to low birth weight baby with poor outcome. If the baby is female one, she will develop as short stature woman and will produce still smaller baby when she is herself pregnant. Deprivations of a woman of food, medicine and expecting healthy baby is like expecting good harvest without adequate water, fertilizer and pesticides.

New born /Infant /Toddler

Female baby after birth till school going age suffers less from diseases and is healthier than their male counterparts of the same age group. Nevertheless, people in general deprive the female baby of necessary food, medicine and other care as against the male sibling. This discrimination tells upon the female child during her adulthood.

Schooling

It is right to say that, when one male is educated, he alone is educated. Moreover, if one woman is educated, the whole family is educated. Still female education receives lesser attention at individual, community and Government levels.

Female education can do wonder and it is one single most important intervention which can change whole society and future of the nation.

One small example will strengthen the point. In a survey of Jhugi Jhopri of Delhi, it was observed that other parameters remaining the same, incidences of diarrhea in children were significantly low when the mother was just literate. Acceptance of community health services is higher in literate women, resulting in lower population growth.

Adolescents

This is the period when the process of sex differentiation is at its peak. This is the period when there should be more and more of psychological and moral support from parents, teachers and society. Nevertheless, mostly all concerned are exploiting this period. Especially, exploitation of girl is alarming.

Sexual abuses of minor girls are on increase. Two aspects of sex abuses need special mention. One is sex abuse by close relatives, where the girl is not able to open her month. If she opens her month, she alone is considered guilty.

The other aspect is rape on minor, which is increasing day by bay. Reporte d cases of rape on minors in India have been 3393, 3986, 4067, 4083 & 4414 respectively for year 1993, 94, 95, 96 and 97.

While rape in itself is a heinous crime, the rape of minor is crime against innocent for which there should be more stringent punishment than for simple rape.

In this regard, it is being debated whether sex education be imparted to adolescents or not? Indian Academy of pediatrics, a national body of pediatricians under the leadership of Dr. M.K.C. Nair, Director Child Development Centre, Thiruvananthapuram has evolved a course module and given it a name as "Family life Education for Adolescents". Kerala Government has adopted it for introduction in school curriculum. This is desirable that the curriculum is introduced at all India level, but lot of homework is needed before actual acceptance of the proposal.

Child Marriage

Adult female is put under two categories for our discussion, one female of reproductive age group (18-45 yrs) and the other of post reproductive age group.

Female in reproductive age group suffers from natural disadvantage. She loses in a substantial way due to much more manual labor.

Age of marriage is another important consideration. Marriage before the age of 18 is against law and undesirable, so it is medically. Nevertheless, late marriages are also problematic. Reproductive capacity decreases with advancement of age. In order to build career there are many who marry late or remain unmarried.

Single Women, by Choice or Design

Institution of marriage is so much deep-rooted in our society that unmarried women are seen as aberration. The need of the hour is to provide all kinds of support to women who remain single either by choice or otherwise. In this connection, two aspects need special consideration. Problem of widows requires another incarnation of Raja Ram Mohan Roy.

Secondly, child out of wedlock should also be provided same social protection and laws have been made where there is no need to mention the name of father in any application form and lot of things have to be done in this regard.

Problems of post reproductive female are immense. Unlike male, where the change is insidious, the changes in female are more abrupt and traumatic. All sorts of medical and social supports are needed for them but less and less is available to them.

Who can be torchbearer?

Certain social and legal institutions can ameliorate the sufferings at individual and society levels. It is beyond the scope of this paper to go into details. Still, I would like to draw attention towards them.

A. Politicians & political masters

Politician and political masters should be first to act against gender discrimination. However, we should expect least from them. After agreeing in principle, they are unable or unwilling to introduce Women's Reservation Bill in Parliament. What can they expected from them?

B. Bureaucrats and Administrators

Bureaucrats and administrators are shadow of their political bosses and we should have similar expectation from them. No doubt there have been notable works done by administrator of individual levels but the examples are few and far between. Moreover they are handicapped by the way of transfer and other problems.

Judiciary

In place of putting forward, my own view I shall like to quote from a recent editorial of "*Times of India*" which is self-explanatory.

"Significantly, an NGO survey of 109 judges revealed that 49 percent felt that a husband was justified in beating his wife on certain occasions, 34 percent felt that there was an inherent cultural value in dowry, and the rest believed the family should be of primary concern to women" Beaten track, 'Editorial' *Times of India*, Patna dated, March 14, 2002.

Now, one can have one's own conclusion.

Intellectuals / Social & Spiritual leaders

The intellectuals and social and spiritual leaders can do a lot and they should leave no stone unturned in this regard, because if they fail to do so the whole nation will fail. As it is amply clear that if we neglect 50 percent of population, health, happiness, development, peace cannot be ours.

N.G.O. & women, individually and/or at organization levels

The dedicated NGO, women's organizations and enlightened women individually can do a lot. Self-help groups of deprived persons can do wonder in ameliorating their sufferings.

A. Medical Ethics

Medicine is a noble profession. If a medical man commits crime like identification of sex of foetus and selective foeticide, he should be simply debarred to practice medicine. There are many vocations where lot of money can be earned. If doctors can't stick to Hippocratic Oath they better leave the profession. Lot of moral pressure should be put by society on them, as law alone can't mend their way.

Women lib movement &Ethics

It is my considered view and of many more that women lib movements sans morality and ethics are more dangerous than the gender discrimination practiced by male dominated society. To give a simple example use of condom reduces the chance of AIDS, in case one has multiple sex partners, but having single sex partner eliminates the chance of AIDS altogether. Choice is yours.

Chapter 46

Gender Bias—
Female Foeticide and Infanticide

K.K. Singh

The highly deplorable gender discrimination is prevalent all over India with its first manifestation beginning before birth. Sex determination of unborn baby is rampant and is being performed with the help of ultrasound all over the country leading to an unchecked practice of female foeticide. Sex determination by this method is not possible before the second trimester of pregnancy. If the foetus is a female, women undertake abortion even beyond 20 weeks. People go for sex determination test without giving a serious thought about the health hazards of the later abortions of the women.

Still others who cannot afford these tests and cost of abortion await the birth of the child and then decide to do away with it if the baby is a girl. Some of the states where female infanticide is largely prevalent are Tamil Nadu, Gujrat, Rajasthan, Punjab, U.P. and Bihar.

Indian Medical Association and Federation of Obstetric and Gynaecological Societies of India have been urging their members to give up these practices of sex determination and female foeticide, but the number is on increase.

The Medical Council of India has recommended derecognition of doctors found supporting the practice of female foeticide by conducting sex determination tests and medical termination of such pregnancies.

According to ICMR risk of maternal mortality is more than 10 fold, even if they are done by experts in Government approved Institutions i.e. 26/100,000 in First trimester abortions against 322/

100,000 second trimester abortions. Sex selective abortions are all second trimester abortions.

Due to the preference for a son discrimination against women begins even before birth, by abortions of female foetuses. Female infanticide may be condemned, but there is indisputable evidence of parental discrimination against female babies. Girls are breast fed for a shorter period than boys and get less nutritious food and less medical attention than their brothers. They are given less education than boys.

Childhood deprivation ends in nutritionally deprived mothers who are themselves undernourished and underweight, producing low birth weight babies. Thus the vicious cycle goes on. Very little attention is given to the mental health of women. The psychological trauma occurs due to sex and pregnancy before the young girl is emotionally mature. Social evils as physical abuse, wife beating, sexual harassment, rape and dowry add to her innumerable problems.

It has been reported that one dowry death takes place every 102 minutes. A rape occurs every 54 minutes. Molestation occurs every 38 minutes. A crime against women occurs every 7 minutes.

Son preference as a distinct characteristic of patriarchal norms finds expression in active discrimination against the girl child. Studies in India reveal three major factors that lead to son preference, with resultant implications for girl child discrimination The first is the economic utility of sons. Sons are more likely than daughters to provide family labour on the farm or in a family business, earn wages and support their parents during old age. Upon marriage, a son brings a daughter-in-law into his family, and she provides additional help around the house as well as an economic reward in the form of dowry payments.

The second factor is a son's socio-cultural utility. This is in the context of India being a patrilineal society, with the family constituted primarily as a patriarchal unit. To add to this is the increasing trend towards patrilineal inheritance.

The third factor is linked to religion. The Hindu religion accords sons the unique responsibility for performing certain religious functions like kindling the funeral pyre of their deceased parents and to help in the salvation of their souls.

Regardless of the social, economic, religious and cultural pressures produced by the environment in which Indian women live, it is clear that many women are seeking sex selective abortion. The motivation to have a son in the family is so strong that women who are otherwise God-fearing, law-abiding and concerned about their health are willing to break the law and risk illness, death and social and legal consequences to avert birth of unwanted girl child.

Desire for a 'boy' in India drives every year about four million women to risk their lives and get illegal abortions done. This leads to dwindling sex ratio. India has less than 93 women for 100 men against the world average of 105. Punjab sex ratio in 1997 had dipped to 751 girls per 1000 males. Haryana and Delhi are not far behind. What a paradox? India the land of Durga, Saraswati, Laxmi and Parvati is killing its goddesses everyday without betting an eye-lid.

The main cause of female foeticide and infanticide is dowry. Anti Dowry Act was introduced but the demand of dowry has been increasing everyday. Previously it was limited to certain states, certain religion and certain castes but now it has spread in all the states, every religion and every caste. There is no political will to implement the provisions of the Act. The female foeticide cannot be termed as an escape route in order to prevent dowry deaths. Can the problem of dowry be eliminated by finishing women themselves? Women are not the problem. The problem is society's attitude towards them. The remedy lies in making daughter, 'Wanted' and 'Welcome' and not in refusing them their existence.

Under certain circumstances the right to an abortion was recognized in 1971 under the Medical Termination of Pregnancy Act 1971. The Act provides that termination of pregnancy by a registered medical practitioner only where its continuance would involve a risk to the life of the pregnant women or grave injury to her physical or mental health or where there is a substantial risk that if the child was born it would suffer from such physical or mental abnormalities as to be seriously handicapped. But in practice this Act provided a license to every registered medical practitioner to terminate pregnancy. Deregularisation has resulted into a new type of criminal behaviour practice by the medical practitioners. The Government being concerned only with its family planning programmes became a willing party to this so-called legalised female foeticide. Ammiocentasis technology added fuel to the fire when after detecting the sex of the foetus, selective abortions were caused.

Amniocentasis technique came to India in 1975 as a measure of detecting genetic disorders and abnormalities, but unfortunately this invention of science has been used by the business minded people (including medical professionals) for determining the prenatal sex. During last decade it appeared as female foeticide has replaced female infanticide demonstrating that the social attitude to the birth of the female child has not changed. Amniocentasis test in India became synonymous with sex determination test, which resulted to sex selective abortions.

There were and there are enough provisions under the Indian Penal Code as well as under the Medical Termination of Pregnancy Act 1971 to deal with the criminal abortions and female foeticide or infanticide, but the Central Government in its wisdom thought to combat this menace by enacting separate legislation and therefore passed pre-Natal Diagnostic Techniques (Regulation and Prevention of Misuse) Act 1994. Since the introduction of this Act the sex determination of foetuses and inturn female foeticide have increased many folds. Just passing legislation after legislation is no solution. The solution is to get their provisions strictly implemented.

In December 1977 U.N. General Assembly adopted a resolution proclaiming a United Nation's Day for women's Rights and International Peace. Its symbols are 'Bread' to represent security and 'Roses' to represent quality of life. The women in general irrespective of caste, creed, religion or functional status are being subjected to plethora of humiliations and subjugations since time immemorial. International Womens' Day is now celebrated through out the world on 8th March every year.

The recent move of the reservation for women in Parliament was smartly scuttled by narrow minded and myopic male politicians who tried to insinuate the element of caste in this group.

The whole journey from childhood to senility is a journey filled with bumps of pains, pangs and agonies. The advent of a girl child in a family is regarded as the advent of misfortune and doom. The female infanticide has put a challenge before the gender equation in the society paving the way for a great turbulence. As per the

1991 census it is estimated that 48 million women are missing from India's' population.

Girls have a greater risk of dying in infancy, have lesser chances of being admitted to school and have higher chances of dropping out from school. Expenditure incurred for a girl's education is considered as a total wastage because she is not the so-called member of the house. She is an alien property destined to be the part of in-laws' house. So the first responsibility of a father is not to impart quality education to his daughter and make her purposeful in society, but to arrange for early marriage and get peace. It is high time to instil the quality of vision in the father's eye towards both genders.

List of Contributors

1. Dr. Abha Singh, Reader, Department of Philosopy, Magadh University, Bodh-Gaya (B.S. College Dauapur Patua) (Bihar.)
2. Professor Tandra Patnaik, Department of Philosophy, Utkal University, Bhubaneshwar-751004.
3. Professor Shyam Narayan Chaudhary, Retd. Professor of Philosophy, R.N. College, Hajipur-844101 (Bihar).
4. Professor R.K. Singh, Head, Department of Philosophy, L.S. College, Muzaffarpur (B.R.A. Bihar University).
5. Dr. C.D. Jha, M.S. College, Motihari (Bihar)
6. Dr. Ravi Kumar Sinha, Department of English, R.N. College, Hajipur-844101 (Bihar)
7. डॉ. विद्यासागर सिंह, अध्यक्ष, दर्शनशास्त्र विभाग, रामचरित्र सिंह स्मारक महाविद्यालय, बिहार, बंगूसराय (बिहार)।
8. डॉ. नवीन कुमार, दर्शनशास्त्र विभाग, रामश्रेष्ठ सिंह महाविद्यालय, चोचहां, बी.आर.ए. बिहार विश्वविद्यालय, मुजफ्फरपुर (बिहार)।
9. डॉ. शैले कुमारी, उपाचार्या, दर्शनशास्त्र, विभाग, संगत सिंह महाविद्यालय, मुजफ्फरपुर-842001 (बिहार)।
10. डॉ. आलोक टंडन, 53, अशराफ टोला, हरदोई-241001
11. डॉ. राजेश्वर सिंह, दर्शनशास्त्र विभाग, बी.आर. अम्बेडकर बिहार विश्वविद्यालय, मुजफ्फरपुर-842001 (बिहार)।
12. डॉ. हिमांशु शेखर सिंह, सामान्य अध्येता, भारतीय दार्शनिक अनुसंधान परिषद्, नई दिल्ली, दर्शनशास्त्र विभाग, बी.आर. अम्बेडकर बिहार विश्वविद्यालय, मुजफ्फरपुर-842001 (बिहार)।
13. श्री राजीव कुमार, दर्शनशास्त्र विभाग, श्री राघव प्ररु सिंह कॉलेज, जैंतपुर, मुजफ्फरपुर-843001 (बिहार)।

14. Dr. Indu Kumari, Lecture's Flat-2, Khabra Road, Muzfferpur (Bihar).
15. डॉ. सुनील कुमार सिंह, दर्शन विभाग, बी.एम.डी. कॉलेज, दयालपुर, वैशाली--844502 (बिहार)।
16. डॉ. श्याम किशोर सिंह, दर्शन विभाग, अवध बिहारी सिंह महाविद्यालय, लालगंज, वैशाली, (बिहार)।
17. Dr. Damoder Singh, Reader & Head, Department of History, B.S. College, Danapur, Patna (Bihar).
18. Dr. Kanupriya, Department of English, L.S. College, B.R.A. Bihar University, Muzffarpur (Bihar).
19. Professor M.R. Kazimi, (Retd) Prof. of Pol. Sc., B.R.A. Bihar University, Muzffarpur (Bihar).
20. Dr. Rekha Singh, Department of Philosophy, B.R. Ambedker Bihar University, Muzffarpur (Bihar).
21. प्रोफेसर हरि नारायण पाण्डेय, दर्शनशास्त्र विभाग, बी.आर.बी.यू. मुजफ्फरपुर-842001 (बिहार)।
22. Professor Nirmala Kumari Jha, University Department of Philosophy, B.R. Ambedkar Bihar University, Muzffarpur (Bihar).
23. Dr. B.V.S. Bhanushree, Asst. Professor, Department of Philosophy, Andhra University, Visakhapatnam.
24. Dr. Rashmi Rekha , Department of Medieval And Modern Indian History , Lucknow University , Lucknow.
25. प्रोफेसर कमला कुमारी, दर्शनशास्त्र विभाग, बी.आर. अम्बेदकर बिहार विश्वविद्यालय, मुजफ्फरपुर (बिहार)।
26. डॉ. इन्द्रा कुमारी, दर्शनशास्त्र विभाग, आर.डी.एस. कॉलेज, बी.आर.ए. बिहार विश्वविद्यालय, मुजफ्फरपुर (बिहार)।
27. डॉ. सरोज कुमार वर्मा, दर्शन विभाग, बी.आर. अम्बेदकर बिहार विश्वविद्यालय, मुजफ्फरपुर-842001 (बिहार)।
28. Dr. Yogini G.Nighoskar, Reader, Dept. of Philosophy, Faculty of Arts, The M.S. University of Baroda, Vadodara-390002.
29. डॉ. पूनम सिंह, W/o डॉ. राजेश्वर सिंह, L/F-47,न्यू रीडर्स कॉलोनी, बी.यू. कैम्पस, मुजफ्फरपुर-842001 (बिहार)।

30. Prabhakar Prasad Singh, Reader in History, B.M.D. College, Dayalpur-844502, Vaishali (Bihar).
31. Dr. Y.V. Satynaryana, Professor of Philosophy, Andhra University, Vishakhapatnam-530003, A.P.
32. Dr. D.N. Mallik, Former Proffessor & Head, Department of Political Science, B.R. Ambedkar Bihar University, Muzffarpur (Bihar).
33. Dr. Anil Kumar Ojha, Department of Political Science, B.R.A. Bihar University, Muzffarpur-842001 (Bihar).
34. Dr. S.B.P. Sinha, Former Professor & Head, Department of Philosophy, B.R.A. Bihar University, Muzffarpur-842001 (Bihar).
35. Swami Brahmeshananda, Secretary, Ramakrishna Mission Ashrama, Chandigarh.
36. Dr. Anima Kumari, General Fellow, ICPR, Department of Philosophy, B.R. Ambedkar Bihar University, Muzffarpur-842001 (Bihar).
37. Dr. Sadanand Prasad Singh, Professor & Head, Department of Philosophy, Nitishwar College, B.R. Ambedkar Bihar University, Muzffarpur-842001 (Bihar).
38. Professor Sachindra Kumar Singh, Pro VC, Kameshwar Singh Darbhanga Sanskrit University, Darbhanga, Bihar.
39. Dr. M.P. Chaurasia, Department of Philosophy, J.P. University, Chapra-8413101 (Bihar).
40. Dr. Shiva Bhanu Singh, Reader & Head, Philosophy Department, Ewing Christian Autonomous College, Allahabad.
41. Dr. Asha Mukherjee, Department of Philosophy, Visva Bharti, Santiniketan-731235.
42. Professor S.Shyam Kishor Singh, Manipur University, Impharl-745003.
43. Dr. Rashmi Rekha , Department of Medieval And Modern Indian History , Lucknow University , Lucknow.

44. Professor (Dr.) Rangila Sinha, Retd. H.O.D. & Director Obst & Gyn. S.K. Medical College, Muzffarpur-842001 (Bihar).
45. Dr. Ram Udaya Sinha, Retd. Professor & Head, Department of Paediatrics, Rajendra College, Ranchi (Jharkand).
46. Dr. K.K. Singh, Former Gerneral Secretary, Indian Medical Council, (Bihar).